C000204431

Dear
Charlotte

THE GOOD HUSBAND

ABIGAIL OSBORNE

Best Wishes

Abigail Osborne

BLOODHOUND
— BOOKS —

ALSO BY ABIGAIL OSBORNE

The Puppet Master

Save Her

For my husband, Jamie

PART I

CHAPTER ONE

NOW

Somehow, Jack knew that his father was there without needing to open his eyes. Like a gazelle that has learnt to sense danger from miles away, Jack could tell. He was puzzled. Why would his father be in his house? They only saw each other at Christmas. In fact, his father had never been to their house. Jack tried to open his eyes but they were heavy with sleep. He attempted to move his arm, intending to wake his wife, Elsie, but his arms wouldn't obey. He tried to force his eyes open but his eyelids seemed to have weights attached.

Jack's heart pounded. Scared by his body's disobedience. Something was very wrong. He tried to recall his last memory. Perhaps that would explain why his body felt full of lead. But as he reached into the recesses of his mind for his memories, they danced away like leaves in the wind.

Concentrating as hard as he could, Jack focused only on trying to open his eyes. Fear pulsed around his body with every beat of his heart. He didn't know where he was or what was happening. Just that he had to concentrate on opening his eyes.

Elsie's voice echoed in his head, *'mind over matter, Jack.'* Her mantra when he had been undergoing physiotherapy after his accident at work. Focusing hard, he demanded his eyelids obey and it worked. An icy white light penetrated his eyes and he had to fight the urge to close them. The room slowly came into focus and Jack looked around startled, this was not his bedroom. The room was white and clinical, a strip light blindingly bright, a collection of tubes and buttons on a panel at the head of his bed and a thin blue blanket covered him. Why was he in a hospital? In a wooden chair next to his bed, sat his father. Head bowed, unmistakably praying.

Jack almost closed his eyes again. He didn't have the energy for him right now. He looked out of the window in the door, searching for Elsie. Why would she leave him alone with his father? She knew better than anyone how volatile their relationship was. Lost in prayer, Jack took the opportunity to study his father. There were only eighteen years between them but his father looked more like his younger brother. Even now, at seventy-three, his father's power was tangible. His strength rippled from every pore. Jack had always thought his father was invincible and it appeared he was right. Immune from the ravages of time. He was every bit as terrifying and awe-inspiring as he was when Jack was a boy.

For most of his life, Jack had both adored and feared this man in equal measure. He had never been the doting father that would sit by his son's bedside in times of illness. So what was he doing here? Jack looked around for Elsie again, needing her like oxygen to breathe. In her absence, he was starting to panic and wilt. He needed her calming presence to help soothe him. But she still hadn't appeared. She was the only person who truly understood his difficulties with his father.

After all, it was meeting her that had led to his freedom from the prison his father had spent Jack's whole childhood building. It was only because of his faith and Elsie's support that he still tried to see the good in his father. Jesus taught

4

compassion and forgiveness and Jack had tried his best to honour that by visiting his father every year at Christmas. It never went well. No matter how much time had passed, his father would never approve of Elsie and the way in which she had changed Jack. Which is why it was so odd to see him here. Sitting at Jack's bedside like a loving father. Was Jack finally going to have a normal relationship with him?

Jack craned his neck to look further out into the corridor. Where was Elsie? A leathery hand took his, startling him. Had his father held his hand before? It felt so strange. Like being embraced by a random stranger off the street. Tears trickled down Jack's face as he locked eyes with his father. Why was he such an emotional wreck?

Inside, he was screaming for Elsie. He wanted her to see this. He knew her happiness would mirror his own. It was starting to annoy him that she wasn't there. He was obviously in a hospital, which meant something had happened to him. Why wasn't *she* at his bedside holding his hand? Jack used his free hand to wipe away his tears and white-hot pain caused him to gasp. His nose. He felt a bandage taped across his face. Using the tips of his fingers, he traced the skin around his eyes and nostrils; it felt hot and swollen.

His father opened his mouth to speak but a nurse barrelled through the door. She was a short, well-built black lady with her hair cropped at her shoulders, framing her round face. She stopped abruptly when she realised that Jack was awake.

'Ah, Mr Danvers. My name is Aisha, I'll be looking after you today.' She smiled at him warmly and moved closer. Jack liked her instantly. He knew Elsie would like her too. They'd be best friends after a few minutes, he just knew it. If they weren't already.

'Where's my wife? Have you seen her?'

The nurse exchanged a look with his father. His eyes flicked between them, attempting to translate the unspoken conversation they were having.

'I'm just going to have a look at your nose and then we will talk about your wife.'

The nurse's hands moved towards him but he swatted them away.

'I don't understand. Why isn't she here? Where is she?'

The nurse sighed. She pulled up a wooden chair and sat next to him. He felt her hand clasp his, skin as soft as marshmallow. Looking at the apprehension in her eyes, Jack no longer wanted to hear what she had to say.

She squeezed his hand gently and smiled at him, her caramel eyes watery.

'Please,' Jack said, nausea rolling in his stomach. 'Please tell me where Elsie is.'

'Jack, I'm afraid you and your wife were involved in a tragic accident.' She looked around the room trying to find the right word. 'I'm afraid your wife suffered catastrophic internal bleeding and died at the scene. You were sedated by the paramedics and brought here.'

The room around him dissolved as an explosion of sounds and images consumed him: Elsie lying on the floor, pale and unmoving. People clawing at him. High pitched screams. Jack fisted his eyes, trying to forcibly remove the memories. He refused to believe it. A wave of grief was about to consume him. A door to his old life was shutting and he couldn't let it. He had to keep it open.

'No.' Jack shook his head emphatically. 'That's not right. Elsie is probably just signing some forms. I think you've got the wrong room.' Jack heard the hysteria in his voice. He sprang up from the bed, startling both his father and Aisha. Before they could react, he had opened the door and charged down the corridor. One side of his brain was trying to convince the other that if he just looked hard enough, he would find her. The hospital was a maze of uniform corridors and staircases. Signs flew past him as he walked, examining every face, trying to spot Elsie. His vision was becoming blurred from tears but he swiped furiously at them and kept moving. He would find her. He just knew it.

Jack followed the staircases, breathing heavily from the exertion. He kept climbing until he was at the top of the hospital. Not one of the people he passed was Elsie. Deep down, he knew it was fruitless but if he kept moving, he could fight off the grief that was waiting to drown him. The pain was coming ever closer. The agonising acceptance that his wife was gone. He wouldn't, he couldn't.

A nurse approached from the opposite side of the corridor, running towards him.

'Mr Danvers!'

Panicking, Jack opened a doorway to his right and followed a staircase up to a metal door. Opening it, Jack was greeted by a slap of cold wind. His gown fluttered and he walked onto the roof. The giant moon shone down on him, lighting him up like his own personal spotlight.

Jack heard footsteps behind him and moved to the edge of the roof. He looked down. His stomach roiled in horror, but his mind considered the sweet relief jumping would give him. He would not have to live in a world without Elsie. Jack had loved her since he was eighteen years old. For thirty-seven years she had been his wife. She made up almost all the pieces in the jigsaw of his life. Without her he would never be complete again, the integral piece would be forever missing.

As Jack lifted his foot, a hand took his and he looked into the steel-grey eyes of his father. He could hear voices behind him, begging him to move away from the edge of the roof. But he ignored them, eyes locked on his father.

'God is the giver of life. He gives and he takes away. Your life is the Lord's. You do not get to decide when it is over, son.'

Jack looked back down at the concrete pavement below. People walked to and from the hospital, never looking up. Hunched over or huddling under umbrellas from the rain. Jack hadn't even noticed the rain, he realised now his whole body was soaked through and he was shivering violently. Jack imagined himself falling through the air, on his way to ignorant bliss, to join Elsie. Taking his place next to her at the Lord's side.

'I can't do it, Father. I can't live without her.' Jack sobbed, tears mingling with raindrops.

'This won't take you to Elsie.' Jack turned to face him. 'Suicide is a sin. Sinners do not go to Heaven.'

The truth behind his father's words brought him to his knees. There was no choice, he had to accept that she was gone. His father gently helped him to his feet. They walked back over to the spectators who had watched with bated breath. Aisha was standing at the front of the group, two porters and a woman in a white coat stood behind her. Aisha held out a hand to him and he took it. Her face was pallid and she looked at him with cautious eyes, hair and uniform both sopping wet. Jack wanted to apologise but he was numb.

They placed Jack in a wheelchair and Aisha wheeled him back to his room. Tenderly, she dried him with a towel, her eyes brimming with compassion. It was as though she was trying to soothe his grief whilst she dried him and helped him into bed. Before she left the room, Aisha told him he would be discharged the next day pending a psychological evaluation.

Jack's father took her place next to him. Jack met his eyes and the emotion that had been trying to escape since he woke up finally broke free. His scream of pain echoed around the corridors of the hospital. The agony in his voice stopping doctors, nurses, patients and visitors in their tracks. Arms came around him and Jack sobbed into his father's embrace, not registering that this was the first time his father had ever held him voluntarily. Grief was slashing through his body like he'd swallowed razor blades. His brain tried to reconcile the fact that the sun he orbited had been extinguished. Suicide is a sin, but how on earth could he carry on? Jack had no reason to live anymore. It had been taken from him by monsters.

CHAPTER TWO

THEN

In one of the fields that surrounded Oakdale Farm was a rock formation lying in the centre. The huge black rocks were uniquely grouped together in a circle to form a crude sort of giant bowl. The weather had beaten them smooth, and Jack could slide from the top down into a shallow pool of rainwater collected in the bottom of the bowl of rocks. For eight-year-old Jack, it was his favourite place in the world. He spent hot days splashing in the water at the bottom, cocooned from the rest of the world.

When he first found it, Jack was convinced if he jumped into the water it would transport him to a different world. Every day he would jump into the water, just in case. It was a quiet, safe place. His imagination was free to run wild and he fought off armies of soldiers and hid from giants and saved the world from alien invasions. Today he had been defending his castle from an army of trolls when he lost his balance. Jack fell backwards. It was like falling in slow motion. It seemed to take an age for him to fall through the air and then slam into one of the rocks. He slid down to the bottom and as he did, a jagged stone he had collected and stored in the bottom sliced his leg.

Winded, Jack stared up at the blue sky. The fluffy clouds idled by as his brain tried to process what had just happened. The shock began to wear off and he sat up gingerly. It was then that he saw his leg. The skin had been ripped away, blood dripping down. The minute he saw it, the pain hit him and he began to cry. It hurt so much.

Slowly, Jack took off his shirt and wrapped it around his leg. His cries intensified with the pain as he pressed the T-shirt to his leg, the material rubbing the broken skin. Getting to his feet, Jack thought only of his mother. She would make it better. He limped his way up over the top of the rocks and jumped down. Fresh tears leached down his face as his leg absorbed the impact of the jump. It took Jack fifteen minutes to get home.

His father was in the garden, working on the vegetable patch. Taking a deep breath, he crept forward trying not to make a noise. He skirted past and as his foot crunched on the gravel driveway, a voice stopped him in his tracks.

'Boy!'

His father was eagle-eyed when it came to Jack. He spun around to see his father straightening up, hands coated with soil. Hastily, Jack wiped at the tears on his face but from the dark, thunderous expression on his father's face, it was too late.

'Are you *crying,* boy?' his father asked, disgusted.

Jack cowered back a few steps, wishing he could run into the house. To the safety of his mother. But with his leg injured, it was futile.

'I said stop.' His father took a step closer. His large frame blocked the sun, casting Jack into shadow. 'What have you done?'

'I hurt my leg, sir,' said Jack quietly.

'What have I told you about crying?' His father stood over him. Not an ounce of sympathy in his cold, stone-grey eyes.

'I'm sorry. Sir. I- I- I couldn't help it. It really hurts.'

'You are eight years old, Jack. Men do not cry. I have raised you to be stronger than that.'

Jack was shaking. The pain in his leg had vanished. Replaced by fear at the promise of punishment in his father's eyes.

'Right. You've given me no choice.'

His father pointed to the other side of the garden.

'Move.'

Fear strangled all protests Jack might have made. He thought he might be sick. But that would have been physically impossible as his throat was closing up. It was becoming hard to breathe. Jack's father grabbed his shoulder, fingers digging into his skin painfully. He led Jack over to the wooden door lying on the ground. It looked innocuous to anyone else. Like it had been left, abandoned by accident and was just now part of the furniture of the garden. But Jack knew better. His father lifted the door up, revealing a roughly dug hole, just the right size to fit a small boy.

'Get in,' his father ordered.

Knowing it was pointless to refuse, Jack clambered in, ignoring the protests from his injured leg. He lay down in the grave-like hole. He was getting too big for it. He curled into a ball, his legs wedged into his chest, no longer able to lie straight. With one swift movement, his father dropped the heavy door over the hole. Blackness descended and Jack had to work hard to stop himself panicking. He remembered all too well the time he had passed out with fear and woke up to find some sort of beetle trying to burrow up his nose. He had to stay calm.

He had lost count of the number of times he had been in this hole. But it didn't get any less terrifying. Jack raised his hands and felt the indents in the wood. Scratches made by his nails when he had tried to claw his way out. Jack swallowed his fear and tried to focus on his breathing. He could feel blood dripping out of the gash on his leg. He prayed that it didn't attract anything more sinister to join him. Unable to control it, his imagination went wild and he could feel the cold skin of snakes slithering over him and the claws of rats climbing and nibbling at his skin. Hyperventilating with fear, Jack counted to ten in his head and recited the names of the planets that he had just learnt at school. He recited the rhyme the teacher had taught him over and over again.

'Many Vile Earthlings Munch Jam Sandwiches Under Newspaper Piles.'

Jack was so squashed, it hurt every inch of him. It was impossible to find a comfortable position. The worst part of being in here was that he had no idea when he would be let out. *If* he would be let out. His father had forgotten him before.

Jack's arm was painfully numb. He adjusted his position but instead of getting more comfortable he accidentally inhaled a mouthful of dirt. The dirt coated the back of his throat and he started choking. Trying to sit up, he smacked his head on the wooden door and lay back down. He coughed and hacked, trying to dislodge the dirt from his mouth. Swallowing repeatedly, he managed to get rid of the soil. Jack felt weak from the pain and fear. To pass the time, he started picturing a world where his father was dead.

It was dark when the air rushed into the hole as his father lifted the door. His mother was stood next to him. Tears ran down her face but she did not rush to embrace him. She couldn't risk it. Not when there was a larger hole at the other side of the house that she inhabited when it was her turn to be punished.

Jack clambered out of the hole. His entire body ached. Dried blood cracked and his skin which had started to knit back together broke, dripping fresh blood down his leg and onto the grass. Jack stood in front of his father, head bowed and waited.

'Well?' his father demanded.

'For–' A sudden coughing fit stopped him talking. 'Forgive me, Father, for I have sinned.'

'What have you learnt?'

'I must not cry. I am a man. I will be strong.'

It took all his effort to stem the tears threatening to fall. He took deep steadying breaths and waited.

His father patted his shoulder.

'As the Bible says, he who spares the rod hates his son, but he who loves him is careful to discipline him,' his father recited.

Bowing his head, Jack's father ordered them to pray. Jack and his mother both bowed their heads and muttered Amen at the end.

Giving them a satisfied nod, his father strode back into the house.

As soon as the front door slammed shut, his mother leapt forward and gathered Jack into her arms.

'I'm so sorry, Jack.'

'My leg.' Jack wept quietly into his mother's shoulder. She rocked him gently. Rubbing his back soothingly. Once he was calmer, she led him into the kitchen and sat him on a chair. She gave him a piece of rope and instructed him to bite down on it. Gently, she cleaned the earth that had embedded into the exposed skin on his leg. As she bandaged his leg with some spare cloths, his father paced up and down in front of the fireplace, muttering to himself. Jack could hear odd words: 'discipline', 'my role', 'sinner'.

'You know that your father just wants the best for you. He wants you to grow up big and strong like him.'

The next day, Jack's mother unwrapped the cloth and gasped. The cut on his leg was a mosaic of green, yellow and angry red. The smell permeated the room in seconds. Jack whimpered, trying not to draw his father's attention.

'We need to get this looked at.'

She quickly wrapped his leg back up. Face white, brow furrowed with concern. She helped him up and Jack swallowed the moans of pain trying to escape. They had made it to the front door when a voice came from behind them.

'Where are you going?'

Jack could feel his mother's body trembling as she turned to face his father.

'Jack needs to see a doctor. His leg. It's infected.'

'Nonsense. He doesn't need to see a doctor. God will take care of it.'

'But–'

'But nothing. If the boy's faith is strong then God will heal him.'

Jack was feeling faint, the throbbing in his leg was making him want to cry.

Jack's father strode over to them and gently stroked his mother's face.

'We don't need a doctor, my sweet. Our faith is strong. God will hear our prayers and His love is all we need.'

He bent down and lifted Jack into his arms. Jack stiffened at the touch. It felt strange. He had never been this close to his father. He smelt like the outdoors, earth and wood. His step never faltered as he took Jack back to his bedroom. Carrying him as easily as a bag of feathers. Jack relaxed into the embrace, the rare closeness to his father momentarily distracting him from his agony. Gently, his father laid him in his bed. The movement pulled the skin on his leg and tears rose in his eyes.

'Hush, child. God is with you. He loves us. Our faith is all we need.'

'Rose,' he yelled, but his mother was already behind him.

For the rest of the night, they knelt at his bed and prayed. Jack tried to stay awake but he was dragged into fitful bursts of sleep. For three days, Jack slipped in and out of consciousness. His whole body burned with fever. At one point he begged his mother to cut his leg off. Longing for just one minute without pain. It took a whole week for his fever to break.

Jack had woken up, unsure of the time or day. But for the first time, the pain had receded to a bearable ache and his mind felt clear. His mother was asleep on the floor. She looked skeletal, her skin the colour of bone.

His father strode into the room; seeing Jack awake a huge smile broke out on his face. He stepped over his wife and lifted Jack from the bed and swung him around the room.

'What did I tell you, my boy? If your faith was strong, He would save you.'

He set Jack down on the bed and hugged his wife who had stirred. Seeing Jack, tears sprang to her eyes and she held him to her, almost cutting off his air supply.

Jack had the best day of his life. His father, exultant at the power of their faith, was joyous to be around. He ordered Rose to cook up a feast. Jack, used to a meagre ration of food each day, scoffed down two helpings of roast potatoes and green beans. By the end of the meal, he felt sick but happier than he could ever remember being. His father's laughter filled up the house, chasing the usual house guests, fear and anger, into the corner for the time being.

CHAPTER THREE

NOW

The next few days passed in a blur of black, grey and white. The world had lost its colour. He could no longer appreciate anything around him. His senses had broken. When people spoke to him, he couldn't hear them. His ears rejected all sounds that weren't Elsie.

People kept ringing about the funeral, but he was not capable of making any decisions. Ignoring his phone, he let all the calls go to voicemail. He was lucky that they were part of such a strong community. Their next-door neighbour, Susan, was spearheading the planning. Luckily for him, she knew Elsie almost as well as he did and so he was able to leave her to make sure it was a funeral to be proud of. He was capable of nothing. Immobilised by pain and grief.

If it wasn't for his father, Jack would have been lying in a coffin next to Elsie. His father hadn't left his side since the news had been broken to him. A tower of strength propping him up. Stopping him from being swallowed by his grief. Opening the front door to his and Elsie's home had broken Jack. The smell of their old life had assaulted him. Just the sight of Elsie's shoes lined up in the corridor had overwhelmed him. He collapsed.

Jack wanted to die. He couldn't go on. He couldn't go in the house. He couldn't live this life. This wasn't his life. Elsie was his life. There was no life without her.

His father led him out of the house. Jack's legs gave way as they left the house. They collapsed in a heap outside the front door. Jack's grief took hold. His body convulsed, seizure-like as he sobbed. He wanted to die in that moment. The pain was too much. He could not live this life. Jack's father held him tightly. Perhaps believing if he held on tightly enough, it would stop Jack falling apart. They stayed that way until exhaustion dampened his grief. He sat up, wiping his eyes, and pulled away from his father. Judging by the stiffness in his legs, they must have been sat like this for a while. Jack felt a wave of gratitude to his father. His unwavering patience and support were exactly what he needed.

'Let's go home, son.' Jack nodded. He turned back to look up at the house behind him. This was no longer his home. The thing that made it a home had been taken from him. Jack stood up, wincing at his creaky knees. He got into the driver's seat and looked across at his father.

'Let's go home, Father.'

Jack gazed up at his childhood home, Oakdale Farm. An imposing grey stone farmhouse set in four acres of land. An array of small stone buildings surrounded the main house, like soldiers circling the general. At the front of the house was a courtyard of gravel. Around the back a green lawn spread for miles until it reached the bordering forests.

The house looked less intimidating to him now. It was smaller and the paint was peeling from the window frames and slates were missing from the roof. There was also a distinct lack of noise. In his younger years the farmyard had had a unique melody composed by ducks, chickens and bleating lambs.

Jack followed his father into the house, stalling at the smell of must and damp that hit him. Had it smelt this bad last time he was here with Elsie? Recovering, Jack marched straight up to his old bedroom, needing to be alone. He laid down and pulled the covers over his head, shutting out the world.

A while later, his father woke him, darkness was misting up the room and he could only just make out his father's shape. His father thrust Jack's mobile at him.

'It won't stop ringing!'

Jack took the phone, it showed forty-one missed calls and three text messages. He opened up the text messages. They were from Susan. He clicked on the most recent.

Please call me. Elsie's funeral is Friday 10th December at 9.30am. I've organised your suit to be cleaned and delivered to my house so you can get it when you are ready.

Jack threw the phone onto the floor and pulled the covers back over his head.

The day of the funeral arrived and Jack looked out at the crowds of people crammed into every orifice of the church and wanted to laugh. His body started jerking slightly as he tried to contain himself. The whole thing was absurd. When he looked over at the coffin that held his beloved Elsie it became even harder to stem the laughter clawing to be let out. How could his Elsie be dead? Good people are supposed to die peacefully in their beds. A natural death from old age with the people who loved her standing around her. Her death was no less than murder. Jack's laughter died away, instantly replaced by his new best friend, pain. It lanced his heart, filled up his lungs. If only. What he wouldn't give to get in that coffin, cuddle up to his Elsie May Danvers and join her in a peaceful eternity together.

Reverend Andrews coughed gently and Jack tried to regain

control of his emotions. He examined the crowd, seeing his grief mirrored on a lot of the faces. So many people had loved Elsie. It wasn't a hard thing to do. You couldn't forget her once you had spent time with her. That type of kindness leaves a mark. She stood out from the crowd in a world full of people who judge everyone solely on their economic worth rather than the type of person they were.

But none of them knew her the way he did. He had had the privilege of knowing her intimately. Jack knew what made her laugh. Knew that she claimed cheese made her sick but would happily devour cheese flavoured crisps in secret. That she had a circular scar on her forehead from chickenpox that she hid behind her fringe. He knew that she was scared of flying. That when she was thinking, her nose would scrunch up slightly. He had had the privilege of bathing in her kindness and beauty every day for thirty-seven years. He had known her for more years than he hadn't. He'd watched her grow from a young girl into a mature, magnificent woman. If only he hadn't had to watch her die.

His mind recoiled at the memory. Instead, he focused on the piece of paper shaking in his hands. On it were empty, pitiful platitudes that he had spent the night before agonising over. Words would never be able to capture the rare, vibrant woman he had loved with every fibre of his being. He opened his mouth but nothing came out. Her loss was strangling him. Gripping his windpipe, making it hard to breathe let alone speak.

A hand wrapped around his and he turned to see the reverend gesturing for him to give him the piece of paper. Jack gratefully handed it over, the kindness on the reverend's face undid him and sobs wracked his body. He glanced at his father, an irrational fear flickered through him, that his father was going to punish him for crying in public. But tears were glistening in his father's steel eyes as well. *He's not like that anymore.* Jack reminded himself.

The pain of losing Elsie was like having locusts inside his body, eating him from the inside out. He wished they would hurry up and finish the job.

The reverend read aloud Jack's words. His voice sombre. Painting a picture of Elsie's journey in the world. He told of how she and Jack had met at eighteen and been inseparable ever since. That they had built a life together in the village of Winterford and the community had become their family. He explained that Elsie was family to everyone and there wasn't a person alive she wouldn't move heaven and earth to help.

Jack managed to rein in some of his emotions. He surveyed the room trying to focus on something else. But that didn't help as when he saw the tears streaming down almost all the faces, his own tears reared in response.

Finally, the service was over and Jack shouldered the coffin. He laid his cheek against the wood, knowing that this would be the closest he was ever going to be to Elsie again. He pressed hard against the wood and tried to pretend it was Elsie's soft cheek against his. A longing to feel her skin on his overcame him. The knowledge that her body was hiding just out of reach in the coffin was a form of torture. He just wanted this to be over but he also wanted to stay standing there forever so that he would never have to say goodbye.

They moved over to the prepared grave, the hole in the ground giving him such a big dose of reality that he almost lost his footing. Jack gripped the coffin tightly. He couldn't let her go, he just couldn't. The knowledge that his Elsie would be languishing in the ground, food for worms and all things living in the soil, it wasn't right. He wanted it to stop. But everyone carried on moving and he had no choice but to help lower his Elsie into the ground.

Jack's feet crept towards the edge of the grave of their own accord, as he contemplated whether he should just jump in after her. To lie on top of the coffin and let them bury him as well. This was a final separation. An official end to his life as he knew it.

The reverend placed a gentle hand on Jack's arm and pulled him back from the edge of the grave. Experience most likely of other grieving parishioners who wanted to jump in after their loved one. He guided Jack so he was standing beside his father.

The reverend moved to the head of the grave and looked around at the large gathering of people.

'Our sister Elsie has gone to her rest in the peace of Christ. May the Lord now welcome her to the table of God's children in Heaven. With faith and hope in eternal life, let us assist her with our prayers. Let us pray to the Lord also for ourselves. May we who mourn be reunited one day with our sister. Together may we meet Christ Jesus when He who is our life appears in glory.'

The reverend proceeded with the committal, but Jack could no longer heed his words due to the internal conflict happening between his brain and his heart. His brain was processing the scene around him, trying to convince his heart that this was it, Elsie was really gone. But his heart was refusing to accept it. Trying to explain to his brain that if Elsie was dead then there was a very good chance that it would stop beating or tear in half. One foot tried to move as his heart insisted it was time to leave, to refuse to be a part of this. But his brain knew he couldn't leave, he had to be here for Elsie. He had to say his last goodbye to the woman he loved.

The wake was held at the community centre behind the church. Jack didn't want to go but the congregation surrounded him and he was swept along with them. He lost track of the number of people that hugged him, shook his hand and patted him on the back. Faces no longer registered in his mind and their words floated away before he could process them. His brain focused only on keeping him standing upright. Jack was lucky that they were part of such a tight-knit community. They had supported him every step of the way with organising the funeral. Susan had even had his suit pressed and he'd collected it from her house. A journey he didn't even remember making.

Susan stood by his side through most of the wake. Now and then she would whisper to him and take his arm. But he was unable to function as a normal human being and ignored her. He knew he was being rude. Responding with only nods of his head when another sympathetic face with no features came in front of him to express their sorrow. Each time he blinked he would see Elsie's coffin being lowered into the grave. Funerals were meant to give you closure. But he had been struck with one thought since the coffin was lowered. What now? How on earth was he supposed to go on without her? There was nothing for him to live for. He had no job, no children. No real family depending on him. Elsie was his sun and without her, he was orbit-less. Spinning pointlessly in the Universe all alone.

The room and people were suffocating him. He needed to get away. A hand grasped his arm and pulled him outside. A sharp blast of wintry wind calmed him instantly. He saw it was the reverend leading him away from the wake. Reverend Samuel Andrews was one of the first people they had met in the village. He was there for the best day of Jack's life, his wedding. He supposed it was only fitting that he was there for the worst day of his life.

Having grown up with his father as his link to God, Jack had struggled to bond with the reverend originally. His father's views on modern-day reverends and their 'soft' teachings of the Bible had still been reverberating in his mind. But you couldn't help but like Sam Andrews. He was down to earth, patient and unbelievably kind. Over the years, they had had many spirited debates and discussed Jack's father's view of the Bible and religion. The reverend, helped by Elsie, had made him see that the Bible could be interpreted in many ways and that can sometimes be used by people to justify their own thoughts and ideals.

Jack could see now that his father's obsession with the Old Testament had stopped him from focusing on the New Testament and the fact that Jesus offered forgiveness and eternal life to all that believed in him. The Old Testament had a focus on the Law of the Lord and many references to power and punishment. On reflection, he could see that his father would choose to emphasise these teachings as he was prone to punishing Jack in the name of the Lord.

Over time, Jack had been able to let go of the belief system his father had drilled into him. He was able to open his heart to love and forgiveness. It had brought him a lot of happiness to be able to enjoy what the modern world had to offer instead of living in the past with his father.

But it had driven a wedge between them, causing them only to see each other at Christmas for one night of unbearable silence. He and Elsie would go to his father's house for dinner. They would sit in excruciating silence or Jack and his father would have a blazing row. Either way, they would always leave after the main course and Jack would vow never to return. But they did, every Christmas. He was his father after all.

As he matured, Jack had tried to see his father more but his visits always descended into an argument when it became apparent that Jack was no longer following the religion as his father had taught it. Consorting with black and gay people would never be acceptable for his father amongst other things. Jack refused to allow his father to dictate who he spent time with anymore.

He thought back to those years he spent isolated from the world. His world had been flat and empty. Once he had met Elsie and moved to Winterford, he soon discovered how vibrant the world could be. Everyone was different and that was to be celebrated not avoided. He admired his father's devotion to his faith but the reverend had shown Jack that it was possible to have a faith and also experience all the wonders that the world had to offer.

The reverend turned to Jack and all he wanted to do was run away. There was nothing the reverend could say to fix this, to make him feel better. He wasn't interested in empty words. What Jack needed was someone to show him how to survive the pit of darkness that was threatening to swallow him up. To explain to him how he was supposed to carry on living when the person he had lived for had been taken from him.

'I thought a bit of fresh air might help.'

Jack said nothing. If he opened his mouth there was a very good chance he would tell the reverend to leave him alone.

'You look so lost, Jack. I cannot imagine the pain that you are in. But we both know that Elsie is with the Lord now. She will be welcomed with open arms.'

'I just don't understand why this happened,' Jack said, voicing what had been going around in his mind since Elsie died. 'She was so kind, generous and beautiful. She put other people first and dedicated her life to helping others. How can the Lord have let this happen to her? Why would he take her from me? She didn't deserve to die.' His voice was getting louder now, a few people standing outside smoking looked over, curious to see who thought it was okay to shout at a funeral.

'Please try and calm down, Jack. This is a really difficult time for you, I understand that.'

'You understand. How can you understand when I don't understand? I don't understand how Elsie was ripped from me in such a violent, painful way. She should have died peacefully in her sleep. She shouldn't have died that way.' He spat the words. Kicking at some flowers that bordered the path.

'Come with me,' said the reverend. He grasped Jack's arm and led him over to a bench away from the smoking spectators.

'It is painful when a loved one is taken from us in a violent way. I understand that. But you have to remember that the Lord gave us free will. If he didn't then we would all just be puppets in this world, not really living. But the gift of free will comes with drawbacks because of how other people choose to use their free will. I know that you are suffering because of other people's choices and decisions. But you have to hold on to the fact that Elsie has moved on. She is going to live in Heaven, eternally by God's side. This is just an earthly death. Elsie is still alive; she is with the Lord. You will be reunited one day.'

'I can't do it. I can't live without her.' Jack leant forward. His face hidden in his hands, tears coating his fingers. The reverend laid a hand on his back.

'Yes, you can, Jack. The Lord is with you. He is always with you. You also have your family around you to get you through this.'

'I have no family. Elsie was my family.'

'Look around you, Jack. Did you see how many people were in that room? Crying with you. Sympathising with you. Suffering with you. Those people in that room love and care for you and we will all support you. You've been staying with your father, haven't you? I know you haven't always seen eye to eye, but the fact he is here in your time of need – that shows you that he loves you. You are not alone, Jack. It might not feel like it. But you do have a purpose still. You are still here. God is with you.

'I know this is an awful time. But you must take comfort in your relationship with the Lord. You must keep living because God created you in his image. You are special and valuable because He says so. You are worth all the effort it took to create this world. You are worth the sacrifice of His son. You need to remember this, Jack. It will help you move forward. With God's love, you will get through this. Your faith will give you all the reasons that you need to keep living. Even when you feel that you have no reason to go on. Which is what I am sure you have probably been feeling. God never gives us more than we can handle.'

The reverend's gentle tone and words made a pinprick in the darkness that was consuming him. He felt a tiny ebb of hope flow through him. Could he really carry on without Elsie? Was his relationship with God strong enough to fill the aching void in his heart?

CHAPTER FOUR

THEN

Spare the rod, spoil the child. These were the words that Jack's father lived by whilst raising his son. In fact, Jack was pretty certain if his father was cut open, these words would be etched into every layer of his body, like a stick of rock. Taken from the Proverbs, it guided his every interaction with Jack. In his father's defence, it had had the desired effect. Jack was so scared of the punishments he would face that he spent all his time trying to follow his father's rules to the letter. But living with his father was like being at sea. Rogue waves would suddenly appear and Jack was powerless to predict or prevent them. How was he supposed to follow the rules when they changed as easily as the direction of the wind?

His mother did her best to protect him. But even she was unable to navigate the choppy waters of his father's regime. If she tried too hard to stand up to his father she was reminded with a sharp slap around the face that the Bible tells wives to 'submit to their husbands and do not cause trouble'. She insisted that his father just wanted him to be a good, faithful man, explaining that his father was terrified that Jack would succumb to evil. His father had warned him many times that he would do whatever it took to ensure that he would never become a 'wayward Neanderthal that doesn't know right from wrong'.

It seemed to Jack that his father's paranoia grew with each passing year. He was convinced the Devil was everywhere and that he had to take precautions to make sure that he did not take root inside Jack.

The rain was bouncing off the roads as he walked home from school. He was soaked from head to toe as he walked into the kitchen. Jack's mother peeled off his clothes and hung them to dry. He sat in his underpants by the oven, warming himself, chatting with his mother whilst she peeled the vegetables. He rocked back and forwards on the chair, seeing how far back he could go without falling backwards.

'There was a new kid at school today. Atif. Mr Moore sat him next to me and I had to look after him all day,' Jack bragged.

'That was nice of you.'

'I showed him everything and I let him play with me at lunch. The other kids don't seem to like him much either.'

At first, Jack had tried to hide the bullying from his mother. But she didn't miss a trick and when she found him troughing his way through his fifth piece of bread and butter, he confessed that the kids at school were stealing his lunch and that they kept calling him a 'Bible-basher' because he made the mistake of quoting the Bible in class. Every day he was subjected to a never-ending campaign of bullying. Books thrown at his head, his pencil case stolen, holes cut in his PE shorts and pulling down his underpants in the changing room.

Jack's mother put down the carrot she was peeling and placed a hand on his cheek and looked at him, eyes burning with compassion.

'I'm sorry you are having such a hard time. Just ignore them, sweetie, they will get bored soon enough.'

Jack looked at his feet, unable to tolerate his mother's pity.

She must be embarrassed having a loser for a son, he thought. He wished he could just make the kids at school like him. But everything he said or did just gave them more ammunition.

'Does it make me a bad person that I'm glad that they are now picking on Atif instead of me?'

'No. That's understandable.' His mother turned back to the counter and resumed peeling the carrots. 'But you should try to be kind to Atif. You know what it is like to be in his shoes.'

'I like him, but he talks a lot about Allah. I didn't know who that was at first. But then he told me he is a Muslim and that is the god that they worship.'

His mother's face drained of colour and she fumbled with the peeler – it slipped from her hand, clanging onto the worktop.

'Don't say that word again, Jack. You know what your father is like.'

'I know. I won't. But, Mum, does being Muslim mean that I shouldn't like Atif? Because he doesn't believe in the same god as us?'

'No, son. You can like whoever as long as you believe they are a good person.'

His mother's eyes darted from the front door to Jack. Looking like a cornered animal. Most likely checking for his father but Jack had seen him fixing the hen coop. She moved over to the radiator and pulled his T-shirt off it and passed it over to him.

'Put this back on.'

He pulled it over his head and enjoyed the warmth still lingering in the fabric.

'Good. Because Atif is good at maths like me. We spent lunch setting each other maths problems to solve.'

'That sounds like fun.'

'It was. Atif invited me over to his house for tea one night.

But Father would never let me go, would he? Because his parents are Muslim.'

Jack asked the question, already knowing the answer but still holding out hope in case his mother might be able to find a way that he could go.

One second Jack was waiting for his mother to answer, the next his father had burst into the room and grabbed Jack by the scruff of his neck. Pulling him off his chair, his T-shirt choked him.

'A Muslim!' his father thundered. Spittle flew onto Jack's face. His father's face was contorted with rage. He raised Jack into the air, his hands around his neck. Jack clawed at them, kicking the air fruitlessly.

'My son! Friends with a Muslim! I won't have it.' He shook Jack violently. Stars danced in his eyes. His head felt like a tomato about to burst, his eyes were swelling in their sockets. 'Have I taught you anything?'

Jack was thrown to the floor. His elbow struck the concrete and he cried out. Cradling his arm he watched through tears as his father rounded on his mother.

'And you!' He poked her hard in the chest. She recoiled in pain. 'You are encouraging him. You may as well open the door and welcome the Devil inside.'

His father strode over to the kitchen and flung open a cupboard door. Jack watched in confusion as his father brought out a large bag of rice. He upended the bag and the grains tinkled across the kitchen floor. His father looked at Jack and his wife and pointed at the pile of rice he had created.

'Kneel. Both of you.' His voice was icy cold, laced with menace.

At first, Jack thought his father had lost his mind. Until his kneecaps connected with the grains of rice. Although tiny, they were rigid and immoveable. They dug into his kneecaps, fighting to penetrate his skin.

His mother was about to kneel when his father grabbed her and pulled off her dress, leaving her standing in her underwear. He then pushed her to the floor and she was forced to kneel without the protection of her dress from the grains of rice. She wrapped her arms around herself, trying to hide her body from Jack. It was covered in bruises of varying colours. Jack felt sick at the sight.

'Now. Don't move. I will not allow you to think it is okay to consort with people who do not follow the word of *our* Lord. Do you realise how heinous it is to create your own deity and worship it? It's an atrocity. I will *not* have you associating with cretins that deny our Lord's existence. You both need a reminder of where your loyalty lies.'

They kneeled in silence. The only sound was his father's rage. It filled the room, stifling the air. The discomfort of the rice soon turned to pain. Jack tried so hard not to fidget as movement only caused the grains to try and burrow further into his kneecaps like pins. Glancing at his mother, he could see beads of sweat forming on her forehead, caused by the strain of trying to remain as still as possible. He tried to catch her eye, but she was staring at the floor, seemingly transfixed. Jack tried looking around the room, desperate to fix his attention onto anything apart from the grains of hell trying to penetrate his skin. The vegetables lay on the side, the peels going hard in the waning sunlight. When he had come home from school the sun had been burning brightly. It was now dipping behind the hills. The air becoming colder with each passing hour.

When it went dark, Jack was sure he was going to cry. The pain in his knees was intolerable. His body was trembling from fatigue and cold which only worsened his pain. He looked over at his mother, trying to find her face in the darkness. Hoping to beg her with his eyes to get them out of this situation. But he couldn't see her eyes. Only her body which was shaking more than his. It looked like she could collapse at any minute. Neither of them had eaten. The meat was still in the fridge waiting to be cooked. Jack's father sat at the kitchen table, watching them intently. Like he was playing a perverse game of musical statues. He hadn't even left his vigil to turn on a light so all Jack could see was his outline in the darkness. Was he going to have to kneel here all night?

The chair creaked and Jack's head snapped towards his father. His father walked over to them, his shoes crunching as he stepped in the rice.

'Have you learnt your lesson?'

Jack and his mother nodded at the same time. He would have agreed that the sky was yellow and pigs could fly if it stopped this torture. The pain was excruciating, he felt like he was being stabbed repeatedly in the knees by tiny blades.

'I will not be friends with Atif or anyone that does not worship our Lord, Father,' Jack added in case his father needed more persuading to let them stand up.

'Good. Now let us pray. Then you can make the dinner, wife.'

Jack's father always called her that. His father didn't use names, preferring to remind them of their roles in this world. The wife and a son, who must obey the father.

Getting up, Jack almost cried out with relief. His knees cracked and little grains of rice fell to the floor as he rose. Jack brushed off the remaining grains that were embedded into his flesh. His kneecaps were a tapestry of angry blotches where the rice had attempted to penetrate his skin. Jack walked tentatively to the table and sat down. His mother pulled on her dress and recommenced peeling the vegetables. Her hands were shaking and every so often Jack watched as she brushed tears from her cheeks, hurriedly before his father could notice. But his father was sat at the table, holding court. Lecturing them about other religions and explaining in great detail why their Lord was the only Lord and what he would like to do to the people that weren't Christian. It was a very long night and they did not eat until gone 10pm. His mother sat at the table picking at her sausages. There were great black bags under her eyes and just looking at her made Jack feel tired. She looked like she was days away from death. Guilt spread over him; most of the time it was his fault she was punished.

The next day at school, Atif tried to catch Jack's eye. He asked him if he wanted to sit next to him in English. But Jack studiously ignored him. Refusing to meet his eye or engage at all. His knees had swollen up and there were bruises that made each movement painful. Jack knew that he was not a good enough liar to maintain a friendship with Atif and remember to lie about it to his father. Jack's knees were still red raw and he thought about the grave outside his father would happily throw him in. No. No friendship was worth that. Jack just needed to remember what his responsibility was in life.

CHAPTER FIVE

NOW

The sun rose and fell after the funeral but Jack was oblivious to it. He ate only because his father made him. He slept fitfully as his dreams brought with them agonising memories of Elsie. His subconscious forced him to watch her die over and over again. Whenever he felt sleep creeping up on him, he'd put his hands under the covers and pull out a hair on his leg. The sharp pain jolting him awake. Jack felt sure he was going to die from grief. It was implausible that his body could keep functioning when it kept sustaining such brutal waves of pain.

Soon God had to put him out of his misery. He was sure he had heard of people dying of a broken heart.

But Jack's father had different ideas. He allowed Jack to wallow for a week before he marched into his bedroom and instructed him to come downstairs. He had spent his childhood in this room and it looked the same now. A single bed with clinical white sheets, plain white walls and no curtains. A rail to hang his few clothes on and that was the extent of the furniture. He had seen prison cells on the television with more personality. But according to his father, 'one had no need of possessions when one had faith'.

Jack registered his father's presence but didn't acknowledge him. He no longer had any desire for words or conversation.

'Jack, I would like you to come downstairs and have dinner with me.'

His father had been bringing his meals up to his room and standing over him while he ate. The food no longer had taste. Jack was only eating out of muscle memory and because his father would push his hand up to his mouth whenever he stopped. If he had not been so lost in his sadness, Jack would have been gobsmacked by this nurturing side to his father. But he had no room in his mind for thoughts. Thoughts were dangerous. Only disconnecting himself from the world helped to ease the pain.

Jack stared at his father, telepathically willing him to leave. Unable to reply. Didn't his father understand, he didn't want to do anything? He couldn't do anything.

'Come on.' His father held out his hand. Jack stared at it. It was the only part of him that revealed his father's age. The skin was papery and veins like tiny purple snakes were embedded in his flesh. The inside of his palm was calloused from the physical work it took to run this house. His father still chopped the firewood as easily as he had in his twenties. Thinking of his father was synonymous for Jack with the sound of an axe cleaving the air. Jack pictured the muscles rippling in his father's arms as he raised the axe well above his head and brought it down on the wood. When he was younger, he would watch his father, awed and terrified in equal measure.

Jack took his father's hand; over his childhood, his father had barely touched him. Intimacy was not a concept he was familiar with until he met Elsie. At first, he had found it uncomfortable how she thought nothing of physical contact. But she quickly taught him to crave it. His body burned with a desire to be held once more. To feel Elsie's face tucked into the nape of his neck. She would whisper, 'I fit here,' her hot breath tickling his skin. Grief lashed his heart and cut off the memory. He focused instead on putting one foot in front of the other and he followed his father down the stairs into the kitchen. Pulling up his trousers as he walked, they were no longer the snug fit he was used to.

They both took their customary seats at the table. Easily slipping back into their routine of his childhood. His father at the head of the table, Jack at his right-hand side. Jack fought tooth and nail to suppress the memory of the last time that he had been at this table. Elsie had been sitting opposite him. In his mother's seat at the table. She had quietly eaten her food, whilst Jack and his father got into another inevitable row.

'We have more important things to discuss.'

'What?'

'Your future.'

'I have no future.' His voice as hollow as his world.

'Don't be stupid. You have a very bright future ahead of you.'

Jack ignored him. He had tried to picture his future but his mind just went blank. Like a satnav telling him there were no alternative routes. There was no way he was living with his father and he couldn't go back to the home he had shared with Elsie. He shuddered at the thought. With the soul of the house no longer there, it was just bricks and mortar that he could never again call home. He could start again, move somewhere else. But just the thought made him feel exhausted. He was fifty-five years of age. That was the time to start to unwind, enjoy the quiet life with the one you loved.

Only last night he had once more considered ending it. One swift motion, a jump from a roof or the swipe of a knife and this agonising pain and misery would end. But just like last time, he was forced to remind himself that suicide was a sin that could cost him his place at God's side, with Elsie. But how on earth was he going to wait until God decided it was his time? His father was still going strong at seventy-three. He could last another twenty years.

Sitting at the dinner table, looking at the father who had bullied him most of his life, the thought of ending it seemed more attractive. Elsie had been the only antidote to his horrific childhood. His father's warped view on religion and how one should live had almost succeeded in cutting him off from the world and confining him to a life without love. He couldn't spend any more time with this man. No matter how much he seemed to have mellowed in his old age. The carving knife lay next to the serving plate. His father had been waiting for him until he carved the chicken. The chicken lay golden, glistening with oil and peppered with herbs. The knife glinted at him, enticing him. One deep cut and he could escape the pain that had crippled him from the minute he saw Elsie take her last breath.

So what if he couldn't join her in Heaven. He had had three decades. He could be content with that if it meant he didn't have to feel this anymore. Decision made. Jack lunged for the knife. His father jumped up, looking at Jack warily. Was that a trace of fear in those steel-grey eyes?

'What are you doing, son?'

'I've made my decision.' The words steadied his shaking hand and he knew he had made the right choice. He had nothing to live for, no reason to exist. He raised the blade to his throat. Taking deep breaths, he prepared himself. This had to be done properly. The cut needed to be deep and firm. He did not want to mess this up. It was his one chance to end the endless torture.

'Elsie had to die and I know why.'

CHAPTER SIX

THEN

As he got older, Jack began to get more adventurous with how far he strayed from the house. He had always kept the house in sight, scared he wouldn't be able to find his way back. But he was going to be nine soon. The farm was ostracised from civilisation, with only fields and forests for neighbours. His mother filled his head with horror stories of little boys that wandered off, fell into streams and drowned. Their bodies never found. But there was nothing new to explore. Jack knew every rock, bush and tree. He could get back to the house with his eyes closed and had even done so. Spending a very entertaining afternoon with his eyes closed trying to get home without falling over.

At the bottom of the field that bordered their house was a river. If he took a run at it, Jack could jump from one side to the other. Today, Jack had decided to follow it to see if he could find where it ended. The sun was beating down, warming him from head to toe. He was tempted to wade through the water to cool down but his mother's stories still rang in his ears. The sound of bees dancing from flower to flower accompanied him downstream. Jack stopped occasionally to skim stones, trying to beat his record of seven.

Jack was starting to wonder if he should turn around, he had to make sure he was back before his father. That was the rule. Tardiness was not tolerated in the Danvers household. Screams of laughter from nearby startled him. Jack followed the riverbank around the corner and stopped. Up ahead, a stone bridge crossed the river. He spotted a group of children underneath the bridge in the water. Some of them looked a similar age to him, some younger and some older. Jack crept closer, watching as they appeared to work as a team. Yelling to each other as they picked up large stones. Unable to help himself, Jack moved closer, sliding down the embankment towards the edge of the water. The boys were topless. Their T-shirts abandoned on a rock at the side of the river.

A large boy with blond hair and a protruding belly spotted Jack. He caught the others' attention and three boys followed him over to Jack.

'Who are you?' asked the boy. He looked suspiciously at him.

'I-I'm Jack.'

'Not seen you round here before. Where do you live?'

He looked at Jack like he was a monkey in a zoo exhibit.

'I live at a farm, about an hour up the river.'

The boy considered Jack, he seemed to be thinking hard.

'Wanna help?'

Jack stared up at the boy, gobsmacked. He nodded his head, smiling gratefully.

'I'm Billy.'

The rest of the boys introduced themselves and Billy explained that they were trying to create a dam. They wanted to try and stop the flow of the river. Jack took off his top, feeling uncomfortable being exposed but he so badly wanted to fit in. It was probably the best day of his life. Jack completely lost track of time. The camaraderie of their mission was addictive. It felt like they were the most important people in the world. That damming the river was the difference between life and death. Jack avoided the girls as much as possible. Too nervous to be near them, he had never even spoken to a girl. Not even at school. They were too giggly and strange. One of them asked him to help her lift a rock. She laughed as his face burned red and he dropped the rock on his foot.

The sun had set off towards the west as Jack sat eating an ice pop. A girl had run home and returned with a big box of them to share with everyone. Jack's was orange flavoured and it was incredible. He had never tried orange before and it was mind-blowing.

Cars had been passing over the bridge and no one paid any mind to them. But the slam of a car door from the road echoed down to them. All eyes looked up. They watched to see who was invading their fun. A man appeared through the gap in the wall that led down to the riverbank.

Jack's ice pop fell to the floor. His heart stopped beating momentarily. He couldn't catch his breath as his lungs seemed to malfunction, as if too stunned to work. Jack's father stomped towards him. His father's eyes were sparkling dangerously and his face was turning the colour of aubergine. The other children looked between him and his father curiously. Jack wanted to make a run for it and never stop running. To have a life where he didn't have to face his father's rage.

Jack stood up as his father closed the distance between them. He had been sitting on a large stone, his feet in the water. The coolness of the water had been helping to counteract the heat of the day. When he was within reach, his father grabbed him by his brown hair. Jack whimpered as each strand was almost ripped from his scalp as his father tugged him back to the car. The children were deathly quiet as Jack passed them by. Silent tears tracked down Jack's face as he saw their terrified expressions out of the corner of his eye. He was humiliated.

At the gap in the wall, Jack's father thrust him through it. Jack's knees hit the tarmac. Tiny pebbles embedded themselves in his palms and knees.

His father climbed through the gap and stood over him.

'Get in the car.' His father's voice frostbite cold, Jack shivered in response. His fear crippled him. He knew if he got in the car bad things would happen.

Reaching down, his father grabbed his hair once more and forced him into the boot of the car. The boot shut and the engine started. A spare tyre was digging into Jack's side every time he took a breath. Whenever the car took a corner Jack was tossed from side to side. A tub of oil hit him in the head. But he knew this was nothing compared to what lay ahead for him. His stomach rolled as he pictured the grave in the grass at home; would his father put him back in there? Just the thought of it made it hard to breathe.

Gravel crunched as the car ground to a halt. Jack's head collided with the metal boot. The boot opened and Jack was yanked out. His father hauled him inside the house. His mother jumped as the door banged open. She put down her sewing, brow creased in concern. She got up and moved towards them.

'Sit back down!' his father ordered.

His mother obeyed immediately. She looked at Jack, her periwinkle-blue eyes filled with a fear that mirrored his own. Fury was coming off his father in waves. Jack saw the vein in his temple was throbbing. A sign that Jack should be very afraid. Terrible things happened when that vein appeared.

Jack wrapped his arms around himself. His T-shirt abandoned by the river. He was visibly shaking now, the room the same temperature as a walk-in freezer. Jack's mother's fingers twitched. It was taking all her restraint not to reach out to him.

His father unhooked his belt.

'I will not tolerate disobedience. You know the rules. As part of this family, you abide by my rules.'

'I'm sorry, Father.'

Jack's father ignored him. He turned to his wife.

'Do you know where I found him? Cavorting in the river with girls, half-naked!'

Jack quaked with fear whilst his father shook with rage. He turned to Jack, breathing heavily like a rhino. He held the belt between both hands, menacingly.

'I will have obedience. I will have an obedient son. I will not stand such disrespect. I raised you better than this. Not to be a foolish hooligan prancing around with the children of the corrupt and faithless.

'You've left me with no choice. I will have to punish you. You will learn what happens when you associate with unsuitable people. Now, turn around.'

Jack started to cry, he knew this would antagonise his father further, but his father was looking at him with a deranged fury and he couldn't stop the tears. He turned his bare back to his father and waited. There was no sound from behind him. Not knowing when it was going to happen was making him cry harder.

He heard the swish of the belt before the pain floored him. His mother screamed, ran forward and gathered him in her arms.

'Get off him!' snarled his father. But his mother ignored him. She clasped Jack to her, stroking his hair and rocked him back and forth making soothing noises. His father grabbed her blonde hair and threw her to the floor, ripping Jack from her arms. He hit her with the belt. The buckle caught her in the eye. She clutched her face and cowered in the corner.

Jack was pulled to his feet and turned around. The belt came down on the back of his thigh this time. He toppled over. Seizing his leg and sobbing into the concrete floor. From his vantage point, he could see his mother crying almost as hard as him. The skin around her eye was already discolouring, her eye almost swollen shut. She reached out and took his hand. He took strength from the feel of her warm, soft fingers wrapped around his.

Jack took deep breaths and calmed himself down. He needed to be strong for his mother. He needed to protect her and stop her from getting hurt. She had only been hit because she had been trying to comfort him. It was his fault. Ignoring the pain in his leg and back, Jack stood up. Turning to meet his father's gaze, he tried to adopt what he hoped was a sincere face.

'Father, I am sorry for what I did. Please can I go to my room to pray for the Lord's forgiveness.'

His father's face brightened instantly. He patted Jack on the shoulder.

'That's my boy. Of course. Off you go.'

Jack walked up to his bedroom, trying not to give away how much pain he was in. He felt a trickle of blood working its way down his back and his leg stabbed with pain every time the skin moved. He would make sure from now on that he obeyed his father. Vowing that he would also keep his mother safe.

CHAPTER SEVEN

NOW

His father's words stole the breath from his lungs. He lowered the knife and stared at him in disbelief.

'What are you talking about? We know why she died. She was murdered!' His grip on the knife tightened. Having spent his life dedicated to helping others, albeit influenced by Elsie, he now detested the human species. Elsie represented all that was good in the world and now she had been snuffed out by the scum of the earth.

'Exactly. There is a reason, son. There is a reason that the Lord took her from you.'

This was not what Jack wanted to hear. He had already discussed this with the reverend and was still grappling with the notion that it was free will that killed his wife.

He was unable to think about his faith. He couldn't believe that God would take Elsie from him. Under his father's roof, Jack had been taught that the Lord was strong and powerful, only rewarding those most steadfast in their faith. But Elsie had shown him that the Lord was loving, kind and helped him to understand what it meant that Jesus had sacrificed himself to save humanity.

'I don't understand,' Jack said.

His father pushed back his chair and moved towards him, his eyes shining and earnest.

'The Lord has taken Elsie from you, to give you the strength you need to carry out his will.'

Jack stared at his father, incredulous. His father, on the other hand, looked like he was going to burst with pride. He reached out and gripped his shoulder.

'You have been chosen, son.'

Jack shook his head, unable to process what his father was saying.

'He has chosen you to carry out his will. He has charged you with the most important task.'

'What task?'

'To rid the world of the sinful. To exterminate those that lie, cheat and steal to get what they want. The depraved people that are a scourge on our race.'

Jack shook his head. His father sounded ludicrous.

'Think about it, son, why else would the Lord have taken Elsie away from you?'

'I talked to the reverend about this. He said that God gave us free will. That it was free will that caused this, not God.'

'Everything is because of God. He is watching us and guiding us. And didn't the reverend also say that God still had plans for you? That you still have a purpose? Well, I'm telling you, this is your purpose.'

The enormity of his father's words pressed down on him and he sank back into his chair. A small part of him was eagerly feasting on this idea. He had been lost in a sea of grief, and a part of him was desperate to clutch this life raft. If what his father was saying was true, then he did have a reason to live. A purpose. His father paced up and down, gesturing with his hands as he spoke. Looking like an enigmatic lecturer.

'Just think about it, son. No one was punished for Elsie's death. It was murder. Her life was stolen by humanity. But it doesn't matter.'

Jack's blood burned his veins as he pictured his wife's last moments. The fact no one had been held accountable was making her death even harder to cope with. There had been murmurs of pressing charges but it had never come to fruition. Elsie's death was considered a tragic accident. No one was rotting in jail. The people responsible were still out there.

'Greed caused Elsie's death. She was murdered by human sin.'

'Okay. But I still don't understand what you expect me to do?'

His father pulled out the chair next to him and sat down. His hand gripped Jack's arm and he stared fervently into his eyes, using his body as well as his words to make Jack understand.

'You've been chosen, Jack. Elsie was killed by the very sin you have to stamp out. It's your destiny.'

Jack's head gave a painful lurch. He rubbed at his temples, trying to ease the pain in his head and his heart. He had spent a long time trying not to think of Elsie. Confronting her death again felt like losing her all over again. His father's words sounded melodramatic and crazy. But there was a small whispering in his mind saying, *what if he is right?*

Jack was suddenly reminded of the plaques Elsie had hung in their downstairs bathroom. *'God works in mysterious ways, it is not for us to question Him, but to trust in Him.'* Throughout their marriage Elsie had weathered any hardship by an innate acceptance that everything happened for a reason. He had heard her counselling her friends that God had a path for them. That God never gave anyone more than they could handle.

When Jack's father had discovered their relationship and

kicked Jack out of the house, it was only Elsie's unshakeable belief that this was part of their journey that had got them both through. Jack had gone to pieces. His father had been his whole world and he didn't know how to exist in this new reality. It was so loud and overwhelming.

But Elsie had guided him through.

'Trust in the Lord, Jack,' she would tell him. 'He has a path for us and we just have to follow it. Everything happens for a reason.'

She had been right. They had found their feet – with a little help from Elsie's parents – eventually getting married and buying a house of their own. Elsie had been resolute in her belief that she was following God's path. Which made Jack wonder, was what his father was saying as crazy as he first thought? Did Elsie die so that he could do this?

'Say you were right. What am I supposed to do exactly?'

His father seemed to be expecting this question and he turned around and picked up his Bible off the sideboard. He placed it down in front of Jack and tapped it with a finger.

'It's all in there, Jack. The word of God will guide you.'

Jack picked up the Bible and his father took the knife from Jack's other hand and walked to the middle of the table.

'Come on, let's eat. You will need your strength for the journey ahead.' He picked up a spearing fork and plunged it into the side of the roasted chicken. Juices spurted out of the hole. His father cut slice after slice off the chicken, until all that was left was bones and the purple stringy flesh Elsie refused to eat. Jack watched in silence. His mind racing with the ramifications of their conversation.

Jack was a good man. He didn't deserve this loss. Until today, Elsie's loss had felt so senseless. Not being able to understand why God would let this happen had made her death too hard to bear. But if there was actually a reason...

Jack thought about the people responsible for Elsie's death. He bet they weren't losing sleep over it. Not caring that Elsie's body was decomposing in a coffin. Jack's fury burned until his blood felt like lava in his veins. He picked up his cutlery and stabbed at the slices of chicken his father had loaded onto his plate. He tore into it. His father was right. He did need his strength. He was going to make the world pay.

CHAPTER EIGHT

THEN

The minute Jack walked through the front door he knew something was wrong. It was his eleventh birthday and his mother wasn't there to greet him. Last year she had been waiting with a cake and a party hat. The smell of baking wasn't emanating through the house. Hairs prickled on the back of his neck as he looked around. The house felt cold and lifeless.

'Mother?'

Silence answered him. With his heart beating furiously, he moved further into the kitchen. The oven door was open, a tray with a baking tin full of cake batter sat on the side. A whisk sat in a bowl of icing sugar, the water yet to be added. It was like someone had pressed pause and then erased his mother from view.

It was when he moved towards the back door that he saw the blood. A smudged handprint, too small to be his father's, was glistening on the floor. On unsteady legs, Jack followed a sinister trail of red droplets that led to the back door. Another handprint graced the door frame. He was reaching for the handle when his father's voice stopped him in his tracks.

'Boy!'

Jack spun around to see his father at the entrance of the kitchen.

'What are you doing here?'

'School's finished.'

'Oh, right.' There was something different about his father. He looked almost scruffy, his clothes were rumpled, and his skin coated in a thin layer of sweat.

'Where's mother?'

'Gone.'

'What do you mean gone?'

His father walked over to him and gestured to Jack to sit at the table. Jack sat down, his stomach fluttering.

'Son, do you know what adultery is?'

Jack shook his head.

'No, sir.'

'You are eleven, not too young to learn. Adultery is when a married woman lies with another man that is not her husband. Do you understand?'

Jack nodded his head. Not quite sure why a woman would want to lie in a bed with another man. It sounded very boring.

'The Bible tells us that adultery is a sin. And you know what a sin is, don't you?'

Jack nodded again emphatically.

'Adultery is punishable by death. It is one of the worst sins you can commit. To do it, lets the Devil in.'

Jack stared at his father. Not understanding exactly what he was trying to say. His father put his elbows on the table and cradled his head. He rubbed his face, looking exhausted. Finally, he looked Jack in the eye.

'I'm sorry to tell you, son, but I found out your mother was committing adultery.'

'No. Mother wouldn't do that.'

Anger flashed in his father's eyes and Jack shrank back in his chair. His father stood abruptly, glaring at him.

'Are you calling me a liar, boy?' His voice deafening and laced with an unspoken threat.

'I abhor lies. To lie is to let the Devil speak through you. Only weak people let the Devil in. Do you think me weak, boy?' His father looked crazed. He picked up a chair and threw it at the wall with such force the wooden legs splintered and cracked. Jack backed his chair away from his father, shrinking into a ball. Would he be the one thrown against the wall next?

'No, sir,' whimpered Jack. Clamping down on the tears that threatened. To cry would result in being thrown back in the homemade grave outside. He couldn't go back down there. He'd rather be here with his father than trapped back in that pitch-black, damp hole struggling to breathe and move. Not knowing if he would ever get out.

'I am an honourable man. I do not lie. Your mother was an adulterer. She cheated on me with another man. And now she has paid the price for her sin.'

'She's dead?' whispered Jack.

Jack's father nodded gravely.

'I had no choice.'

His father moved in front of him and bent down until his nose almost touched his own.

'I will not hear her name spoken in this house. She has dishonoured us both. We must turn our back on sin and show the Lord we are faithful, loyal servants.'

Jack nodded his head once more.

'Good. It's just you and me now, son.'

His father stood up and ruffled Jack's hair. He left him alone to stare at the beginnings of the last birthday cake his mother would ever make him.

CHAPTER NINE

NOW

B y the end of their dinner, Jack was convinced that his father was right. It was the only thing that made sense. He retired to bed with the Bible in his hands. As a child, he had read the Old Testament but now, it was as though he was reading a completely different book. Past readings of the Old Testament had never evoked such emotion in him before. He could almost feel the Lord's presence in his room. He no longer felt like he was reading words on a page. It felt like the Lord himself was sat on the end of his bed speaking directly to him. Charging him with this most important mission.

Jack drank in the commands. *Romans chapter 13: verse 4: For the one in authority is God's servant for your good. But if you do wrong, be afraid, for rulers do not bear the sword for no reason. They are God's servants, agents of wrath to bring punishment on the wrongdoer.*

Closing the Bible, Jack laid there staring up at the ceiling. He felt happiness stirring inside him. Elsie's death had exsanguinated him but this knowledge that there was a reason for her death, that he was God's disciple with a vital mission, was now returning the blood to his body, bringing him back to life.

Waking up the next morning, Jack felt rejuvenated. He had slept a dreamless sleep without a single image of Elsie plaguing his mind. His father came into the room and saw the smile on Jack's face and returned it.

'Praise be to the Lord, my Rock, who trains my hands for war, my fingers for battle,' recited Jack.

'That's my boy,' he said and he turned and left the room.

Jack was revitalised by a sense of purpose and almost leapt out of bed. He was ready to do God's work. He just needed a plan. As he made his way downstairs, he could hear bacon sizzling in the pan, the smell perfuming the whole house. His heart lurched as he saw his father and not Elsie. The pain was strong but no longer as debilitating. Not now he understood why she was gone. He almost felt closer to her. That her spirit was following him, spurring him on. She had spent her whole life doing God's work. Working in the inner city with her parents supporting the homeless. Volunteering for more groups and charities than Jack could remember. She would approve of him doing God's work. He just knew she would be proud of him for not letting his grief destroy him.

'Morning, Father.'

Jack took his place at the table and his father placed a bacon sandwich in front of him. The thick bread coated liberally with butter and what looked like an entire packet of bacon inside. He could just picture Elsie's disapproving face. As they advanced in years, so too did her obsession with health and living longer. Which to her meant not eating the things you loved.

'This looks lovely, Father. Thank you.'

His father sat down and smiled.

'It's fine. You need feeding up.'

Jack inhaled his sandwich in a few bites. Bitterly disappointed when it was gone. His father raised his eyebrows. Jack smiled sheepishly.

'It's been a long time since I've had a bacon sandwich. Elsie was trying to make us eat healthier. You know she once even tried to make me eat Facon. Some weird fake bacon she thought was healthier. It tasted like fried cardboard.'

His father barked with laughter.

'You can't beat proper meat. God intended us to be carnivores. It makes my blood boil when I see all these vegans and vegetarians bleating on. It's God's will for us to eat meat. It's the circle of life.' He thumped his hand on the table, a full stop to his rant. Jack smiled inwardly. This was more like it. His father's rants had been a daily occurrence through his childhood. It was nice to know that side of him was still there. Jack had been feeling wary living with this version of his father who seemed kind, thoughtful and caring. It was nice but so unlike the father he had grown up with. It was good to see a more familiar side of him.

Jack agreed with his father and they both sat in a companionable silence enjoying their breakfast. Finishing his cup of tea, Jack wasn't sure what he was supposed to do with his day. It felt like the first day of the rest of his life. Every action he took needed to be momentous and fulfilling his new purpose. But he was at a loss of how to start.

'Father, about what we decided last night. You know, about me doing God's work.' It sounded so silly when he said it out loud. Who was he to decide he was capable of doing God's work? It felt like announcing he had decided he was a superhero.

'What about it?'

'Well. How?'

'What do you mean how?'

'What am I supposed to do? How do I go about ridding the world of greed? I don't even know where to start.'

'Son, God has charged you with this mission, he will show you the way. You just need to watch for a sign. He will give you one and you'll know it when you see it.'

It wasn't very much to go on.

'What sort of sign?'

His father bristled. His mug of tea paused in the air as he stared at Jack with flashing eyes.

'For Pete's sake. Why do you insist on being so impatient? God will reveal your path to you when it is time. Not when you want him to. Just wait.'

Jack felt his heart hammering in his chest. He may be in his fifties but he had not forgotten how easily his father could succumb to violence. Instantly, he was reminded of the hole in the ground that only lay a few metres from him outside. He hung his head, chastised.

Jack's mobile phone interrupted them. The old-school ringtone piercing the room, a sound Elsie was forever complaining about. Susan's name flashed across the screen. He sighed. Susan had been their first friend when they had moved to Winterford. They had not even had time to unlock the door for the first time when Susan had appeared from nowhere like a ghost. Back then she had been a leggy blonde with two toddlers clutching each of her legs. Elsie had fallen in love with all three of them at first sight.

Susan's husband, Tim, had passed many years ago and the loss encouraged her to embed herself firmly in their lives. Elsie became Susan's emotional crutch and Jack a reluctant surrogate husband to lift anything heavy and fix leaky taps. He had given up being irritated by Susan a long time ago, realising she was like a small splinter he couldn't remove so then the skin had grown over it. Reluctantly accepting her as an interloper that could not be excised. To be fair to Susan, she had taken the loss of Elsie almost as hard as him. They had been friends for over thirty years. Elsie had helped her raise her children and they had been inseparable most of their adult lives.

Jack stared at the phone. He didn't want to talk to Susan. She reminded him too much of what he had lost. He needed to focus on his mission. All his attention must be on spotting the next sign that would show him what to do next. But he pushed the answer button, knowing it would be what Elsie would want him to do.

'Jack. Darling. How are you?'

'Hello, Susan. I'm holding up, how are you?'

'Dreadful, it still hasn't sunk in. I haven't been able to work, I can't sleep, I'm a wreck. You are so lucky you don't have to work. I just can't face other people. They don't understand. I need to be around people that understand how much I miss her.'

Susan began to cry. Hysterical, she was gasping for breath, her words no longer intelligible. Jack didn't want Susan coming to his father's home. He would never get rid of her if he did. He'd learnt the hard way that once you invited Susan in she never left. She invaded like Japanese knotweed.

'Don't cry, Susan. I'll come and see you. Why don't we go for a drink? I'll come over today. I can meet you at the Noble at about 5pm? Is that all right?'

Susan's hysterics stopped abruptly. The pub was Susan's second home. Newcomers often mistook her for the landlady. The Noble Arms wouldn't be recognisable if it didn't have Susan propping up the bar. Elsie used to tease her saying she was a part of the furniture. It struck him that he had never been there without Elsie. In fact, now he thought about it, he hadn't gone many places without her.

Jack had worked on a digger for a local quarry, a job Elsie's father had managed to get him. He had slowly worked his way up until a freak accident caused by a defective piece of machinery stole his career from him. He was left with permanent damage to his knees and a large compensatory cheque. Elsie thought it was fantastic as they were set for life. The money had paid off their mortgage and there was a lot left over. But Jack had been devastated at first. He had lost his reason to get up in the morning. The pain in his knees was a constant reminder of the career he once had. But he soon realised that the accident had actually been a blessing. He got to spend every single day with Elsie. Everywhere she went, he went. But not anymore. The thought caused him to punch the wall in his bedroom. His knuckles bleeding, his blood smeared on the wall. He took bracing breaths, reminding himself that he needed this pain if he was going to succeed in his mission.

CHAPTER TEN

THEN

In the days after his mother's death, Jack hated his father with a vengeance that burned inside him. He had taken away the only person who had loved him. Jack's father didn't love him. Not the way his mother did. Jack remembered the way her face had lit up each and every day he returned from school. The way she opened her arms wide for a hug and would never let go until Jack prised her off him, giggling.

His mother may have committed a sin, but she didn't deserve to die. Surely all the good things she did should count for something. The way she looked after his father and Jack. She always made home-cooked meals, she washed all of his father's clothes and went to church. The house felt soulless now she wasn't filling it with her warmth and affection. His father seemed to be trying to make up for her lack of presence with his own. Usually, he spent a lot more time at church and outside but now he seemed to have decided being with Jack was more important. Only Jack didn't want him there. Whenever they were together it was triggering murderous and violent thoughts.

The night his father had killed his mother, Jack's father had called him downstairs. There were two pieces of bread and some cheese on a plate. He motioned at Jack to sit down and he devoured the food in a matter of minutes whilst his father stood over him, waiting. His father picked up his plate and replaced it with two pieces of lined paper and a pencil. On the first piece of paper, his father had written:

If a man commits adultery with the wife of his neighbour, both the adulterer and the adulteress shall surely be put to death. Leviticus, chapter 20, verse 10.

For the whole evening, Jack's father had him copy the quote from the Bible over and over until both sides of the sheets of paper were full. He sat at the kitchen table, copying the quote slowly, knowing nothing good would come if he made a mistake. The fire crackled in the hearth while he carefully drew each letter. His father sat at the other end of the table, reading from his well-worn Bible. By the time he had finished, Jack's hand was aching from holding the pencil so hard. His father inspected his work and nodded. Picking up the paper he threw it into the fire. The flames quickly devoured the sheets, burning away the words he had painstakingly crafted.

'Bed,' ordered his father.

Jack lay in bed and pictured his mother. If he screwed up his eyes and put the pillows to the side of him and stroked his own face he could almost convince himself she was there. That it was her hand caressing his cheek. Telling him how much she loved her 'Jack the lad'. The next day, Jack refused to get out of bed. He couldn't stop thinking about his mum. His arms ached to hug her. Just when he thought he had cried his last tear, more would come. The skin around his eyes was raw and he was crying so hard that he kept losing his breath, making him choke.

The thought he was going to be left with his cold, violent father for the rest of his life was unbearable. He wanted his mother. For three days Jack lay on his bed. He had wet the bed several times, but he didn't care. Jack was drowning in memories of his mother. Whenever he closed his eyes he would see her smiling at him. He'd remember the games of tig that they would play. Running round and round the house, laughing until they fell in a heap on the floor. The nights when his father went to a local prayer group and she would run him a bath and wash his hair, lathering bubbles so that she could make a shark fin on his head. Sometimes he wouldn't be able to picture her at all and that terrified him.

On the third day, Jack heard footsteps outside his door. His father didn't knock, he just strode into the room. He wrinkled his nose in disgust. Marching over to Jack, he grabbed him by his arm and tossed him over his shoulder like he was a knapsack. Jack clung on as his father marched him into the bathroom. Jack was dropped to the floor and in a matter of moments his father had stripped him down and then chucked him into the bath. The hot water scalded his skin. Jack cried out but it fell on deaf ears.

'Wash,' his father ordered, handing him a cloth.

The habit of obeying his father was stronger than his grief and he began to wash himself. Unable to look his father in the eye. His father stood there, watching him. The water seemed to wash away not just the dirt of the last few days but his self-control. His anger at his father caused his body to start shaking. He stood up, rage boiling over. Jack wanted to lash out at him. An urge to start punching and kicking his father stirred within him.

'Wash, boy,' his father sneered. 'You're disgusting.'

'Yeah, well I'd rather be disgusting than a murderer!' shouted Jack. He made to get out of the bath but his father was quicker.

'What did you call me?' he snarled. Lurching forward, his hands closed around Jack's throat. He scratched and pulled at his father's hands but he was no match for his strength. Jack stared into his steel-grey eyes that blazed with unbridled anger. He wondered if they would be the last thing he ever saw as his vision was beginning to darken around the edges.

His father loosened his grip and Jack gulped in air. The relief was short-lived. In a blur he went from standing to being held underneath the bathwater. Jack's brain reeled in shock. He ingested a lungful of water before clamping his mouth shut. Water penetrated his nose, creating a painful burning sensation. He tried twisting and bucking to break free of his father's grip. His lungs strained, bereft of oxygen. Terror flooded him and he kicked and pushed at his father. *He's going to kill me.*

He was pulled out of the water and thrown onto the bathroom floor like a rag doll. Jack gulped in the air, coughing and spluttering on the floor. His throat burned in pain and his chest heaved. His limbs were shaking and he felt weak and exhausted. Jack looked up as his father approached him and bent down. His eyes full of fury, pinning him to the spot. He was so close Jack could see all of his eyelashes and some nose hair peeking out of the bottom of his nose.

'I. Am. Not. A. Murderer.' He punctuated each word with a finger, jabbing it into Jack's chest. 'I follow the word of God. I act as he instructs me. One day you will see, I had no choice. Your mother was a sinner. She had to be punished accordingly. One day you'll see that.

'But if I ever hear you call me a murderer again you'll go the same way as her.' He pointed to the bathtub. 'Next time I won't pull you out.'

Jack fled the bathroom on shaky legs. He sat in his bed and wrapped himself in his urine-soaked sheets. Shivering with fear and shock. Jack had felt the claws of death on his skin. He cried himself to sleep wondering if that was what his mother had felt in the seconds before she died.

Morning broke the next day and his father woke him at 5am.

'Time to get up and do your chores before school.'

For the next two hours, Jack washed all the bed linen and hung them out on the washing line. He made them both some toast and fed the chickens and collected their eggs. Strangely, he felt closer to his mother, doing the things that she used to do. Jack avoided his father the whole morning. Every time he came close to him, he shied away. Flinching if his father moved too fast. School time couldn't come soon enough.

'I told your teacher you had a fever and that's why you haven't been in. I expect you to tell her the same thing.' The look in his eyes had Jack nodding his head vigorously. The feeling of drowning under the water flashing through his mind.

Jack raced through the school gates and spent the whole day pretending his mother was still alive. By the end of the day, he had almost convinced himself that it had been a bad dream and his mother would be waiting for him in the kitchen. She would open her arms wide and envelop him in a hug that he would refuse to let end. He would stay there forever, wrapped in her beautiful, loving arms. Instead, his father was waiting for him at the kitchen table.

'Sit.'

Jack sat down at the table.

His father laid another two pieces of lined A4 paper in front of him and a pencil. On one of the pages, the words *If a man be*

*found lying with a woman married to a husband, then they shall
both of them die, both the man that lay with the woman, and the
woman. Deuteronomy, chapter 22, verse 22.*

'Copy it.'

Jack opened his mouth to protest but the look in his father's
eyes warned him not to argue. For the next hour, Jack
painstakingly copied each letter. He was slow and meticulous,
not wanting to give his father an excuse to punish him. The only
sound was his pencil on the paper and the crackle of the flames
in the fireplace. His father was sat at the other end of the
wooden kitchen table, reading his Bible and glancing up at Jack
every few minutes. Jack didn't really understand why his father
needed to read it when he knew it off by heart.

At last, he had finished and he threw down the pencil. At
the sound, his father looked up. He checked it for errors and
threw the paper into the fire again. The flames leapt up as if
gratefully devouring Jack's work within minutes. His father
moved to the side and picked up two plates containing a quiche
and salad. There was no way his father knew how to make
quiche. It had to be a store-bought shop. The injustice burned.
He always made his mother cook everything from scratch.

It was only as he got into bed that night, that he wondered
what had happened to the person his mother had committed
adultery with. According to the Bible, he should be put to death
just like his mother. Had his father killed him as well? Part of
him hoped so. Because that way the police would come and
arrest his father. Then he might escape and live somewhere he
didn't have to spend nights copying lines from the Bible,
kneeling on rice and being trapped underground.

CHAPTER ELEVEN

NOW

A t 5pm, Jack walked into the Noble Arms. From the outside, it looked unloved and unattractive. The N on the sign outside had fallen off and the plant pots were now a graveyard of rotting flowers. The noise inside the pub assaulted his ears.

Jack had forgotten how different living in the countryside was compared to the cities and towns. When they had moved into their first home together, even though it was only a village, he found it incredibly hard to adjust. He had thought his eardrums were going to explode from overuse. He had spent his life growing up with almost complete silence in the evenings, only disturbed by the gentle sounds of nature, the hoot of an owl. The worst and loudest sound was the mercurial weather. He had been awoken occasionally by the rain lashing at the windows or the wind shaking the window frames. But in the village, he was unable to sleep for a long time. The sounds of passing cars, people slamming doors or shouting at each other had tormented him until finally he had learnt to ignore them. He'd only been back at Oakdale Farm for a few days and already he was relishing the tranquillity it offered.

The inside of the pub was the antithesis of the outside. Here some actual care and attention had been paid. The tables had recently been replaced and battery-powered candles adorned all the surfaces along with fancy wine glasses, funky placemats and a menu board that broadcasted swordfish as the latest special.

The locals steadfastly congregated around the bar, ignoring the glamour of the restaurant tables. Squeezing in like sardines. Preferring to lean on the bar and ignore their aching legs.

Jack felt all eyes turn to appraise him as he walked in. Judging him disinteresting, they resumed their conversations and like a large swarm of bees had entered the room, the humming intensified once more. Susan was at the end of the bar, her hand gently gripping the arm of a muscly young man. She was wearing a short black skirt, legs bare and her feet stuffed painfully into sky-high shoes. Her blue blouse was much too tight and revealed much too much cleavage. Well, for Jack it did, judging by the glances the young man was giving her cleavage, he did not agree. The young man must have been at least twenty years her junior. Wearing ripped jeans, a rugby T-shirt and a shaved head, he was exactly the type of prey she went for. Jack watched as Susan gazed up at the man through her eyelashes. Ever the seductress.

It was a move he had watched her make numerous times. Tim had been Susan's one true love and she had never had a desire to replace him. Instead, she had contented herself with meaningless encounters. It was the only thing she and Elsie ever disagreed on and to save their friendship Elsie was forced to ignore it.

Susan spotted Jack and immediately walked away from the man. The young man looked crestfallen as his sure thing had now vanished. He threw Jack a dark look and stalked off to the other side of the room. Susan threw her arms around Jack. Suffocating him with a cloud of cloying perfume. Susan squeezed him tightly and her hair tickled his face. Jack tried to move away but she clung on to him.

'Oh, Jack.' He felt her shoulders shake and realised she was crying. His face heated and he felt eyes on them. Jack patted her back awkwardly. Susan was one of those people who didn't understand personal boundaries. She couldn't comprehend a world where a person wouldn't want to hug another person. Jack could quite happily live in such a world. One-armed hugs were wrangled from him. Except for Elsie. His arms ached with the emptiness, a longing to wrap his arms around his wife consumed him and tears pricked his eyes. Susan's bony body in his arms felt foreign. He felt a wave of nausea and forcibly unclasped her hands from around his neck.

'Let's sit down, Susan.'

Susan led him to a table at the back of the restaurant. Instead of taking the chair opposite him, she chose the one next to him. Shuffling as close as possible. Her hand reached out for his and she clasped it hard.

'How are you, my darling Jack?'

'I'm okay, Susan. Muddling through.'

'It's just terrible, isn't it? To lose Elsie that way.' She shook her head. 'If only you hadn't gone shopping on Black Friday.'

'Black Friday?'

Jack looked at her, confused. He tried to pull his hand away but she held tight. Stroking the back of his hand with her thumb. It made his skin crawl, like a bug was walking across it and he desperately wanted to swat it.

'You're not saying you don't know what Black Friday is?'

Jack looked at her blankly.

'Oh, Jack. Elsie always said you were a bit of a dinosaur but honestly.' She laughed. A tinkly noise like breaking glass.

'Black Friday is this one day a year, where all the shops offer massive discounts before Christmas. I think it started in America but it's everywhere now. There can be some real bargains.'

Her face looked stricken as it seemed to hit her once more that a sale was the reason Elsie was dead.

'So, it was because it was Black Friday, that's why the store had that sale?'

'Yes, it's really famous. In fact, I think it's called Black Friday because so many people have had black eyes from fighting over the sales. I saw something where these people were fighting over this one remaining TV on a shelf. I think they both ended up in hospital over it.'

She dug out her phone from her back pocket.

'There are loads of videos online.'

Susan shoved the phone into Jack's hands and he watched as two women ripped each other's hair out in the middle of a shopping centre. He could see children in the background watching open-mouthed. Jack couldn't see what they were fighting over but they were both grabbing onto something black and hitting and kicking each other with their free arms. In horror, Jack saw the women fall to the floor, kicking and shrieking at one another like vicious animals. Another woman tried to break up the fight but walked off when she got kicked in the stomach. The clip ended with two men ripping the women apart.

Then the phone told him a new video was starting in five seconds called *'Brawl at the Mall'*. A whole crowd of people were in a shop. He could see two security guards grappling against them. He saw a male security guard pull a woman around her neck to the floor. The woman was defenceless because both her hands were preoccupied holding on to a large box with what looked like a DVD player. The crowd pressed around them as the security guard wrestled the woman to the floor. Putting all his weight on her back. The camera panned out and Jack could see boxes flying across the room as people seemed to be throwing things to each other. It looked more like a raid than a sale.

Another clip loaded, *'Asda Black Friday Madness'*. Asda staff were barricading the door, stopping the massive crowd from entering the shop.

Then the doors opened and the huge crowd burst through the entrance, shoving others out of the way violently. Animal instincts had taken over, their hunger and selfishness had possessed them. Someone fell to the floor and was immediately trampled on by the swell of people. Jack dropped the phone and it clattered onto the concrete floor. His hands were shaking violently and bile rushed up from his stomach. Again, he was assaulted with memories of Elsie.

Susan's cry of frustration died on her lips when she caught sight of Jack's face.

'Oh, Jack. I'm so sorry, I didn't think.'

She clutched him to her and he was clamped between her breasts. Jack was too distraught to care. It was hard to breathe as he tried to purge his mind of the memory of watching his wife die. After a minute or two he regained his composure. He pushed Susan away and moved his chair back, firmly distancing himself from her. She stooped to pick up her phone and he saw her wince at the shattered screen. The images he witnessed had triggered rage like he had never felt before. He sat on his hands as the urge to pick up the wine glasses near him and throw them at the people in the pub consumed him. *Humanity is disgusting. The immorality. The wickedness.* He could understand completely why God called forth the flood in Genesis. Only he wouldn't have saved any of the people, only the animals deserved saving. Humanity was wicked. Evil. They have given in to the Devil.

Misunderstanding the tears of anger in his eyes, Susan changed the subject. Not realising the battle that he faced inside. The urge to destroy everyone in the room with them.

CHAPTER TWELVE

THEN

Jack had fallen into a rhythm, after school he would write lines and then his father would make them dinner. Everything was cold as it seemed it wasn't just Jack that had relied upon his mother for her culinary expertise. But today, there was no pencil and paper waiting on the table. Instead, his father pointed at the oven.

'You are old enough now to start taking on more responsibility in the house. You can make the dinner tonight.'

Jack stood rooted to the spot. He didn't have a clue how to cook. He had watched his mother, flitting around effortlessly, stirring, chopping and frying food with ease. But he'd never really taken an interest in what she was doing. It hadn't entered his mind that there may be a future where his mother would not be there to do it.

His father had walked off, presumably to his workshop in one of the stone outbuildings surrounding the house. Staring with horror at the oven, it seemed to be taunting him. *Surely there hadn't been that many dials when his mother had used it.* Jack clenched his fists as hopelessness and anger flared within him. It was bad enough that his father had taken his mother from him and now was expecting him to cook him his dinner. He should be cooking for Jack, trying to make amends for taking his mother away.

Putting down his school bag, Jack rummaged through the cupboards and fridge. Locating some sausages, he decided they would have those and salad. After much searching, Jack found a tray that looked like the one his mother would have put in the oven. Taking the sausages out of the packet, he grimaced at the slimy feel on his skin. *Gross.* Not sure why the sausages were tied together, he laid them in the tray and walked over to the oven. He stopped and stared at the dials, no idea which one he needed. After careful examination he worked out that four of them were for the hobs and that just left two others. One had numbers and the other had symbols on it. Jack kicked the oven. Tears of anger and frustration threatened. His mother should be here. She should be doing this. Or his father even.

Giving up, Jack took a punt and turned both dials at random and placed the sausages into the oven. He had no idea how long he was supposed to wait and so he sat down, cross-legged in front of the oven to wait. Jack could just make out the sausages through the glass window of the oven but it wasn't a clear view owing to the number of stains covering it.

Head in his hands, Jack waited. Before long, he could start to smell the faint aroma of cooking sausages. It filled the kitchen and his stomach gurgled in gleeful anticipation. His bottom started to go numb from sitting on the cold tiles and he moved over to his school bag to retrieve his homework. Mrs Mills had set him some maths homework and he was looking forward to starting it. Most of the subjects at school were boring but Jack liked the way his brain felt when he did maths. It was like running but for his brain. Thinking about the maths problem in front of him, he could feel his brain straining to work it out. The happiness he felt once he had worked out the answer always gave him a buzz. Mrs Mills said he was a natural at maths. It gave him a glow inside. No one apart from his mother had ever told him he was good at something.

Jack was engrossed in his homework. He had moved on to the next page of questions even though they were for next week. Hoping that he would get another impressed smile from Mrs Mills. He was just picturing her telling all the class how clever he was when a smell distracted him. It smelt like burning. Jack jumped from the chair and raced to the oven. He opened the door and retreated from a blast of smoke and hot air.

Blackened lumps that used to be sausages sat on the tray in the middle of the oven. Panicking about what his father was going to say, without thinking about what he was doing he reached in to pull them out. The pain was immediate. He screamed as he felt the burning hot metal binding to his skin. The tray fell to the floor and he stared at his hands in horror.

The back door slammed open and his father raced in. He took in the sight and a strange look crossed his face. Before Jack could try and understand it, his father moved swiftly towards him. Gently, his father guided him to the sink and held his hand under the tap. It was pure torture. The cold water cascaded onto his hands. Jack thrashed and bucked, trying to get away but his eleven-year-old muscles couldn't budge his father. Jack's father held him firmly in place until Jack could no longer feel his hands. Silent tears streamed down his face. He dared not look at his father. Not wanting to be punished any more than he already was.

Eventually, his father turned off the tap and inspected Jack's hands. Bright red welts lined his fingers and palms. His father guided him to the chair and sat him down. He rummaged around in a cupboard, pulling out random items until he found a box at the back.

'Your mother thought I didn't know she had this,' he said,

giving Jack a smile as he brought the small box to the table. It contained creams, plasters and bandages. Jack stared at him open-mouthed. Seeming to read Jack's mind, his father spoke again.

'Now I know that God will heal this for you, as long as you are faithful and loyal. But I suppose there is no harm in speeding up the process just this once.' He gave Jack another smile. With a tenderness Jack would not have thought possible, his father then daubed the welts with cream. It hurt at first but the coolness quickly soothed the burns. His nerve endings were no longer screaming in pain but grumbling tolerably.

Jack stared at his father. Unable to believe what he was seeing. It was like a stranger in his father's body. If Mr Moore at school hadn't showed them in science class, definitive proof that aliens weren't real, he would have firmly believed his father had been replaced by one. Not in a single memory had his father ever done anything remotely nice for him. His motto 'spare the rod, spoil the child' had governed his parenting style. Jack had spent his entire life fearing his father. Terrified he would do something wrong that would result in another terrible punishment. He couldn't reconcile this version of his father. It made his brain hurt. He was so confused. Was his father going to be nice to him now?

Whilst Jack tried to fathom this change in his father's behaviour, his father cleaned up the mess Jack had made. He didn't berate or yell at him. Just binned the cremated sausages. When he was finished, he pulled some ham and cheese out of the fridge and proceeded to make them both a sandwich. To Jack's astonishment, his father cut his into small pieces and proceeded to feed them to him.

Jack couldn't stop staring at his father. This man was now feeding him food as if he cared. That didn't make sense to Jack, given the violent and cold outbursts he had experienced his whole life. The simple act of putting some cream on his son's hand and feeding him food felt abnormal. Feelings of gratitude were swirling in his stomach and despite himself Jack couldn't help but nurture a hope that this side of his father was here to stay. A pang of guilt rose within him. This man had murdered his mother.

His father finished his own sandwich and cleared their plates. There were another two pieces of paper and the pencil lying on the bureau that his father would sit at to do his paperwork. His father looked over at Jack and then put them away in the drawer of the bureau.

'We will put some more cream on them before bed.' He held an arm out to Jack. 'Let's go into the living room and do some reading.' They passed a peaceful evening with his father reading his favourite passages from Matthew. His Bible so worn that some of the pages he had to hold in place so they didn't fall to the floor. Despite himself, Jack couldn't help but listen, his father had an enchanting voice. The words that were just boring and underwhelming when Jack had read them on the page, came alive in the hands of his father. The passion and emotion he breathed into each word was captivating. Jack's father was devoted in his adoration of the Lord. So much so that it was infectious. It made Jack want to feel that strongly about the Lord too. He lived to serve and it was awe-inspiring. It explained why his father would be able to commit murder, if commanded to by the Lord he served so faithfully.

By the end of the following week, Jack was facing an internal battle. The hole in his life left by his mother was gaping and painful. But it felt like God was trying to send him a message. Why else would his teacher have chosen that week to start teaching them about the Ten Commandments?

'He stole money. Lots of money. God found out and the

next thing, he's being shot by the police,' Peter said to the class. He used his fingers to mime shooting a gun. 'Bang. Bang.'

'That doesn't mean he died because he broke the Ten Commandments,' retorted Jack. Unable to help himself, his mother in his thoughts.

'Of course it does. Everyone that breaks a Tenth Commandment will die. Everyone knows that, stupid.'

'Peter. Don't say things like that,' rebuked Mrs Halfpenny.

'Is that true, miss?' Jack asked in small voice.

Mrs Halfpenny looked uncomfortable.

'Yes, Jack. The Bible does say that those who break the Ten Commandments should die.' She carried on but Jack could no longer hear her. His ears were ringing. His father had been telling the truth. His mother really did have to die.

It would have been easier to hate his father if he was still a violent bully every moment of the day. But there were times that Jack started to feel a genuine bond with his father. His father teaching him the basics of growing his own food. He talked him through everything and patiently watched as he tried to replicate his father's actions. They now cooked together and his father would tell him about the world. How important it was to be self-sufficient. There were times where he actually liked his father. But then he would be wracked with guilt in the early hours of the morning, as he remembered that his father had killed his mother.

His father didn't even shy away from it. Whenever his mother came up in conversation, he would sigh and express his regret that she had not been obedient and followed the word of God.

'It's in the Bible, son, wives *must* obey their husbands.'

Once his hands had healed. The lines returned and Jack was instructed once more to write the same words over and over again every night. He started to resent his mother's behaviour as he was being punished for it. In the same moment he felt awful.

Jack's thoughts on his mother's murder were becoming murkier. His father was telling him over and over again that his mother was a bad person. Even the teachers at school had confirmed that the Ten Commandments had to be followed. But it was hard for Jack because he had loved his mother fiercely. It was hard to think of her as a bad person when all she had ever shown him was love and affection. Why should he listen to the man that had spent most of Jack's life scaring and punishing him? A vision of his father gently rubbing the cream into his palm crept into his mind. Maybe he wasn't so bad after all?

CHAPTER THIRTEEN

NOW

'Oh, I know.' Susan looked around the pub and moved closer to Jack, as if about to tell him a government secret as opposed to some idle village gossip. 'Eileen told me that Winterford has its very first tramp.'

'A tramp?' Jack asked.

'You know, a homeless person.' Her nose wrinkled with disgust as she spoke. 'Eileen saw him sitting against the wall outside the pub. Dirty hair, dirty clothes. A plastic cup in front of him and asking everyone that walked past him to spare some change.'

Jack knew if Elsie had been sat with them she would have been off to find him. She would have stayed with him until she had got him off the street.

'According to Mary, he's been doing the rounds of all the villages, begging for money. He chooses popular dog-walking routes so he is guaranteed to be seen by a lot of people. Apparently, he's been doing very well out of everyone. I suppose it's that time of the year, people are always more generous when it comes to Christmas.' Susan looked disgusted but her eyes were lit up with excitement. Nothing made her happier than spreading gossip. 'But the worst thing is, my friend, Jennifer – she works in reception at the police station in Redditch – said apparently, this homeless man isn't actually homeless. They've been investigating him as it seems he's got a house in Redditch,' Susan crowed. Eyes wide with fake disbelief. She told this story with a practised nuance that informed him he was not the only person she had said this to.

'He's just spending his days begging instead of going to work. According to Debbie, he gets up at 5pm on the dot and walks out of the village. Isn't it awful, Jack? Scamming us hard workers out of hard-earned money instead of doing a hard day's graft. I don't know how he lives with himself. I haven't seen him, but I will give him a piece of my mind when I do. Mark my words.'

But Jack was no longer listening. A light bulb had gone off in his mind. He could hear his father saying, *'God will give you a sign.'* This was it. This was the sign. This fake homeless man was his first target.

'Do you think he'll be there tomorrow?' Jack asked, trying to appear nonchalant.

'I'd imagine so. Mary said he seems to do a week in each village before he moves on. The bloody cheek of him. I tell you, there is a real lack of human decency at the moment. What with what those folks did to poor Elsie and now we've got a tramp trying to steal our money. It could really get you down if you let it.'

Jack had to bite his lip. He wanted to tell her that that she didn't need to worry. That he had been chosen to fix exactly that. But if he told Susan, then within minutes, her network of whispering women would be spreading the word. Jack knew that not everyone would understand. They might even get in the way and stop him from accomplishing God's work. It was too important to risk. So, he held his tongue and allowed Susan to carry on talking. He was lucky that she was the type of person that thought their voice was a beautiful melody that everyone wanted to hear, so she didn't require or want much more than a nod or grunt from him. Whilst Susan spoke, Jack was pondering what he was going to do. The path he was taking had suddenly become very real. He wasn't sure that he was up to the task but then – just as God intended – he remembered how Elsie died and his conviction was renewed.

He pulled up at Oakdale Farm as his father was coming out of the church. Jack noticed it was starting to look very run-down after decades of battling with the wind, rain and snow. He remembered his father spending weeks erecting it. It was nothing more than a wooden box with a cross pinned to the inside wall but to his father it was palatial in its worth. This was where he communed with the Lord. It was his sacred space. To Jack it was a place of punishment. The nights he had spent in there, ordered to pray for forgiveness from the Lord whilst he slowly froze as the temperature plummeted in the early hours of the night.

Jack followed his father into the house, speaking quickly in his excitement.

'Father, I've had a sign. I know what I need to do.'

His father put the kettle on and pulled down two cups from the shelf before turning to face Jack.

'Brilliant. Tell me everything.'

Jack filled him in on the tramp in Winterford.

'I mean if that wasn't a sign – a con man in the village I lived in with Elsie.'

'I agree, son.'

Jack looked out the window, trying to choose the right words. Something had been bothering him all the way home.

'Father, what am I going to do with the man? Like, I know

God wants me to extinguish greed. But how am I supposed to do that exactly?'

His father let out a large sigh. 'I thought we'd already had this conversation.'

'I know I'm supposed to... supposed to kill' – the word felt foreign in his mouth – 'him. But how do I do it?'

After all, his father had first-hand experience of murder. Jack pushed the threatening memory away. Now wasn't the time for a trip down memory lane. He needed to focus. To plan his next move.

'I'm going to say this one more time. The Lord will show you the way. He will be with you, guiding your hand and showing you the path. You just have to trust him and listen.'

His father was right, he just had to trust in the Lord. He was the Lord's vessel. When the time was right, He would show him the way.

'We need to make a plan.'

They brainstormed late into the night over a dinner of spaghetti bolognaise and garlic bread. Neither of them well versed in kidnap but eventually they came up with a plan. Jack went to bed with butterflies in his stomach. He wanted to do this right. Elsie's life had been sacrificed so that he would have the strength to do this. He would not let her death be in vain.

CHAPTER FOURTEEN

THEN

When his mother died, Jack swore he would never forget her and always hold on to his hatred of his father. But it was getting harder to keep that promise. His father was evolving slowly in his eyes and Jack was powerless to stop it. They had developed a routine. Each morning they got up at 5am and his father would teach him things. Currently, he was showing him how to sow seeds in the garden. They spent hours as the sun rose slowly behind them hoeing the ground, getting it ready for seeds. Every evening they would pray together before bed. Taking it in turns to lead the prayer. Jack's father was treating him with the respect that he had craved his whole childhood.

He took Jack to church with him each Sunday and he would talk to Jack all the way there and all the way back. On the way there, he would point out all the trees and plants, teaching Jack the names.

'That there is an oak tree. Did you know that oak trees can live for over two hundred years?'

On the way home from church, Jack would then identify the ones he remembered. Enjoying the rush of pleasure at each nod of approval from his father. Over dinner, they would discuss the sermon and his father would test him to see how well he had been listening. Then after dinner, Jack would read from the Bible out loud to his father. Jack was beginning to understand why his father was so intensely obsessed with his religion. With his father's guidance, he could see the magic of the Lord in everything around him. He wanted nothing more than to serve the Lord as faithfully as his father did. That desire seemed to bring them closer as father and son.

They cooked together each night, they worked on the garden and cared for the animals. Jack's father taught him everything about the land. He showed him which plants were poisonous, how to tend to the chickens and maintain their land. They even played chess together some nights. Those were Jack's favourite nights. It got to the point where Jack was desperate for school to end because his father would be waiting for him at home.

Jack would spend his nights coveting the penknife his father had presented him on his birthday, feeling the smooth bone under his fingers. It had flabbergasted him as until this occasion, his father had refused to partake in the traditional concept of birthdays. 'It's the Lord that should be celebrated, for giving you the gift of life,' was his customary rebuke after his mother had finished singing to him. Whilst his father hadn't baked him a cake or a special tea, he had given him this present.

'This penknife was given to me by my father on my birthday and his before that. I think it is time you had it. Use it well.'

At night, he would sit in his room, flicking out the blade and then folding it back into the handle. Examining every inch of it. The engraving of the company had worn away. But despite its obvious age, the deadliness of the blade had transcended time. Jack found any opportunity to use it. Gutting rabbits with his father and cutting open bags of animal feed. He would have used it to eat his dinner had his father not drawn the line at this.

Jack slowly forgot his fear and hatred for his father. Unable to sustain it in the face of the connection that was forming between them slowly. Getting stronger every day. It was almost as though they were becoming best friends. Punishment was no longer needed as Jack was now becoming devout and honourable like his father had always wanted. He understood now that his father had only been so strict with him to ensure that he did not take a wrong path. He was following God's word.

CHAPTER FIFTEEN

NOW

Jack's knuckles were white as he gripped tightly to the steering wheel. His hands were sweating. This was the beginning of his destiny and Jack was terrified. There was a part of him that was concerned that when it came to it, he would just stand and stare at the man, frozen in place by fear.

His father sat in the passenger seat. He looked inquisitively out of the window, taking in the passing scenery. His demeanour that of someone going out for a jaunt into the countryside, not about to kidnap a man and put him to death. But then, this wasn't his father's first time killing someone. Plus, it was Jack that would be doing everything. His father had insisted that he was only coming along for moral support. Jack had been chosen. This was his burden to bear.

They followed the road into the village, the sun was running away and the day was turning to night. It was 4.58pm. According to Susan's intel, the man would soon be leaving to go back to his house in Redditch. As they came into the centre of the village, the pub on his right, he pulled up on the left side of the road keeping the pub in view. To leave the village, the man would have to walk past Jack's car. He squinted out of the window and could make out a scruffy man leaning back against the small stone wall that bordered the pub. With black tracksuit bottoms and messy brown hair. He had a thick, navy-blue puffa jacket that looked like crows had pecked at it, the white lining poking through numerous holes. The man must have been freezing. Jack had only turned the car off minutes ago and already the frigid December weather was leaching the heat from his body. As Jack watched, a young woman walked towards the pub from the lane that led to the church. She was walking her greyhound and her pace slowed as she neared the man. Jack watched as she rummaged in her pockets and then tossed something into the polystyrene cup in front of the man and then carried on walking.

Looking at the clock, he could see it was now 5.01pm. The man outside the pub was reaching into his trouser pocket. He pulled out a phone and the screen lit up his face. He didn't have the gaunt appearance of most homeless people he had seen. There were no bags under his eyes. In contrast, his face was round and he appeared to have the makings of a double chin. Putting the phone away, the man stood up. He stretched his muscles and then began to walk towards Jack. He passed in front of Jack's car as he crossed the road to get to the pavement. The road was straight for a mile and Jack watched until the man was almost out of sight. Checking for cars, Jack indicated and pulled out. Slowly he crept after the man. He hadn't got far until he saw the man heading up a side street. Jack indicated left and followed him up the street. Holding back so it wasn't obvious he was stalking him. The man stopped at a BMW that was parked on the side of the road. The light was almost gone, the street lights had kicked in and Jack could just about distinguish the registration plate of the car. It was from this year. The man reached into his pocket and pulled out some keys. Orange lights flashed in response.

'This is it, son. This is your moment,' his father urged. Jack felt sick. All the planning in the world hadn't prepared him for the reality of what he was about to do. Not wanting to let his nerves get the better of him, Jack looked over at his father. The look in his father's eyes fortified him. He would make him proud. Jack opened the car door and hurried over to the man who was taking off the coat and throwing it into the back of the car. Jack conjured the last moments of Elsie's life. He pictured her broken body. He saw the hungry, angry, greedy faces flash in his mind and he felt his body transform. It was no longer being controlled by his brain, but by the powerful rage that had claimed him. With each step, it felt like he was being possessed by a spirit far more powerful than him. He was no longer a fifty-five-year-old man. He was a weapon of the Lord. His eyes trained on the man who was going to pay for his sin. The man glanced up as Jack approached.

Jack's mouth opened. He had no idea what he was going to say but the words came. As if put there by someone else.

'Excuse me, sir, could I trouble you for some help with my car? The blasted thing won't start.' Jack faked a chuckle.

The man shrugged at him.

'Sorry, mate, I'm in a rush. Can't help you.' He turned his back on Jack. Dismissing him. But Jack had planned for this.

He reached into the waistband of his trousers and withdrew his father's hammer. It was old and rusty, more of a relic than a useful tool. Jack buried the hammer in the back of the man's head with a sickening thud. The man collapsed to the floor like he had been deboned. With a quick glance around, Jack holstered the hammer back in his trousers. The curtains of the surrounding houses were all drawn, the street abandoned. Jack grabbed the man under his arms and heaved him along the pavement to his own car. The man was a dead weight, but Jack was no longer an ordinary man. He was a man vested with the blessing of the Lord. He could do anything. At any moment he could take off from the ground and start to fly, such was the adrenaline coursing through his veins.

When he reached the boot, Jack dropped the man to the floor and opened it. Taking out the rope, he hastily knotted the man's hands and legs together. He heaved the man upright and wrangled him into the boot, wrestling with the arms and legs until he was able to shut it. Lit up by a street lamp, Jack could see the broad grin on his father's face. His father's eyes were bright, he was happier than Jack could ever remember seeing him. As Jack started the car, his father slapped him on the shoulder.

'I'm so proud of you, son! Mark my words, this is the beginning of your new life.'

His heart was beating so hard in his chest it could explode at any moment. But he couldn't help but return his father's smile. For the first time since Elsie died, he could picture a future for himself. Was there a more noble cause than fighting the Devil with the support of the Lord? The power he had channelled was intoxicating.

'Now then, you remember the next step. When we get him home?'

Jack's smile faltered. His certainty extinguished like a tiny flame exposed to sudden gale-force winds. Could he really take the life of another human?

CHAPTER SIXTEEN

THEN

School was becoming harder for Jack. It had been two years since his mother died and everything his father taught him made him start to think that his father knew a lot more than his teachers. It became hard to tolerate the others in his class, they were so focused on music and girls and didn't care about religion. Graham, a boy who Jack had struck up, not a friendship, but an acquaintance born of the fact they attended the same church, was starting to really irritate Jack.

He no longer wanted to discuss sermons or religion at all. No, Graham wanted to talk about Scarlett. He had a crush on Scarlett and wanted her to be his girlfriend. But Scarlett wasn't interested in him. Scarlett liked Alex. Scarlett also smoked cigarettes behind the back of the bike shed. Jack had seen her and Alex kissing and smoking after school when he'd had to stay late because he'd got a detention after he told Mr McDonald that gay people should be put to death as homosexuals were sinners. Jack tried to tell Graham that Scarlett was a sinner. That she was smoking and kissing other boys. Graham had punched Jack.

After that, Jack returned to being a loner. Choosing to sit in the school library reading the leather-bound Bible his father had bought him for his thirteenth birthday. It was his most cherished possession. Mainly because his father had never bought him anything in his entire life. It was a symbol of their new relationship and Jack never let it leave his sight. He had it with him wherever he went.

Instead of avoiding him, Graham had teamed up with Peter who still hated Jack, channelling Scarlett's rejection into anger at him. In the library, Jack was safe under the watchful eyes of Miss Burns. To get home was an altogether more challenging experience. Jack lived in the Malvern Hills and used to take the bus home but Peter, Graham and their goons, Ian and Charlie, also took that bus. One journey with them throwing books and anything else they could get their hands on at his head was enough to have him walking home. It took an hour and a half to get there. Jack didn't mind too much, he whiled away the time naming the trees and shrubs he could see on the way back, used to walking to church and back in all weathers. Jack thought he was so clever. He had outsmarted Peter and Graham. They would just have to be content with sending spitballs at him in class. Or so he thought.

Coming out of the bathroom, Jack returned to class and saw Peter scampering away from his desk. Laughing as he joined Graham, Ian and Charlie. Jack checked his seat for booby traps before he sat back down and continued to answer the questions in his exercise book. Bursts of laughter erupted from Peter and his gang. Apprehension caused Jack to look up and see what they thought was so funny. Jack caught sight of something in Ian's hands. He was thumbing through a book. Not just any book. Jack's blood ran cold. He reached down into his bag. Desperately seeking his Bible. It was gone.

Red coloured his vision. He strode over to the boys.

'Hello, Jesus,' crowed Peter cheerfully.

'Give it back,' said Jack. His voice low and menacing. He felt no fear in that moment. Only pure rage that inflamed the blood in his veins.

'Give what back, Bible-Basher?' The boys laughed heartily. Looking Jack in the eye, Peter took the Bible from Ian and opened it. His eyes boring into Jack's, gleeful and exultant. He ripped out a page and dropped it onto the floor. Without knowing he was going to do it Jack placed his hands around Peter's throat and squeezed. His anger fuelled his grip and he squeezed with all his might. It felt like a release. How dare he steal from him? His most prized possession. Peter's eyes widened in shock. His hands tried to pull Jack off him but Jack was lost in his rage.

'Jack!' Mr Moore cried out in shock. Jack felt strong arms trying to pull him away. He held on as tightly as he could. But he was grabbed around the waist and heaved away from Peter. His fingers slid from around Peter's throat.

'No! Let go,' Jack yelled. He kicked at the air furiously. His hands clawing to reach Peter who was cradling his neck, slumped in his seat, panting.

Jack was half carried, half dragged to the headmaster's office. Mr Dobbs' mouth fell open in shock as Mr Moore recounted what he had witnessed. Jack stared defiantly at him, breathing hard. Unwilling to show any remorse. Jack watched in angry silence as he called his father. He sat waiting for him, staring at the tartan carpet. Letting his mind go blank so he could stop the panic brewing in his belly. His father was going to be so angry. It had been a long time since he had been thrown in the grave outside the house. He shivered as he recalled the terrifying darkness.

His father appeared in front of him, as if conjured by his thoughts. He knelt down in front of Jack.

'What happened?' his father asked.

Jack's words spilled from his mouth. He didn't know if he was making any sense but he wanted to make sure his father knew that it wasn't his fault. That Peter had been picking on him for months. That he had torn a page out of his Bible.

'It was so disrespectful, Father. Destroying the Bible. I just lost my temper.'

His father patted his knee and got to his feet. He disappeared into the hallway, leaving Jack alone in Mr Dobbs' office. Jack held his breath, not sure what was going to happen now. Raised voices came from the hallway.

'Now really,' cried Mr Dobbs. 'Mr Danvers, I must ask you to calm down.'

Jack got up off his chair and crept closer to the door.

'How do you expect me to remain calm when you are exposing my son to sin. Have you no shame?'

'Mr Danvers, I can assure you–'

'You can assure me of nothing. My son's Bible was damaged by another student. What sort of students are you teaching here? Do they have no respect for God's word? It's despicable and I won't stand for it. We are leaving.'

Jack backed away quickly and fell onto his seat, rearranging his features into what he hoped was a nonchalant expression.

His father entered the room.

'We're leaving.'

Jack leapt to his feet and followed his father from the room.

Mr Dobbs looked flustered. His cheeks were pink and he kept running his hand through his wiry grey hair.

'Sir, there is no need for this. We can sort this out. Jack acted completely out of character. I think a suspension will suffice.'

'A suspension? I think you'll find that Jack will be coming nowhere near this school ever again. He shouldn't be the one that is being punished. Defacing a Bible. The word of God.' His father was visibly boiling with anger. Like a bull ready to trample everyone in sight. 'That boy should be flayed. It's an outrage.'

Clasping Jack's shoulder, he wheeled them both around and steered them from the building.

And that was the end of Jack's school education. He had mixed feelings; he was relieved to be getting away from Peter and the rest of the children in the school. He couldn't connect with them and was fed up with being the pariah. But he would miss the lessons. Especially maths.

CHAPTER SEVENTEEN

NOW

W hen they pulled up at the house, Jack couldn't get out of the car straight away. He wanted to put off the moment he would actually have to take this next step. Jack kept telling himself that he was doing this on behalf of the Lord. That he had been instructed to do this. That the man in the boot *deserved* this. He was evil and part of a disease that was infiltrating humanity. The disease that had taken his wife. It was his job to eradicate him. He repeated this but he couldn't convince his conscience. His stomach was in knots, beads of sweat formed on his forehead. His hands twisted on the steering wheel as he tried to convince his brain to open the car door.

The choice was taken from him when his father got out of the car.

'Get out.'

Jack obeyed. Obeying his father was as instinctive as breathing. His body remembered vividly the pain of disobedience. Once he was out of the car, his father took him by the shoulders.

'Look at me.'

Jack looked from the floor into his father's stern, grey eyes.

'You can do this, Jack. I have faith in you. The Lord has faith in you. Make me proud.'

Taking a deep breath, Jack nodded at his father. He could do this. Jack walked over to the boot and opened it. The man was still unconscious. Pulling him from the boot was harder this time as he no longer felt possessed with the strength of the Lord. Instead, he was filled with a reluctant resignation. As he dragged the man into the house, he tried not to think about what he was about to do. He focused all his attention on getting the man into the cellar. He would deal with what came next then. Jack's muscles burned as he hauled the man down the cellar stairs. It was surprising the man didn't wake up as his legs bounced off each step.

Once they were in the cellar, Jack let go of the man and bent over, trying to catch his breath. The cellar was empty except for an old workbench. On it, Jack had put the rope he had found in his father's workshop. His father was watching him closely. Waiting for the next step. Recovered, Jack stood upright and picked up the rope. Tying the man's legs together, Jack withdrew his penknife from his pocket. It was the penknife that his father had given him on his twelfth birthday. It was Jack's most prized possession.

Jack glanced at his father. He was standing at the bottom of the stairs, arms crossed. He nodded at Jack, encouraging him. Jack looked down at the man. He was younger than he first thought. His eyeballs darting around under his closed lids. Jack bent down over him. Up close, he could see the man's chest moving up and down. It was hard to think of him as evil when he looked so vulnerable.

The knife glinted in his hand. Jack couldn't do this. He wasn't strong enough. He stood up and backed away. Disgusted with what he had almost done. How had he been so stupid? He let his father convince him this is what the Lord wanted but now he was here, standing over the unconscious figure, the absurdity had woken him up.

'I can't do it, Father.'

'Yes you can.'

Jack shook his head emphatically.

'No. No. This isn't what the Lord wants. What we are doing is wrong, Father.'

Jack's father prowled towards him. Jack cowered at the anger flashing in his father's eyes.

'Who are you to question the Lord, Jack?'

'I can't hurt him. He's just a human being.'

'Just a human being. Is that what you think of the people that sent your wife to her death?' His father lifted his foot and stamped it to the floor. Jack flinched. The action triggering memories of Elsie's death. His father looked at him more softly. He put a hand on his shoulder.

'Look, I know you are nervous. What you are doing is scary. But it is right, Jack. The Lord chose you. He gave you the tools to do this. So you need to go over there and imagine that this man is one of the people that killed your wife.'

His father steered him back towards the man. He pointed down at him.

'This man killed your wife. Can you remember her screams of pain, Jack? Do you remember the light leaving her eyes?'

Jack's mind was filled with Elsie's screams of pain. The way her eyes rolled back into her head as she collapsed to the floor. The blood trickling down her face. Tears leaked from his eyes as anger boiled inside him. He felt like a kettle, slowly reaching boiling point. When Jack looked at the man he no longer saw an innocent human. He saw his true colours. He may not have killed Elsie but his *kind* had.

Jack bent down and his hand was steady as he brought the blade to the man's arm.

'Good. That's better, son. I knew you could do it.'

His father patted him on the back. Jack twisted the man's arm, revealing the delicate skin at the of crook his elbow. Jack looked up at his father who was smiling encouragingly.

Jack pierced the skin with the blade. Blood burst from the wound and the man jerked awake. Jack wheeled back, pointing the blade at him. The man blinked and looked around the room. His eyes fell on Jack and then on the knife.

'W-what's going on?'

The man looked down at his elbow, the cut was only shallow but blood was still trickling down. The man winced and raised an arm to the back of his head. When he brought his hand back, it was gloved in red. Jack stared at his father, panicked. He had not accounted for this. He had been sure the man would stay unconscious.

What was he supposed to do now? His anger had faded and been replaced by shock.

'You can do this, son. Remember Elsie.'

Jack gulped back his fear and moved towards the man slowly, keeping the knife outstretched. An idea came to him suddenly.

'Don't move,' Jack said.

'What are you doing?' the man asked. As Jack came closer with the knife, the man lurched away but his hands and legs were bound, making movement impossible.

Jack grabbed the man's arm. The man moved his other arm, intending to fight back but Jack put the blade to his neck. Instantly, the man froze.

'I said don't move. I'm going to cut your arm.'

'W-why?' Jack could see the fear in the man's eyes.

'I'm going to give you a chance at redemption. If you pray for God's help. If your faith is strong and you survive the cut then I will let you go. But if you don't, well...'

His father harrumphed behind him.

'What are you doing? Just kill him,' his father yelled.

'No. I'm going to let the Lord decide his fate.'

He wanted to give the man a chance. This was the one way to be sure that his death was sanctioned by the Lord. Jack ignored the waves of disapproval coming from his father. He had to trust his instincts.

'What if he lives?' shouted his father. Moving closer, clearly agitated. 'You let him go and he tells everyone what you did? How are you going to carry out God's work from prison?'

'I trust the Lord, Father,' he said, turning to face him. 'You said yourself that God is watching over me and has chosen me. I feel like this is what he would want me to do. After all, you did the exact same thing to me, remember?'

'Please. Please don't do this. I haven't done anything wrong. I don't deserve this. Please just let me go,' the man begged.

A salty tear tracked down his face, it almost landed on the blade Jack had digging into his neck. The man's words reignited Jack's anger.

'Nothing wrong?' His eyes drilled into the man's. The blade shaking in his hand. 'So you haven't been pretending to be a homeless man, begging for money, when you have a car and a home?'

The man swallowed and the movement of his Adam's apple touched the blade, causing it to nick the skin. A single bead of blood bloomed and slowly meandered down the man's throat. The man didn't reply, giving Jack the answer.

'Now, don't move or I won't give you this opportunity, a chance to repent. I'll just kill you right now.' Jack's voice was steady and menacing. Belying the nerves that he had at the thought of what he was about to do. His anger was bubbling under the surface but the prospect of taking the life of another filled him with apprehension. Like evolving from a herbivore to a carnivore.

The man watched with bulging eyes and ragged breath as Jack dug the blade into the crease of his elbow. The man let out a hiss of pain and jerked. Jack held him still and dragged the blade downwards to the man's wrist until the knife reached the rope binding the man's hands together. A trail of blood following in its wake. Jack pulled the blade out of his wrist and at the same time the man's arms spasmed. A spurt of blood burst from the man's wrist. It fired into the air like lava from a volcano. Jack tasted metal as it coated his face.

The man screamed and shuffled away from Jack. With his wrists bound, he could do nothing to stem the flow of blood fleeing his body.

'Help me!' begged the man. He stared up at Jack with unadulterated terror. His face deathly pale. In a last-ditch attempt to save himself, the man brought his hands close to his face and tried to use his cheek to stop the bleeding. His face now slick with blood.

'Help!' he cried again.

Jack was paralysed. He forced his eyes away from the bleeding man to look at his father. Seeking guidance. A big smile was splitting his father's face. He was watching the man struggle for his life like it was entertainment. Nothing more than a captivating television show.

The man lost his fight and collapsed. Blood ran freely from the wound. The sight sparked Jack's conscience and finally spurred him into action. He knelt over the man and clutched his wrist with all his strength. But the blood made the skin slippery, he struggled to cling on and plug the wound. He could feel little pulses of blood fighting to be free of the palm of his hand.

'Father. Help me.' Jack looked over his shoulder at him. 'We need to stop the bleeding!'

But his father just crossed his arms, still smiling. Jack looked back at the man. His skin was bleached of all colour apart from the smeared blood from his attempt to save himself. It was as though his life force was being drained out of him through the cut on his arm. Was he breathing? Jack reached his spare hand to the man's face and held it close to his mouth and nose. No breath. His hand trembled violently as he reached to the man's neck and felt for a pulse. Nothing. The man's whole body had relaxed, all his muscles had lost their tension. His skin sagged and a vile smell of faeces filled the room.

Jack let go of the man. He fell backwards, staring in terror. This was not meant to happen.

His father hauled him to his feet. Jack's legs wobbled and he thought he might faint.

'Son. Calm down. This was always what was meant to happen. Don't you see that?'

His father walked over to the man and picked up the penknife out of the puddle of blood it had been dropped in. The white bone handle coated in blood.

'God was guiding your hand. You killed him because you were supposed to kill him. You said you were going to let God decide. And he did.'

Jack couldn't speak. Bile raced up his throat and he vomited on the floor. He wiped his mouth but the smell of the blood coating his hand made him retch again.

His father watched impassively.

'I'm proud of you, son. You have taken the first step on the journey to your destiny.'

Jack looked down at the body on the floor. The man who had been breathing only minutes ago was now dead. Because of Jack.

'This isn't right. I shouldn't have done that. I-I don't even know his name.'

Jack couldn't take his eyes off the dead man. All the rage in the world could not counteract the guilt gripping him. He was a murderer. No better than the people that had killed his wife.

'Not this again.' His father sighed. 'How many times are we going to have to go through this. Just when I thought I'd got through to you, you revert back to that pathetic snivelling child you once were.'

Jack flinched at the venom in his father's words.

'Do you know how angry I am that you were chosen instead of me?' His father stalked towards him, rage inflating him so he seemed to take up the whole room. 'I would not be hesitating. I would be delivering the Lord's justice with a steady hand. But I trust the Lord. I listen to Him. For some reason, He has chosen you. So, I will help you. I will guide you. But I will not stand for this pathetic display any longer.'

Fury pulsed in his father's eyes and before Jack could blink, his father had raised his hand and slapped Jack around the face. He heard the slap before he felt the pain explode in his face. He grabbed his cheek, shocked at the strength behind the blow.

'I dedicated the best years of my life to raising you. I did everything I could to teach you to be a strong and faithful man. I tried to teach you that the Lord comes first and everything else last. I raised you to be strong enough to do whatever the Lord demands of you. I will not let you fail. You will serve the Lord. You will abide by his will. Or as the Lord is my witness, I will kill you myself.'

CHAPTER EIGHTEEN

THEN

After leaving school at thirteen, his father spiritedly took up his education.

Sitting at the kitchen table, only a Bible in hand, his father beamed at Jack.

'I think this is going to be great, Jack. I can finally teach you what it means to be a man. To serve the Lord and bask in his love. Now, you already know your sums and how to write. So we can skip the boring stuff and spend our time learning the important things.'

The Bible became his exercise book and they debated and discussed it at length. 'You see, son, there are some out there that don't believe that God wrote the Bible. They think that it was written by people inspired by God's actions. These misinformed people don't believe in the descriptions in the Bible of how the world was created. It's disgusting. It is vital that you understand that this is the word of our Lord.' He held up the Bible reverently. 'Don't let anyone try and convince you otherwise.'

His father was determined that not only would Jack learn

the word of God by rote, he would also understand the meaning behind each word.

'God destroyed the ancient cities of Sodom and Gomorrah because of homosexuality. It states in the Bible that the sin of "Sodom" is homosexuality. So that tells us that homosexuals are sinners.'

Jack frowned. This was not what he had been taught at school.

'But Mr McDonald told us in RE that Sodom was destroyed because the whole town wanted to assault the angels, not the homosexuals. So he told me I was wrong to think that gay people are sinners.'

'Yes, but don't you remember Leviticus?'

'You shall not lie with a male as with a woman; it is an abomination,' Jack recited.

'Well done, son. You are picking this up quickly.'

Jack basked in his father's praise.

They developed a harmonious living routine. Every day was the same. They got up, did their chores, read from the Bible, discussed the Bible, had lunch, then did more chores, had dinner, said Grace, read the Bible, discussed the Bible and then went to bed. Life would have been perfect if it hadn't been for their Sunday visits to the local church.

Church was becoming contentious. Each visit was making his father more and more frustrated.

'The reverend is losing sight of what the Lord really wants. Preaching peace and forgiveness. Why isn't he reminding people of their duties to the Lord? To stay away from sin and actively fight the Devil?' his father said, his voice so loud and angry it startled a few birds from a nearby tree. 'Not once has he mentioned the Devil. He's going soft. He's not focusing on our roles as devout followers. As reverend it is his job to make sure we follow the word of God. But how is anyone supposed to know what that is when he doesn't tell anyone?'

The vicar was too focused on the teachings of the New Testament and seemed to disregard the lessons of the Old Testament.

It was the black people that tipped him over the edge. Jack had just shaken hands with the vicar and made to follow his father into the church, when he collided with him because he had stopped moving abruptly. Jack looked around him to see what the hold-up was. Jack just had time to glimpse two people he didn't recognise.

A young couple with dark skin were taking seats in the pews at the back of the church. The woman, dressed elegantly in a navy dress and her black hair swept into an elegant bun, was jostling a baby on her hip. She smiled around and returned waves from people in the congregation. Before he could process any more, his father grabbed his arm and yanked him out of the church.

His father strode through the grounds, ignoring the questioning looks from the regulars. His fury appeared to electrify him. Jack would not have been surprised to see the earth scorched where his father had walked. When they reached the lane that would lead them home his father exploded.

'Did you see that?'

'See what, Father?'

'Those people!' His father seemed to swell with anger, his face red and blotchy. Eyes sparking. 'I can't believe it.'

Jack broke into a run to keep up.

'I know, Father.'

'Coloured people. In *our* church? It's despicable.' Spittle flying from his mouth as he spat out the words.

All the way home, his father raged. The veins in his head

popping. Jack was unable to placate him and his tirade carried on all evening, disrupting the flow of their usually relaxed Sunday evenings. His father marched up and down the kitchen, unable to calm down.

Something woke Jack in the black of night. At first he thought it was the winds, but he could also hear a repetitive sound he couldn't place. He turned on the lights and dressed. The clock in his room told him it was 3am. He crept downstairs, wincing at the cold concrete on his feet. The wind was battering the house, like the big bad wolf was outside, determined to blow the house down. Reluctant to leave the safety of the house, he opened the back door. The darkness was impenetrable. He waited for his eyes to adjust and then stepped outside. Immediately, the winds attacked, bruising his skin with icy blasts. All around him, it tore at the trees and rattled the wooden sheds and greenhouses. As he rounded the corner of the house, he saw his father in his workshop, housed in one of the stone outbuildings. The metal blade of the handsaw twinkled in the light of the lamp his father had lit.

'Father, what are you doing?' called Jack.

No answer. Jack moved closer and could see his father sawing a long piece of wood he had taken from a large pile that had been gathered outside.

'Father.'

His father stopped and turned to look at him.

'What are you doing, Father?'

'What does it look like I'm doing?'

'It's three o'clock in the morning.'

'I had no choice.'

Jack looked at him. His father glared back. His eyes

bloodshot and crazed. All his usual composure had been replaced by a maniacal energy. His father's bedclothes were rumpled, smeared with grass and sprinkled with wood shavings. He was barefoot and could easily have been mistaken for an escaped lunatic.

'Father, come to bed. We can do this in the morning.'

'I can't sleep. I tried. But I just lay there, unable to reconcile the direction our church has taken.' He waved the handsaw around as he spoke, apparently forgetting it was there. Jack took a step back just to be safe.

'But then He spoke to me. He told me what I needed to do.'

'What did He tell you to do?' asked Jack.

'He told me that I needed to build my own church.' He indicated to the piles of wood he had gathered. 'The reverend can no longer be trusted to lead the congregation. So, I must do it instead.'

Jack wanted to laugh but the look in his father's eyes stopped him.

'Son, I have been charged with ensuring that God's word is not dirtied by those people. That his message is only delivered to the faithful and deserving.'

Over the next three months, building materials would turn up at the house and slowly but surely, his father's church was built. The day it was finished, his father had tied a bow between the handles and handed Jack a pair of scissors.

His father was bouncing around with happiness. Jack cut the bow and the church was officially open. From now on, his father delivered the Sunday service in front of the cross he had nailed to the wall of his wooden church. It only had enough room for two people. Jack would kneel on the floor whilst his father gave the daily sermon.

CHAPTER NINETEEN

NOW

The body was cold. The blood congealing before his eyes. Jack started to cry. Harrowing sobs that wracked his whole body. His father stood over him, furious. Jack looked up at him, afraid of the anger emanating from him.

'Come with me,' his father instructed. The menace in his voice spoke to Jack's subconscious mind and he found himself getting to his feet. Jack wiped his face and nose on his sleeve and followed his father up the stairs, out of the cellar. He reached back and grabbed Jack's arm and pushed him through the doorway. Jack stumbled and managed to right himself before he hit the floor. His hand on his back, his father continued to shove him towards the front door. They walked around the side of the house. With a growing dread, Jack realised exactly where they were going. Around the back of the house, where the chickens used to roam was the grave from his childhood. The old battered front door still lying next to it. Ready to trap him inside.

As they reached the edge of the grave, his father shoved him again and Jack fell face first into the hole. Winded, he turned to see his father pushing the heavy door over the hole. Jack tried to wriggle out of the hole but the wood crushed his legs and held him in place. His father moved to the top of the door, ready to push it into place over his upper body. He pushed the door as if it weighed nothing more than a bag of feathers. Again, his body, that of a thirty-year-old man, not a man in his seventies.

'Lie down,' his father ordered. It had been many years since Jack had been forced into this grave, but he felt just as terrified as the first time. His heart thudded. He couldn't breathe. The thought of being trapped underground again was stupefying him. His mouth opened, ready to argue. He was in his fifties. A grown man. He wasn't a child anymore. But the look in his father's eyes stripped him of his resolve. Time was rewinding, turning him back into that snivelling, terrified little boy. He couldn't disobey his father. The Bible forbade it. The wrinkled skin of his father's face that betrayed his father's old age, did nothing to lessen his dominance. Jack's flicker of resistance was powerless against years of obeying this man. His eyes drilled into Jack's, demanding submission. Jack's words died on his lips and his legs folded under him. His memories of the consequences of disobedience all too near to the surface, increasing the haste with which he obeyed.

Jack leant back into the earth's caress. Trying to ignore the soil clambering into his hair, coating his clothes and clinging to his hands. The cold ground penetrated his clothes, chilling his limbs. The air felt like treacle, and he was finding it hard to force it into his lungs. He was taking gasping breaths. Jack watched as his father pushed the door into place. Any minute now he was going to be trapped under it.

'Please,' he begged. But his father either didn't hear him or chose to ignore him. Jack watched as the door slid across his face. The wood inches from his nose. The darkness was not as impenetrable as it used to be. The door, ravaged by the wind and rain and the passage of time, had gained small holes that allowed pinpricks of light to pierce the darkness.

Jack put his mouth to one of the holes. A tiny breeze brushed his lips. But it wasn't enough air. He was suffocating. The door was pressed across his entire body, pushing him into the ground. There wasn't enough room for his lungs to expand. He was going to die. His lips tingled. His lungs stopped moving. Death was coming for him.

The edge of his vision was going black. He could feel his heart beating furiously, trying to keep him alive. But he couldn't breathe. His lungs screamed for air. Jack beat furiously at the door but it didn't move. An old-fashioned, heavy door, designed to withstand the brutal wind and rains, let alone his feeble punches. He clawed at it. His fingernails finding the scratch marks already etched into the door from his childhood imprisonments. He felt a droplet of blood fall on his cheek. One of his nails was bleeding. Weakness flooded his body, his arms dropped to his sides. His vision was getting blacker. He was dying.

He opened his mouth to scream, but nothing came out. His lungs had collapsed. Blackness.

The cold slap of the wind woke him up. Jack's father was standing over him, his expression seeming cold as ice.

'Get up.'

Jack sat up. Exhaustion washed through him. He looked around, confused for a moment until the memories hit him. Jack scrambled out of the grave before his father changed his mind and trapped him in there again.

His father walked back to the house and Jack followed. He wanted nothing more than to go to sleep, every fibre of his being was crying out with fatigue. They walked into the kitchen and

Jack moved towards the door, hoping he could go upstairs and rest. His hand reached out for the door handle.

'Sit down.'

Jack's shoulders slumped and he trudged back to his seat at the kitchen table. It had been worth a try. His father had made himself a cup of tea and sat down at the head of the table. He cupped the drink and stared at Jack.

'I trust you have learnt your lesson.'

Jack nodded his head.

'I'm sorry I had to do that. But you needed to calm down. You need to grow up and find the strength to follow your destiny.'

Jack said nothing. Thoughts eluded him, he felt numb inside.

'I know you can do this, Jack. I know you have the strength to see this through. I just need you to believe it.'

Jack looked up at his father. His grey eyes full of sincerity. His intensity had the desired effect.

'I won't let you down, Father.' And he meant it.

CHAPTER TWENTY

THEN

A s Jack reached seventeen, he started to feel restless. Since his mother's death, he had been living in his father's world of devout religion. He was happy to do so, he understood the importance of serving God. But part of him wanted more. To see what else the world had to offer outside of Oakdale Farm. He loved his father and their life together. But there was a part of him that wondered what the rest of the world was like. It seemed a long time since he had been in the real world. Since he had left school, his life had become ritualistic. Their house had become his whole world. He used to get out every Sunday for church but after his father built his own, Jack didn't go anywhere. Jack had offered to take over the grocery shopping duties but his father had been outraged.

'Son, the Devil and his subjects are everywhere, you are not yet ready to face them. You are still too naive and therefore vulnerable to their tricks. It is not safe for you to leave. Not yet. Not until your will is as strong as mine.' He had then instructed Jack to sit and pray in the church for six hours. The pain in his knees from kneeling had stopped him from asking again.

The only freedom Jack now had was his hikes. His father

had seemed impressed when Jack had told him he wanted to start walking in nature, to be closer to God. But really, he just wanted to escape the claustrophobia of the house. It was starting to feel like the walls were closing in around him.

Jack had trekked through the patchwork of forests surrounding the house, climbed all the hills and waded through the streams. Oakdale Farm was tranquil with a few animals and nestled in the Malvern Hills. The nearest neighbour was a half an hour walk away and the nearest village was an hour's walk.

Jack had taken to going over to their neighbour's house, March Farm. Oakdale Farm was really only a farm in name. Whereas March Farm was a fully functional agricultural farm. It was fascinating. Jack had found a copse of trees that bordered the property and spent many hours watching as if it was his own personal television show. Machinery chugged around, animals herded here and there. But Jack's favourite thing to watch was the girl. Brown-haired and beautiful, she worked as hard as any of the farmhands.

Wearing overalls that matched her father's, she and her dog were always doing something on the farm. He had once followed her to one of the fields and watched from afar as she fixed one of the fences. Jack found her fascinating. She appeared to be the same age as he was but she held herself with such confidence. Jack watched entranced as she laughed and talked with all those that she met. The wind would carry her laughter to him and he couldn't help but smile. She looked so happy. Every day. He had never seen her sad, angry or upset. An aura of sunshine surrounded her and he wanted to bask in the light and warmth she emitted. Just seeing her made him feel happy.

Each day, his addiction to her grew stronger and he spent longer and longer outside, watching. He found excuses to avoid time with his father and would take every opportunity to be out there. The need to be near her became consuming. When the weather prohibited his trek over there, it would feel like a physical pain. He couldn't focus on anything. He felt twitchy and jittery. Like he was going through withdrawal from something.

His father began to notice his strange behaviour and started giving Jack more tasks around the house and the farm. Keeping a closer eye on him, Jack presumed. It meant that Jack had less time to go to Elsie. He had discovered her name by chance. A burly man, with curly blond hair had stood at the door of March Farm house and shouted the name 'Elsie' so loud it caused birds to burst from the trees. The girl had come running and that's when he finally knew her name. He said it out loud, enjoying the sound of it.

CHAPTER TWENTY-ONE

NOW

Jack went down the cellar stairs and stared at the body. Whereas earlier he had felt severe anguish and guilt, he now looked down at it dispassionately. Jack had once seen a woman on the television, on one of those soap operas Elsie used to watch, in hysterics, and someone slapped her around the face. It brought her back to her senses. Snapped her right out of her craziness and restored her sanity. His father had done a more extreme version of that with the grave. Jack was thinking clearly again. Able to see the bigger picture, and register and regret his weakness. He would not let this happen again. He was ready now. Jack had stumbled at the first hurdle. But he had got back up and he was ready to win the race.

Trying not to breathe in the fetid aroma of death, Jack bent down to pick up the body. He hefted it over his shoulder and slowly moved up the stairs, out of the cellar. When he reached the kitchen, his father was still sat at the table, reading the newspaper. Deep grooves lined his forehead as he glared at the paper. His father could never read the news without getting angry. He didn't look up as Jack clumsily carried the dead man outside. Not even helping as Jack struggled to open the front door without dropping the body.

When Jack was younger, he never truly appreciated how lucky he was to live in such a beautiful place. He also did not realise how fortunate his father was to own an estate of four acres that was fenced off by forests on all sides. The privacy it offered had never really registered with Jack until now. There was no one around to know what he was doing. God knew that they had the perfect place to dispose of the sinners.

The ground was stiff and resistant to his shovel. It was in hibernation for the winter and did not appreciate being disturbed. It took every ounce of muscle to shift the earth and dig a grave. Jack reluctantly admired his father's dedication to punishing him now he was getting experience of how hard it was to dig a grave. The repetitive movements of shovelling the earth became a form of mindfulness. He focused on the physical task and it quieted his mind. Stopping a few times for a rest, it took him over two hours to dig a grave big enough for the man. He had flirted with the idea of putting the man in the punishment hole behind the house. But that was Jack's hole. The place where he paid for his sins. The man needed a punishment hole of his own.

Jack jumped down into the grave and laid down, checking it was deep and long enough. A spider darted across his chest and he jumped to his feet, spooked. Satisfied it was suitable, Jack hefted the man into the hole. The man dropped in like a dead weight. Jack jumped in after him and turned him over onto his back. His face white as paper, smooth and free of emotion. Jack moved the man's hands so they were crossed over his chest like a mummy in a Sarcophagus.

Taking one last look at the man, Jack began to toss the earth back onto him. Covering him from head to toe, a baptism of soil.

It took less time to restore the earth than it did to dig it up.

Soon he had shovelled the last of it into place. Jack threw down the shovel, his hands bleeding from burst callouses. Bowing his head, he felt the urge to say something. But he didn't even know the man's name.

'For the wages of sin is death, but the free gift of God is eternal life in Christ Jesus our Lord. Romans, 6:23.' He crossed himself and looked down at the grave. 'You have been found guilty of sin. With your death, your sin has been expunged. May you repent and may the Lord have mercy on you.'

Walking back to the house, it was like he'd been in a washing machine on the fastest spin cycle, every part of him felt battered. But his spirit was deeper than it had been before. A sense of righteousness had enveloped him, like the Lord was patting him on the back saying, 'good job, son'.

His father was at the stove when he opened the front door. The delicious scent of cottage pie cloaked him and his stomach rumbled eagerly. His father brought him a plateful. Jack sat at the table and wolfed the food down whilst his father sat watching him, smiling at him benignly.

'I'm very proud of you, Jack.'

Jack inhaled his last mouthful of mashed potato and looked up at his father, beaming.

'Thank you, Father. I'm sorry about before. But I'm ready now, I promise.'

As they were relaxing on the sofa, listening to the radio, Jack's phone rang. He groaned, full of food and exhausted from the events of the day. He forced himself to his feet and hobbled into the kitchen, wincing as his knees clicked in protest. Susan.

He did not have the energy for her. But for some reason he found himself pressing accept.

'Hello.'

'Jack, darling. How're you?'

'I'm fine, thank you. How are you?'

'I'm missing you, Jack. I've lived next door to you almost all my life. It's so strange seeing your house empty. I hate it. Are you planning on coming back?'

'No!' he shouted unintentionally. The thought of going back to that house filled him with dread. It would break him. 'No,' he said more quietly, 'I can't, Susan. I just can't be there.'

'It's okay, Jack,' Susan soothed. 'I do understand. Why do you think I hate living next door without you there? I miss her too.'

He didn't, couldn't reply.

'So how have you been? Is your father taking care of you?'

'Yes, he's been brilliant. I really don't know how I'd get through this without him.'

'It's strange, from what Elsie said, I didn't think you guys were very close.'

'We weren't. But you know, things like this. Well, it changes things.'

'I'm glad you aren't alone. But you'll never be alone. I will always be here for you. Promise.'

Jack smiled despite himself. She really could be quite nice sometimes.

'Anyway, you'll never guess what,' and she reverted to the annoying gossip from next door, 'you know that fake homeless man I was telling you about?' Jack could tell she was brimming with excitement at having such juicy gossip to tell him. It's like she thought he was Elsie. They used to spend hours in the kitchen gossiping about all the other villagers. 'Well, he's only gone and done a runner. His wife, Sally, is now going around all the villages trying to find him. Jim told me she'd been into the shop with a missing poster of him. "Have you seen my Harry?" she asked him.' Jack's heart was pounding in his chest. He almost lost his grip on the phone as her words registered in his mind. 'We reckon she must have been in on the scam. I mean, how else would she know where to look for him?' Susan paused. Obviously hoping for some reaction from Jack. When none was forthcoming she carried on. 'I do feel for her though, poor lass. According to Jim the police are being no help as they think someone rumbled his scam and he did a bunk and is hiding out somewhere. To make matters worse, my sister, Jennifer, has a friend who lives next door to them and she said there were bailiffs outside their house, banging down the door. Poor woman.'

His name was Harry. Jack felt shaky. People were looking for him. What if they came here? He shook his head; *be sensible, Jack.* Why would they come here?

'Hello? Jack?'

'Sorry, I got distracted. What were you saying?'

'Oh, never mind,' she said, irked. 'Have you spoken to Debbie recently?'

Debbie, another neighbour that he and Elsie had been quite close to. She was much more tolerable than Susan. Jack had often accompanied her on dog walks around the village. He had a fondness for her Jack Russell, Cooper.

'Er, no I haven't. I've been keeping to myself, I'm afraid. You understand.'

'Well, you might want to give her a ring. She's going through a hard time at the moment. The poor thing has been scammed by some dodgy builder.' And just like that, Jack had his next target.

CHAPTER TWENTY-TWO

THEN

I t was six months later that Elsie spoke to him. A day that
would be etched into his memory as the best day of his life.
Jack had been shadowing Elsie as usual, using bushes, trees and
rocks to keep hidden. Or so he had thought. He followed her
into the shade of the trees, but when he came out of the other
end, she had gone. Turning a full circle, he looked for a glimpse
of her but she had vanished. Presuming she had gone out a
different way, he turned to go back into the forest. A weight
knocked him flat on his back.

Elsie had launched herself out of a tree and landed on top of
him. She was smirking down at him, enjoying the look of shock
on his face.

'You're the Danvers boy.' It wasn't a question. But he
nodded anyway.

Elsie reached out a hand to help him up.

'Apologies for knocking you over.' She smiled at him
impishly, not sorry in the slightest. 'I just got fed up of waiting to
see if you were ever going to talk to me.'

Jack took her hand. Her touch set off fireworks in his body.
He felt electrified, reluctant to let go. Jack got to his feet and

THE GOOD HUSBAND

brushed the mud off the back of his jeans. Face burning bright red, he berated himself. S*top blushing. Stop being an idiot. Say something.* Jack opened his mouth but no words came out. Apparently his brain no longer functioned.

Elsie laughed, the sound was melodic and made his heart swell. He smiled at the sound of it in spite of his embarrassment.

'Can you tell me your name at least?' she asked. She was examining him like he was a fascinating new species she had discovered. At last, forcing his brain to engage, his ability to speak was restored.

'Jack.'

'Hi, Jack, my name is Elsie.' She held out a hand to shake his. Elsie was even more beautiful up close. Sunlight danced off her brown hair, her brown eyes were bright and expressive. Her smooth skin was unblemished and tanned from her days spent in the elements. Her body was muscular and strong. Jack stared intently at the scar running down her palm, a faded red. He reached out a shaking hand and took it in his. Her grip was firm. Their eyes met as they shook hands and Jack felt a balloon inflate in his chest. He dropped her hand, unable to cope with the upwelling of feeling he was experiencing. The moment felt immense. Like it was the start of something profound.

'Would you like to go for a walk, Jack?' Elsie asked. Apparently unaware of the jungle of emotions her touch had caused him. She was playing with a strand of her hair, twisting it around her finger and letting it go, then catching it again. He stared, mesmerised. Jack nodded at her. Struck dumb once more.

They meandered through the countryside, Elsie chattering nine to the dozen. She showed him the borders of their land. Then took him to meet her favourite pair of cows that she had named Macbeth and Lady Macbeth. Elsie clambered over rocks, waded through streams with the same ease he had when he rambled

121

through the land around Oakdale Farm. Jack had the best afternoon. He had never been this far before and he loved seeing the world through Elsie's eyes, sensing her obvious passion for nature that matched his own. Until he had found her, and began watching her from afar, nature and his father had been his only companions.

The sun beat down on them, the wind unwilling to bless them with its presence and cool them down. They could hear the song of the bees as they feasted on buffets of wildflowers. Birds swooped lazily into the shade of the trees.

'So what's the deal with you?'

The question took him by surprise and Jack lost his footing, tripping on a clump of mud. Elsie put her hand on him to stop his fall. She was so tactile it was like an electric shock each time she touched him. Jack hadn't had another person voluntarily touch him since his mother's death. He had become immune to the need for affection. Taking solace in his relationship with his father and with God. Jack hadn't thought he was missing anything. But the strength of the feeling that surged through his body just at the merest touch of Elsie, had awoken a desire he didn't know he was capable of feeling.

'W-what do you mean?'

'Well, what school do you go to? I haven't seen you around at Chesterfield High. Do you go to a boarding school or something?'

'No, my father homeschools me.'

'Oh, okay. What about your mother?'

'She's not around. She left when I was eleven.' The standard line he fed anyone that asked. Jack now understood what his father had done. The pain of his mother's death was a dull ache that he was able to live with now that he had the same profound understanding of the Lord and the rules that come with a pious life. At first, Jack hadn't told anyone what his father had done for fear of his own life. But now he was old enough to understand that true faith was being diluted in society. There were very few devout believers that would understand what his father had done.

'It's safer not to tell anyone, Jack. Let sleeping dogs lie,' his father had once said to him. It hadn't been much of an issue as Jack had only seen people at church and they soon got bored of asking about his mother when they realised there was no juicy gossip to be had.

'I'm sorry, Jack. I don't know what I'd do without my mum. She's my favourite person in the world,' Elsie replied.

'It's okay. I have my father. And He is always with me.'

'Your faith?'

'Yes, I'm never alone. I have Him.'

'What's your father like? My father said he is a bit of a recluse and no one really knows that much about him.'

They carried on walking for a while, Jack trying to work out how to describe his father.

'My father is a loyal, strong man. His relationship with God is the most important thing to him. He spends each day trying to serve the Lord in the best way he can. At first I didn't understand him. I feared him even. But over time I came to realise that he was just trying to show me the power and strength of faith. Of serving God and being a loyal faithful servant. That is my role in life. Nothing else matters.'

The words had tumbled out. Jack was surprised at himself. It was the most he had said in one go in a very long time. His father usually dominated their conversations. Jack had become used to being the one that listened. But with Elsie, he found himself wanting to speak. He sensed that she genuinely wanted to hear what he had to say. Elsie gave him a searching look. It took a while for her to respond.

'I'm glad you have a good relationship with your dad. Race you to the stile.'

By the time he began to walk home, his cheeks ached from smiling. He felt lighter, like happiness was giving him buoyancy. He half expected to start floating his way home. As he reached the door to the house, it was wrenched open before he could touch the handle. His father drew himself up to his full height, filling the doorway.

'Where have you been?'

'Just walking outside. Like I always do.'

His father inspected him, a human lie detector if there ever was one. Jack met his gaze. Emptying his mind, he thought only of the fact his father's eyes were the same grey as the slates on the roof. He could not risk his father finding out about Elsie.

CHAPTER TWENTY-THREE

D ebbie Hodgetts was a thoroughbred Winterford villager. Still living in the house that she was born in. She was part of the fabric of the place, an integral cog, as important as the post office and the pub. There wasn't a day you didn't bump into her somewhere. Tending to the flowers and graves of those in the churchyard, walking her dog, Cooper, the same route at the same time, every day. She had a special place in everyone's heart. The house she lived in was old and historic. Since the passing of her husband, the garden had been invaded by nature and she was too proud to ask for help.

When a seemingly lovely young man offered her a cash price to fix her crumbling roof for her then and there with some tiles, she bit his hand off. All day she waited for him to come back with the tiles from another job. He never came back.

Debbie reported him to the police but there was nothing they could do. All she knew about the man was that his van was white, he said that he lived somewhere on the outskirts of Worcester and had two kids, Aidan and Jessica. Debbie wasn't completely stupid; a retired lecturer, she was as sharp as a whip and had a very good memory. She was able to give the police the first two letters of the man's van registration plate. But unfortunately, due to cutbacks, her case was not given the priority it deserved. It was an unspoken secret that Debbie had no money. She was living off her meagre pension and it wasn't unnoticed by visitors that family heirlooms seemed to be disappearing at an increasing rate.

There was communal outrage from the villagers at what had happened to Debbie. None more so than Jack. Debbie had been the first person they had met when they moved to Winterford. She'd baked them a large casserole and it was only after a few months he had realised that that would have taken a large chunk out of her meagre shopping budget.

Jack and his father discussed at length how they were going to track this man down. For it was obvious that this man was the next target in his mission. God had shown him the way and he would not let him down. Not again. They agreed that taking Jack's car was too risky after the first kidnapping. Better to use his father's car.

The rusty Morris Marina was a relic and belonged in a museum. However, Jack couldn't be more thrilled to be behind the wheel. His father had had this car for as long as Jack could remember and it had been a bone of contention when he was sixteen that he wasn't allowed to learn to drive. It was Elsie that taught him to drive in the end. His father hadn't seen a need for Jack to know how to drive and refused to teach him, believing they both had more important things to do with their day. Jack had given up asking and watched with frustration as his father disappeared down the drive in the car, leaving Jack behind to finish his chores. But now here he was, driving the Morris Marina he had lusted over all those years.

They bumped down the track, the years eroding the driveway, making it a maze of potholes he tried and failed to avoid. His father had seemed happy for Jack to drive but every now and then he would reach out to grip the dashboard and close his eyes, grimacing. Jack tried not to smile. Unable to help himself, he enjoyed being the one in control for a change. Jack may have jerked the wheel a bit harder around the corners than he might normally have done. His father clutched the grip handle above his door with both hands. Both his lips were white.

Driving back into Winterford took the wind from his sails. Every inch of it was tainted with memories of Elsie. Pulling up at the church, he parked the car and gazed at the solid, ancient stone building, unsure if he was strong enough to do this. He hadn't been back since Elsie's funeral. It felt unfamiliar to him now. No longer a place he and Elsie went every Sunday. It was now a place where his pain and suffering were anchored.

His father stayed in the car and Jack opened the door. He made his way up the pathway, pulling the collar of his coat up to block the invading icy wind. Opening the lychgate, his gaze was drawn as always to the plaque proclaiming the men that had lost their lives so long ago. Passing through, he followed the stone path, walking between rows of graves, unable to find the strength to look in the direction of Elsie's.

Every Sunday since they had moved to the village, he and Elsie would sit on the bench just behind the church. It overlooked the rolling hills and the view was captivating no matter what the weather or time of year. They would sit there for hours, cuddled up. Drinking in the ever-changing landscape. Elsie loved nature. He supposed it was inevitable given she grew up on a farm, helping lambs give birth when she was eight years old. Being able to look out at the arable landscape and watch a distant tractor rumbling around, to hear the lambs bleating in the field directly below, was restorative for her. It recharged her. They would come back home and it would be like she had a new lease of life, she would be laughing more and smiling brighter. Rejuvenated by time spent breathing in the fresh air and being at one with Mother Nature.

Jack took his seat on the bench. Elsie always sat on his left. He rubbed at the plaque on the bench. *In Loving Memory of Chubbs.* The hours they had spent wondering who Chubbs was and what his life had been like. Jack closed his eyes and pictured Elsie. He tried to conjure her in his mind and felt her presence wrap around him like a hug. Never wanting the moment to end, he was irked when the sound of footsteps chased Elsie's presence away.

Debbie appeared at his side. Jack smiled up at the sky. *Thank you, my Lord.* Once again, the Lord was orchestrating the way of things so that he and Debbie crossed paths.

'Jack, I thought that was you.' She beamed at him. Cooper darted over to greet him and covered him in wet kisses. But quickly lost interest when he couldn't smell dog treats on him. Cooper moved off to sniff the grass around them. 'Can I join you?' asked Debbie.

'Of course, please sit down,' Jack replied. Debbie sat, quiet for a moment as she absorbed the view.

'I haven't seen you since Elsie's funeral.' To the point as ever, Debbie hadn't changed. 'It was a beautiful service. The reverend did a fantastic job. She would have loved it. All those people there. Celebrating her life.' Debbie turned to look at him. 'I'm sorry, Jack. I didn't mean to upset you.'

Jack hadn't realised he was crying. He wiped at the tears that were tracking down his face, into his grey beard. If Elsie could see him now, she would not be impressed. She was forever reminding him to shave and cut his hair. He must look like a wild animal by now.

'It's okay. It's just still so raw.'

'I can only imagine. When I lost Dennis, it was like my world became dull and less appealing. I still feel like something is missing. Every day. It gets easier, but it never goes away.'

'I can't– can we talk about something else?'

'Of course. How have you been getting on since the funeral? I take it you aren't staying in the village?'

'I've been staying with my father. It's too hard...' He trailed off.

'That's nice for you. I don't think I ever met your dad. Is he local?'

'Not really, he lives in Malvern, up in the hills. He's been great. Came straight to the hospital when he found out.'

'I'm so glad, Jack. It's not good to be alone at a time like this.'

'Thanks, how are things with you? I heard from Susan you had a bit of bother recently?'

Debbie grimaced. The skin of her face creasing like parchment. She shook her head and sighed.

'It's my own fault, Jack. A foolish old woman's pride getting the better of her.'

'Elsie thought the world of you, Debbie. Both of us care a lot for you. And you may be many things, but foolish is not one of them.'

'Oh, but I am, Jack. I trusted a complete stranger. I could have asked anyone for a recommendation but I didn't want to admit that I needed help. I've lived alone for too long. I've got too independent. I like to be the one people come to for help, not the one asking for it.'

'Tell me what happened.'

'Well, my roof has been leaking for a while. I haven't had the money to fix it. But buckets were no longer working and I was ashamed I let it get as bad as it did. I didn't want to use anyone I knew. You know what it's like round here. Gossip is like oxygen.'

Jack did his best to suppress a smile, Susan coming to mind.

'I saw a card in the post office written by a man advertising building services including roofing. So I called him up. I always thought I was a good judge of character, Jack. He seemed like such a decent lad. Charming. He reminded me of my Dennis when I first met him. He said it would be no problem to fix and he'd do me a cash price so that it wouldn't cost as much.'

Debbie gazed out over the fields as she spoke, unable to look at him.

'I should have got some reviews. Asked people if they knew him. Looked him up online. But I didn't. I just took him on face value. I handed over the last of my savings and I never saw him again.'

Debbie hung her head.

'I haven't told anyone this. But things aren't looking good for me. My mortgage was paid off when Dennis died. But that big old house is expensive to run. It's freezing cold and every day something else breaks or needs fixing. With just my pension to live off, I can't afford to fix half the things that are wrong with it.'

Tears of shame were brimming in her eyes. She looked at him with such sadness it stirred his heart.

'I knew something wasn't right when he asked for payment up front. But I didn't listen to my instincts. He reassured me he just needed it to go and buy the materials and he would be back within the hour. I was so stupid, Jack.'

'Susan said you reported it to the police. Aren't they helping?'

'I didn't even get a visit. They just called me up and took the details over the phone. It was embarrassing. I could tell the girl on the phone thought I was a daft old biddy.'

'I'm so sorry, Debbie. Have you got any idea who he is?'

'Oh yes.' She pulled out a battered-looking business card from her coat pocket. 'Dan Beckett. I'm showing it to everyone. It's a dent to my pride but I need to spread the word so that no one else gets conned by him. It turns out, I'm not the only one. Quite a few people have been stung by him. They have the same business card but the number is different on each one.'

'Which noticeboard did you find his card on?' He tried to keep his tone light. But inside his heart was hammering.

'The post office in Redditch. You know the one on Astwood Lane. Someone else got theirs at the Studley post office. It seems anywhere there is a noticeboard, there is a card. I've been taking down the ones I see and dropping them off at the police station. I've also been warning as many people as I can.'

'That's really good of you, Debbie. Will you be okay? You know, money-wise. I could–'

Debbie visibly bristled. 'I'll be fine, Jack. I've managed this far. We are made of tough stuff us Hodgetts.'

She stood up and shouted for her Cooper. Debbie made to walk away but stopped and turned back to Jack.

'It's been really lovely to see you, Jack. I know this is a hard time for you. But don't be a stranger. Winterford is your home. You have got family here too.' She grasped his shoulder and squeezed it. The gesture more affectionate than a hug coming from Debbie. He watched her walk away and then returned to looking at the view. He could feel Elsie's spirit cloaking him. She was there beside him. Encouraging him. He knew what he had to do. He would avenge Debbie.

CHAPTER TWENTY-FOUR

THEN

His whole life had been spent wearing glasses crafted by his father. Seeing only what his father wanted him to see. Spending time with Elsie was reducing the power of his father's glasses. The more time he spent with her, the more of the world she revealed to him. A world that had been hidden from him by his father. All Jack had in his life was his father and the farm. Before Elsie, that had been enough for him. He had thought he was happy. But now, he realised he had been coasting through his life.

With Elsie by his side, the landscape he had spent his childhood roaming around was transformed. He saw things through her eyes and began to see how much he had missed out on, not having a friend his own age. They played immense games of hide and seek, acres of forests, fields and bushes offering places to hide. They waded through the stream trying and failing to catch fish. They climbed trees to see the world from a bird's perspective.

But more revolutionary for Jack was their conversation. At first, spending time with Elsie had been jarring. His sheltered life had not prepared him for her extroverted personality. But she didn't seem to mind. In fact, she took it as a personal challenge to expose him to things he hadn't experienced. Taking great pleasure in his shock.

'I can't believe you've never tried Coca Cola before,' she exclaimed, laughing as he swallowed the bubbly drink, the fizz making his eyes widen in astonishment.

It was also hard to let go of his father's decree that his days should be spent communing with the Lord. But Elsie was a magnet and he was helplessly attracted to her. She burned as bright as the sun and he couldn't help but want to be around her. Her wide smile, infectious laugh and wicked sense of humour made every minute with her fun and addictive.

Jack's nights were spent trying to work out how he could carry on seeing Elsie without his father finding out. There was no doubt that his father would not approve of Elsie. She was a Christian, but her approach to religion was completely out of kilter with his father's. It appeared she was one of those that took the Bible conservatively. When she had told him she thought the Bible was written by humans, it had taken every fibre in his body not to lose his temper.

It showed the depth of his feelings for her that he was able to swallow his objection to her beliefs. He couldn't risk telling her she was wrong. Elsie was confident and opinionated like his father. He was sure that if he disagreed with her, she wouldn't want anything to do with him. His father only put up with him because they were blood relatives.

Adding to his internal strife was the fact that the more time he spent with Elsie, the more he realised that he did not actually have any of his own opinions. Each time he opened his mouth, his father's words came out. This became a problem when Elsie forced him to justify and defend those words.

Today they were nestled on the side of a hill, the whole of Worcestershire spread out before them.

'It's like one of those rugs my mum got me for Christmas.'

'What rugs?'

'You know, the ones with roads and villages and you would get your toy car and drive it around the roads visiting the different places.'

Jack looked at her nonplussed.

'Come on. Everyone had one.'

His cheeks flushed.

'I didn't have any toys. My father doesn't really believe in frivolities.' His voice was quiet. Worried his father might hear him being disloyal.

'But what on earth did you play with?'

Jack thought back over his childhood. He didn't really spend that much time playing with physical toys. The only times he remembered playing was with his mother. She had the most amazing imagination. He remembered they would play epic games of hide-and-seek that spanned into the forest. There had been no need for toys when he was with her. The memory stirred feelings he had long since buried. Jack tried not to think about his mother as a rule. A rule that became easy to follow as time progressed. If a stray memory rose, unbidden, he would banish it by repeating 'Thou shall not commit adultery' in his mind until the memory was buried again.

But this time it was different. He could hear the squelching of their wellies as they splashed in the puddles outside the house. Shrieks of laughter echoed in his mind as he recalled his mother dancing around the trees. He could feel the sun on his back as he chased around after her. Another memory took over; his mother lying on the floor after his father had punched her. Yelling at her for ruining his wheelbarrow. Jack shook his head. His father wasn't like that anymore. Anyway, he needed that wheelbarrow to provide for them.

'What are you thinking?' Elsie was staring at him curiously.

'About my mother.' The words slipped out before he could stop them.

'You don't talk about her much,' Elsie observed.

'She was a bad person.' His father's words once more.

'Really? What did she do?'

'She committed adultery.'

'Oh.' Elsie looked like she wanted to say something, but she picked at the grass, twirling the blades between her fingers before throwing them into the air, to be carried away by the wind.

'What?'

'Well, being unfaithful doesn't necessarily make her a bad person.'

Anger flared within Jack. He jumped to his feet, looking down at Elsie, incredulous.

'Yes it does!' He began to recite the lines he had written all those years ago. 'Exodus, chapter 20, verse 14, thou shall not commit adultery. Hebrews chapter 13, verse 4, marriage is honourable in all, and the bed undefiled: but whoremongers and adulterers God will judge. Proverbs, chapter 6, verse 32, he who commits adultery lacks sense, he who does it destroys himself.'

'Well, yes I understand that. But it also says: "For I will forgive their wickedness and will remember their sins no more." Hebrews, chapter 8, verse 12.'

'Leviticus, chapter 20, verse 10, if a man commits adultery with the wife of his neighbour, both the adulterer and the adulteress shall surely be put to death.' He was breathing heavily, his mind reeling. Unable to cope with Elsie disagreeing with him.

'Things have changed since the Bible was written. Society has become more complex. Nothing is black and white. If everyone in the world was punished according to the laws of a

Bible written over 3,000 years ago, there would be no one left. Humanity would perish.'

'No they wouldn't! People that follow the word of the Lord are good, faithful and true, and will not perish but have eternal life! John, chapter 3, verse 16.'

'Look, I'm not trying to upset you. I am a Christian; I believe in God. But the Bible is open to interpretation. It's there for moral guidance but it isn't a mandatory rulebook. I bet your mother was a good woman. I bet she loved you more than anything. She probably just made a mistake. That doesn't mean you can never speak of her again. She should be given the chance to atone for her mistakes. The Bible clearly states that if we confess our sins that the Lord will forgive our sins.'

Elsie was looking at him fiercely. Shoulders back, eyes bright with conviction. Pain flared in his chest as his mind was bombarded with repressed memories of his mother. He remembered her holding him, rubbing his back gently. Jack threw away the memory. Unable to cope with it. Anger rose within him. How dare Elsie come along and interfere with things she didn't understand.

'No! You are wrong. My father has studied the Bible his whole life. His relationship with the Lord is stronger than anyone's. He knows what the Lord thinks and wants. The Lord views adultery as a sin. Therefore, my mother was punished according to the word of the Lord.'

Elsie looked quizzically at him.

'What do you mean *punished*?'

Jack stopped breathing. His anger at Elsie had almost tripped him up. He floundered for words.

'I just–' He ran a hand through his hair, he was sweating. 'I just meant she was made to leave by my father. Her punishment is that she will never see her son again.' He didn't wait to hear her reply. Jack felt sick at what he had almost done. His brain felt frazzled. It was getting harder to breathe. Desperate to escape her, Jack started to run up the hill, his muscles burning as he pumped his legs up and down. Jack heard Elsie yell up at him.

'The Lord our God is merciful and forgiving, even though we have rebelled against him.'

CHAPTER TWENTY-FIVE

NOW

'Another round, boys?' called Dan as he strode into the pub. It had been a spectacular day and now he was going to celebrate. The lads pulled apart to make space for him and he gave them all the customary one-armed hug before ordering four pints.

'Someone's in a good mood,' observed Dave. 'Who's the lucky lady?' He jabbed Dan in the side, winking at him. The result made him look like he was having a fit. A gangly lad with floppy brown hair he was forever pushing out of his eyes. Most of the time Dan just tolerated Dave. He didn't have much personality, but the way he hung on Dan's every word made him bearable to have a pint with. Plus, it didn't hurt that when he was stood next to Dave, his muscles and sleek black hair looked more attractive to women.

'Lady Luck, my friend,' replied Dan, winking back at Dave.

It was busy in the Copcut Elm tonight; a loud hum of conversation and the football playing on the big screen made it hard for them to hear each other. Dan took a long swig of his pint, sighing in satisfaction as the cold liquid hit the back of his throat. There was nothing like a pint after a hard day's work.

Although Dan couldn't say it had been a hard day's work exactly. He had never experienced one of those and didn't intend to.

'Come on, mate. Tell us what has put you in such a good mood.'

At that moment, Tanya, the red-headed landlady, came over with the last of the two pints. She was large with a fantastic pair of breasts that she was more than happy to share with the world. Framing them in barely-there tops so everyone, no matter where they stood, got a good view.

'That's £15.50 please, Dan.'

Dan pulled out the large roll of notes he had been keeping in his back pocket. He kept his face blank, but eagerly watched the look of shock and envy that graced his friends' faces. They stared at him open-mouthed.

'Where did you get all that?' asked Alex. His eyes were fixed on the money. His bald head beading with sweat from the heat inside the pub. He could understand his friend's shock. Alex had probably never seen so much money in his life.

Friends from school, Dan had watched Alex fall for the same outdated sense of obligation to his ancestors that his father subscribed to. The farm would never do anything more than break even and Alex was never going to make anything of himself thanks to the noose that was the family legacy that had been placed around his neck. Being the firstborn, it was his birthright to ensure that the Thomas family continued to run the farm for years to come.

Alex was forever moaning about the early starts and the unreliable prices of milk. Dan felt sorry for him. He worked harder than Dan ever intended to and would never be wealthy no matter how much he slogged away. Dan couldn't understand why someone would work so hard for no return. But Alex lacked his ambition and drive. Alex might whine about his lot in

139

life, but he would never do anything about it. Farming was in his blood and that was what he said when Dan had lined up a new job opportunity for him.

'Wow, look at all that dosh,' said Dave, almost salivating as Dan passed over a twenty-pound note to Tanya. A virus no one wants, Dave was persistently unemployed and living off his jobseeker's allowance. Pointlessly applying for jobs but his lack of brain cells and insipid personality, combined with a well-known unreliability, meant no one wanted to take him on. Dave had been fired from more jobs than Dan had had hot dinners. He was always whinging about living with his mother and the measly amount in benefits he was getting. Dan bet he had never even seen a fifty-pound note and made sure to fan the cash in his face.

'Where did you get that?' asked Ollie. He was looking at Dan suspiciously. Dan smiled back coyly. Ollie was another childhood friend and he knew Dan better than any of them. Dan's useless layabout mother used to forget to feed him and so Ollie's mother often took pity on him. Letting him stay for tea a few nights per week. Dan and Ollie were unlikely friends. Ollie was as straight as they came. Prefect in school, head boy and did so well in his GCSEs that everyone thought he was going to be a hotshot lawyer or a doctor. Whereas Dan was not a fan of the straight and narrow. He wanted to have fun and played to his own rules. He wasn't book-smart but the parade of nefarious men that frequented his mother's bedroom had taught him to be street-smart.

Dan soon realised that he was not going to be able to get anywhere through education. He wasn't patient or clever enough to follow the traditional route to success. It didn't help that he had a natural aversion to being told what to do. Dan was smart enough to make it on his own. He didn't need anyone. As much as it had been hard being raised by a drug-addicted whore, Dan believed it was actually his mother's greatest gift. He had been forced to become independent and learn to fend for himself. Dan wasn't one of these babied millennials that had been wrapped in cotton wool and had everything handed to them on a plate. Dan's upbringing had taught him life skills that would help him succeed.

No one could understand why an A-star student would be hanging around with the likes of Dan. But their friendship had started in preschool. Dan had kicked Andrew Danfield in the shins when he broke Ollie's glasses and that was that. What people didn't see was that they helped balance each other out. Ollie helped Dan with his homework and ensured he didn't go so off the rails that he'd be kicked out of school. Dan helped Ollie loosen up and have some fun. Dan knew if he hadn't been around, Ollie would never have left his room during GCSE and A-levels. Ollie was Dan's conscience and Dan was Ollie's reminder not to take life too seriously.

'Seriously, Dan. Where did you get it?' pressed Ollie.

'Well. That would be telling.' He smirked at Ollie and jabbed Dave in the side.

'It better not be anything illegal, Dan.' Ollie stared at him, unsmiling.

Dan pretended to be offended. 'Now, Ollie. Is that any way to talk to your oldest friend? Like I would do anything illegal.'

Alex choked on his pint and Dave barked a laugh.

'Seriously, Dan. Where did you get it?'

Dan wasn't flustered, he'd had many years of dealing with Ollie's judgemental attitude. What he didn't know couldn't hurt him was his approach to Ollie.

'If you must know, I got a new customer. I'm doing some roof repairs for her. She insisted on paying me half up front.'

What Dan didn't add was that he had absolutely no intention of going to complete said work. He also didn't tell them that it had been *his* suggestion that she paid half up front. Dan had got the idea for the scam from reading one of those crappy magazines at the dentist. It had been serendipitous. He was in a bind and desperately needed money. He'd spent a bit too much at the pub lately. And lo and behold, he spotted the article when flicking through the magazine out of boredom.

The article told of how a woman with two children had been scammed by a rogue builder. It was perfect. Dan had been working as a car salesman, he was perfect for it as he had the gift of the gab. He could charm Eskimos into buying ice, as his boss was always saying. But the pay was rubbish and he wasn't designed for being an employee. He wanted to be his own boss. Dan had this voice in the back of his head telling him he was destined for more. Reading that article, he just knew it was the blueprint for his future. Only he wasn't going to get caught like the halfwit in the article.

After leaving the dentist, Dan had called his boss and quit. He used the rest of the money in his bank to buy a nondescript van and had some business cards made. After that, all he had to do was buy twenty or thirty burner phones and cycle through them as required. It was the perfect scam. The whole of Worcestershire was at his mercy. He was cleverer than the idiot in the article though. He targeted old codgers in remote villages. The ones whose brain cells were dying off. Dan didn't feel guilty, they had had their time. It wasn't fair that they got to sit in their big fancy houses that they bought for peanuts. Stockpiling their money like dragons. He deserved that money. He had his whole life ahead of him unlike them. Dropping his cards into small local villages had been a stroke of genius, only the elderly used the noticeboards these days.

Today he had been in Winterford. One of those villages that had retained and celebrated its history. It had a collection of thatched houses, intimidating mansions and some chocolate-box new builds bolted onto the sides. Dan drove past two pubs, competing with each other from opposite sides of the road. He passed the village green, a huge Christmas tree lit up with so many lights it was probably visible from space.

As he drove towards the church, he was filled with a burning desire to live there. He swore to himself, one day he would have a house like one of these. A mansion with spires and a gated driveway. That life would be his one day. As he drove up the driveway to Winterford Cottage his anger kicked up a notch. One woman lived in all of this? The injustice burned through his veins. Winterford Cottage was not an accurate name. It had a crenellated roof giving it the appearance of a castle. He could just picture guards standing in between the gaps in the stone, looking for threats. The rest of the house was fitted with arched windows and moated by large hedges that gave it privacy from the road. Jack parked up in front of the house and watched as the old lady opened the door.

'Hi, Debbie. Pleased to meet you.' She proffered a hand. Her grip firm and assured.

He instantly sized her up. From the way she held herself it was obvious that she was a proud woman. Dan would need to tread carefully with this one.

Walking into the house, he could just picture himself living there. This woman didn't need all this room. She led him around and he saw the back of the house gave views over the fields that were to die for. Who needed pictures on the walls when you had a vista like this? Envy was burning within him. It wasn't fair. He looked at Debbie, what had she done to deserve this? There was nothing special about her. She was just a dumpy old woman that had just won the birth lottery.

Dan pretended that he was looking at the work that needed doing. He made all the right noises, his face the picture of concern. At first glance, the stately home seemed perfect. But it was actually tired and very old. It was starting to show its age and would soon need a lot of investment to fix the erosion it had faced at the hands of time. With a keen eye, he had noticed the Aldi shopping bags, the radiators turned off in most of the rooms. The fact Debbie had two cardigans on and three blankets on the sofa. That and the fact she had called him and instantly accepted his stipulation to be paid in cash only. She was desperate to get the work done, for the cheapest price possible.

'Right, Mrs Hodgetts. We need to get this fixed for you. If you leave it much longer the roof is going to cave in completely. It's not safe at all.'

'Really?' She looked aghast, her hands cupping her face and fear in her eyes.

'Don't worry, I can see exactly what the problem is and I can get it done for you today if you like?'

Dan saw the relief in her eyes.

'I just need £1,000 cash to get the materials and then the rest you can pay me later. If I get going now I can be back within half an hour.'

He checked his watch as he spoke. The trick with any con was confidence. It was important to believe the lie yourself. He spoke as if he had every intention of coming back within half an hour. His confidence sold it. It also helped that he had a trustworthy, handsome face that seemed to put people at ease. It would have been a lot harder if he was an ugly runt like Dave.

Dan pretended to look at the view out of the panoramic window as Debbie emptied out the cash from a milk jug she had taken from the back of a shelf in the kitchen. Her hands trembled as she counted out the notes. Dan took them from her and bid her a good day, battling a sudden urge to skip down the driveway. Debbie may have won the birth lottery, holed up in her fancy house in a posh village, but he was on his way to make megabucks. It was just so easy. Like taking candy from a baby.

Getting into his van, Dan took the burner phone out of his pocket and pulled out the SIM card. He snapped it in half and put it in the cup holder where it joined a collection of other snapped SIM cards. Taking out the notebook and pen from the glove compartment, he drew a line through the number and wrote Debbie's name next to it. All the way home, he hummed along to the radio revelling in his cunning. He couldn't wait to get to the pub and show off all the money he'd earned this week. His next job was already lined up. He wondered if he should ask for more when he went to see Jack Danvers the next day. Maybe he could get a ton off him?

CHAPTER TWENTY-SIX

THEN

Misery became Jack's best friend. Having glimpsed a life where he could have fun, laugh and be happy, returning to the tedious routine after Elsie was agonising. Jack's father even noticed his melancholy.

'What's the matter with you?' he asked one night as Jack stared morosely into the fire, unable to garner his usual enthusiasm listening to his father quote scripture. Startled, Jack scrabbled for something to explain himself.

'Oh, I'm just not feeling too well. Think I might have caught a chill.'

'Well, you know what to do.'

Cursing himself for not thinking of something else, Jack got up and put on his coat. He made his way to his father's church. Puddles of rainwater that pockmarked the yard were invisible in the dark. He winced as cold water flooded one of his shoes. Pulling open the wooden door, Jack walked in and shut it behind him, blocking out the cold night. Jack kneeled on the red pillow before the wooden cross his father had nailed to the wall.

He tried his best to think about the Lord and talk to him.

But Jack had never felt that connection the way his father had. Not once had God ever spoken to him the way he did to his father. His father would happily spend hours in here communing with the Lord. But Jack could never find the closeness that his father seemed to garner from being here. All he felt was pain in his knees and a draft coming from underneath the wooden door. It smelled like sodden wood inside and it was bitterly cold. Jack warred with his mind, refusing to think of Elsie and how much he missed her. But it was futile. Hands stuck under his armpits for warmth, he couldn't help thinking of how much he would love to hold her hand right now.

But she wasn't a true believer. His father would be appalled. Jack had been born to serve the Lord. To follow his word and let it guide him through his life on earth. But Elsie, the things she was saying, they were not the words of a true Christian. But the longer he sat there, feeling stiff and cold, the more he longed for her. His mind was playing dirty, forcing him to relive the touch of her skin as they held on to each other, wading through the river. The way the sunlight bounced off her hair. The way her hair had tickled his face when she had given him a hug before leaving to go home. He pictured her dimples that only appeared when she smiled at him.

He had only spent a few weeks with her but she had wormed her way into his heart and mind. He needed her and wanted to be near her. When his father called him in to go to bed, his knees cracked with pain as he stood up. He looked up at the cross on the wall and sent up a silent prayer of thanks. It had come to him suddenly. A bolt from the blue. Was it God talking to him? He didn't know but in a moment of revelation he realised that the Lord had sent Elsie to Jack so that he could teach her what it meant to be a Christian. A true, devout

Christian. If he was honest, he had no choice but to ensure that Elsie met his father's high standards. He tried hard not to think about what happened when the only other woman in his life did not abide by his father's beliefs. The hairs on the back of his neck rose as fear for Elsie's safety enveloped him.

CHAPTER TWENTY-SEVEN

NOW

I t was surprising the number of post offices there were in the surrounding area of Winterford. Jack had used the local one for as long as he could remember. He had banished Elsie from going to the post office as she was constantly being coerced by the lady that ran it into buying things she didn't need. He pictured her sheepish face as she came in with a shopping bag, pulling out an incense stick thing and some candles.

'Elsie, you went in to send a parcel, how on earth did you end up spending forty-five pounds?' he had said.

'But Cathy said that they are struggling to keep the post office going. That if they don't sell anything they will have to shut it down. So, I had no choice but to buy these things.'

'Oh, Elsie. That's the oldest trick in the book.'

She had moved over to him and kissed him on the lips. His annoyance had evaporated.

'You are officially banished from the post office.' Her laughter rang in his ears as the memory faded.

The pain of losing Elsie was like living with a dagger in his heart. His mission was distracting him from it, but he knew it was there. But memories like this dislodged the dagger and caused a ricochet of fresh pain. But Jack was learning to focus on the anger that came with the pain. He made himself remember that he would never hear Elsie laugh again because of the greedy, selfish people he was tasked with eradicating. It filled him with renewed strength and determination.

Jack and his father searched every noticeboard in every post office. They even tried the local supermarkets. Just when they were about to give up, Jack remembered the village shop in Feckenham.

'I'll wait in the car, son.' Jack could see why, his father looked exhausted. The lines on his face were more prominent and his usual energy was missing. His eyes were heavy and Jack could tell he was struggling to stay awake. For the first time, Jack truly appreciated that his father was becoming an old man.

The bell tinkled as he opened the door and he inhaled the aroma of coffee. The village shop was also home to a small café with only three tables and a few more outside. Walking over to the counter, he saw the noticeboard next to it. His eyes darted hungrily from each notice and then he saw it. A small white business card with a cartoon of a hammer. Just like the one Debbie had been holding that morning. Dan Beckett.

'Gotcha.'

Jack unpinned the card.

'That didn't last long,' said the woman behind the counter. She had curly blonde hair that stuck up at all angles. Her eyes were beady and she was scrutinising Jack. A stereotypical gossipmonger if ever he saw one. 'He only put that up this morning. Such a charming young man. I'm sure you'll be in good hands there. Poor lamb, he was telling me he has just been through a nasty divorce. Wife won't let him see his kids and so he lives all alone. I felt ever so sorry for him.'

'That is sad,' said Jack. He turned on his heel and strode from the shop. Wired with anticipation. This was it. Scum like

Dan Beckett didn't deserve the gift of life. They were a scourge on this earth and he was the one that had been tasked to handle it. He would make sure that people like Elsie, so pure and beautiful, were no longer in danger from people like Dan Beckett. A woman with greying hair knocked into him as he walked towards his car. Her shopping bag fell to the floor and the wind started to steal it. Jack snatched it and placed it back in her hand. She beamed at him before turning and hurrying into the shop. Jack felt like he had seen her somewhere before. But before he could consider it further his father was striding towards him.

Jack brandished the card at his father. Like a child who had got full marks on a test, he waited for praise.

'Well done, son. That's brilliant. You know what you have to do.'

They walked back to the car and once settled, Jack took out his phone and dialled the number on the card.

'Dan Beckett.'

'Oh hello, my name is Jack Danvers. I just spotted your card in the village shop and was wondering if you could come around and give me a quote for some building work that I need doing?' Jack forced his voice to sound watery and old.

'Of course I can. Whereabouts are you?'

'We live in the Malvern Hills. It's just me and my father. But we are both getting on and can't do what we used to. I'm afraid we need some help.' Jack could practically hear Beckett rubbing his hands together.

'Not to worry, Mr Danvers. I can help you. How does 9am tomorrow sound?'

'That would be perfect. I'll text you the address.'

'Brilliant. I'll see you tomorrow. Oh, just a heads-up, I only work for cash, Mr Danvers.'

'That won't be a problem. See you tomorrow.'

ABIGAIL OSBORNE

Jack hung up and looked over at his father. Apprehension rose even though he had done this before, he knew he could do it.

'Corinthians, There hath no temptation taken you but such as is common to man: but God is faithful, who will not suffer you to be tempted above that ye are able,' his father recited.

Jack started the car. It was getting dark and they had a lot of work to do.

CHAPTER TWENTY-EIGHT

Their reunification was one of the most magical days of Jack's life. It felt like his heart would burst out of his chest when he realised that Elsie had missed him almost as much as he had missed her. The morning after his epiphany, he rose with the sun and made his way over to their special place, on the side of the hill – a large rock half embedded in the hillside, engraved with J & E when they had proclaimed it their place. He sat with his back leaning against the rock. He watched the birds cavorting around in the skies, tiny cars travelling around tiny roads. Jack's whole body burned in anticipation. But there was a small voice in the back of his mind that whispered to him, warning him that she might not come.

For seven days, Jack visited the hill, every spare minute he could steal away was spent sitting and waiting. He thought about going to her farm, to watch her like he used to. But he couldn't cope with the thought of what he might see. What if she had new friends? What if she was happy and not thinking about him anymore? What if this was only a way to pass time for her, that she had never really liked him and was just curious to find out about the weirdo from Oakdale Farm.

On the eighth day, the heavens opened and Jack was drenched within minutes. His jumper was happily guzzling the rainwater. When he squeezed one of his sleeves, water poured out of it onto the floor. But still he sat there. His mind kept telling him that she wasn't coming. That she didn't want to know him anymore. That the connection he believed they had was all in his mind. But his heart didn't want to let go. It reminded him of how happy he had felt around her. That was worth taking the brunt of a bit of rain. He raised his face up to the sky, trying to enjoy the rain as it trickled down his face. Thankfully, it was a mild day with next to no wind.

'What are you doing, you crazy idiot?' said a voice from behind him. He whirled around and wiped water from his eyes. Unsure if he was conjuring her from pure desperation. Elsie stomped down the hill towards him, not waiting for an answer. She grabbed his arm and dragged him down towards the shelter of the forest that lined the bottom of the hill. The relief of being out of the rain was short-lived when Elsie shoved him. He almost fell over but caught hold of a tree trunk and stopped his fall.

'What were you playing at?'

'I was waiting for you,' he replied, unable to meet her eyes. Instead, he looked down at his sodden shoes.

'Well, I know that. But what sort of lunatic waits for someone in the pouring rain?'

He didn't have an answer that didn't make him sound like an idiot so he said nothing.

'You could have caught a chill out there. Didn't your mother teach you any–' She broke off, realising what she had said. The wind seemed to leave her sails and she calmed down.

'Honestly, I've never seen anything so stupid.'

A thought struck him.

'What were you doing out in the rain?'

It was Elsie's turn to avoid his gaze. She looked out towards the hill, stepping from side to side.

'Were you looking for me?' His heart swelled and he tried to contain a smile that was bursting to escape. 'You've been looking for me?'

'Well, you've been looking for me more. I mean, who sits on a hill for seven days straight! It's pathetic.' Her cheeks were flaming red and she refused to meet his eye. He moved closer to her, smiling so broadly his cheeks hurt.

'Who watches someone waiting for someone for seven days straight?' he asked, still smiling at her. He wanted to reach out and touch her so badly. The air around them seemed to spark with anticipation, an electric current wrapped around them.

Elsie whirled around, her eyes bright and fierce. He thought she was going to yell at him again but then she threw her arms around him and her lips were pressing firmly against his. At first he was paralysed with shock. But then instinct kicked in and he wrapped his arms around her waist and kissed her back.

Jack had heard about kissing when he was at school. But he could never have known how intense it would feel. The world around him vanished and all he could do was feel wave after wave of desire. He pressed Elsie to him, he wanted to mould them together and never let go. Her lips were soft and she smelled of rain, hay bales and sunshine. Her hand gently stroked his face and a ferocious heat ripped through him. Feelings exploded in his mind and body and he never wanted the moment to end.

His lips numb and sore, his breath ragged, they pulled away, looking into each other's eyes. Elsie giggled nervously. The flush of her cheeks and the fact her body was trembling made him think that she had felt what he had felt. It had been his first kiss, but it had also been the first day of his new life. As he looked down into Elsie's eyes, he knew that his life would never be the same. That she was the woman he was meant to be with. He looked up as the sun parted the clouds and the rain retreated. The abrupt change in the weather convinced Jack that God was giving his blessing. They wandered the hills together for the rest of the day. Lost in the bliss of being together. Their argument completely forgotten.

Jack returned that night with his lips swollen. He had to work especially hard to suppress the smile that wanted to adorn his face. His father would not approve just yet. He had to show Elsie the error of her ways before he could introduce her to his father. Once she understood, then his father would give them his blessing. They would be married and his life would finally be perfect. The piece he hadn't realised was missing would be filled.

CHAPTER TWENTY-NINE

NOW

Returning to the grave of the man he now knew as Harry, Jack set to digging a grave next to it. As the hole became bigger he could almost feel his fear rising at the memory of lying in the pitch black. Hearing the rustle of the creatures, feeling them scuttle over his body. The fear that he would never get out. Beating his fists on the immovable wooden door of his prison. Unable to move it and escape. The fear had been paralysing and he couldn't think of a better way to punish someone. Yes, this would be the perfect home for Dan Beckett and the rest. They would suffer for their crimes before they eventually died.

His father stood watching him, a pleased expression on his face. It was so nice to make his father proud again. He understood that the beatings, the strictness, it had all been leading him to this moment. Without his father helping him to nurture his relationship with God, he would not have realised his life's purpose. Elsie had been the catalyst, the trigger that would propel him on his destiny. A destiny he could only fulfil because of his father's support.

His hands bled quicker this time. Only a few minutes

digging had his hands slipping and sliding on the shovel handle. Every so often he would be forced to stop and wipe the blood on his trousers. His knees ached in protest and pain radiated up his back, reminding him of his age. But he ignored the pain, it felt good to push his body to the limits. It was a different type of pain to grief and he welcomed it.

'Enough,' instructed his father. It was pitch black and only the portable floodlight lit up the surrounding area. The trees around them whispered and crows cawed menacingly. When he was younger, the crows used to make the hairs on the back of his neck stand up. He could never see them, only hear their creepy calls echoing around him. Making him feel like he was being watched by someone invisible. But now, he was so used to them, it was like being surrounded by old friends.

Jack heaved himself out of the hole, his shirt sticking to him, and he wiped sweat from his forehead. Looking down, he was pleased to see a man-sized hole, ready to swallow Dan Beckett.

'Now, a lid for our prison.'

Jack followed his father back to one of the outbuildings that was used as a workshop. He found an old back door covered in cobwebs at the back of the shed. It was thick and heavy, just perfect for keeping Dan Beckett in his hole. He also found some barbed wire that his father had used to keep the foxes away from the chickens. With great difficulty, they dragged it over to the forest. Jack could barely breathe when he got there, his lungs on fire.

Jack headed home covered in cuts, bruises and mud. Lining the hole with barbed wire had been the ingenious idea of his father. Although he had just watched as Jack lined the grave with it, suffering many cuts and scratches in the process. His father slapped him on the back as they returned to the house. After Elsie died he thought he'd never be happy again, but here he was saving the world with a large smile on his face with his father marching with him into battle.

The hardest job of all came next. Jack had to go home. There were things he needed that were at their house. Slowly, he drove back to Winterford. His good mood from before fading. He pulled up on their driveway. Thankfully, Susan was in bed, all the lights in her house turned off. Jack looked at his old home. A semi-detached chocolate-box house. It had once been his pride and joy, but now it seemed dreary and miserable, like it too was grieving her loss.

Jack prepared himself for the smell of Elsie as he unlocked the front door. It was only his father's hand on his back, bracing him, that stopped him collapsing this time.

'Remember your mission. Remember what you are here for,' whispered his father, seeing Jack's step falter as they reached the kitchen.

Jack clamped down his emotions and strode to the internal door that led to the garage. Inside, he pulled down a large box covered with dust. It was a home security system that Elsie had purchased on Amazon after one of their neighbours had been burgled. It had several cameras that connected to a phone. Jack had been meaning to put it up for many years but, due to his aversion to technology, it had continued to slip his mind. But his father insisted that they needed to be smart. To keep an eye on the prisoner at all times.

Going back into the kitchen, Jack held his breath as he rummaged through the cupboards. This was strictly Elsie's domain. He could almost hear her shooing him out of the kitchen. Tears lined his eyes as he pulled some bags of rice out of the cupboard and piled them on top of the CCTV box. He grabbed the laptop that was on the kitchen table. He held it like it was china. Elsie had been using it just before they left that day. She had been looking up holiday destinations. Pain pierced his heart and he felt like the lid of his grief was seconds from being ripped off.

Jack's father was examining pictures on the walls. But Jack couldn't look. He was only just holding himself together. A thought of going upstairs to get some more clothes crossed his mind, but his feet held him in place. He couldn't do it. The thought of going into the bedroom was too much. It would break him. They left and Jack locked the door. Breathing hard and trying to remember his mission. To focus only on that and not the memories of Elsie that were diving at him like birds, trying to peck their way through his barriers.

Whilst Jack battled his rising tide of grief, his father alternated between sitting in silence, staring out the window, or turning to Jack and quoting the Bible at him. He knew his father was trying to help him, the only way he knew how. But he did wish he would just shut up. The Bible was his father's answer to everything, but it was not the salve that Jack needed to heal his grief right now.

The further he got from the house, the better he began to feel. The mission was almost ready to begin. Tomorrow, he would finally be able to get justice for Elsie.

That evening, Jack made himself some tea whilst his father headed for a shower and then to bed. Humming to himself as he fried eggs, he was excited for the coming day. Nervous, but excited. He was ready for this. To do good in the world. To have a purpose. He thought back on his conversation with his father earlier that day, as they drove back from the shop after finding Dan's business card.

'This is great, Jack. Your life revolved around Elsie. Now, that's not a bad thing,' he added, raising a conciliatory hand as he saw Jack open his mouth to argue. 'But you were meant for more than that. I brought you up to do God's work. Now you are finally ready to live the life you were meant to have.'

'But being around Elsie made me happy,' he argued.

'Yes, son, but there is more to life than happiness. What about everyone else's happiness? The greed that has contaminated the human race is devouring their happiness. You are the only one that can fix that. Isn't it worth sacrificing your happiness to save your fellow man? There is no more normal a cause.'

The words had hit hard. Had he been wasting his life with Elsie? Was he selfish for focusing only on them and no one else? Not thinking of the greater good?

He shook the thought from his mind. This was his path. Without this gut-wrenching loss, he wouldn't have had the strength to do it before. But now, God had shown him the pain that gluttony and greed were causing in the world. By sacrificing Elsie, he had revealed to Jack his true destiny. Jack ate his ham, egg and chips and pictured the events of the next day. Dan Beckett had the Devil in him, and that Devil was in for a shock. Dan thought he was going to make some easy money but he would be getting a lot more than he bargained for.

CHAPTER THIRTY

THEN

Introducing Elsie to his father was Jack's ultimate goal. Jack was tutoring Elsie in the ways of his father. It turned out to be easier than he thought as she was fascinated by his upbringing. She peppered him with questions about his father's way of life. Jack had noticed her biting her lip a few times. He could tell she wanted to say something but she seemed to be keeping her own counsel. He didn't press her as it would take time for her to truly understand that his father had the most sacred bond with the Lord. A bond that people could only dream of. It had taken him many, many years to truly understand. For a long time, he had hated and resented his father's seemingly cruel, tyrannical reign but that was because he was ignorant.

It was getting easier to spend time with Elsie. His father had been to the livestock market in Worcester to buy some new chickens. Whilst there, he met a man whose beliefs mirrored his own and they had struck up a friendship born out of their desire to make people realise what true faith was. The bonus of this was that his father was now spending more time away from home so that Jack could be with Elsie. Their bond was becoming stronger each day.

Neither of them would consider sex before marriage, but the desire was building between them. Elsie just had to smile at him, a twinkle in her eye and his desire electrocuted him from inside. His longing for her was more than just physical. When they weren't kissing, they were talking. Elsie was teaching Jack so much. He was beginning to realise the almost hermit-like existence had shrunk his world to the acres around the farm. Jack had never heard of many things Elsie referred to and he hung on her every word as she described technology, people and events he could never have dreamed of. She told him of record players and bands that she loved, her current favourite The Human League. Jack had only ever heard the songs of praise. Elsie tried to sing him some of their songs, laughing at herself. Her enthusiasm to show him all the world had to offer outside of his bubble was infectious, and he longed to see the world she had seen.

At nights, he would listen to his father and feel restless. Now he knew there was a whole world out there, it was impossible to be satisfied with the monotonous routine of their lives. Jack became resentful of his father as he was allowed to go off to the city whenever he liked, but Jack was kept at home like some perverse Cinderella. A nickname Elsie had given him. He hadn't been offended at first because he didn't even know what she was talking about. But when she explained the story to him, he got it. He was being kept at home, looking after the animals and maintaining the farm. Whilst he understood his father wanted the best for him, Jack was starting to feel like what was best for him should be his decision now.

They began to get braver. His father had settled into a new routine where he went out all day on Mondays, Wednesdays and Fridays. He set Jack a list of jobs and homework to do whilst he was away. Jack would complete them all as quick as lightning and then at 10am on the dot, he would open the door to Elsie. It was equal parts exhilarating and terrifying having her in his home. The first time, she had walked around open-mouthed and he had tried to see what she was seeing. He supposed it was very minimalist.

'Where's your TV?' she asked.

'Father said that TV is just a device for brainwashing, designed to push political propaganda.'

They went up to his room. As Elsie surveyed the room, he noted the look of sadness in her eyes. He looked at it through her gaze. The only personality in the room came from various stones that he had pulled out of the river because he liked the look of them. Apart from that, he supposed it was quite sterile with just a bed, white sheets and a rail that contained his five pairs of trousers, seven white T-shirts, four jumpers and a white shirt for church. He wondered what her room looked like. They had agreed not to go to her house yet, as there was always someone around. They needed to get both parents onboard first. Jack had a feeling that Elsie's parents wouldn't want her hanging around with the 'crazy Danvers boy'. Elsie couldn't quite meet his eyes when she denied this.

They fell into a very happy routine. Elsie was free for the summer holidays. She had applied to colleges to train in nursing but wouldn't be going until the following year. She had deferred a year so that she could help her parents on the farm. The following year, her brother would be old enough to take her place and she could then go to nursing college. Their days were spent rambling around the Malvern Hills, having picnics. Elsie was enjoying Jack's astonishment as she introduced him to weird and wonderful foods he had never heard of. She had also brought him some magazines, as part of his education on the real world, as she put it. Although *Jackie* seemed to be a magazine for girls and not something that really appealed to him. But he pretended to find it fascinating.

It would have been a magical summer, if it hadn't been for his father's unexpected return one Friday afternoon. They had been lying on the sofa intertwined like shoelaces. Jack had been running his hand through Elsie's hair. Enjoying the silky feeling between his fingers. Elsie's head was resting on his chest. She nuzzled into him and they laid there, enjoying the fizzing connection between them, fighting the sexual tension. They had the radio tuned to a station that Elsie loved, Radio Luxembourg. She had promised to put it back to the pre-programmed station, insisting his father would never know. The music had made him feel comfortable at first. The drumbeat had given him a headache, he found it jarringly repetitive. But after a while, he got used to it and he began to rather enjoy it. The unpredictability of the lyrics was refreshing after listening to hymns he knew by rote.

The front door slammed open. His father strode into the room and called out to Jack.

'Well, that was a–' He stopped stock-still. His eyes wide. He took in the scene. Jack and Elsie together. Fear jolted through Jack's body. He sprang to his feet, dislodging Elsie who almost fell to the floor and squeaked with fear as she did so. Jack helped her to her feet and she readjusted her T-shirt which had ridden up, and pulled up her jeans. Jack saw his father's gaze burning into her. He watched as his fists balled at his sides and the vein in his head twitched forebodingly. Jack could barely breathe. An invisible force was gripping his windpipe, preventing the air from getting in.

'What is this?' whispered his father. He was shaking now, anger flashing in his steel-grey eyes and Jack felt a fear akin to that of his childhood. Jack moved in front of Elsie and opened his mouth.

'Father, I can explain.'

His father's rage exploded.

'What is the meaning of this! How dare you, bringing a woman into my house!' he roared at Jack. He grabbed Jack's jumper and pulled him up by it. Spitting in his face as he yelled at him.

'Have you no shame? Have I not taught you better than this?'

He threw Jack down on the floor. He moved towards Elsie who backed away. But not quickly enough. His father grabbed her arm and threw her out of the living room into the kitchen.

'Get out of my house, serpent witch. I banish you.'

Elsie crawled backwards as Jack's father marched towards her. The ferocity on his face and the terror on Elsie's triggered Jack. He stood in front of Elsie, blocking his father's path.

'You will not lay a hand on her, Father.'

His father tried to shove him out of the way but Jack was immoveable. He was no longer a weak ten-year-old boy. His father had succeeded in turning him into a strapping young man, his equal in strength.

'Get out of my way. You have been duped, boy. This witch intends to seduce you. To let the Devil in.'

There was a collision of fear and fury in his father's eyes. Jack knew he was doing this out of genuine fear for his son's soul. But Jack would not tolerate violence towards Elsie.

'No, Father. I love her and she loves me.' They hadn't said the words yet but Jack knew them to be true. Despite the gravity of the situation a flush of pleasure spread through him.

'Rubbish. Don't fall for it, son. I've taught you better than this.'

'I promise you, Father. Elsie is not the Devil. If you just got to know her–'

'Never! I will not have that whore in my house! You will stop seeing her immediately.'

'No, Father. I won't. We are going to be married when we turn eighteen.'

His father stared at him, incredulous. Jack felt guilty for deceiving him, it must have come as such a shock. Without warning, his father dived around Jack and seized the front of Elsie's T-shirt. He moved his hand back to slap her but Jack grabbed it. In one swift motion he twisted his father's hand behind his back. Fury rising in him at the thought of his father daring to hurt Elsie.

'You will never hurt Elsie.' Jack twisted his father's arm even higher up his back, forcing him to bend over. His father cried out in pain, unable to move or he risked breaking his arm.

Jack threw his father forward and he crumpled to the floor. In a flash he was standing again. His father's body vibrated like he was being electrocuted. Jack could tell he wanted to kill him for his insubordination. But Jack was no longer scared. Not when Elsie's safety came into play.

'Come with me, Jack. Let's go.' Elsie's voice came from behind him and she wrapped her delicate hands around his arm, tugging him gently.

'If you go with her, you are no longer welcome in this house.'

Jack gaped. His father didn't mean it. Surely. The thought of abandoning his father was hard. He knew his father wasn't perfect. But he had raised him the best way he knew. Jack glanced at Elsie and his jaw set. He couldn't give up the life that Elsie was offering him. No matter how much he loved his father.

Jack turned his back on his father and slammed the front door behind him. He took Elsie's hand and they set off down the road. To their new life together.

CHAPTER THIRTY-ONE

NOW

I t was like being a child at Christmas. Not that Jack had ever experienced that as his father did not follow the 'corporate scam' that was a traditional Christmas. The first time Jack had even heard of Santa Claus was when he started school. He had asked his parents over dinner whether Santa knew where he lived as he had never seen him before and had never had any presents. His mother had lowered her head, unable to meet Jack's eye. His father had jumped up, outraged. He had informed Jack that Santa Claus was in fact a product of capitalism designed to convince people to spend their hard-earned money. There was no such thing and he was never to mention it again.

To ensure it never happened, Jack's father forced him to spend every Christmas writing out Matthew's Gospel, the story of Jesus. It would have been useful if he was cast in the nativity but his father forbade that too. When Jack had come home and made the mistake of requesting a sheep costume from his mother in earshot of his father, his father had lost his rag. The next day, he marched Jack into school and demanded to speak to the head teacher. Jack had stood their shamefaced as his father yelled at Mrs Smith.

'A sheep? You expect my son to take part in the nativity, one of the most integral events in the Bible, and you cast him as a sheep? It's blasphemy. It's a mockery. I will not have it. My son will not be part of your nativity. I am disappointed, Mrs Smith. The birth of Jesus Christ seems just to be entertainment to you. But you wouldn't be here if it wasn't for that pinnacle event in our history. Perhaps you will give it the respect it deserves in future.'

After that, Jack was ostracised from the class. Peter told Jack that his dad was a 'crazy lunatic' and no one wanted to be friends with him because they might become crazy as well. Jack had watched from the sidelines as his class discussed what they were asking from Santa. Jack had told them he wasn't real, that it was a corporate scam. But no one listened to him. They loved to ignore Jack and eventually he had given up trying. Until Elsie, he had given up on talking to anyone apart from his father.

But now, waiting for Dan Beckett, he could imagine it was what waiting for Santa Claus felt like. He had shaved and washed and now sat impatiently. Every few minutes, he looked out the window but all he saw was the empty driveway. Just as he was making a cup of tea, more for something to occupy himself than to satisfy his thirst, he heard the crunching of tyres on gravel. The cup fell out of his hand; he made a grab for it but it hurtled to the floor and smashed into pieces on the concrete. A knock at the door startled him and he stared at the broken cup and then at the door, a flicker of indecision running through him. Leaving the cup, he answered the door, his father appearing behind him.

'Hi.'

'Mr Danvers?'

'Yes, come in, come in.' Jack hunched over; he clenched all his muscles so that his hands and arms shook. He spoke in a weary voice and tried to act just like the old men he had seen in church with Elsie. Jack could see his father holding back a smirk. Dan Beckett was handsome. Muscles, sleek black hair and a clean-shaven face, he was sure to melt many people's hearts. He did not look like a builder. His clothes were as immaculate as his hair.

Jack watched as Beckett's shrewd eyes surveyed the house. It was like stepping back in time to the sixties. Modern developments had not been embraced here. Jack's father had kept everything, from the old wooden table with dents, stains and scratches to the old-fashioned olive-green sofa that looked haggard and unloved. Beckett spotted the cup on the floor and Jack grinned apologetically.

'My hands aren't what they used to be. Always shaking now. The price of old age, I'm afraid.'

Beckett bent down and began to pick up the broken cup.

'Don't worry, Mr Danvers. I'll help you. It's a lovely place you have got here. I bet it is worth a fortune.'

Trust Beckett to be thinking about the value of the house.

'I don't know. My family have lived here for generations. My father,' he indicated to his father, 'he was born here, as was I.'

'How lovely,' Beckett replied, not even deigning to look at them. He put the pieces of the broken cup into the bin and wiped his hands. 'Now what is this work you need doing?'

'I'm afraid it is down in the cellar. We've had terrible weather lately and there is now a huge leak. I don't go down there often but I needed to get something and found half of the things down there completely ruined.'

Beckett looked fidgety, obviously wishing Jack would stop talking. How did anyone think this man was charming?

'Not a problem, Mr Danvers. I'm sure it's nothing I can't fix. As I said on the phone though, I take cash only and I'd need half now to cover costs. I'll go and have a look at the problem, then I will go and get the supplies I need and then I'll be back to do the work later today.'

Jack decided to have a little fun.

'But how do I know you will come back?'

Jack was hoping to wrong-foot Beckett. But he replied, completely unfazed.

'Oh, you wound me, Mr Danvers.' He gave Jack a wolfish grin and clutched his heart, pretending to have been physically wounded. 'Of course I'll come back. I can give you the numbers of hundreds of people that I have worked for. They will all tell you I'm reliable if you need a character reference. I just need some money up front to cover the cost of materials. That's all. I only take cash as it means I can give you the best and cheapest price for the job. To be honest, bank transfer would be easier for me but my customers come first. I always want to give them the best price.'

'No, that's fine. I trust you. I pride myself on being a good judge of character.'

Jack led Beckett to the door for the cellar. It was hard to remember to walk slowly and slightly bent. His knees ached from the unusual position. Jack let the pain show on his face.

Opening the door, he motioned Beckett to go first.

'I won't join you, Mr Beckett, if you don't mind. My knees can't take the stairs these days.'

Beckett nodded and moved past him. Jack held his breath. He watched as Beckett lifted his foot to take the first step. When his other foot lifted up to follow, Jack struck. Summoning all his strength, he pushed Beckett as hard as possible. The man was off balance which made him powerless to Jack's shove. Beckett flew downwards; his head thudded as it made contact with a concrete step. A crack sounded as his leg hit a different step. It was over in a matter of seconds. One minute Beckett was walking down the stairs, the next he was a crumpled heap at the bottom.

Following Beckett down the stairs, Jack kicked him so that he was lying on his back. He smiled as he saw Beckett's carefully groomed hair coming out of place, strands of midnight-black hair sticking up. Jack stepped over him and picked up the ropes on the workbench. He yanked Dan's legs together and tied them tightly. Turning him over, he then tied Beckett's hands behind his back. Jack dragged him over to a wall and leaned him up against it. Searching Beckett's pockets he found a roll of notes, some business cards, a scratched, basic-looking smartphone and a packet of cigarettes.

Beckett's eyelids fluttered and then opened. He gazed up at Jack, uncertainty in his eyes. Reality seemed to hit him as he tried to move his arms and legs. He looked up at Jack, terror in those previously smug eyes.

'What's going on?' Beckett looked up at Jack and his father. 'Why are you doing this to me?'

A trickle of blood escaped his hairline, etching its way down his face.

'What is wrong with you? Say something!' Beckett yelled.

'You are a sinner, Dan Beckett.'

'What are you talking about? You're crazy! Let me go.' He struggled against the binds to no avail.

'You are a sinner. Do you deny taking people's money?'

'What? I haven't taken anyone's money!'

'Now we both know that isn't true.' Jack stared down at Beckett, meeting his eye. He felt a cauldron of anger bubbling inside him. Every lie Beckett told just added more potency to the anger inside. This man disgusted him.

'Seriously, you've got the wrong guy,' Beckett pleaded, his eyes beseeching.

Jack bent down so he was at the same level as Beckett, shaking his head at him.

'So, you don't remember my friend, Debbie? Lives in Winterford?'

Beckett's face lost all of its remaining colour. His mouth opened and closed, fish-like. Most likely trying to conjure another lie.

'Ah, so you do remember?' Jack gave Beckett a predatory smile.

'Listen, I'm sorry, okay? I didn't realise she was your friend. I'll give you the money I took from her. I promise. Please.'

Beckett may not have struck the killing blow that took his Elsie's life, but Jack knew he was just the same, just as evil as the ones that did. It was his responsibility to exterminate this evil from the world. Jack looked down at Beckett, a snivelling, disgusting rat. He stole from innocent people and he wasn't even sorry. Just concerned about his own skin. Well, Jack would soon see to that. He punched Beckett in the face. The weight of his anger behind it. The warbled scream of pain that erupted from Beckett was like beautiful music he could listen to all night.

'But, Mr Beckett, what about all the other people whose money you stole?' he shouted over Beckett's screams.

'I'll give it all back!' pleaded Beckett. His face panic stricken. 'I'll never, never do it again. I swear. Please, just let me go!'

'I will never let you go, Dan Beckett. You will pay for the wrong you have done. You will suffer as those you have wronged have suffered.'

With that, Jack walked back up the stairs; at the top of the landing, he turned off all the lights. Let Dan sit in the darkness, be alone with his thoughts. While he still could.

That night, Jack and his father had a roast dinner and toasted to their success. Watching Beckett sobbing on the CCTV whilst they ate.

PART II

CHAPTER THIRTY-TWO

'Please, Mummy.' Ten-year-old Poppy gripped Adina's leg. Adina tried to move but the girl gripped on to her leg tightly, sitting on her foot and clinging to her like a koala bear. No longer as light as she used to be, Adina could no longer sweep her over the floor, pretending she was a mop.

'Poppy, get off.'

'Not until you say yes,' Poppy insisted.

A knife pierced Adina's heart. Here she was again, disappointing her girl. Thanks to her, Poppy lived in a flat outfitted by Oxfam. The sofa was her friend Sally's that had been molested by dogs and young children who had left permanent stains all over it. Adina had put a bright-red blanket over it to cover the worst but it didn't help, the flat cushions made it almost as comfortable as sitting on a gym mat. Their TV was tiny, a small grey box that she had put on a shelf to try and give the illusion that it was bigger than it was. It was a stupid decision as Poppy moaned on a daily basis that she couldn't see the *Tracey Beaker* reruns she was obsessed with.

The wallpaper was coming away from the wall and the carpet was threadbare and stained. If she thought about the stains for too long she would shudder and feel nauseous. It was run-down and all that she could do was put patches over the worst of it, but there was no hiding the shabbiness. It wasn't meant to be like this. When she had fallen pregnant she had been living in a detached house on a beautiful estate of new builds in Worcester. She had been able to tell people that she lived in Warndon, one of the richest parts of the town, until the bailiffs turned up at the door searching for Brian, her husband (now ex-husband) who she thought was on a business trip in Dubai.

On the whole, Adina knew she had come through the experience stronger. With no sign of Brian, Adina had no choice but to leave the home they had built and take the then three-year old Poppy to a friend's house. Adina had hit rock bottom, been forced to sofa surf until the council finally gave her a flat and a meagre amount of money each week. She could have gone to her sister's but she would have had to have been an inch from starvation before that happened.

Unwilling to be a benefit whore, Adina had begun making handcrafted cards using plastic that she found by the riverbanks. Poppy used to think it was the best game in the world and was desperate to go out and explore and see what treasure they could find. With a rubbish laptop that only worked if she hit it three times every half an hour, she started a Facebook group and slowly the money began to trickle in. Her first sale was for £2.50 and when the money arrived in her bank, she had taken a delirious Poppy to McDonald's for the first time in her life. Adina had watched with a lump in her throat as Poppy, brown eyes wide with wonder, tucked into her first ever Happy Meal. Sucking on the chips and nibbling at the chicken nuggets whilst clutching the figurine that came with it.

Everything she had ever done was to make Poppy happy. And Poppy seemed to have cottoned on to this by the way she was strangling the blood from Adina's leg and using her best begging voice. Adina knew that Poppy was aware they didn't have much money. As much as she tried to shield her little girl from their dire situation. But there were times when the pressure to fit in with the other girls became too much for Poppy.

'I just can't, Poppy.'

'But all the girls in my class have one. It's not fair.' She let go of Adina's leg. Realisation dawning that she wasn't going to get her way this time. There was a big difference between a new pencil case and an iPad. Adina would have to sell thousands of cards in order to buy Poppy a new pair of shoes let alone electronics. She couldn't even afford a proper smartphone, she was still using a basic phone that couldn't even connect to the internet.

Adina looked at her daughter's disappointed face and tried to stem the tears. It was bad enough that she turned up to the school gates red-faced and out of breath because she had to walk three miles to come and get Poppy. All the other mums breezily stepped out of their cars, looking glamorous and so relaxed. They huddled together whilst Adina stood on the fringes. Her poverty was a scent that kept the other mothers at bay. It killed her inside as she had listened to them bragging about the new things they had bought their kids and the karate and dance lessons they were taking them to.

Before they were aware of her social standing, they had good-naturedly handed over cards for different classes they thought Adina might want to take Poppy to. Obviously not noticing that Adina had worn the same threadbare coat to school pick-up and couldn't even afford a car. Each word had hit home that Adina would never be able to give Poppy the life these kids had. When they realised that Adina couldn't afford the same lifestyle as them, they slowly backed away, as if concerned her economic situation was infectious.

But how was she supposed to earn any money when Poppy needed her to be there? The cost of childcare was more than anything she could earn. Having got pregnant at sixteen, she had no qualifications and she was only able to work school hours. So, the best she had been able to get was some cleaning work and combine that with the small amount of money she made crafting cards. She was doing the best she could but it wasn't enough.

Poppy stomped off to her room and Adina finally gave in to tears. It wasn't Poppy's fault she had been born to a mother with no prospects. Adina looked around the room to see what she could sell. But there was no longer anything of value. Moving into her bedroom, Adina walked over to the windowsill. She took out her grandmother's ring. When the bailiffs had searched the house, she had just enough time to hide this in her bra. The diamond glistened in the sunlight coming through the window. She had no curtains to keep out the rays so they baked her room, slowly turning it into a furnace.

The gold band was twisted around the diamond, it was intricate and breathtaking. Nanny had given her this ring shortly before she had passed away. Nanny had always had a soft spot for Adina and they had spent a lot of time together when she was growing up. It was the only thing she had left of her family. Could she really part with it? The disappointment in Poppy's face rose in her mind. She pictured handing her a brand new iPad and watched as her brown eyes sparkled and her face lit up with surprise and happiness. Her excited screams would echo off the walls. For once in her life, she could go into school with the latest gadget and show off to her friends.

Adina's guilt gnawed at her. Her nanny had intended that ring be passed down through the family. She was supposed to give it to Poppy when she was sixteen. Not pawn it for an iPad. But the possibility of having money was too tempting. After years of having nothing, her resolve was weakening. Just this once she wanted to give her daughter something she wanted. Adina put back the ring and flopped down onto her bed. Unable to make a decision. Memories of curling up on Nanny's knee fought with Poppy's giant smile of excitement. Picking up the laptop, she logged in to her online banking, already knowing what it was going to say. Maybe if she stared long enough the £21.39 would morph into £2,000.

Her phone rang, making her jump, and she reached over to get it but tripped on the charging cable of the laptop. Instead of grabbing the phone she knocked it onto the floor. The accompanying crack made her heart sink. There were already so many scratches and cracks on her phone, she couldn't send any messages with the letter 'm' because of one particularly nasty crack. With trepidation, she saw another freshly laid crack in the corner of the phone. She blew out a breath. Not the worst it could have been. A missed call registered and she saw it was Scarlett.

Looking at the time, she realised they were late, jumping off the bed and yelling at Poppy to get her shoes on. Adina raced to the wardrobe. She put on her one good jumper, saved for occasions when she needed to impress. There was no one she needed to impress more than Scarlett. Her older sister was thriving and successful and wasn't afraid to show it. Every time they met Adina came home feeling like more of a failure than she had when she arrived.

Scarlett had two boys and a husband, Adina reminded herself. *Of course she was thriving*, she thought bitterly. Adina would be if she had someone to share the burden with. But she hadn't clapped eyes on Brian since he'd left for his supposed business trip to Dubai. His phone number and interest in his wife and daughter had disappeared overnight and she had no idea where he was and if he was still alive.

Just before they reached the café where she met Scarlett every other Monday, Adina pulled Poppy to one side and deftly French-plaited her hair. She turned the girl and examined her face, wiping a smudge of chocolate from her cheek. Poppy looked at her with serious brown eyes, so like her father's it was uncanny. She wished fervently that one day Brian would come back to them. Not because she still loved him but so that Poppy could have a father.

Her parents had both died when she was eighteen. Although they weren't happy with her getting pregnant at sixteen, she had known that they both loved her. She wanted that for Poppy. That knowledge that she had a mother *and* a father that both loved her. Anger burned as she was once again reminded that the money her parents had left her, that Brian convinced her to invest in the house, was now gone. Maybe Poppy was better without that sort of person in her life.

'Are you crying, Mummy?'

Adina rubbed her eyes, wiping away the escaping tears she hadn't noticed.

'Yes I am. Because you are so damn beautiful, little bear.' And she wrapped Poppy in a bear hug, squeezing her until she heard her giggles.

'Now come on, we are late to see Aunty Scarlett.'

Poppy did an eye-roll that reminded her of herself so much, it made her heart swell. She lived for these mini-me moments.

The doorbell tinkled as they walked in and heads swivelled to look at them and then swiftly away. Scarlett didn't even look up, she had Logan bouncing on her knee, his chubby hands stabbing at the iPhone screen she was holding in front of him. Peppa Pig was prancing around the screen much to his delight. Thank God Poppy no longer watched things like that. *Peppa Pig* had to be one of the worst shows ever made. Mind-numbing in every sense of the word.

Adina looked at Logan and felt her heart twinge. She would love nothing more than to have another baby. But she had had to go without meals for two weeks in order to replace Poppy's school shoes. How would she cope with another mouth to feed?

'Hiya,' Adina said. Forcing a cheerfulness into her voice that she didn't feel. It was going to be an hour of torture but family was family. She didn't have anyone else and it was important for Poppy to spend time with the only family they had.

'Hi, darling,' Scarlett drawled. She got up and gave Adina a half-hearted hug, Logan balanced on her hip. A scream forming as it dawned on him that he no longer had the iPhone.

Poppy and Adina squeezed in at the other side of the table and Poppy immediately joined Joshua at his iPad. They began a whispered conversation and Adina smiled. In her gut, Adina believed Joshua had been switched at birth. There was no way her devil sister had produced such a gentle, intelligent young boy. Both his parents were loud, selfish and competitive. Everything that he wasn't.

'How's work?'

At least let me get a coffee first before you start with the jibes, thought Adina.

'Shall we order?'

She tried to catch the eye of the blond waiter who was walking around studiously looking at the floor in case someone asked him to do something. But unfortunately, he came too close to their table and Adina took advantage of his proximity to force his attention.

'Excuse me.' So loud he couldn't pretend he hadn't heard.

He looked up and drew closer, reluctantly drawing out his pad from the pocket of the apron.

'I'll have another coffee. But can you try not to butcher this one, please. That last one tasted worse than cat pee,' requested Scarlett, not even bothering to look up at the waiter, and said before Adina could even open her mouth to order. Adina was tempted to ask how Scarlett knew what cat pee tasted like but knew it wouldn't be worth the tantrum it would elicit.

'And for you?' asked the waiter. His disgust at Scarlett's attitude evident on his face as she smoothed Logan's hair and jiggled him up and down. Adina paused, wondering if she actually wanted something as there was every chance he may actually spit in their drinks. Scarlett misinterpreted her silence and said loud enough for the entire café to hear:

'Get what you want, I'll pay for this, don't worry about the cost.'

Adina's cheeks flushed. Both Joshua and Poppy had looked up from the iPad. Poppy looked nervously at her. An elderly man at the table next to them was studying her intently. His newspaper lowered as he watched. It seemed he was hoping for some sort of drama. God, why did Scarlett have to treat her like this? She could afford a bloody coffee. Well, not really, but Scarlett didn't know that.

'No, don't you worry. I will get it. It's my turn, I absolutely insist.' She looked up at the waiter, trying to hide her embarrassment.

'I'll have an oat milk latte and a hot chocolate and...' She turned to look at Poppy. 'How many flakes do you want, Poppy?' The girl's face lit up and she bit her lip as she thought. 'Erm... four?'

'Four it is. Oh, and throw in as many marshmallows as you can fit in the cup.' Poppy squealed with delight.

The waiter walked off and Scarlett stared curiously at Adina. Four years older than her, Scarlett didn't look a day over twenty-five. Her bouncy brown hair was shoulder length and straight, not a single frizz or hair out of place. The cream jumper and perfectly fitted jeans made her look youthful and sophisticated. Her face was free of lines and her make-up was expertly applied.

Adina used to watch her sister applying her make-up to go out with her friends. As a young girl, she had been mesmerised and had always begged Scarlett to teach her. But for some reason, her older sister had always kept her at arm's length. She refused to let Adina in and they had never shared the bond that Adina had always wanted. It seemed to Adina that Scarlett resented her birth. Wishing to have their parents to herself perhaps, it was the only explanation she had for the contempt Scarlett had shown her for her whole life. Adina was sure that the only reason Scarlett insisted they meet up was so she could check she was the superior and more successful sister. Even though their parents were no longer there to be impressed.

'How are you going to afford that? Robbed a bank, have we?' Scarlett snorted, as she wiped away a bit of dribble from Lucas's face. If only she could be as nice to Adina as she was to her son.

'Well, a lot has changed since we last met up. I didn't want to say anything until it was all sorted. But I have set up a business.' The lie was spilling out before she could stop herself. She didn't even know what she was going to say next. All she wanted was to wipe the smirk of superiority off her sister's face. For her to look at Adina with respect instead of pity.

'A business? You've set up a business?' Scarlett looked at her incredulously. Her derisive tone made Adina's veins burn with anger. She may be making it up but who says she couldn't start a business.

'Yes, Scarlett. Me. I have a cleaning company. I've got a team of women working for me. They go and do all the work and I get the money. It's genius if I do say so myself. All those days spent doing the cleaning myself when I can get other people to do it for me. I get to sit back and relax whilst the money just pours in.'

As she was talking, Adina realised that this would actually be quite a good idea. If only she had had this brainwave earlier, instead of as a reaction to her sister's constant jibes. Maybe she could make this lie a reality? Who was she kidding. She wouldn't even know where to start. Scarlett had said something but Adina hadn't been listening.

'Sorry, what did you say?'

'I said, I can't imagine there is much money to be made in cleaning.' Adina could see her sister seemed less certain of herself. Inside, Adina felt a flush of pleasure. For once, Scarlett was worried that her reign as successful sister may be under threat.

'Ah well. That's where you are wrong. I can understand why you would think that. Not having had to work, you wouldn't know what the demand is like out there. In the real world.'

Scarlett's cheeks flushed red and her eyes flashed. She opened her mouth to retort but Lucas chose that moment to vomit all over himself, the table, Scarlett's iPhone and her hand. Scarlett cried out in disgust and got up and took Lucas to the bathroom to change him.

Adina smiled in victory. It wasn't often that she dared stand up for herself when she was with Scarlett. She was too scared of losing the only family she had left. In Scarlett's absence, Adina glanced over at Poppy and she wanted the ground to swallow her up. Poppy had evidently been listening to every word. She stared at Adina with confusion in her large brown eyes. Her lips were parted as if she wanted to ask a question. A question that Adina did not want to answer. *Oh, Poppy.* How could she have been so selfish? How was she going to explain this to her?

Scarlett came back to the table, Lucas sporting a new Ralph

Lauren polo shirt.

'That top is nice,' Adina said.

'Yes, but not as nice as the other one. Such a shame I had to bin it. I'll just have to order another one.'

Adina wondered what it was like to have so much money you could just throw things away. She took hold of one of Lucas's chubby hands in hers. The feel of his cotton-soft skin seemed to swell her ovaries, her longing for more children was overwhelming sometimes. She had always dreamed of a house full of children. Scarlett did not know how lucky she was.

'Can I?' She gestured to Lucas and Scarlett passed him over. The room disappeared as Adina breathed in the intoxicating baby smell. She cradled Lucas to her chest and smiled over at her sister.

'You are so lucky. He is adorable.'

'Yes he is.' The sisters' eyes met and for the first time, Adina felt a sense of connection between them. A bond stemming from their shared love of being a mother. 'You'll be able to have more now you've got a steady income.' And just like that, the feeling disappeared and Adina was left with a sour taste in her mouth. Scarlett looked over at Poppy appraisingly. 'But if I were you, I'd start with getting Poppy a haircut and treating the girl to a few new clothes. She's worn that jumper every time I've seen her this year. Poor lamb.'

Adina's hackles raised. She was fine with her sister criticising her, but she would not tolerate Poppy being the subject of her scrutiny. Desperate to shut her sister up, she began talking without really realising what she was saying. Word vomit poured from her as she fought to defend herself against Scarlett's accusations.

'Actually, I'm already working on that. You wouldn't believe the stuff I've ordered for Poppy. A personal shopper has selected a seasonal wardrobe for her and she is booked in with Tony and

Guy next week for her hair. She is going to get the best of everything. I've ordered her an iPhone, an iPad and a MacBook which should be coming tomorrow. Poppy's life is going to be very different now. I can assure you of that. My little girl is going to want for nothing.' Her voice had become louder as the lies flew from her mouth, and she noticed that the old man at the table by the door was staring unabashedly at them. Adina could feel Poppy's eyes burning into the side of her head but she couldn't look at her. Nausea rolled in her stomach as shame began to creep in, dissipating her anger. It was time to leave before she did any more damage to Poppy. Adina got to her feet. She was amazed that Scarlett didn't question her. Her words sounded ludicrous and unconvincing to her own ears. But Scarlett's mouth was opening and closing as she struggled for words.

'Now if you don't mind, we have an appointment at Jaguar. We are doing a test drive of the new model they have just released.' Unable to look at her daughter, Adina moved towards the exit, trusting Poppy to follow her out.

In her haste to escape the disgusting lies she had just told she didn't see the child running out of the bathroom. At the last second, Adina noticed him and jumped out of his way, slamming into the old man's table. His cup upended, covering his trousers in hot coffee before it smashed to the floor. Adina, unbalanced, lost her grip on her handbag and watched as it fell, dispersing her lipstick and small change across the tiled floor. Groping on her hands and knees, Adina grabbed her things. Briefly, she considered offering to replace the man's coffee. But she only had £20 to last them the month. Pretending she hadn't noticed the spilt coffee, she took Poppy's hand and strode out of the café. Head held high. Feigning confidence, when inside she felt like the worst person in the world. Before that coffee, she had been poor but at least she had been respectable and decent.

Now she was rotten. What sort of example was that for her daughter?

Poppy was quiet all the way home. Adina kept opening her mouth to explain but she couldn't find the words. Should she tell Poppy the truth? Was she too young to understand the complexities of being a human? That people don't always get things right, that making mistakes is a part of life. Poppy still saw things in black and white, could she understand that her mother was just fed up with being the runt of the litter?

They were almost back at their street when Poppy took her hand. Her soft skin wrapped around Adina's and it made her heart constrict with happiness. It was the same every time her daughter touched her. Adina gently stroked Poppy's hand with her thumb.

'Mum. What you said before to Aunty Scarlett wasn't true, was it?' she said quietly.

'No, sweetie.' Shamefaced. Adina couldn't look at Poppy.

'It's okay. I understand,' said Poppy, her tone matter of fact. She jumped over the cracks in the pavement as they walked.

Adina stopped and finally looked down at her daughter.

'I once told a girl at school called Fiona that we were getting a puppy.' Poppy looked up at her, face earnest. 'She told everyone else and all that day everyone was really nice to me because they wanted to know about my puppy. They asked me to bring it in for show and tell. I had to tell them that you had changed your mind and they stopped talking to me again. But it was worth it, for that one day of being allowed to join in.'

Adina's heart broke. Tears fell from her eyes and she sank to the floor and pulled Poppy into a fierce hug before she could see them.

'Mum,' Poppy mumbled into her coat.

'Yes?'

'I don't want an iPad.'

CHAPTER THIRTY-THREE

The pain hit Jack before his brain could understand what had happened. He jumped up, rubbing at the hot liquid spreading like a flame, burning the skin beneath his trousers. He cried out as coffee stains bloomed across his beige pants, making it look like he had fouled himself. A shattering sound filled the café as his mug fell to the floor and crashed to the ground, an explosion of white pottery. Everyone in the café seemed to take a collective breath and turned to look in unison. The woman seemed oblivious to his cries of pain and anger. Her bag had fallen to the floor and she scrabbled around, ignorant to everything except sorting herself out. Her hair was raven black but he could see roots of brown staining the top of her head. She did not look up as she snatched at the lipstick and coins that were making a bid for freedom. He waited for her to apologise, to look at him and offer to make amends. Her daughter looked stricken and reached down to pick up a few more coins that had gone under a different table. The woman threw everything back into her bag and stormed from the café.

He stood staring after her open-mouthed. The woman's

sister came over to him. She sneered as they watched her walk down the street.

'I'm sorry about her. She's always been selfish and rude. Can I get you another coffee?'

Jack sat back down with a fresh coffee, still dabbing at his trousers uselessly. He hoped the stain would come out. They were his favourite pair. Elsie had got them for him in a bid to encourage him to 'join the twenty-first century'. He could remember her smile when he had tried them on. Exclaiming he had never looked so handsome. Jack pushed away the memory and focused on his anger instead.

The woman's face came into his mind's eye. The way she had gloated that she was paying her staff to clean houses whilst she sat back and did nothing. Jack could just picture her, sitting in a fancy office, reaping the profits her staff brought in. It made him nauseous. He recalled the swagger in her voice as she reeled off all the things she was going to buy her daughter. *Eight iPads?*

The daughter was a beauty. Long dark-brown hair that glittered in the lights of the coffee shop. An angelic oval face with large brown eyes. His heart filled with sympathy and concern. What chance did this young girl have when she was being raised with such a materialistic monster? She couldn't even stop to apologise for knocking over his coffee. The thought struck him like a bolt from the blue. He could save her. Jack could eradicate the evil from her life. She was better off being raised in foster care or with lovely adoptive parents instead of that woman. He had the power to do that.

God had a new plan for him. Why else was he in this coffee shop at this time? It had been a spur-of-the-moment decision. He had just abandoned Beckett's van on a side street near Rainbow Hill in Worcester. It was always crammed with vehicles and there were no yellow lines. He didn't think it would be found for a while. If anyone even bothered to look for

Beckett. He couldn't imagine a man like that had many friends. As Jack had walked to the bus stop, he remembered that he wasn't far from the coffee shop that Elsie was forever dragging him to after a day of shopping at the retail park. After years of living in a vibrant, busy village, he was used to seeing people every day. In a moment of madness, he changed direction and headed there. Knowing it was going to incite painful memories, he still went in. Unsure what was driving this need to be around people in a place that he and Elsie used to visit. But now he realised it hadn't been an impulsive decision, it had been the Lord, whispering in his ear.

As Jack wondered how he would find her again, he spotted a business card bathing in the spilt coffee. It was a company called Spik 'n' Span, and on it was the name 'Adina Carter' and a mobile number. Jack smiled to himself, thanking the Lord for giving him a clear sign. Adina would be next. He left the café, his mind lost in planning his next attack. Not noticing the car trailing him.

'Father, Father. We've got the next one.' Jack burst through the door. The business card held aloft. He was breathless with excitement. His father looked up from the paper he was reading.

'Calm down, boy.'

Jack took some deep calming breaths and took a seat at the table. He explained everything to his father and flourished the business card.

'It's perfect, Father. All I have to do is call her up and get her to come over.'

'And you are sure she is one of them?' questioned his father.

'You should have heard her, Father. She was bragging for

everyone to hear about how she runs an empire of cleaners, does no work and "the money just pours in".' He did air quotes as he spoke. 'It was disgusting, but more importantly, it was in front of her daughter. She was so young, impressionable. We have to help her. We can save her from turning out the same way as her mother.'

His father steepled his fingers and rested his head on them, seemingly lost in thought.

'Anyway, you weren't there, it was like she was meant to spill coffee on me, I was meant to do this. Why else would her business card just happen to fall out and land under my table? He wants me to do this. He is giving me a sign.'

His father nodded.

'Right then, we best get to work.'

He walked over to Jack and rested his hand on his shoulder. 'I am proud of you, son.'

Happiness radiated around Jack's body. Intertwining with the anticipation of punishing Adina Carter.

CHAPTER THIRTY-FOUR

The phone rang but Adina ignored it. She wasn't in the mood to talk to anyone. Despite her best efforts, she wasn't sure she was ever going to forgive herself for the lies she had told. As a mother, she had to set an example for her daughter. Why hadn't she given a thought for the impact of her words on Poppy? It must have been so hard for her to hear her listing all the things that they were never going to have. She felt like the scum of the earth.

Poppy deserved someone who could give her the things that Scarlett could. Not for the first time, she had thought about asking Scarlett to have Poppy. But she could never go through with it. She had always told herself that Poppy would rather have a mother that loved her with a fierce intensity that money couldn't compete with. She couldn't let her daughter go. Or she would lose the only reason she got up in the morning. Poppy was her whole world. Plus, Scarlett was a stuck-up cow with as much empathy as a shark. Until today, Adina had always considered herself the better person out of the two of them. She shuddered at the thought of Scarlett's face when Adina had to admit she had made it all up.

The insistent buzz of her phone disturbed her thoughts and she picked it up, worried that it could be Poppy's school. She didn't recognise the number and answered warily.

'Hello?'

'Hello, is that Adina Carter?'

'Speaking.'

'Oh, hello there. My name is Jack Danvers. I saw you at the coffee shop today.' *Oh no,* she thought. 'I'm afraid you were in such a hurry to leave you spilled my drink over me.' He laughed genially and she groaned inside, her face heating up even though he wasn't in front of her.

'I'm so sorry about that–' He cut her off before she could continue to grovel.

'My dear, please don't apologise. I know it was an accident. Anyway, I had been about to come over and talk to you before you dashed off. I expect you are wondering how I got your number?'

'Erm, yes I was,' she replied.

'Well, as luck would have it, your business card fell out of your bag and underneath my chair.'

Adina was unsure what he was talking about for a few seconds. But then it came to her. Months ago, her company had given them all business cards and promised a bonus for every new customer they signed up. Adina was surprised the card was still legible. It had been in her bag for months.

'Oh right.' She paused, feeling extremely uncomfortable and unsure what this man could possibly want with her. It wasn't going to be good. Nothing good ever happened to her. 'You said you were going to talk to me about something?' she asked.

'Well yes, I am sorry for eavesdropping. It's a dreadful habit I picked up ever since my wife died. I admit I spend as much time as I can in public places just to enjoy the sound of conversation. It gets ever so lonely.'

Adina could hear the pang of loneliness in his voice. She pictured him again, salt-and-pepper hair, brown eyes and a smart corduroy suit. Her heart swelled in pity. She knew exactly how he felt. After Brian left, Poppy had been a baby, incapable of decent conversation. She had had a visceral longing for her father that had her crying herself to sleep. It had been a dark and lonely time.

'I can understand. I lost my parents at a young age and felt the same way.' She didn't usually tell anyone this but the man sounded so bereft she wanted to reassure him that he wasn't alone. She heard him taking deep breaths on the other end of the line and waited patiently for him to compose himself.

'Thank you, my dear. Anyway, as I was saying, I overheard you talking about your cleaning business. I was very impressed with your entrepreneurial spirit, it reminded me of myself at that age.'

'Oh, thank you.' Shame enveloped her again. *See, this is why you don't lie, Adina,* she reprimanded herself. It just leads to more lies.

'I've been meaning to hire a cleaner for a while. It's just me rattling round in this big old house. I'm ashamed to admit, my late wife did all the cleaning and the dusting and I'm afraid it's getting a bit out of hand. Would you be able to come and give me a quote?'

Adina was taken aback, having spilt coffee on this man she was expecting to be yelled at. Not offered a job. But what would he do when he realised it was just her? That she did not in fact run a team of cleaners that serviced wealthy clientele across the county. Well, he didn't need to know that, she reasoned. She could *really* do with the money.

'It would depend on if we covered your area. Where are you?'

'I live up in the Malvern Hills. A little bit in the wilderness I'm afraid. Down a dirt track in fact. A satnav won't find us but I can give you directions. Could you come tomorrow?'

Well, that was that. Without a car she would never be able to get there. She didn't think the buses frequented dirt tracks.

'Erm. I'm afraid my car is in the garage at the moment being repaired.'

Another lie, *what a wonderful human being you are, Adina*.

'That's not a problem. If you get the bus to Malvern I can come and collect you. Just this once. It will work out better this way as then you can see how you get to my house so you will know for next time.'

'Er... I'm not sure. I would need to check my diary.'

'I'm happy to pay the going rate. I had a look online and I think twenty-five pounds per hour is the average amount.'

Twenty-five pounds per hour. That would be life-changing money. She would be able to have actual milk in her cereals instead of water. But something didn't feel right. Why was he so eager to have her come over tomorrow? What was the rush? Plus, how would she explain that her car isn't in the garage?

'I'm sorry, but we aren't taking on any new clients at the moment. We are just too busy.'

He paused for a minute. She breathed a sigh of relief and prepared to hang up.

'I'm sorry, I don't mean to come across as pushy, but it has been really hard coping with the loss of my wife. I finally feel ready to move on and start living again. So now I've made this decision, I just want to get started. Does that make sense? Please can you reconsider?'

Adina thought back to the bleak period of time after her parents had died. She had been all alone with the baby. Brian jetting off on business trips she now knew were bogus. Adina would have given anything for another human being to spend time with back then. A bit of sunshine in the dark pit of grief. She had lost her parents and her marriage in one fell swoop and she never thought she would be happy again. The sadness in Jack's voice touched her. She might actually be doing something good here. Something that might make up for the lies she had told. Adina could help him move on and manage his grief.

'Okay, if you give me your address I'll book you in my diary.'

She pretended to make notes whilst he spoke and they arranged a pickup point at a local bus stop near Great Malvern. She'd deal with the lack of car situation later. Coming off the phone, Adina grinned. Perhaps she would be able to buy Poppy that iPad after all.

CHAPTER THIRTY-FIVE

Jack turned on the light and set off down the stairs into the cellar. The smell of urine made him gag as he got to the bottom of the stairs. Beckett was lying huddled in a corner, whimpering in pain. There was blood on his fingernails and as Jack got closer, he could see dark red rings around his wrists. Smudges of blood, a telltale sign he had been trying to escape.

Once again, he allowed the memory of Elsie being killed to flood his mind. The cracking of her bones echoed around the cellar and he attached Beckett's face to the violence of her demise. His vision turned red. Jack could quite easily rip him to shreds, such was the power of his rage. A wave of desire to inflict pain rose within him, he wanted to trample and crack his bones. He wanted to hear each whimper of pain and dance to the beautiful sound. The sound of atonement.

Beckett had been in the cellar for a day and a half now. Jack had left him a bowl of water but no food. He could only imagine the hunger Beckett must be experiencing. As Jack edged towards him, the man recoiled.

'P-please, don't hurt me!' he begged, his voice whiny and

laced with fear. Gone was the arrogant man he had first met. If only Debbie could see him now. He wished there was a way that he could tell her that he had sought justice on her behalf. That this man would never hurt anyone again. But his father was right, his duty was too important to risk ignorant fools trying to stop him.

Jack took a small square of bread from his pocket, the size of a postage stamp. Beckett's eyes followed him as Jack placed the square of bread in between them.

'Eat it. I dare you.'

He gave Beckett an evil smile that said what his words didn't. He turned on his heel and stomped back up the stairs, his mind filled with revenge and justice. He was punishing Beckett for his sins. Punishing him for being part of the species of denigrates that had killed his wife. And he was going to enjoy every minute of it.

Jack appeared back in the kitchen and he gave his father a wide smile. He felt energised, powerful. As if he had the power of the Lord running through his veins. His father came over to him and handed him a spade.

'Time to dig another hole.'

It didn't take as long to dig a hole for Adina Carter. His body was used to the hard labour and his hands developed thicker callouses that no longer bled as he wielded the shovel. As he dug, he replayed Adina's boastful words. The disgust at her bragging tone and his need to protect the child fuelled his muscles. Before he knew it he had gone deeper than he needed to. Wiping the sweat from his head with his T-shirt, Jack looked over at his father. He passed Jack the barbed wire and he lined the grave with it, wincing as the barbs caught hold of him. They had not been able to find another door to cover her grave. But they had decided they would just cover her with soil.

Whilst making a cup of tea, Jack happened to glance at the laptop screen. He saw Beckett was lying on his front, staring at something on the ground. Jack moved closer to the screen and could see that Beckett was looking at the square of bread. Jack was impressed with the quality of the image as there was only a small amount of light in the room, coming from a fading ceiling bulb that really needed to be changed.

Beckett picked up the square of bread with trembling hands. He put it to his mouth but at the last minute pulled it away.

'That's right, you greedy piglet, I knew you couldn't resist.' When Beckett popped the piece of bread into his mouth Jack looked over at his father.

'He's eaten it.'

'Not surprising. You know what you must do.'

Jack didn't hesitate. He leapt towards the cellar door. He was doing God's bidding. He was punishing Beckett for his sin, a mortification of sin. After all, those who trust in their riches will fall, but the righteous will thrive like a green leaf. He had read those words so many times but never had he appreciated them the way he did today. At the bottom of the stairs, he undid his belt.

Beckett quailed, starting in horror. Tears tracking down his face, which was streaked with dirt from his writhing around on the floor. Unable to move properly due to his hands being bound behind his back and his legs tied together. Jack let his fury build. He could almost feel God's presence embracing him. Encouraging him.

Jack stood in front of Beckett.

'I'm going to take off your trousers. If you try to escape, I'll take this belt, wrap it around your neck and strangle you until you are dead.'

Beckett looked stricken. He didn't move or speak, just stared wordlessly at Jack.

Jack put the belt on the floor and undid the rope binding Beckett's legs. He pulled off the trousers, trying not to breathe as the smell of faeces cloyed the back of his throat. Tossing the trousers to the other side of the room, he retied his legs. Making sure the rope dug into the skin.

He stood.

'Dan Beckett. You are sinful and greedy. You shall be punished accordingly. If the wicked man deserves to be beaten, the judge shall then make him lie down and be beaten.'

Without giving Beckett time to process what he was saying, Jack whipped the belt through the air and watched as the buckle sliced into Beckett's thighs. He did it three more times until Beckett's screams pierced his eardrums, so loud he almost covered his ears. Satisfied, Jack walked away to the sound of the Devil's sobs. When he emerged from the cellar and saw his father, he was struck by the memory of him whipping him with his belt. Of the pain he had felt and the weeks it took for the scabs to heal. The pain of walking and moving around with welts on his thighs. He pushed the memory away. His father had had no choice. Jack had deserved it. He knew that now.

That night, Jack couldn't sleep. Images of Elsie and their life together kept slipping out of the place he had locked them away. He thought about the person that Elsie was. Her kindness and generosity. How every month she went to Tesco and did a food shop and put it all in the donations basket at the exit to go to the food bank. The work she did with the church, always volunteering and raising money for different charities.

A beautiful, selfless person had been ripped from the world. It was his job to avenge that. He had been charged with this mission, a mission only he had the strength to do. They had always disagreed on what she called 'his father's religion'. She said it was archaic and self-serving. But God had spoken to him, he had taken Elsie and reconnected him with his father for a reason. He was meant to do this. But that was why God had chosen him. Only he had the strength to do what needed to be done. People were put on earth to do God's work. Elsie was there to spread kindness and he was there to rid the world of sin.

CHAPTER THIRTY-SIX

The next morning, Jack woke up to a loud chorus from the birds that slept in the tree near his bedroom window. Their gentle song was an idyllic alarm clock. Jack felt renewed from his sleep. He was confident and ready. It was like he had a career once more. There was a reason to get up and a plan of action. For the first time in a while, he had a purpose.

At 10am, he set off for Adina. He wanted to get there and find the right parking space. His father was going to stay at home and keep an eye on Beckett on the monitors. The journey to Malvern was pleasant, he enjoyed the peace of not having his father in the car, silently criticising his driving through winces and sighs. The rolling hills surrounded him and he could just spot the dot-like outlines of walkers as they ascended towards The Beacon. It was the highest point in Worcestershire. He remembered going there with Elsie years ago, the wind whipping her hair into his face as he tried to remind his lungs how to breathe properly. Elsie hadn't wanted to come back down, she was enthralled by the view, turning this way and that as he sat on a concrete step, leaning back on The Beacon, trying to ignore the stars in his vision.

The bus stop came into view and he drove past it, turned around and slowly crept back up the road. Looking for the best place to park. It was a tiny bus stop, not even a bus shelter, just a pole with a sign atop with the numbers of the buses that stopped there. There was barely any traffic on the road, and no pedestrians. He wasn't surprised, the roads in Malvern were notoriously steep and if there wasn't a phenomenal view it just wasn't worth the energy.

He sat in the car and waited. He hoped she wouldn't be late. It would just be like her, to keep other people waiting, running to her own clock. Jack pictured her in her large house, with her fancy gadgets and big car. Earning money off the backs of her staff whilst she deliberated over what dress to wear. He was quite surprised she had agreed to get the bus and not decided to get a taxi. But he was not one to look a gift horse in the mouth.

He was pulled from his thoughts at the sound of an engine. The bus grumbled up the hill and came to a hissing stop at the pole. The doors swung open and he saw Adina get out. He faltered for a minute. She had looked so sophisticated and egotistical when he had met her yesterday. But her demeanour was completely different today. She looked up and down the street, she seemed almost nervous.

But then, he remembered the Lord's warning about Satan transforming himself into the Angel of Light. So what if she looked innocent. She had the Devil within her, he had heard and seen it for himself. He must not be fooled by the Father of Lies. He tightened his grip on the steering wheel, imagining it was Adina's neck.

Jack then opened the door and got out. He walked towards Adina with a broad smile.

'Hello, Adina.' He greeted her like an old friend. When she shook his hand, he ignored the desire to recoil. He felt dirty just touching her.

'Hi, Jack.' She smiled politely back at him.

'Right, let's go.'

She followed him to his car and got into the passenger seat. He indicated and pulled onto the road, forcing the car up the slope, ignoring the protests of the engine.

'There are some steep hills around here,' said Adina.

'Yes, there sure are.'

They lapsed into awkward silence. Until Jack, unable to stomach it, spoke.

'So, tell me about your business?'

Out of the corner of his eye, he could have sworn she blushed. But when he turned to look at her face, it was composed.

'Erm. There's not much to tell really. I manage a team of cleaners.'

'That's brilliant. Especially at such a young age. I admit I was quite poor at your age. It must be so wonderful to have money to do what you want with.'

'Oh yes, I do okay.'

Jack felt flustered. Her personality was so different to yesterday. Where was the brash, bragging woman? The confidence and arrogance had dripped off her yesterday. Was this an act? Maybe it was part of her ploy to ensure that he hired her.

'I bet you spoil that little one of yours rotten?' he asked.

'Yes, she has everything she could ever need.'

'And more I bet.' He forced a laugh.

'Yes, I suppose.'

Jack was feeling very disconcerted. This was not what he expected. Thinking fast, he thought of a way he could draw her out.

'I was talking about you last night.'

Adina looked alarmed.

'Nothing bad.' He smiled to reassure her. 'Just to a friend of my late wife. My wife, she was a big part of the church in Malvern. She used to do all sorts down there, she was forever raising money for this and for that. So I was talking to this friend and they are looking for a sponsor for the football team. I thought you might be interested. You would just need to donate enough money to buy them uniforms. The uniforms would have your logo and then all the games they play would raise money for charity. It is a wonderful cause. I could take the money today and pop it down to them for you. If you were interested? It would be a great way to give back.'

He tried to focus on her face but he needed to look at the road. In the glimpses he caught of her, she appeared to look uncomfortable.

'That's kind of you to think of me. But that's not the sort of thing we do.'

What, give money to charity? He just managed to stop himself from saying it. According to her diatribe yesterday she was rolling in it. But not enough to share it with others evidently.

They pulled up at the house and Adina exclaimed, 'Wow. What a beautiful house.'

'Thank you.'

He led her to the front door and unlocked it. She was looking around, apparently awestruck. They moved into the hallway and he offered to hang up her coat. As she passed it to him, he noticed a hole in the sleeve and the colour was fading. It looked like she'd worn it every day for years. He guided Adina into the kitchen. She didn't even acknowledge his father, instead she seemed to be gathering herself. She carried on walking through the house, examining everything. When he followed her into the living room, he found her gaping out of the window. It was a charming view of the forest. Little did she know her final resting place was going to be amongst those very same trees.

CHAPTER THIRTY-SEVEN

'There are a few cleaning supplies in the cellar and I was also hoping that you could have a look at maybe helping me clear it out. There is a lot of my late wife's belongings down there. I'm afraid I boxed them up and tossed them down there in the early stages of my grief,' said Jack.

Talking about Elsie was hard but he was sure it would help lower Adina's guard. When she talked about the loss of her parents, he knew that their shared grief would be a way to garner her trust. He gave her a small smile and led her to the cellar. He opened the door and gestured for her to go down the stairs.

'No, after you, Mr Danvers. I'm rather afraid of the dark. I'd feel better if you went first.' She gave him an apologetic smile and he had no choice but to lead her down the stairs. What was he going to do now? This wasn't how it was supposed to go. If she didn't see Beckett straight away she would smell him soon enough: Beckett turning into a soup of urine, faeces, blood. He got to the bottom of the stairs and waited for the inevitable. He sighed, closing his eyes as her scream pierced his eardrums. He turned slowly to look at her.

'Oh my God!'

Her hands were over her mouth, eyes wide with shock. Before she could react, he grabbed her top and dragged her down the rest of the stairs, putting all his weight into the movement. Adina tumbled down the stairs and landed hard on the concrete floor. It seemed he had at least managed to wind her. He called up the stairs to his father for help and then approached Adina. As he came closer, she backed away, trying to get to her feet. Jack was about to grab her arms to restrain her when she flung herself at him. It was so unexpected that he stumbled backwards, momentarily stunned. Adina scrambled to her feet and was about to run up the stairs when he grabbed her hair. Jack yanked as hard as he could and she was forced back into the room. Her screams echoed around the walls. It really was a good job they had no neighbours.

Adina whimpered as he pulled her into him. He put his arm around her neck and squeezed. Not hard enough to kill her but enough to subdue her. Satisfied he had her under control, he led her back to the opposite side of the wall from Dan. He forced her down onto the floor. She tried to resist but he pulled back his leg and kicked her as hard as he could in the ribs. He watched her clutching her chest, trying to breathe. Moaning in pain. Taking advantage of the distraction, he reached for the rope he had placed on the workbench and bound her hands and feet. He tied her up as tightly as he could. She was a fighter this one. Not a weak and pathetic rat like Beckett. Grabbing her phone from her pocket he left the cellar, smashing it against the stone wall as he went.

CHAPTER THIRTY-EIGHT

U naware of how much time had passed, Adina finally gave up trying to escape. At first, she had concentrated on trying to untie the rope from around her ankles and wrists. But there was nothing in the cellar that she could use to help her. The room was empty apart from a small plastic bowl that held a few inches of water and a solid wooden workbench. There was nothing sharp, just concrete floors and immoveable stone walls.

Adina had tried to stand up but with her arms bound behind her back, she kept losing her balance. She succeeded once only to fall as soon as she tried to hop towards the staircase. Without being able to use her arms to brace her, she had fallen flat on her face, her head colliding with the concrete floor. The pain had caused her to vomit, adding to the foul aroma of the cellar.

There were nasty red welts around her wrists and ankles from the bites of the rope. A small amount of blood was trickling into her shoe. But she couldn't feel the pain. The cellar was freezing cold and had numbed her entire body. The cold had seeped into her bones and her body wouldn't stop trembling.

Each breath she took was complemented by a searing pain from the ribs she was sure he had broken.

Adina had tried to talk to the man on the floor. But he wouldn't speak to her. He stared through blank eyes but she didn't think he was actually seeing her. She was irritated at him for ignoring her but then she had caught sight of the bloody welts on his legs. One of them appeared to be yellow and green inside. The man looked like he was inches from death and that terrified her the most. How long would she be kept here? Was she looking at her future? Would she become a broken husk of a human like this man?

'Please. Talk to me. If we work together, we could escape!'

Adina pleaded with him to talk to her. But he just continued to look at her with his unseeing eyes. He could have been handsome, but the dirt, blood and grime obscured his features. His black hair was greasy, sticking up in all directions. His face was gaunt, pale and his blue eyes had no life in them. No spark of emotion, like doll's eyes, glassy and expressionless. She couldn't understand how he had got into this situation. He looked like a strapping young man. He couldn't have been more than thirty years old and looked like he could easily overpower their captor. Jack was what, fifty? Sixty?

With great difficulty, Adina gritted her teeth and slowly crawled over to the man. It took a monumental effort to ignore the protest of her muscles as she pulled her bum forwards by locking her legs together. She was panting from the effort until she finally got close to the man. She felt herself sliding in faeces. Her nose wrinkled and she wanted to be sick again. But she forced herself to keep moving.

'Please. Talk to me. Help me!'

She shouted in his face. But she may as well have spoken to the walls. She turned her back on him and tried to clutch at the rope binding his legs together. Maybe if she could get him free, he would wake up from whatever trance he was in. Adina couldn't loosen the rope. It was tied in a complex knot and she gave up after several minutes. The pain of having her hands tied behind her back was starting to become all-consuming. She returned to her position on the other side of the cellar, as far away from Dan as she could, unable to cope with the smell around him.

For the first time, she let herself think about what had happened. Jack Danvers had invited her to quote him for a cleaning job. She pictured him, slightly greying hair, genial brown eyes twinkling at her. He looked so normal. Until she had followed him down the stairs she had no idea that it was all a mask. How had this happened to her?

Her thoughts turned to Poppy. *Oh God, Poppy!* She was probably waiting outside the school for her. Wondering where she was. In her entire life, Adina had always been there on time to pick up Poppy. Always there to greet her with a big smile and a cuddle. Her heart ached as she pictured Poppy's anxious face. What would happen to her? Presumably, the school would ring her sister when they couldn't get hold of her. Adina wasn't lucky to have a choice in who she listed as an emergency contact.

Would her sister call the police? Surely she would call them, she'd be worried – right? They had never had a good relationship, but Adina prayed that their bond as sisters would be strong enough for Scarlett to raise the alarm. She just had to stay alive long enough for the police to find her. Thinking this way helped calm her down. The police could track her phone, couldn't they? Although it was a crappy ten-pound phone off eBay. It wasn't a smartphone; did phones that old even have GPS? Goddammit, why did she have to be so poor? If she wasn't desperate for money this would never have happened to her.

The door opened to the cellar once more and Adina prepared herself. She would fight him. She would not let him kill her. Poppy needed her. She would get back to her daughter.

CHAPTER THIRTY-NINE

Adina braced herself at the sound of heavy footsteps on the stairs. Curiously, it reminded her of *Jurassic Park*. Each thud of the tyrannosaurus had made her feel like her heart was going to stop. It was much worse now. She'd give anything to be safe at home watching a horror movie. But this was real life. Jack's shoes came into view and she closed her eyes. Unable to face the fact that she might be about to die. She had no idea what was going to happen. Jack Danvers thudded down the last of the stairs. Something small in his hand. He placed the smallest piece of bread she had ever seen in between them, no bigger than a square of chocolate. Equal distance between the man and herself. Was this a good sign? He wouldn't be feeding them if he planned to kill them, would he? She barely breathed as he turned to the man.

'I'll leave it to you to explain,' he said, addressing the man. Jack moved back up the stairs. Adina was sure that she could see a wince of pain as he lifted his leg to take the first step. But she couldn't be sure due to the dimness of the light. She moved over to the piece of bread. It was tiny, the size you might give a baby when you are weaning it off milk. A small piece that would fill neither of them and was hardly worth tearing in half. But it was better than nothing, she reasoned. The man hadn't made a move to the bread. There was no point asking him if he wanted any. No, she would have it all to herself. Adina lay down on the floor, with hands tied behind her back she couldn't use them to eat. Which was exactly why he'd put it there. *Sick bastard*, she thought. Her mouth was open and her tongue poked out, almost touching the bread when a voice yelled:

'No!'

She jerked back as if stung.

'What's wrong?' Adina struggled back into a sitting position.

The man lifted himself slowly. Using what was left of his energy. Sweat was forming on his brow and his hands and arms were shaking. He looked like a terminal cancer patient, pale and clammy.

'Don't eat it. It's a trap,' he said. His voice was wheezy and weak.

Adina struggled around to face him properly.

'What sort of trap?'

'The first night I spent down here. He put the same thing in front of me. He told me not to eat it. Spoke a load of religious mumbo jumbo. Something about me being wicked or a sinner. I resisted as long as I could but in the end, I ate it.'

He shuddered at an unseen memory in his mind.

'The next time he came down and saw that I'd ate it. Well...' Dan gestured to his bare legs. In the dim light she could see the welts lining his thighs. Up close she could see one of them was mottled green and yellow, definitely infected and looking worse than before. 'He took my jeans and then gave me three lashes with his belt.'

The man leaned back into the wall, resting his head. He was breathing heavily, talking was using up what little energy he had left. Adina stared in horror. Thoughts collided in her mind;

how was she going to get out of this? What was going to happen to her?

'I'm Dan, by the way.'

'Adina. Do you know why he is doing this?'

'He's a lunatic. Absolutely crazy. What my mum would have called a religious nutjob.' Dan laughed but it died off quickly. He could no longer hold himself up against the wall and sank back to lying on the floor.

'How long have you been here?' Adina whispered. Her heart was hammering. She did and didn't want to know the answer.

Dan glanced at her, compassion in his eyes.

'I have no idea. Two days, three days maybe?' His voice was weakening and she saw his eyes close. Her next question died on her lips.

She looked over at the bread. She wasn't hungry. Fear was suppressing her appetite. How long would it take for her to begin to starve? Glancing over at Dan, she could see his eyes were open again. He was staring at the bread like she had seen tigers on documentaries stare at gazelles before they pounced. She could almost imagine saliva building in his mouth. His longing was palpable. She wondered how strong her own willpower would be. Given that she had been going without for so long to make sure Poppy had enough food, she was hopeful that with all that practice she would be able to hold out.

Hold out for what? an evil voice inside her mind asked. She brushed it away. Someone would be looking for her. She had a child. God, she could just picture Scarlett's face. Moaning at the inconvenience. But when she couldn't get hold of her, surely she would start to worry – wouldn't she? Their relationship was so entrenched in competition and dislike. Did their blood ties run deep enough to overcome that? Adina moved so her back was leaning on the wall. It hurt her arms but it was the only vaguely comfortable position she could find. She would not curl up in a ball like Dan. She would stay alert and strong.

But that was hard to do when her only hope of rescue was the sister that had resented her for their whole life. Of all the people that she would rely on to rescue her, she would never choose Scarlett. Hopelessness shrouded her and she began to cry. She tried to swallow the tears, not wanting Dan to think he was trapped with a weak, pathetic woman. Even though it was true. Anyone else would surely be trying to get out, but she had just sat doing nothing.

A rustling startled her and she saw Dan manoeuvre himself and before she could say anything, his mouth fell on the bread. As he chewed, he made a moan of pleasure. His eyes were closed, lost in the satisfaction of eating something. He swallowed reluctantly and then his eyes flew open. He stared at Adina in abject terror.

'What have I done?' he whispered. His whole body vibrated with fear. Struggling upright, he looked around the room. Desperately searching in case there was a piece of bread that he could use to replace the one he had eaten.

'No. No. No.' He rocked backwards and forwards.

The door opened. All the remaining colour in Dan's face evaporated. Dan moved back, wincing in pain as he tried to tuck his legs behind him. It looked like he was attempting to burrow into the wall. Each footstep sounded more menacing than the last. Adina could barely breathe. Dan's fear was infectious. Possible scenarios floated in her mind, each more terrifying than the last. Adina tried to conjure up Poppy's face, wanting it to be the last thing she saw before she died. But her vision was entranced by the black boots of Jack Danvers as they came into view.

He moved silently through the room until he was standing

over the cowering form of Dan. Dan looked up, reluctantly meeting his eyes.

'Oh dear,' said Jack.

'It wasn't me. It was her,' Dan said, jerking his head at Adina.

Adina's heart stopped as the man looked over at her. Anger at Dan warred with the fear that Jack might believe him. As Jack examined her, she was struck once more by how ordinary he looked. She had always thought bad people *looked* like bad people. His clothes were standard and his greying hair was freshly washed and he was clean shaven. On the television, you could always tell who the bad guy was. They seemed to give off a vibe. But Jack Danvers had a mask like no other. His was the most superior camouflage she had seen.

Jack looked down at Dan and shook his head sadly. His face filled with loathing. He looked at Dan like he was a bug he would very much like to step on and kill.

'Does your depravity know no bounds?' Jack questioned.

Jack pointed to the ceiling. She had never noticed but there was a red light, a tiny pinprick. As she focused on it, she realised what it was.

'I've been watching you, Dan. I see everything.'

Dan began to cry, his underpants darkened. The stench of fresh urine wafted over to her. Adina couldn't look away. Shaking with fear but she couldn't close her eyes. Her eyelids were frozen open. A desperate urge to try and escape filled her, but the twinge of pain in her shoulders reminded her she couldn't even hop one step without falling over.

Jack was holding something bulky in his hands. He turned it upside down and she heard a gentle hiss as something began to fall from the bag. When the bag was half empty, he put it down on the floor. Silently, he moved over to Dan, stepping behind him and lifting him onto his knees. Dan's mouth moved, trying and failing to formulate words. Dan was so weak, a mere rag doll for Jack to play with.

Dan was dragged to where Jack had upended the bag. Dan winced as his bare knees came into contact with whatever was on the floor. Jack moved back and surveyed his work. He nodded to himself.

'Stay.' He ordered Dan like he was a pet dog.

Then he turned his attention to Adina. As her eyes locked with Jack, she felt terror choke her. His eyes were cold and menacing, his lip was slightly curled in disgust. The rest of him was ordinary but those eyes. There was nothing human about the way he was looking at her. Hate rippled from him. But how could he hate her when he didn't even know her? What had she ever done to him?

Jack picked up the bag and moved over to her and she found herself subconsciously copying Dan's earlier attempt to burrow into the wall, overcome by a need to put as much space between her and the man stalking towards her. A menacing predator she had no chance of escaping. Once again, Jack turned the bag upside down and emptied the rest of the contents on the floor in front of her. Grains of rice bounced off and landed on her jeans. Jack stepped towards her and undid the bindings on her legs. As her legs were freed, the thought of running crossed her mind. Jack must have known as he glared at her.

'Don't even think about it.' The promise of pain in his eyes quelled any thoughts of escape. He pulled off her trousers and then retied the rope around her ankles.

Adina met Jack's eyes. She would not cower and beg like Dan. He would not break her.

'Why are you doing this?' Furious at the sound of fear in her voice. 'What have I ever done to you?' He ignored her. 'I haven't done anything to deserve this.' At this he snorted contemptuously. The cold air was attacking her bare skin, but she refused to react.

Jack came behind her and, shoving his hands under her armpits, he hauled her so that she was kneeling in the rice. Instantly, she could feel almost every individual grain attacking her kneecaps. With all her weight on her knees the grains dug painfully into her skin. Every minuscule movement made each grain move and bite at her skin. Seemingly satisfied, Jack grunted and moved towards the stairs.

'Do not move until I tell you to.' He pointed at the red dot on the ceiling. 'I'll be watching.'

Unable to contain herself, Adina screamed at him. 'Why are you doing this to us? What have we ever done to you? You're a lunatic!'

For some reason, maybe it was the wildness in her eyes, or the loudness of her scream or the words themselves, his eyes lit with fire and he marched over to her, his body shaking with anger. He reached out and grabbed her face in his hand, holding her so tightly his nails dug into her skin.

'What have you done to me? You and your *kind*' – his mouth was curled in disgust – 'you killed my wife!' he roared in her face, spittle flying out of his mouth and landing on her cheeks. Jack let go and began pacing the room.

'What are you talking about? I've never even met your wife.' He was mad. Deranged.

'No. Maybe not. But your *kind* are the reason that she is dead. So it's my job to get rid of you. Greedy, disgusting vermin that must be stamped out!' He mimed stamping on an invisible insect with his boot. Jack was breathing hard, his face mottled red with rage.

'What are you talking about? My kind?'

'Sinners! You are greedy. That greed is toxic. It is infiltrating society and destroying innocent people's lives. I have to stop you.'

Tears leaked from her eyes. His anger was terrifying her. He looked at her like he wanted nothing more than to punch her and not stop until she was dead. All hope that she could reason with him was beginning to evaporate. But she tried again.

'But we aren't greedy. We are just people. Innocent people.'

The man looked at her incredulously.

'Innocent!' he bellowed and turned abruptly and moved so he was stood in front of Dan.

'This guy,' he said, pointing at Dan, 'takes money from the elderly. Tells them he is going to do work on their house but needs cash for materials, and never goes back.' Without warning, he kicked Dan in the side, knocking him to the floor. Dan cried out in pain, gasping for breath as he clutched his side.

'Kneel,' ordered Jack.

Dan, coughing and spluttering for breath, clumsily tried to lift himself to his feet. But it was impossible with his hands and legs bound. The man grabbed Dan's hair, forcing him to rise. Gathering tears made her vision kaleidoscopic. She blinked furiously to clear them. Whatever Dan had done, he didn't deserve this.

'Wh-why don't you just kill us then? If we are so evil.'

A sadistic smile spread over the man's face.

'That would be too easy. You need to suffer for your sins before I give you the sweet relief of death. Believe me, you'll be begging me to do it soon enough. It's called the Mortification of Sin. I want you to realise you are a sinner and to suffer for your sins. Only then will I give you the sweet relief of death.' He roughed up Dan's hair like a kind uncle might do to a favourite nephew. 'Isn't that right, Danny-boy?'

Dan cowered away from the touch. He was crying in earnest now, his breathing erratic. Snot and tears merging on his face. He was a wreck of a man. Jack turned away and left the cellar. It was only when he shut the door that Adina realised that she hadn't asked him why he thought she was greedy? She hadn't been scamming people out of money.

Adina tried as hard as she could to ignore the grains of rice that were attempting to burrow into the skin on her kneecaps. Every time she moved it was like a blade of glass digging into her skin. Unbidden, an image of Poppy rose in her mind. Fat tears dripped from her eyes and her heart contracted in pain. *Oh, Poppy. Mummy loves you.*

CHAPTER FORTY

J ack came down the stairs into the cellar and beamed. Dan and Adina were staring at him and he could smell their fear. He refilled the water bowl with a cup and then placed the cup on the bottom stair. He had very much enjoyed watching them lapping up the water with their tongues like the animals that they were. But it was time to get serious. There were more people that needed to be punished and eradicated. He didn't have the time to keep playing games. It was time for one final game. For one of them.

Smiling, Jack stood in front of them both. Adina glared at him and he felt as though he could see the evil coming from her pores. The insolent look she gave him was proof she was harbouring the Devil inside. Never mind, he would soon snuff that out. He looked over at Dan. He looked lifeless, close to death. It was time. But not before he had taught them another lesson.

Jack pulled out his penknife. He stepped over to Dan. The man tried to escape but it was ineffective. With one stride, Jack was stood behind him, the knife to his throat. He looked over at

Adina. Her face was pale and she was shaking. But still she looked at him defiantly, trying to hide her fear.

'Let's have a little chat, shall we?' he said to Adina. 'I'm going to ask you a question. If you lie to me, Dan over here will suffer the consequences.'

Adina just stared at him. She was shaking harder but still she held his gaze.

'Are you a sinner?' he asked her.

'No.' Her voice was firm and she looked at him with hatred in her eyes.

'Now now, Adina, what did I say about lying?' He placed the knife on Dan's arm and cut. Red blood glistened in the light of the cellar, streaming from the wound. Dan whimpered. He didn't seem to have any energy to scream. He wasn't even trying to get away.

'I'll ask you again. Are you a sinner?'

'Yes,' Adina mumbled. The word came reluctantly. She didn't really believe it.

'What was that? I didn't hear you?'

'Yes!' she shouted, her eyes burning brightly with unrestrained anger.

'That's better. Now, are you a greedy, poisonous stain on humanity?'

'No. I'm a good person!'

He forgot to cut Dan in his surprise. She was not playing the game.

'A good person? A good person? I heard you, Adina. You work your team of cleaners to the bone and pay them a pittance, raking in all the profit for yourself so you can buy the latest car!'

Adina looked stunned. Her eyes wide with shock.

'N-no. No! Oh my God. No!' She tried to stand up but fell backwards. 'You've got this all wrong. I'm not who you think I am.'

'I know exactly who you are, Adina. You are just as bad as him. Liars. Cheats. Greedy disgusting rats.' He folded away the penknife and grabbed Dan under his shoulders.

'It is time for you to die, Danny-boy.' He heaved the man to the stairs. Dan didn't even try to fight. But his eyes were wide with horror.

'No. Let me go! No!' Dan screamed as Jack lugged him up onto his shoulder. Adina was howling at him. Demanding he let them both go. The language coming out of her mouth was dreadful. Before he left the cellar he shouted down to her.

'Don't get too comfortable, Adina. I'll be coming back for you.'

CHAPTER FORTY-ONE

Getting up the stairs with Beckett wriggling, trying to get free, was hard work. Jack reached the top of the stairs and threw Beckett to the floor in the kitchen. His father didn't even flinch, just continued to drink his cup of tea, staring down at Beckett with a disgust that mirrored Jack's own.

'It's about time,' said his father. 'I'll get my coat.'

Taking down his coat from the hook by the front door, his father watched as Jack resumed dragging Beckett.

'Aren't you going to help?' complained Jack, his body aching from digging holes.

'The Lord chose you for this, Jack. I'm just here for support. You are the chosen one, it has to be you.'

The closer they got to the forest, the more Beckett screamed and tried to resist. It was a slow journey and Jack's muscles burned with pain and fatigue. If only he would stop bucking and rolling. Jack felt like Jesus carrying the cross to his own crucifixion. Both of them on a mission to save humanity.

When they reached the grave, Jack could see that Beckett's eyes filled with terror as he took in the awaiting grave. The patch of trees was dense, but dapples of sunlight broke through the branches. He had thought about waiting until nightfall. But what was the need? No one was going to come up here. Birds chirped happily, leaping from tree to tree. Jack stood, his sides heaving. He closed his eyes and enjoyed the sounds and beauty of the forest whilst he caught his breath.

'Ready, son?' his father asked.

Jack moved so he was stood right next to Beckett's head. Jack began to recite.

'Whoever makes a practice of sinning is of the Devil, for the Devil has been sinning from the beginning. The reason the Son of God appeared was to destroy the works of the Devil. John, chapter 3, verse 8.'

Jack locked eyes with his father. He nodded his head at Jack.

'Please. Please don't do this. Please.' Tears poured from Beckett's eyes. His nose running as he pleaded for his life through gasping sobs. 'Please. I'll never do it again. I promise you. Please.'

'I'm sorry, Mr Beckett. But the Lord is very clear, I have to stand against the schemes of the Devil. I have no choice. You have to die before you ruin any more lives.'

Placing his hands under Beckett's armpits, he forced Beckett into the hole. It wasn't easy. Beckett was fighting for his life, tossing and turning, trying to kick out with his legs. Just as he got Beckett under control and was about to push him into the grave, the memory of all the times he had been thrown into a grave as punishment overwhelmed him. He felt Dan's fear as if it was his own. His hands began to shake and his breath came quickly.

A hand squeezed his shoulder and he looked up into his father's face, smiling warmly at him.

'You can do this, son. Think of Elsie. Think of what they did to her.'

Images of Elsie's face before she died rose into his mind. His anger ignited like a match to a flame. An explosion of fire flooded his veins and he felt the urge to kill. He looked down at Beckett, writhing on the ground in front of him. *He must die.*

With hands that now trembled with wrath rather than fear he rolled Beckett into the hole. Watching with grim satisfaction as Beckett cried out in pain. Sharp metal cut into his body as he landed on the barbed wire. Jack looked down at Beckett. He stared up at Jack, his whimpering barely audible over the wind dancing merrily with the leaves of the trees around them. It really was a beautiful winter's day.

Jack moved the wooden door with great difficulty, dragging it over the hole. Beckett's last moments would be spent the exact same way Elsie's had been, terrifying and painful.

'You did well, son. Elsie would be proud.'

They turned away from the final resting place of Dan Beckett and walked back to the house. Jack breathed in the cold air and thought he could smell snow. He smiled a real smile for the first time since before Elsie died. His breath came easier and he knew without a shadow of a doubt, that the rest of his life would be dedicated to this.

CHAPTER FORTY-TWO

It was all Sean's fault, thought Isabella as she angrily cleaned the worktops in the kitchen. If he hadn't left her and taken his salary with him, this would never have happened. Who leaves a marriage because of money? The vows say for better or for worse for a reason. So what if she was spending a little bit more than she should be. She deserved to as she was going through a bad time.

Made redundant from her job at MPG Boilers, she was feeling bruised and lost. Who cared that she didn't like the job and had never meant to stay for as long as she did? It was still hard to be told you are no longer needed and tossed out like a used Coke can. Not so much as a thank you for giving them five years of your life. Just a couple of months' pay and a promise of a reference.

Sean said it was her opportunity to work out what she wanted to do with her life. Like having a career was what defined you. Just because he had known he wanted to be a police officer since he was five years old, didn't mean she should. Isabella would love to know what she wanted to do with her life. She asked herself the same question every day as she sat in front of the television watching *Castle*. The truth was, she had no idea.

Isabella's parents had really encouraged her to have dreams. They never expected to have a child and Isabella's shock arrival was not an altogether pleasant surprise. She knew that deep down they loved her. But she had not been part of the plan. They carried on their lives together and Isabella was just something they had to deal with rather than a child they wanted to raise. Her mother had returned to work at her law practice only a few weeks after giving birth and Isabella was raised by an au pair they flew in from France.

Her mother hadn't even helped her journey through growing up, forgetting to tell her about periods and what she should do when they started, let alone sitting down and discussing her future prospects. They just let Isabella get on with her life. They didn't enrol her in ballet classes, they didn't go on family holidays or even out for meals. It didn't even occur to them to take Isabella with them when they went out for dinner.

Isabella knew that she wanted more from life. But as an average student with average looks, she had no talent. She was just, well, average. How were you supposed to know what you wanted to do with your life when you have no obvious talent or skills?

Out of sheer desperation, Isabella had filled in countless aptitude tests and skills tests, but it turned out answering *'it depends'* on all of the questions because she wasn't sure made it hard for even these tests to tell her what she should be doing, only suggesting vague options like retail and hospitality. They were stupid tests anyway. What sort of question is *'I like to see things through to the end'*? What things? A murder? A project? A burglary?

Everyone dreams of not working. When Isabella used to

drag herself out of bed in the morning for work at MPG Boilers, she used to fantasise about long lie-ins and days spent relaxing, chatting with friends. Having time to do all those things she couldn't do because eight hours of her day were spent chained to a desk answering stupid emails about boiler parts. Pretending she knew what the hell a flue pipe was and when the customer could expect delivery of said flue pipe.

But the reality was that not working was actually the most boring thing in the world. For the first week she had revelled in it. Slept in, had pyjama days and generally pissed about. Luxuriating in doing absolutely nothing. But unless you have infinite money and all your friends are also not working, it becomes horrific.

The house suddenly becomes a prison. Grocery shopping the highlight of the day, like the routine exercise a prisoner gets. Dawdling each aisle, desperate to stay away from the house. But then, the inevitable happens, it is time to go home. After putting the groceries away, there is nothing left but to sit on the sofa and watch crap TV to the sound of brain cells shrivelling up and dying from lack of use. Naps become an integral part of the day because it is something to do and plus it is tiring being bored. The days become about mealtimes. Trying to decide when it is too early to have lunch, just because making it is something to do. At first, extravagant meals are made, making the most of cooking all those fancy recipes that there had never been time for. But it soon becomes pointless. No one is there to rave about the food and self-congratulations are not fulfilling at all. Instead, takeaways become the norm as there is no motivation to do anything. Boredom has sapped all energy and desire for life away.

No one else was free during the week and so the hours between 8am and 5pm have become Isabella's personal hell. Every night Sean has told her how jealous he is and has suggested things that she can do with her free time. But he doesn't understand a lack of work has turned her into an unmotivated slob. She has no energy or inclination to do anything apart from mope around the house feeling miserable. It turned out, although working at MPG boilers was unsatisfactory and a rubbish job, having a reason to get up in the morning and people to chat to throughout the day was an amazing gift she had churlishly not appreciated.

Isabella used to have a work coach who she met with twice. After the second meeting she was no longer entitled to Universal Credit or John's help because she was turning down perfectly acceptable jobs and was not spending thirty hours a week searching and applying for them. But John didn't understand that Isabella didn't want just any old job. She wanted to find *the* job. Although, the way she was feeling at the moment she was tempted to just take anything. But she kept telling herself she had been given a gift. The luxury of time. To discover just what Isabella Stewart was meant to do. She knew she was meant for more. It was just proving difficult to know what.

Sean had told her to consider what her passions were. But Isabella's only passion was shopping. She had flirted with the idea of being a personal shopper but discounted it immediately because she didn't want to help other people spend their money. She couldn't think of anything worse than watching other people leaving a store laden with bags and none of them were hers. No, that wouldn't work.

Isabella loved money and shopping. She just needed to work out a career that made her lots of money and allowed her to spend all day shopping. Imagine that, shopping all day, every day. Oh, the things she would buy, it would be heaven. So really, it was all Sean's fault. He was the one who had encouraged Isabella to think about her passion. If he hadn't, she was sure her shopping addiction would not have become such a problem.

The trouble was, Isabella was an emotional shopper. When she felt down, miserable or upset she would shop. The worst part was, she didn't even want what she bought. A couple of weeks ago, she had gone onto Hollister's website and put everything she liked in her basket. It came to about £500 in total and she had no intention of buying it all. It was just a daydream about what she could buy if she had lots of money. But somehow, she ended up clicking the checkout button. With her card details stored in her internet browser, it was over within a couple of clicks. The buzz it gave her was worth it though. She had paced up and down the living room waiting for the parcel to arrive. Squealing with excitement as the van drew up. She opened the box of clothes and did a quick Instagram video to show off to all her friends. Then she tried all the clothes on and put them away carefully in her drawers. As she sat on the bed, her happy glow began to fade. What now?

Isabella hadn't even worn half of the clothes that she had bought. It was the thrill of the purchase and the receiving that she lived for. Technically, it didn't matter what she bought, she just wanted to spend money and receive a parcel. The Instagram post had been her downfall. Naively thinking that Sean didn't really look at her Instagram, she had been shocked when he had come home, slamming the door with such ferocity the whole house shook. He had thundered through to their bedroom, pulling out all the clothes, tossing them onto the bed.

'These have still got bloody tags on,' he yelled at her, brandishing the dress in his hand and throwing it to the floor. 'This has got to stop. I checked our online banking today, after seeing your little spending spree. You've withdrawn all our savings! That was our emergency money. What do you think you're playing at?'

Isabella looked at the floor, she had no defence. She had been lucky that Sean didn't really pay attention to their finances. As long as there was always money in the accounts he didn't really monitor what they had and where it went. But she had crossed the line. She hadn't meant to. At first, she was only spending small amounts so that the money only trickled out. She had told herself she would put the money back once she was working again. That she deserved it as she had worked hard. Well, used to work hard.

'I've had enough, Isabella. I don't deserve to be treated like this.'

She gaped at him. He never used her full name. She had known he would be mad when he found out but she hadn't even contemplated that he might leave her.

'You're breaking up with me? Over something so trivial?'

He moved towards her like he wanted to shake her but stopped short, right in front of her.

'Trivial?' He stared at her, searching her eyes in disbelief at what he was hearing. 'Trivial? Iz, you lied to me. You kept secrets and you have spent over £10,000 in a matter of months. Without telling me. You've betrayed me.'

She scoffed at him.

'Don't be so melodramatic. We can always earn more money.'

'Isabella, it took us years to earn that money. We have nothing now. We can only just afford to pay the mortgage. I can't believe you have done this to us. I'm the only one earning, remember?'

Isabella didn't like the way he was looking at her. Like he didn't recognise her. She knew she had done wrong but she didn't feel it warranted this reaction. She reached out and stroked his face.

'Look, I know I've done wrong, but really it's not like I've murdered anyone. I just spent a bit of money.'

'I've had enough.' He shook her hand off him and walked around the bed. 'I don't even recognise you anymore.' She followed him and her heart began to flutter with panic as she saw him reach for his gym bag. He thrust clothes from his drawers into it and the panic hit like a steam train. Sean was leaving. He was actually leaving. She felt tears fall from her eyes. He couldn't do this.

'No, Sean. Please, I'm sorry. We can work this out.' She grabbed a handful of his clothes out of the gym bag and tossed them onto the floor. 'I won't let you leave me.'

'I'm afraid you've been calling the shots in this marriage for far too long. I want out.' He left the gym bag and walked down the stairs, ignoring her pleas for him to stop. She raced after him and jumped past him, barring his exit. He looked down at her, stony-faced.

'Get out of my way.'

He pushed her to one side, forceful enough to move her but not hard enough to hurt her. As the door shut, her heart broke and she curled up into a ball by the front door and cried herself to sleep.

CHAPTER FORTY-THREE

Isabella woke up, face moulded to the cold PVC front door. Her neck twinged with pain and she stretched, trying to alleviate the aches caused by sleeping on a hard floor. Standing up, she caught sight of her puffy red eyes in the hall mirror, gaunt face and tangled dyed blonde hair. Taking some deep breaths, she gave herself a pep talk. It was no good letting herself go to pieces. Sean just needed to cool off. He was in shock. He'd soon be back.

She just had to wait.

After having a shower and eating some breakfast, Isabella felt much better. She was convinced that any minute Sean would reach out to her. They had been married for six years. There was no way that he was going to turn his back on her. He was too loyal for that. Sitting on the sofa, watching the day pass by outside, it became harder to stay positive. The house felt emptier now that there was a possibility Sean might not come home tonight. Switching on her favourite detective show, *Castle*, she tried to lose herself in the murder. But her mind kept reliving the look of loathing on Sean's face. He had never looked at anyone like that in the ten years that she had known him. Sean was one of the most placid men she had met. Sometimes infuriatingly so. He rarely bitched or moaned about anyone, always choosing to see the good in people. It drove her crazy as she loved nothing more than having a good old bitching session. Why couldn't he see the good in her this time? Surely he could see she hadn't meant to spend all their money.

Looking out the window, she saw an Amazon delivery driver taking a parcel up to her neighbour's house. Her hands twitched as she longed for a delivery. Now she had spent all their savings and maxed out her credit cards, she couldn't order anything. She *needed* a delivery. She wanted something to open. To satisfy the aching inside. *God, I really do have a problem.* In the background, Castle and Beckett are still denying their love for each other whilst closing in on the murderer. It was only 11am and they were already solving murders. All she had done was shower and eat and snoop on the neighbours.

Checking her bank accounts, Isabella was horrified to see that Sean had removed all the remaining money from the joint account. There was just £20.83 left in there. How was she supposed to survive off that? Nauseous, she snatched up her phone. It took a couple of attempts to unlock it, her hand was shaking she was so angry. *Who was he to take their money?* She dialled Sean's number. Each ring just added fuel to her rage. A weary voice answered the phone.

'Hello.'

'Sean. How dare you take out all the money from the joint account. How the hell am I supposed to live?'

'Oh, like you asked me if you could spend all of our savings?' His voice matched her own fury.

She faltered. What could she say to that? The wind out of her sails, she tried a different tack.

'But, Sean, how am I supposed to live? I've got nothing. I

need money for food and things. How will we pay the mortgage?'

He sighed. A sigh that made tears prick at the corners of her eyes.

'I'm sorry, Isabella. But I can't be your financial crutch anymore.'

'Oh for God's sake, that's your mother talking!' Isabella screeched.

'No, Iz, you've brought this on yourself. I will continue to pay the mortgage until we can arrange to sell the house. But as for the rest, you'll have to... I don't know. Sign on or something.'

Isabella swallowed, her throat constricted as she held back her tears.

'Sean. Please. Don't do this. Surely we can work this out.'

'You've betrayed me, Iz. I don't think I can ever get over that.'

'I'm so sorry. I promise I'll never do it again.'

'I can't trust you. How can we have a life together if I can't trust you? I'm always going to be worrying that you are going to do it again.'

'I won't. You can take all my cards. Take complete control of the money. I promise. I'll never lie to you again.' She couldn't hold back the tears. 'Just please don't leave me,' she begged.

'I'm sorry, Iz. I just can't.'

'Don't you love me? You can't do this if you love me. Our vows. For better for worse. This is for worse. You have to stand by me.'

'Those vows go both ways. You broke our vows first. Of course, I love you. But I don't trust you. You've been keeping secrets from me for God knows how long. You can't have a marriage without trust. You know how important trust is to me.'

'Please, Sean. I love you so much. I was just going through a hard time. This is my wake-up call. I know I need to change. I will. I won't do anything like this again. Please.' She slumped to her knees, as if the posture would enhance her plea even though he couldn't see it.

'I'm sorry, Iz. It's over.'

The call ended and so did Isabella's life as she knew it. For the next few days, she stayed in bed. Unable to cope with a world without Sean. Every few hours, she sent texts that remained unread. No blue ticks to show that he had read them. It was torture. Knowing he was out there, her Sean, but unable to be with him. She had driven to his parents' house. But his mother wouldn't let her in.

'Go home and sort yourself out,' she had shouted at Isabella, nose turned up like Isabella was some sort of street rat. With hindsight, she supposed it would have been better to have brushed her hair and got out of her pyjamas. Isabella had driven home with tears blurring her vision. She couldn't decide if the pain was worse than if Sean had died. Would it be better to know that he was dead than the fact he was alive and actively choosing not to be with her?

The days bled into one another and Isabella became a shadow of her former self. She tried to take out another credit card but it seemed no one wanted to give her free money anymore. Living off crackers and black tea, she knew she was going to have to do something about her situation soon. She presumed that because the lights were still on, Sean was paying the utilities for her. Just thinking about him brought a fresh set of tears. She wondered at the human capacity to cry. Would she ever stop?

Her days were spent staring out the window. She used to do this before Sean left, but that was to watch for her next delivery. The happiness that had sparked was foreign to her now. Would she ever be happy again?

With now only thirteen pounds to her name, she wouldn't

be able to buy anything for a while. Plus, spending money was what had got her into this mess. Another Amazon parcel arrived for her neighbour. Their home was in a row of detached houses in Malvern. It was a sought-after area because it was well known for being safe and respectable. It was the type of place where you could forget to lock your door and nothing would happen. It was like all the criminals had had a consortium and agreed to leave parts of Malvern alone.

There were a few kids that sometimes made trouble, but nothing really terrible happened in this part of Malvern. Having said that, they had lived there for six years and had no idea who their neighbours were. The era of 'love thy neighbour' had long since died out. Apart from the perfunctory greeting in passing, she couldn't have picked any of her neighbours out of a line-up. Which was fine by her, as until recently, her world had been full up. All she had needed was Sean. Now she had nothing.

Isabella watched from the bay window as the scruffy young lad dropped the parcel onto the doorstep. He dropped the box and ran back to the car. Seemingly racing an invisible opponent back to his van. She watched as he rustled in his van. Clutching a bigger parcel now, he delivered it two doors down. Almost salivating over it, Isabella felt an overwhelming itch to open that parcel. She bet there was something really good inside it. God, she was pathetic. Lusting over other people's deliveries. She needed to get her life back on track.

But as she turned away from the window and moved into the kitchen, she was still fantasising about what could be in the parcels. Grabbing some crackers for lunch, she raced back to the bay window and took a seat. She had begged Sean to build this window seat for her when they had first moved in. She had intended to use it to read and relax at the weekend. But until she lost her job she had never used it. Now it was her only window to the world outside.

The postman came and went. She watched as he walked up the pathway to her house. She saw a glimpse of red and knew that it was more yelling from the credit card companies that she had 'forgotten' to pay back. Now back at his van, he drew out a box that had the word *'fragile'* stamped over it in large red letters. Her interest was piqued and once again, her mind was racing with thoughts on what it could be. A new dining set, an ornament, a new vase? The desire to know, to be the one to open the parcel and see what was inside was consuming her.

Her fingers were twitching and she watched as the postman rang the doorbell of number seven. No one answered. He put a slip through the door and turned back to his van. Isabella was overwhelmed by the urge to run outside and rugby tackle the postman and run off with the parcel. Luckily, she managed to resist.

Isabella put her head in her hands. She needed to get a grip. Stalking the postman and having visions of decking him to steal parcels was not normal behaviour. She needed to get some air. Quickly, she got up and stuffed her feet in one of the six pairs of Ugg boots she had bought on a whim when she hadn't been able to choose a colour. They suffocated her feet but she was sure they would loosen their death grip on her toes eventually. She just had to wear them in. Isabella opened the coat room. Where normal people had one or two coats, she had around twenty. All purchased in the last month and most of them hadn't been worn. But she had been so happy when they arrived. The anticipation was electrifying. She picked out a black Karen Millen coat and trod on a pile of envelopes on the mat as she left the house. Studiously ignoring the red letters warning her she was in trouble.

The wind whacked her in the face as soon as she opened the front door. But it wasn't an unpleasant feeling, she drank in the fresh air and set off down the street. She knew she was going to regret this walk as no matter where she went it would involve walking up a massive hill. The penance for living in an area of outstanding natural beauty no one warned her about. Although Sean had laughed when she moaned, after all, she was the one that had wanted to move to the Malvern Hills. 'The clue was in the name, Iz. Malvern *Hills*.' He had chuckled as he dragged her up to the top of The Beacon, the first and last time she climbed the Malvern Hills that she had been so desperate to live near.

Despite the hills, the walk was refreshing. She felt like she had escaped her life for a moment and was able to focus on the fresh air filling her lungs and the signs of winter around her. People were getting ready for Christmas already. Houses were begging Santa to stop here and others were making sure he couldn't miss them by suffocating their houses with enough lights to land a plane. They never did Christmas lights on the house. Sean had wanted to but she had stopped him. She had an irrational fear that they would burn the house down. Sean had laughed when she had confessed and kissed her on the nose. He never asked her again and settled for turning their living room into Santa's grotto instead. How was she going to have Christmas without him?

Her parents were living the American dream over in Florida and she was an only child. A medical miracle that couldn't compete with the hot sun and sand in America. Her mother was forty-five when she had Isabella and retired on Isabella's eighteenth birthday. She recalled how they had sat her down, given her a tennis bracelet and the news that they were retiring to Florida and she could come if she wanted. Isabella had turned down the less than enthusiastic invitation and moved to Birmingham for university. She had been ready to live a life alone and independent. But then she had met Sean. A geeky IT nerd that had turned her world upside down.

She could go to America she supposed. But she had only spoken to her parents on video calls once a month. In their early seventies now, they felt more like strangers she was obliged to speak to. How could she go to them and admit her life was in tatters? No, she was going to have to sort this out herself.

Resolved to sorting her life out, Isabella turned back to her house. Trudging up the hill that led to her street was harder than it should have been. She supposed a diet of tea and crackers was to blame. Starting to feel dizzy, she stopped and took a breath. The street was empty and the darkness was mixing with the sunlight making her surroundings look slightly hazy. There was still just enough light to see but it wasn't going to be long until it was pitch black.

She was about to continue walking when she saw it. There were hedges along the footpath, broken by fences leading to the posh, fancy houses that cost more than she could make in her lifetime. Just up ahead, resting on a black metal gate was a brown parcel. Isabella creeped closer and stopped in front of the gate, staring down at it. It looked heavy and the label said John Lewis. Looking through the metal gate, she couldn't see the house, the driveway was longer than she would have anticipated and trees hid the house from view. Coincidentally also hiding her from view. Her eyes searched the gate. No camera or intercom. No one would know she had been here.

Hang on. What the hell was wrong with her? *Am I seriously considering taking this parcel?* Snorting with derision at her stupidity, she set off up the hill. But she stopped only a few steps later. A magnet was pulling her backwards. She hadn't decided to stop. It had just happened. Why was she turning around and walking back down the hill? It was like someone else was controlling her. She watched in horror as she bent down and picked up the parcel. *Put it back!* she yelled at herself. *What the hell are you playing at?* But her admonishments were drowned out by a sense of adrenaline. A giddiness rose inside her and she all but ran up the hill, her lungs burning. She didn't stop until she reached the front door. Putting the parcel at her feet, she clumsily shoved the key in the lock. Both the excitement and fear raging through her body, impairing her dexterity.

Picking up the parcel, she dashed inside the house and slammed the door behind her. With bated breath she took the parcel into the kitchen. For the first time since Sean had left she had forgotten what a shitshow her life had become. Instead, she was thrilled and filled with delicious anticipation. It was like opening an advent calendar but a hundred times better. Taking a knife from the drawer, she sliced open the parcel and fought with the bubble wrap and Sellotape inside. She jabbed and cut at it, wielding the knife like a machete, frustrated it was prolonging the moment. Cutting through the last of the protective layers, Isabella pulled out a beautiful lamp. It was gorgeous. A stone hare, pewter coloured, was standing on a stack of books perched underneath a silk lampshade. No wonder it had been so heavy to carry. A statement piece. There was paper in the bottom of the box and she pulled out the receipt. It was £230.00. She squealed with happiness.

Pulling the plug free of the wrappings, Isabella moved into the living room. She unplugged her boring geometric print lamp from beside the sofa and replaced it with the new lamp. It was perfect. The room looked more homely and sophisticated. She stroked the stone body of the hare, it glittered as it was bathed in the glow from the light bulb above. For a while, Isabella felt happy and content. She kept glancing at her new lamp every now and then. But then her happiness diminished when she realised she had no one to show it to.

The next day, Isabella felt just as sad as the day before. Not even looking at her new lamp helped. It's 'cheer up' powers had worn off. Bored and miserable, she went for another walk, choosing a different coloured pair of Uggs and a North Face coat. She didn't want to be in when the postman came with more demands for money she didn't have.

Isabella tried to convince herself that she had not gone out for a walk with the intention of taking another parcel. She had only gone out to get some fresh air. But somehow, when she was only one street away from her house, she saw an Amazon parcel lying on a doorstep. All of a sudden she was looking around her for people and then for cameras. Finding none, an alien chose that moment to possess her and she found herself picking up the Amazon parcel and hustling away back to her house.

It was the only way she could explain it. It wasn't her doing the stealing, something or someone was taking over her mind and making her do these crazy things. But her shock at her actions was banished by her desire to know what was in the parcel.

This time when she got home, her thrill at getting the parcel was for nothing. She opened up the box, almost breathless with the suspense. But what she revealed was dog-poo bags. It was gutting. All that excitement for nothing. She threw the poo bags and the parcel in the bin. Huffing like a sulky child. She was about to go and sit on the sofa but at the last minute, an impulse to get back outside overcame her. Before she knew it she was back outside, the rain pattering on her hood as she walked around the streets for her next target.

After a few days, Isabella's ratio of finding good things was getting better. She used her walks to scope out which houses it was safe to take from and this time, she would do due diligence on the type of people and the boxes that she took. It filled her days and she thanked the Lord that internet shopping was the new normal. Isabella focused all her time on staking out the houses and was going further afield to avoid suspicion. Her new hobby stopped her from longing for Sean and worrying about her future. It was an addiction and she hadn't even realised it had consumed her. All she knew was that she needed the fix of adrenaline she got every time she got home with a new parcel. She had never felt anything like it. Plus, it was a victimless crime. All the people had to do was report it not delivered and they would get a refund or replacement.

Isabella had well and truly fallen down the rabbit hole. Not once did it cross her mind that she might get caught. Had she not lost all her sensibilities and been so focused on her next fix, she might have noticed that an elderly gentlemen in a Morris Marina had watched her steal a parcel and run away.

CHAPTER FORTY-FOUR

They had run out of rope and food. Jack had no choice but to go out and get supplies. Driving back from the local garden centre, the lights turned red at a crossroad. These lights were notorious for staying red as if someone was playing a game of 'infuriate the drivers by staying on red for eons'. Bored and frustrated, he happened to glance down the street to his left. He watched absent-mindedly as a plump, short woman, in a large coat with a fur hood obscuring her face from view and furry brown boots walked down the pavement towards him. Something about her drew his attention. The way she kept looking around her, as if she thought she was being followed.

As he watched, she stopped in front of a house and appeared to survey the area. The street was deserted. Like an eagle pouncing on its prey, the woman darted to the front door of the house, grabbed a parcel off the doorstep and ran away. A car horn blared, making Jack jump. The traffic light was now on green. On an impulse, Jack turned left instead of carrying on and drove slowly down the street the woman had just ran from. At the bottom of the street he saw her walking away. He tailed her, pulling in and waiting for her to turn up another street before setting off again. He watched as she turned up another street but when he rounded the corner, he saw her unlocking a front door. He parked up and watched her enter the house.

Did he really just watch this woman steal a parcel from someone else's house? He replayed what he had seen in his mind. One minute she had been standing on the street, the next she had picked up the parcel and ran off with it. She hadn't slowly meandered away, she had walked quickly off. The way she was acting, it was obvious it wasn't her parcel.

Jack noted the house number and the name of the street and drove away. As he pointed the car towards home, he thought about the likelihood that he was in the exact right place to witness this woman's crime. Of all the traffic lights he could have stopped at and all the directions he could have looked in, it was as if he was meant to see her. Once more, he realised that it was the Lord guiding him again. After Adina, there would be no one left. But now he had his next target.

Jack was blown away by the audacity of the woman. He hadn't been able to see her face but the speed with which she moved off and the way she surveyed the street for witnesses spoke of experience. He couldn't believe someone could be so immoral that they would steal parcels from strangers. It was disgusting behaviour. She looked so normal. Just an ordinary woman. When in fact she was committing heinous crimes against her neighbours. Did she even think about the impact of what she did? That the person she stole off maybe didn't have the money to replace what she took? That they maybe vitally needed what was in the parcel. His rage flared and he knew what he must do. Adina's death would have to wait. Jack's blood burned with a desire to take this woman. To punish her. She must be his focus for now.

Pulling into the driveway, he parked the car and walked into his house. The front door slammed behind him as he took out his anger on it. His father looked up from where he had been dozing on the chair beside the fire. Jack stalked over and tossed more logs onto it. Watching the flames lick the side of the wood, hungrily feasting upon them.

'I've found another one.'

He recounted what he had seen and was gratified to see the same look of repugnance on his father's face.

'Well, you know what you must do, son. He has shown you the way.'

'I know, Father. Have I not shown you already the depth of my commitment? Isn't there a man out there now, starving to death in a grave I dug for him? Inches from death if he hasn't succumbed already.'

His father raised a hand in defence.

'Calm down, son. I wasn't patronising you. Merely supporting you.' He got to his feet and looked at Jack, meeting his eyes. 'I could not be prouder. My son. Chosen by the Lord to carry out this most important duty.'

Jack smiled and warmth flooded his body.

'Anything from the rat?'

'Nope. She hasn't moved.'

'I was going to move her tonight but I am shattered from yesterday. Once I've caught this other rat, I'll get rid of her.'

'As you wish, son.'

That night, Jack was unable to sleep. Each time he closed his eyes, he kept seeing the woman stealing the package. It ignited his hatred and made sleep impossible. He had to fight his desire to go and get her right this minute. Drag her out of her house by her hair. But he needed to be smarter than that. He had a lot more people to deal with, he couldn't get caught.

She would wait until tomorrow. He smiled into the night as

he pictured the look on her face when she realised retribution was going to be delivered. Would she grovel? Would she fight him like Adina? Or would she snivel and beg like Beckett? He was going to enjoy whatever she did. Punishing the evil was more delicious than the finest feast.

CHAPTER FORTY-FIVE

O ver breakfast, Jack and his father brainstormed what to
do about the package-stealing woman. She lived in an
affluent area of Malvern and would not be as easy to get to.
Especially during the day. Just as he was picking up his keys to
go and stake out his new target, his mobile phone rang. Susan.
He took more deep breaths and answered.

'Jack?'

'Hello, Susan.'

'Where on earth have you been? I've been so worried.'

'I told you. I am staying with my father for a while.'

'But it has been ages and no one has seen hide nor hair of
you. Debbie said she spotted you the other day but no one else
has seen you. Jack, you need to come home. We are your family.
You know we all support each other.'

'I'm sorry, Susan. I just need some space.'

'There are things to sort out, Jack. You need to move on.
Part of the grieving process is acceptance. You are avoiding it.
You need to come home.'

'It's too hard. I'm not ready.'

The thought of going back to his house brought him close to

tears. He couldn't do it. He didn't think he would ever be ready. No. He had to stay here and focus on his mission.

'I know, Jack, darling. We all miss her. But we miss you too. You have been a big part of our lives for so long.'

'I know. I miss you too.' It wasn't a lie. As much as he found her irritating and only tolerated her for Elsie's sake, it would seem he actually did like her. Her voice was soothing and a reminder of the old times. A time when he had been happy.

'Right, that settles it. I'm coming to see you. Give me the address. I'll get in my car right now.' Panic flared. He could not have her coming here.

'No! I'll come to you. I'll meet you at your house. I'll set off now and I can be there in an hour.'

Jack hung up and chose to ignore the disapproval on his father's face.

'Shall I come with you?' his father asked.

'No. I best go on my own,' Jack replied. 'I won't be long.'

'You'd better not. We have work to do,' replied his father, looking pointedly in the direction of the cellar door where Adina was waiting.

'Just keep an eye on her. The sooner I go the sooner I'll be back.'

Jack parked up on his driveway automatically. He hadn't even realised what he had done until he had got to the front door and had placed his key in the lock. Jack jumped back like the door had electrocuted him. He gazed at the number six, remembered how Elsie had kept him at B&Q for over an hour trying to decide which style of number six she liked best for the door.

Stepping away from the door, he moved over the patch of grass that divided their house from Susan's. It was well trodden, less grass more dirt now. A well-trodden path was all that was left to symbolise the friendship between Susan and Elsie.

Jack raised his hand to knock but the door swung open. The smell of stale smoke and cloying perfume hit him instantly, causing his stomach to roll. He had made it his business to avoid going to Susan's house. She never seemed to let him leave. Always found excuses to extend his visit. *'Oh you wouldn't mind just looking at the washing machine. The thing's on the blink again.'*

Susan opened the door and embraced him, suffocating him with her perfume and squeezing him so tightly he could barely breathe. He patted her back lightly and resisted the urge to push her away. Eventually, he was released and he followed her into the living room. Her house was a carbon copy of their house in layout. But that was where the similarities ended.

Susan had filled her room with every ornament she laid eyes on. Creepy pigs and porcelain children gazed at him from all angles. Whereas their house was stylish and clean with everything in its place. It was like Susan had been to a car boot sale and said, 'I'll take it all'. Nothing matched and it made the room feel claustrophobic. The mantelpiece looked like a horizontal Jenga. There were so many knick-knacks that a stray wind would risk knocking them to the floor. Which wouldn't necessarily be a bad thing. Susan caught him staring at a particularly vile stuffed squirrel. *Who stuffs a squirrel?* Its beady eyes were boring into him. The hairs on the back of his neck raised.

'It's beautiful, isn't it?' Susan reached out and stroked the squirrel's body affectionately. 'It's so soft. Touch it. Go on. Touch it.' Jack moved away and sat on the sofa. He grunted in pain as he sat on something sharp. Reaching under him, he pulled out a stiletto. *Of course, why wouldn't you keep your shoes under a cushion on the sofa.* Susan chuckled.

'Ooh silly me.' She took the shoe off him and threw it into the corner of the room.

Susan took a seat next to him. She was too close, her leg pressing against his. He could see down her top as she leaned towards him. Her breasts were smashed together, creating a line that looked like two bum cheeks rather than cleavage. He leaned back and tried to edge away but she just moved closer. Susan took his hand and looked at him with pity in her eyes. She used to be pretty when they had first met. But the cigarettes and alcohol had slowly eaten away at her good looks. Tarring her teeth and staining her skin. Her face once slender was now bloated and puffy.

'How have you been, Jack?'

'Oh, you know, getting by.'

She stroked his hand gently and he wanted to slap it away.

'Now, Jack. You can talk to me. How are you really?'

'Just missing Elsie as you can imagine.'

Susan nodded, her eyes filling with tears.

'I miss her too. That's why we need to stick together, Jack. Only we can help each other through this terrible time.'

'Er, yes. I suppose.'

'Yes, Jack. Exactly. We are all we have now. Just you and me. I will help you get through this. We can grieve and move on together. I am the only one that understands what you are going through. I loved her too.'

'Well, I don't know about that. I know she was your best friend. But she was my wife.'

He needed to leave. Jack looked at the door longingly. Being here, talking about Elsie. It was too much. His heart couldn't bear it. Being in this room, with Susan, it just reminded him of what he had lost. He stared at the door and wished that Elsie would walk through it. Looking at him with laughter in her eyes because she knew how much Susan irritated him. His throat swelled with unshed tears. He needed to leave.

'Actually, Susan–'

She cut him off before he could say more. She threw her arms around him. 'Oh, Jack. I've missed you so much.'

His arms were pinned down by his sides. He couldn't get her off without tipping her from the sofa.

'Have you missed me too?' she whispered. Her breath was stale cigarettes and it made him nauseous. He wanted to stop breathing to prevent the toxic smell from entering his system.

'Er, yes I have. But–'

'Oh, Jack.' Susan looked up and moved into him. Her mouth puckered inches from his own when he realised she was about to kiss him. Aghast, he pulled his arms free and pushed her. With more strength than he intended, she thumped to the floor. Tears were in her eyes and she gaped up at him in shock.

'I'm sorry, Susan.' He reached down to help her up but she recoiled from him.

'How could you?' she cried.

'I'm sorry. I just don't feel that way about you. I love Elsie.'

She sniffed and rubbed her arms. He really hadn't meant to hurt her.

'I should go. I'm sorry if I misled you in any way.'

He got to his feet, awkwardly, backing away slowly like she was a coiled snake.

Susan glared at him.

'What's wrong with me? I thought you liked me?'

Jack stopped moving. He felt bad for her.

'I'm sorry, Susan. I will only ever love Elsie. No one else. She was my soulmate. The only one.'

His voice broke and his legs almost gave way under him as the strength of his loss hit him all over again. He took deep breaths, trying to calm himself and regain his composure.

Susan's face clouded. She got to her feet, looking every inch a sulky child.

'Oh yes, perfect Elsie. You have no idea what she was really like.'

He stared at her, confused.

'What are you talking about?'

Susan's eyes flashed with anger and she looked at him scornfully.

'She never deserved you!' she shrieked at him. 'I deserved you,' she spat. Pointing at herself. 'She treated you like shit. She bossed you around like a little bitch baby and you let her.'

'Now hang on a minute.'

But Susan wasn't listening. The words pouring out of her like they had been waiting there for years, desperate to be said.

'From the moment I first met you, I knew we were destined to be together. That Elsie didn't deserve you. That you should be with me. But there was nothing I could do. I knew you were a man of honour and would never leave her. So I just had to sit there and watch her disrespect you and treat you like a slave.'

'Susan, I don't know what you are talking about. Elsie and I were happy. She would never disrespect me. We loved each other.'

'Oh yeah. You sure about that are you?' Susan looked at him, a nasty smile spreading across her face.

'Yes. I know Elsie loved me. I don't understand where this is coming from.'

He backed away, turning to the door. Unwilling to listen any longer. His hand reached out to the handle and then he heard the words that paralysed him.

'Elsie had an affair.'

CHAPTER FORTY-SIX

B lood pounded in his head as Susan's words smashed into his brain. Shattering the world as he knew it. His first thought was denial. There was no way. Elsie would never. He turned to Susan and wanted nothing more than to strangle her. His hands clenched at his sides as fury pulsed through his veins.

'How dare you!' he roared. 'How dare you tell such a lie.' Susan was unperturbed by his anger. If anything, she seemed to be feeding on it. Her eyes were wild and her smile split her face. She puffed out her chest.

'It's not a lie. Dear old Elsie was a good-for-nothing cheat.'

Jack was moving before he knew it. His hands closed around Susan's throat. Her whole body stiffened, but she didn't try to stop him. Just smiled up at him.

'Ah now I've got your attention.'

Jack shook her forcefully.

'You're lying. Admit it. You're lying!'

'It's not a lie, Jack. About three years ago Elsie came over to mine and confessed the whole thing. Unable to keep it a secret anymore, she had to tell someone and she chose me. Gave me all the sordid details.'

'No! Stop it! You are lying.' He tried to stop himself but his wrath was like a wild beast, out of control. His fingers clenched harder around her throat and she tried to prise his hands away. Her fear was evident now.

'I'm not,' she wheezed, struggling for breath, 'I promise you. She told me she had been having an affair for six months. But she had finally broke it off because she wasn't sure she could live with herself.'

Jack let go. Stunned at what he was hearing.

'I begged her to tell you. It would have been perfect. I could have swooped in, comforted you and we could have been together instead. Like we were always meant to.' Susan rubbed at her throat, taking deep breaths. 'But she wouldn't tell you. I thought about telling you myself. But I couldn't cause you that pain. Plus, I didn't think you'd believe me over *Saint* Elsie.'

She was right, he would never have believed her. He still didn't.

'You are just a bitter, twisted drunk. Trying to get back at me because I don't want to sleep with you.'

'Think what you want. But I'm glad the bitch is dead. She got what she deserved. The adulteress whore.'

Jack's control shattered. He couldn't think. He couldn't see. He was nothing but infernal rage. It consumed him. It propelled him back into the house. It placed his hands around Susan's neck. It forced him to strangle the life from her body.

When the red mist faded away. He was standing there, Susan hanging limply by her neck in his hands. Her eyes were looking at him, red spots surrounding her iris. Nail marks and scratches lined his hands where she had tried and failed to stop him. Jack was breathing heavily. The realisation of what he had done suddenly struck him. Horrified, he pulled his hands away and Susan flopped to the floor.

Jack backed off. What had he done? This was not part of the

plan. This was not meant to happen. Jack dropped to his knees and caressed Susan's face.

'No. No. Please don't be dead,' he begged her. But her lifeless body ignored him. He fell backwards, his head in his hands, and began to cry. He had killed her. The woman he had lived next to for ten years. The one who had brought him soup every day when he was first home from the hospital after his accident at work. The person who had bought him a new tie for Christmas every year. She may have been irritating and brash but she didn't deserve to die. Bile rose in his throat and he began to shake uncontrollably. This was not part of his mission, God would not approve of this. This was murder. He was a murderer.

Jack stood up and stumbled out of the house. He had to get away. He fled, racing to his car. Once behind the wheel, he took deep calming breaths, trying to stop himself from slipping into a total breakdown. He thought of Susan's body, lying there. He couldn't leave her. Jack got out of the car and returned to the house. The sight of Susan so obviously dead made his stomach heave. *I am a monster.* Jack knelt down and picked her up. She was a dead weight and with some difficulty he carried her to the car. It was only later that he realised he should have checked that no one was watching. But he was too caught up in self-loathing and disbelief at his actions to think clearly. Gently, Jack laid Susan down in the boot of the car. Her eyes stared at him, accusatory. *How could you, Jack Danvers?* they seemed to say.

Tears clouded his vision and he wiped furiously at his face as he returned to the driver's side. He pulled away and drove home, becoming more distressed with each mile that passed. *I am a monster.* He could feel Elsie's presence in the car. He couldn't look to his left, convinced she was sat there, staring at him. Screaming at him. *Murderer.* The word kept rebounding in his mind. By the time he pulled into the driveway at Oakdale

Farm, he was a shadow of the man who had left. He burst through the doors and fell to the floor at his father's feet. His father jumped up, concern on his face.

'What's happened, son?'

Jack couldn't speak, he was hysterical. Suffocating on unshed tears. He curled up like a foetus on the floor. His father forced him to a sitting position and slapped him across the face with the back of his hand. The action had the desired effect as Jack stopped crying instantly. The shock distracting him from his anguish.

'Tell. Me. What. Happened,' his father commanded.

'I killed her,' Jack murmured. He waited for the revulsion to spread across his father's face. He deserved nothing more. He was a monster. A killer.

'Susan?'

Jack nodded. He felt hot tears pouring from his eyes.

'What happened?'

'I killed her.' He covered his face with his hands. His father pulled them away. His expression severe.

'Tell me what happened.'

'I didn't mean to. Sh-she said that Elsie was having an affair. I just snapped. One minute I was leaving, the next. The next I was strangling her.' Jack grabbed his father's shirt. 'You have to believe me, Father. It was an accident. I didn't mean to kill her.' He searched his father's face, trying to decipher his expression. For the longest time, his father stared into space, apparently lost in thought. Tears tracked down Jack's face as he tried to force the images of Susan out of his mind. The vivid red marks around her neck from where he had squeezed until no air could pass to her lungs.

'It's okay, son,' his father said quietly. 'It's going to be okay.' Slowly, his father helped him to his feet and they both sat on the sofa.

'You said this woman said Elsie was having an affair?'

'Yes.'

'Do you think she was telling the truth?'

'No!' shouted Jack. Even now, he still couldn't believe that his Elsie would have an affair. There was no way. Theirs was a love told of in films and fairy tales. A bond spanning thirty-seven years. They spent almost every day together, he would know.

'Well then, there is your answer. She is a liar. She has been punished accordingly.'

Jack stared at his father in shock.

'She was my friend, Father. I have known her for years. I shouldn't have killed her. She was just lashing out because I rejected her. She didn't deserve to die.' Jack shook his head. Unable to understand why his father was so accepting of the fact he had taken an innocent woman's life.

'Son, from what you told me she was a drunk and a liar. What good did she bring to society? No one will miss her.'

'Yes they will, Father. She was a big part of our church. She may have been a drunk but she was always helping people when she could. Raising money and visiting people. She will be missed by everyone in the village. She had flaws but she was a good person, Father. And I killed her.'

Jack got up, pacing, unable to sit and consider what he did. He ran his hands through his hair. This was not what he was supposed to be doing today. He was supposed to be doing God's work. Not killing someone because he didn't like what they said.

'Son. You need to calm down. What's done is done.'

Jack turned and looked down at his father open-mouthed. 'What's done is done?' he repeated incredulously. 'How can you be so calm? I am a monster. I just killed someone. Someone that didn't deserve it.' He was shouting now. Jack felt out of control. Unable to cope with the idea that he had killed Susan. He felt unstable. All he wanted to do was scream and shout and throw things. He wanted the ground to swallow him up.

'I need to go to the police. I need to tell them what I have done. I need to be punished.'

'You need to pull yourself together, son.' Jack wasn't listening.

'That's it. I'll take her body and hand myself in. Someone else will have to carry on the Lord's work. I have failed. I am a monster.' He looked at his hands. He had blood on these hands. He had spilled innocent blood. *Oh, Susan.*

Jack started to move towards the door.

'Oh no you don't!' snarled his father. 'We've come too far for you to fall at the first hurdle.' His father clutched his arm. A grip so strong it was painful. He dragged Jack from the house. Jack tried to protest but his father wasn't listening. He ignored Jack's attempts to break his hold. He held on tighter and Jack was forced to follow him into the church his father had built all those years ago. His father threw him down before the cross.

'You are going to stay here until you come to your senses. Repent for what happened with Susan. But understand this. You were chosen by God to eradicate sin from this world. Nothing is more important than that. You are going to stay here until you realise that.'

'But, Father–'

'But nothing! Yes, you maybe shouldn't have killed her. But I understand exactly why you did it. Heck, I would have done it myself if I was in your position. Elsie was the love of your life. How dare that woman try and destroy your memories of her. Who is she to besmirch Elsie's name when she is not here to defend herself? It was despicable and if you ask me she deserved what she got.'

With that, he turned heel and slammed the doors. The key turned in the lock. Jack heard him leave, his father's last words echoing in his mind. His anger at Susan started to stir in the pit of his stomach. It was despicable, the things that Susan said. She knew how deeply Jack loved Elsie. How could she try and ruin that?

Jack turned to face the cross that his father had nailed to the wall. He knelt down to pray. The motion triggered pain in his knees and he relished it. The physical pain gave him a chance to focus on something else. It quietened his mind as he allowed himself only to feel the pain in his knees. He began to pray. He prayed for forgiveness. He prayed for guidance. He was still in the kneeling position when his father unlocked the doors the next morning.

CHAPTER FORTY-SEVEN

S itting in front of the fire, Jack relished the heat that was defrosting his bones. The pain of walking from the church back into the house was so strong, it was only with his father's help that he managed it. He swore he could hear his bones cracking as he walked.

The fire was roaring and the welcome heat was thawing not just his frozen limbs but also his despair. Spending the night in church had had the effect his father had hoped. Being close with God, he was able to repent for his actions but also to refocus on his mission. He knew that he had done wrong, but by carrying on this sacred work, he would be able to right that wrong. Jack was more determined than ever to make amends for what he had done, by eliminating every sinful person he came across.

He had been so conflicted for most of the night, as he himself was now a sinful person. But he reasoned, he was repenting and trying to make amends. The people that he was targeting weren't sorry. They didn't see what they were doing to humanity, the pain they were causing others. Slave labour, scamming people out of money and material goods. It was disgusting. Which is why his mission was so important and he couldn't let anything get in his way.

Jack took the cup of tea from his father, smiling gratefully.

'Thank you, Father.'

'Are you feeling better today, son?'

'Yes, Father. I'm sorry about last night. I've had a long time to think and you're right. The mission is too important. I won't fail.'

His father nodded sagely.

The sun was breaking through the clouds and the rays shone through the window, highlighting his father's face. Jack could see the deep-seated wrinkles and was once again struck by how old his father was getting. In this light, without his personality to mask it, he looked every inch the old man he was.

Jack was glad that they had finally managed to reconnect in this way. He didn't know how he would have got through Elsie's death without his father. A rush of emotion spread through him. If his father hadn't helped him see that Elsie's death had happened for a reason, he would never have survived. He would never have achieved his life's purpose. Nor would he have developed this deep connection with the Lord. He smiled warmly at him.

'What are you looking at me like that for?' asked his father, his voice gruff.

'I'm just grateful for your support,' replied Jack. Feeling shy at being so emotionally open with his father. It wasn't their style.

'Get on with you. Don't be soft.'

'Sorry, Father.'

'Never mind being sorry. What's the plan? We need to make a plan. We have to be smart, son. The Lord is depending on us to get this right.'

'I know. I know.'

'So, we need to do something about the body in the boot.' Jack couldn't help but wince at his words. He swallowed down the guilt that was waiting patiently like a Venus flytrap, ready to ensnare him and eat him alive. It would do no good. He had to be pragmatic and focus. 'We've also got the one downstairs. And you said yesterday that you found another target.'

'Yes, I think we should get her first. Then deal with them both together.'

'And the body in the boot?'

Jack took a deep breath.

'I will deal with that, Father. You can keep an eye on her.'

By the afternoon, Susan was resting in a grave marked by a large stone and some of the finest flowers he could find. He had chosen to bury her in one of his favourite places in the forest. Nowhere near the sinners. No, Susan had a lovely view of the Malvern Hills, buried just on the edge of the forest. He had wrapped her body in a rug, unable to stand the sight and the smell of her. The smell had made him gag and he forced himself to avoid looking at her. Her body was evidence of his sin and he just could not look. He had carried her to the grave and placed her gently inside. He recited what a vicar would have said and tried to make the burial as nice as he could. It was the least she deserved. When he shovelled the last of the dirt onto her grave, he felt a lot better. Placing the stone and the flowers, he left and was determined to never look back. He had left his guilt and remorse behind mixed in with the soil that was now embracing her body. Jack had a job to do and nothing or no one was going to get in his way. Jack walked off, his mind deliberating how he was going to kidnap the thief he had identified as his next target. He was so lost in thought he failed to notice the figure watching from behind a tree to his right.

CHAPTER FORTY-EIGHT

I f Jack had needed any more proof that the woman he saw was meant to be his next target then he was given it hand over fist the next day. Getting up with the dawn, Jack had fed Adina just enough water to keep her alive with another scrap of bread. He had treated her to another day of kneeling in the grains of rice. He had left her with his father, who had promised he would ensure she stayed on her knees whilst he was gone. Jack was happy to see that Adina's spirit was beginning to fade. She was no longer glowering at him with obstinate looks. She was compliant and almost grateful when he brought down the water and scraps of food. Perhaps a few days lying in her own filth had finally brought her down a peg or two. Each time he went down there, she tried to convince him that she wasn't sinful. That she didn't belong here. But he wouldn't listen. As far as he was concerned her words were poison. He would not let that poison take root in his mind.

Sitting outside of the woman's house, he waited patiently, reading the paper. Confident that the Lord had led him to this woman for a reason, he knew that he would be rewarded for his patience. After lunch, the green door opened and the woman came out. The antsy way she walked made Jack think that she was planning another 'shopping spree'. Jack got out of his car and followed. One of the benefits of being old was that eyes tended to slide right past him. Old age blessed him with powers of invisibility. No one would suspect him of following her. He was just an old man out for a walk to get the daily paper. He tucked a paper under his arm to add to the effect.

The woman walked for fifteen minutes, she seemed to have a direction in mind. He watched as she scoped out her surroundings, constantly on the alert. Following her onto New Road, he stayed behind a large aerial post that shielded him from her view. She walked up the street extremely slowly. He realised she was assessing each house, looking for parcels and witnesses.

Jack's fists clenched as he watched with growing anger as she gave one last look up and down the street and walked up onto someone's driveway. She picked up a large brown box and turned and strode quickly back down the driveway and up the street. Going a different way back, he hurried to catch up. A plan formulating in his mind.

As they neared the woman's house, Jack increased his pace so that he was no less than a few metres from her. Just before she turned into her driveway, Jack lurched forward and fell hard onto his knees. He did not have to pretend to cry out as the white hot pain in his knees was very real. The woman turned at the sound of his voice. He watched as she stared at him. She appeared to edge slightly towards the house, as if contemplating leaving him there and so he let out another moan of pain. It worked; the woman placed the parcel on the floor and rushed over to his side.

'Sir, are you okay?' asked the woman. She put her hand on his shoulder, looking down at him with concern.

Jack let the pain in his knees show on his face.

'I'm afraid I took a bit of a tumble. My legs aren't as strong as they used to be.' He let his voice wobble. He needed her to feel sorry for him.

'Are you okay? Are you hurt?' she asked.

'I've just hurt my knees.'

'Can you stand?'

'I'm not sure. Let me try.'

Jack lumbered to his feet, letting out more moans of pain as he did so. The woman placed an arm around him, trying to help him to his feet.

'I don't suppose it would be too much trouble for you to help me back to my car. It's just there.' He pointed in the direction of his car. Jack watched as the woman glanced back at her house, specifically at the parcel and then back at Jack.

'Okay.' She tried and failed to hide the sigh in her voice. She did not want to help him.

'Thank you so much, dear.' Jack smiled at her brightly. 'My name is Jack.'

'Okay.' She reached an arm around him and took one of his hands. In his mind, he was squeezing her hand until he felt the bones breaking and she was screaming in pain. But in reality, he smiled at her pleasantly and began to lead the way to his car. He acted the old doddery man and they made slow progress to his car.

'What's your name?' he asked her. Surprised she hadn't offered it to him already. Did she have no manners at all?

'Isabella. How much further?' she enquired whilst looking to check her parcel was still where she left it. Wouldn't it be ironic if someone stole it? Jack smothered a laugh and led her to his car. He pointed at it and felt her pushing him forward, trying to increase his pace. As they reached the back of the car, Jack took a deep breath. This was the crucial moment. Everything hinged on this. His only advantage was the element of surprise.

'Would you mind getting my driving shoes out of the boot?' Jack said, and he reached into his pocket and withdrew the keys. He passed them to Isabella so she had no choice but to help him. He gave her what he hoped was his most grateful smile, ignoring the look of frustration and the huff she made when she took the keys from him. She turned her back and put the key in the lock. As she lifted the boot open, Jack moved so that he was right behind her. As she bent down to look for his shoes, he pushed her as hard as he could. With lightning-quick reflexes, he grabbed her legs and thrust them into the boot. It was over in a matter of seconds. Isabella didn't even have a chance to panic or fight back before he shut the door. His heart was beating so loudly in his ears, it was almost louder than the sound of Isabella banging on the boot and screaming for help.

Jack nimbly darted back to the front of the car and climbed into the front seat. Putting the car in gear, he drove quickly away. His heart rate slowly returned to normal and he began to feel jubilant. He was doing it. He was slowly but surely getting rid of the disgusting people that were tainting the human race. Jack was making the world better and safer. Had he not been so wrapped up in his joy, he might have noticed that a brown Vauxhall had pulled out of the street at the same time as him and followed him almost all the way back to his house.

CHAPTER FORTY-NINE

The door banged open and a cacophony of screams ripped Adina from her slumber. Quickly, she jumped up and returned to a kneeling position, holding back the scream of pain when her knees connected with the rice. Each time she felt like giving up, of finding a way to end it all, she conjured up Poppy's beautiful smiling face and her resolution to survive was restored. Adina had worked for the last few days on the ropes binding her arms but had got nowhere. Now she was too weak from lack of food. Her arms screamed in pain with the slightest movement. They were now cemented in that position and if she ever did manage to escape she was sure they would stay that way for the rest of her life.

Adina looked at the floor. Meeting his eye and being confrontational did not work. It aggravated him and seemed only to increase his conviction that she was evil. She needed to find a way to get through to him. To connect with him. If she could just get him to listen to her and hear what she had to say then he would let her go. But each time she had tried to explain, he walked away, refusing to listen.

Adina had no idea how long she had been down here but with every second, she began to feel that she was living on borrowed time. When Jack came and took Dan away, she had spent the next few hours trying and failing not to picture what had happened to him. She felt sick with the knowledge that she was next. But he seemed to be toying with her. Keeping her guessing as to when he was going to kill her. Just coming down to give her water and make sure she was still kneeling in the rice. Taking pleasure in her swollen knees and tears of pain.

Her body was a tapestry of cuts and bruises that would heal. But if she ever got free, she doubted that she would ever recover from the mental torture. The fear of the dark, the dread that he was going to come downstairs. The anxiety that he wouldn't come downstairs and she would die in this cold concrete prison. As more time elapsed, her mind retreated from her reality and escaped into memories of Poppy. If she was going to die, she wanted to do so thinking of Poppy, not her current circumstances.

Although Adina was starting to think something had changed. She had fallen over, weak from lack of food. Unable to summon the energy to try and get up and kneel in the rice again. She laid there, waiting for him to come and beat her. But nothing happened. Adina fell into a fitful sleep, knowing that when she woke up she would be punished for her disobedience. But too exhausted to care.

When she woke, there was still no sign of anyone. The hours were long and the pain relentless. The concrete floor was so cold and hard, it was impossible to get even slightly comfortable. The minutes ticked by endlessly. She regretted thinking about the passage of time as she started hearing an imaginary ticking clock that she couldn't unhear. Her body felt so weak and her need for food was overwhelming. She had licked the spot where the bread had been placed just in case there were any crumbs. But all she got was dust, dirt and the taste of concrete. Her stomach was eating the rest of her body. At one point her mind convinced her that she could actually hear it. Adina was very close to losing her grip on reality. If she hadn't already. She had no concept of time and being alone in the dark was wearing her down. All she had to keep her going was Poppy. She had to get out of this alive for Poppy's sake. Her daughter needed her.

The screams got louder as a pair of legs in blue jeans came into view, they were thrashing up and down. When Jack appeared, his face was red and strained as he fought to keep hold of the screaming woman. His face was bleeding from a vicious scratch. But despite the ferocity with which the woman was fighting him, she was unable to break free as Jack carried her down the stairs over his shoulder. When he reached the bottom, Jack lowered the woman down onto the floor. He captured her hands in one of his and placed his other hand around the woman's throat. She kicked out at him and Jack used his grip on her throat to push her back into the wall. Her head thudded into the concrete and she looked momentarily dazed. But not for long, she resumed her screaming and kicked and fought against Jack.

Adina felt ashamed, she hadn't put up half the fight this woman had. She was literally fighting for her life. The wildness and strength in her green eyes, the desire to live in every kick of her limbs. She would not be subdued easily. But Adina also knew that Jack was stronger than he looked. The genial old man was hiding a strong, capable lunatic who was resolute in his mind as to his purpose in life. When she had asked him why he was doing this, he would keep telling her she was evil and had to be punished. That he was ridding the world of scum like her under God's instruction. His certainty that he was doing the right thing was giving him the strength to ignore the fact that they were human beings.

Adina locked eyes with the woman. She tried to encourage her with her eyes to keep fighting. At the sight of Adina, the panic in the woman's eyes grew. She kicked and clawed at Jack more forcefully.

'Get off me,' screamed the woman. She managed to kick Jack between the legs and for a minute Jack staggered backwards, clutching his crotch, grunting with pain. Adina watched, unable to breathe as the woman raced back up the stairs.

'Father,' Jack croaked. As he looked at the woman the realisation that she was almost at the top of the stairs seemed to break through the haze of agony. He stood up, taking deep breaths, pain etched on his face.

Go on! Go on! Get out of here! Get help! This was the miracle Adina had never dared hope for. Before Jack moved, Adina dragged herself over to him. She was well practised at moving with her legs and hands bound now and was in front of the staircase before he reached it. He looked down at her as though she were an irritating bug that he was going to swat away. Jack moved to step over her and Adina lay down on her back. She swung her legs in the air, colliding with Jack's legs and he tripped over her mid-step. He fell forward and she thought she heard his head hitting the concrete step. Their legs were tangled together and Adina wriggled, trying her best to stop him from being able to get up. Jack grabbed her legs and threw her to the side.

'Stupid bitch.'

And then she was gone. Adina hoped with every fibre of her being that the momentary delay she had caused had given the woman the head start she needed. With no idea where they were, she had visions of the woman running, screaming at the top of her lungs until she found someone to save her. To save them both. With bated breath, Adina waited at the bottom of the stairs. Jack had slammed the door behind him when he left the cellar. She wriggled until her back was against the wall and she was facing the staircase. Staring intently at it. Waiting for her rescue. The woman had to have escaped. Poppy needed her. Someone had to help her get out of here.

A loud thump came from outside the cellar. Then the cellar door banged open. She began to cry as she saw Jack coming down the stairs. The woman was once more over his shoulder, but this time she wasn't moving. Adina's heart broke. Leaning her head against the wall, she sobbed. She was never going to see her daughter again.

Jack smiled at her.

'See, Adina, this is what happens to people that are evil. People that sin. God is not on their side.'

Adina looked over to him. He had laid the woman flat on her back where Adina used to sleep and was now tying her up. Adina was now where Dan used to sleep, the next in line for execution.

'What do you mean?'

'Well, I was all set to chase the lovely Isabella into the forest. But she wasn't looking where she was going and fell over. It seems she hit her head. There she was, lying sprawled out on the floor.'

Adina didn't answer. She looked at the woman. Beads of blood dripped from an angry gash on her forehead.

'The Lord prevented her from escaping. She is sinful and must be punished. So, he intervened.'

'Why is she sinful?'

'I spotted her, brazenly stealing parcels from people's doorsteps. Can you believe it, Adina? What sort of human being steals from their neighbours?' He laughed and looked over at her. 'Sorry, I forget who I am talking to, of course you can believe it. You are just like her.'

'No, I'm not.'

'Come now, Adina, we both know what you are.'

Adina took a deep breath and launched into her pre-prepared speech that she had been preparing in her mind should she ever get the opportunity to talk to Jack properly.

'Do you know what I am? I'm poor. I have no money. I can't afford to feed both myself and my daughter so most days I go without food so that she has enough to eat each day. I scrape every single sliver of butter out of the tub to prevent having to buy some more. I don't have a car in the garage. I lied. I don't even own a car. I walk three miles to my daughter's school every day even when it's pouring down with rain. I bought this top in a charity shop five years ago and wear it most days because I have no money for clothes for myself and most of my other tops have holes in them. Everything I get goes on my daughter. I make £7.50 an hour cleaning people's houses but I can't work full-time as I can't afford childcare.' Her voice got stronger as she spoke, encouraged by the fact he actually seemed to be listening.

'I don't believe you. I heard you in the coffee shop. And on the phone you confirmed it.'

'I lied!' she screamed at him. An amalgamation of snot and tears were dripping down her face but with her hands behind her back she could do nothing. 'The conversation you heard in the coffee shop. It was my monthly visit with my sister. She has the perfect life and wants for nothing and spends every single visit bragging about how much money she has and what she is buying for her children. Whilst adding in the occasional dig about how unsuccessful I am compared to her. I just snapped. For once, just once, I didn't want to be the failure of the family. I wanted to be able to brag about my own accomplishments. So, I lied. I made all that stuff up, the cleaning company and making loads of money. I have £20.83 in my bank account and that has to last me until the end of the month. I couldn't even afford to offer to replace your coffee after I spilt it or I wouldn't have been able to feed my child.' She was crying in earnest now. He had to believe her. 'As soon as I was outside the coffee shop, I felt like the worst person in the world. My daughter had just heard me tell the most awful lies. I was so ashamed. I didn't mean to do it. I just couldn't stand my sister looking down on me all the time. Couldn't cope with her reminding me how much she is able to give her children whilst I struggle just to make sure Poppy has shoes that fit. I snapped and made one of the worst decisions of my life because it landed me here.'

Adina blinked the tears away and stared Jack in the eyes, trying to make her eyes mirror the honesty of her words. 'I promise you, Jack, I'm not greedy or evil. I told a lie in the heat of the moment. But that doesn't make me sinful. I am just a mother, with barely two pennies to rub together. I do not deserve to die.' Jack stared at her. His face impassive. 'Please. Please let me go home to my daughter. I don't even know if she is safe. If she has someone looking after her.'

Jack didn't speak to her. Abruptly, he moved to the staircase and began to climb. *No!* He couldn't leave. He had to believe her.

'I can prove it!' she shouted after him. Jack stopped, but he didn't turn around.

'Have you got a computer?'

She took his silence as confirmation and continued.

'Go onto the Barclays Bank website. I know my login details. The username is adinapoppy1402, the password is my daughter's date of birth, 230801. Log in. You'll see I'm telling the truth. You'll see I'm not greedy. That I don't deserve to be here.'

Jack went up the remainder of the stairs and closed the door behind him. Adina sank back into the wall. She had done what she could. But a small voice told her it was pointless. Even if Jack did realise that he had made a mistake was he really going to let her go? How could he? It wouldn't matter if she swore that she would never go to the police, he was never going to take that risk. She just had to accept the fact that she was going to die. That this was it. A groan broke her misery and she shuffled over to the woman whose eyes were fluttering open.

'Are you okay?'

The woman groaned and tried to get up. She was short and curvy with piercing green eyes and hair which was blonde but judging by the dark-brown roots poking through it wasn't natural, in fact, it reminded her of Poppy's hair colour. Realising her arms were bound behind her back, the woman looked at Adina, with eyes full of terror. Adina almost told her to not bother being scared and just come to terms with the fact they were both going to die. But that would be cruel.

'What's going on?' the woman asked. 'Who are you?'

'My name is Adina. Is your name Isabella?'

The woman nodded and began to look around the room, absorbing her new surroundings. The blood had stopped dripping from her cut. The red trails it had left stood out on her pale face.

'What's happening? Who is that man?'

Adina sighed. Should she be brutally honest or sugar-coat the truth?

'His name is Jack. I believe he is on some sort of religious crusade to kill sinful people.'

Brutal honesty it was.

'What?'

'I know, he is crazy. Some might say, a religious nutjob.' She snorted darkly, realising she was quoting Dan. 'He mentioned something about you stealing?'

Isabella blushed and looked down at her knees.

'Oh my God. I can't believe this is happening.'

Isabella began to cry and Adina longed to put her arms around her. But all she could do was rest her head on Isabella's shoulders.

'I didn't mean to do it.' Adina sat up and looked at Isabella. She looked so young, it made her think of Poppy. She wondered what Poppy would look like at that age. Her heart contracted with pain when she realised she would never know.

'Do what?'

'You have to understand, I've lost everything. My job, my marriage. I've been so depressed.' Isabella was looking at Adina with pleading eyes. Begging her to understand. 'I went for a walk one day and saw a delivery driver leave a parcel on the side of a road. Anyone could have taken it. I didn't even know I was going to take it. It just happened. I took it home and opened it. And for the first time, in a long time, I forgot how rubbish my life was.'

Adina tried to swallow her judgement. She had no money but not once had it crossed her mind to take from other people. But she refused to judge this woman. If she did, she was no better than Jack. Everyone made mistakes. At the end of the day, Isabella hadn't murdered anyone. She'd stolen a few parcels by the sounds of it. It was unfathomable to her how Jack saw that as an offence punishable by death.

'What did you do?' Isabella asked Adina. 'What did you do that made him take you?'

Adina sensed that the woman wanted to know that Adina was as flawed as she was. It would make her feel better about herself to know that she wasn't the only one that had done something they weren't proud of.

'It's a long story. Jack overheard a conversation I had and got the wrong end of the stick.'

'Is that his name? Jack?'

'Yes, that's all I know about him. There is just him and his father up there. I don't even know where we are. I know we are near Malvern but I don't know exactly where.'

'The middle of nowhere. I got near the front door before he dragged me back and then I fell. All I could see was forests and fields surrounding the house and a long driveway. I didn't see any other houses. We drove for ages from my house. But I was in the boot so I don't know exactly where we are.'

'Jack drove me here. I wasn't paying attention to where we were going.'

'He drove you here. Voluntarily?'

'He was hiring me for a cleaning job. I got the bus to Malvern and then he picked me up and we drove to his house from there. He seemed like such a lovely man. I can't believe I got it so wrong.'

'Don't beat yourself up. That's how he got me too. He pretended he had fallen over. I almost left him there. God, I wish I'd left him there.'

Isabella was shivering with cold. She only had a thin red raincoat with a yellow T-shirt with Care Bears on it. Her jeans were stained with mud and she was missing one of her Uggs. Even so, she was doing better than Adina who only had her knickers and a thin jumper on. Adina moved closer and tried to share what little warmth she had with Isabella.

Isabella rested her head on Adina's shoulder and they sat in silence, both lost in their own thoughts.

'Adina, why does it smell so badly in here?'

Adina grimaced. Isabella was very naïve and seemed not to have a grasp on the situation. 'Over in the corner is the bathroom. We haven't been given a bucket or anything so...'

282

Isabella looked nauseous.

'How am I supposed to go to the bathroom with jeans on? I can't take them off with my hands behind my back?'

'Isabella, I think you have bigger things to worry about than going to the bathroom, don't you?' Adina said through gritted teeth. She wasn't going to see her daughter again and this girl was more concerned with not soiling herself.

'How long have you been here?' Isabella asked. Adina recalled asking Dan the exact same question. Adina took a deep breath and decided to be honest. It wasn't fair to hide the gravity of the situation from Isabella. She would need to prepare mentally, just as much as Adina was trying to.

'I have no idea. I know that it was Monday when I arrived here. But I've lost track of the days. When I got here, there was someone else here.'

'Someone else?' Isabella squeaked. 'Who?'

'His name was Dan. I think he was Jack's first victim.'

'Dan? Where is he?' Isabella was looking around the room as if she had missed someone, as if they had been hiding from her.

'He's gone.'

'He escaped?' Isabella was looking at her with such hope that Adina almost couldn't answer her.

'No. Jack came, dragged him out of the cellar and I haven't seen him since.'

'So he could have escaped. Or Jack changed his mind and let him go.' Adina shook her head sadly.

'When I asked Jack where he was, he just said the same place I would be going.'

'No. You don't know that. He could have been lying.'

Adina didn't bother replying. They both lapsed back into silence, Isabella fidgeting as her arms tried to adjust to being behind her back. She wanted to tell her they would soon go numb but found herself unable to speak. The hopelessness of their situation was oppressive. Adina was ashamed. She couldn't look at Isabella. Scared that she might work out what Adina was thinking, that she was really glad that she was not alone anymore.

CHAPTER FIFTY

The laptop lay open on the table in front of him, a sign on the screen saying that the account had been logged out due to inactivity. He had checked out Adina's bank balance and what she said was true. There was a meagre amount of money in there. Each month she played with the limits of her overdraft, depositing only small amounts in cash each week. Her bills were astronomical and any transactions appeared only to be for food.

When his father came in from the church, he had tried to talk to him about his concerns, not realising the fury he was about to engender.

'Father, I think I've made a mistake.'

'What do you mean? What mistake?'

'With Adina. I don't think she is the one I was meant to punish.'

'But you told me you heard her bragging. That she was working people to the bone and taking all the profits.'

'She was lying, Father. She said she was making it up to impress her sister.'

His father took a seat at the table. He was quiet for a

moment, his hands steepled and his head resting on the tips of his fingers.

'How do you know she isn't lying now? She would say anything to get out of here alive.'

'But I checked her bank account, she gave me the password. She has no money.' He gestured to the screen, urging his father to look at it.

'She could have another account. These people are master manipulators, son. You know that.'

Jack shook his head emphatically. 'No, Father. I believe her. I think she is telling the truth.'

'Well. It doesn't really matter if she is, does it?'

'Of course it matters. The Lord has charged me with exterminating and punishing the guilty, the greedy, the evil of this world. If she isn't one of them then I have no choice but to let her go.'

'Are you really that stupid?' His father gaped at him, a look of incredulity spread across his face. The condescension hit him like a hammer. Jack didn't reply. Just stared at his father, feeling hurt and confused.

'It doesn't matter if the stupid bitch is innocent or not. You cannot let her go.'

'Why not?'

Jack's father stood up abruptly. 'Why not? Why not!' he shouted, looking at Jack like he had just said the earth was flat. He prowled towards him, bending down and putting a hand on each arm of the chair, bringing his face right up to his.

'Listen to me, boy. What do you think the first thing that woman will do if you let her go?' He straightened up and walked away, turning back to speak again. 'Say you drive her back to her house, reunite her with her daughter. What is the first thing that she is going to do, the minute you drive away? Come on, tell me.'

'But I could reason with her, Father. Convince her not to say anything. She will be so grateful I haven't killed her that she will keep my secret. I'll sit her down and explain it. Make sure she understands the importance of our mission. That it's God's work. Once she understands that, she won't say anything. I'm sure of it.'

Jack tried to convey his confidence in the plan in his voice. But a small voice inside was telling him his father was right. After what he had done to her already, would he really be able to guarantee her silence? Jack was trying to ignore that voice because he did not think his soul could tolerate killing another innocent person. Susan's face rose in his mind. Her ghost was haunting him.

Everywhere he went, her spirit appeared to be following him. When he turned too quickly he was sure he had caught sight of her in his peripheral vision. As he ran a bath, he could see her outline in the steam filling the room. He smelt her pungent perfume when he woke up in the morning. Killing Susan had poisoned his soul. A virus in his blood that was slowly driving him mad until finally it killed him. Only his will to complete God's work was diluting the poison for now. If he killed another innocent person, did he even deserve to live? Could he call himself God's soldier if he was killing as many innocent people as guilty? It would make him just as bad as those that he was eradicating.

'I can't–' He took a deep breath. 'I can't kill another innocent person, Father. I have to let her go.'

His father was incandescent with rage.

'You are a useless, good-for-nothing idiot. I knew I should have got rid of you the minute you were born.' Jack couldn't look at him. Choosing instead to stare at his knees while his father paced around the room. Apoplectic with rage to the extent that all his veins were bulging.

'I should have taken you outside, got a bucket and drowned you. I knew as soon as I laid eyes on you that you were pathetic. So tiny and weak. Not the young strapping boy that I should have had.'

'Father, I'm sorry.' Jack felt miserable. His father's words more cutting now than when his father had whipped him with his belt. Just when he thought he was making progress. He had ruined everything, let him down.

'Sorry isn't good enough, boy.'

'I just–'

'I don't want to hear it. You are too weak and pathetic to do what needs to be done.'

'I'm not, Father.'

'I spent your whole life trying to instil in you the importance of following the Lord's word. Of devoting your life to Him.'

'I know, Father. I just–'

'And now you are questioning Him? You have the audacity to think you know better than the Lord Almighty? The man who created the earth and all the creatures in it?'

'I didn't say that–'

'The Lord had spoken to you, boy. He charged you with the most important task. More important than anything. Has he not shown you the way every single day?'

'Yes,' Jack mumbled. Shame consumed him.

'Do you know how lucky you are? To have the Lord following you, protecting you, trusting you to carry out this most sacred work?'

'I know. But–'

'But nothing!' His father slapped him forcefully around the back of his head. Not expecting the blow, his head was propelled forwards and smacked into the table.

'Do you think Elsie would be proud of you? This weak, snivelling weasel?'

'Elsie was a good person. She would want me to let Adina go.'

'No, son. That is your cowardice talking. Elsie was a religious woman who followed the word of God. She was murdered by human sin. If she knew that you had been chosen to carry out the work of God she would be here now, screaming at you to stop being so pathetic. To avenge her death and purge the world of human scum.'

The tears fell unbidden. Jack knew that his father was right. Elsie was murdered. Her death needed to be avenged.

'Did we not agree,' continued his father, 'that Elsie was taken from you, so that her loss would give you the strength to do what had to be done?'

'Yes,' answered Jack. His head was bowed, he couldn't look at his father. His temples throbbed in pain as thousands of thoughts collided and crashed in his mind.

'Well, where is that strength? Are you going to do what has to be done? To honour your wife's death. Or maybe you didn't love her as much as you said you did?'

It was as though a match had been lit and ignited the rocket of his rage. Jack grabbed his father around the neck and slammed him against the kitchen wall with such force that the cross that was hung there fell to the floor. Jack's nose was inches from his father's and he wanted nothing more than to slam his fist into his father's smiling face.

'Don't you ever question my love for Elsie again,' he said through gritted teeth, trying to hold back the paroxysm of anger that was straining to escape. It wanted nothing more than to punch, kick and tear at his father's body until it was a soup of bones, blood and flesh on the floor, unrecognisable as a person. It was the same anger he had felt when Susan had accused Elsie of having an affair. A red mist clouded his vision but Jack was breathing heavily, fighting back the anger, unwilling to lose control once more. That was not who he was. This was his father. He could not kill his father. That would be unthinkable.

Jack kept repeating this until his anger reduced from boiling to simmering. He let go of him and stormed out of the room. His father had not flinched. He had grinned at him the whole time, as if this was what he wanted. Jack stood outside the house, breathing in the cold air. Looking around at the frost that was melting under the glare of the winter sun.

Jack heard his father stop just behind him.

'You know what you have to do, son.'

Jack didn't turn around. He still didn't trust himself not to hurt his father.

'I know.'

And he did. Although he was furious with his father, everything that he had said was true. Elsie died so that he could carry out this sacred work. With every war, there was always collateral damage. He was stupid to think that this was going to be easy. Nothing worth fighting for was ever easy. Jack didn't want anyone to suffer the way he had because of the blight of greed that had poisoned humanity. He would see this through.

Once again, appearing to read his mind, his father stepped forward and grabbed his shoulder.

'Let's get this done.'

CHAPTER FIFTY-ONE

The crashing and screaming she heard upstairs filled her with dread. Isabella had fallen into a fitful sleep and Adina was trying to pretend she was Poppy. It was easier to do when she was asleep. When awake, Isabella swung between self-pity, denial, and a conviction they were going to be rescued. That her husband would realise she was gone and come and find her. Adina had a split second of hope when she realised that Isabella was married, but it shrivelled up and died when she discovered they were separated because Isabella had used up their entire savings buying things for herself to ease her depression.

Adina knew deep down that Isabella had an addiction and needed help. But it was very hard to warm to her when she compared their situations. It was impossible for Adina to understand how someone could spend that much money on crap. If she had that sort of money, there was no way she would fritter it away. She would actually be able to buy decent food for her child. However, the prospect she might be killed any minute was helping her ignore the resentment she felt towards Isabella. They were only four years apart in age but the hand Adina had been dealt meant she was a great deal more mature that her. She reminded herself that at the end of the day, they were only human. People made mistakes. It didn't mean they should be murdered because of it.

They heard something heavy fall to the floor and Isabella awoke with a start. There was silence and they waited with bated breath. But nothing happened. They heard the front door slam. A burst of motivation filled her. She turned to Isabella.

'We need to get out of here. I don't think it will be long until he decides to kill us.' Her determination rose. She couldn't pinpoint what had triggered this. When she had been feeling so hopeless for ages. But she was suddenly aware of the air filling her lungs and had this primal need to ensure that it stayed that way.

'I'm going to turn around and we will try and line our hands up. Try and see if you can undo my rope. I've been trying for days, I might have loosened it a bit.'

'Why do I have to do yours, why can't you do mine?' Isabella asked petulantly. Adina swallowed her next words, sure that calling Isabella a spoilt brat would not help the situation.

'Because I've been trying for days. I might have loosened it a bit,' she repeated. 'Just do it!' she ordered, using her mum voice.

Adina winced as Isabella's long nails scratched at her skin as she tried to undo her rope. White-hot pain shot down her spine as she tried to extend her arms further to give Isabella more leverage.

'It's no good,' Isabella huffed. 'I can't see what I'm doing. They are too tight.'

'Do you want to die in here? Keep trying.' Isabella's face crumpled and Adina relented. 'Here, let me try yours.'

Isabella swivelled around. Adina tried to visualise the knot and pulled as hard as she could but she couldn't get enough purchase on the rope to make any headway. It was infuriating but she refused to give up. Adina conjured Poppy's face each time she could feel herself thinking of stopping. Her fingers were raw from pulling and scratching at the rope.

Isabella had fallen asleep again. Adina had made no progress either and the pain in her fingers finally forced her to stop. She dozed on and off, her head against the wall. She had no idea how many hours had passed until she heard the telltale sound of the door opening. Jack came down the stairs. Isabella stirred. She backed away from Adina as he moved closer to them. He reached Adina and she cringed as his arms wrapped around her. She felt the bindings around her wrists come loose and a cry of pain escaped her as her arms returned to their natural position.

Adina looked at Jack, trying to get a clue as to why he had untied her. He then unbound her legs and passed her the jeans he had taken. Watching as she dragged them over her legs. Wincing as the rough material grazed her swollen kneecaps.

Adina stared up at Jack, terrified. Why was he doing this? With Dan, he had carted him off over his shoulder. A look of revulsion on his face. But Jack seemed to be looking at her with an expression of pity. Remorse in his eyes. Adina tried to stand up, but days of sitting in one position with only centimetres of water to keep her alive had weakened her. Her legs couldn't hold her up, they shook uncontrollably and black spots appeared in her vision. She felt herself falling but before she could hit the ground strong arms encircled her waist. Jack slowly helped her to her feet. His grip was gentle as he guided her to the bottom of the staircase.

'What about me?' screeched Isabella. 'Don't leave me here!' Adina saw Isabella shuffling over to them. She reached to the bottom of the stairs and Jack's body turned. He kicked Isabella hard in the face. The force sent her reeling onto her back. Blood spurted from her nose and she howled with pain. Adina's heart lurched. She wanted to go to her, knowing Isabella couldn't even wipe the blood away because her hands were bound. But Jack was leading her up the stairs. She did not know why, but as she looked up at Jack, she saw no malice in his eyes. Was it possible? Did she dare even dream that she was going to be freed?

At the top of the stairs, Jack opened the doors and the bright lights were blinding Adina. The light in the cellar was a dull yellow that did not excel at its purpose and she had become used to seeing very little. Her eyes could not tolerate the vibrancy of the colours around the room. The smell hit her as she stood, surveying the house she had been held captive in. Her mouth filled with saliva as the delicious aroma of a roast beef tickled her taste buds. How long had it been since she had last eaten?

Jack led her over to the long kitchen table. It was one of those traditional farmhouse oak tables that dominated the room. Adina's mouth dropped open as she saw it was laden with food. Her eyes were drawn to the huge roast beef, sitting on a serving dish surrounded by a wreath of roasted potatoes, carrots and parsnips. Bowls of Yorkshire puddings, stuffing, cabbage, and pigs in blankets were crammed onto the table. There were three place settings; a napkin, cutlery and a wine glass bordering a black table mat. Jack pushed Adina gently into a seat and moved over to the kitchen worktop. He brought back a jug full of water and poured it into her glass.

Jack glanced out of the window as he sat down.

'Let's eat. I don't think Father is going to join us. He doesn't agree with my decision.'

Jack stood once more and began to carve the beef. Adina's stomach rumbled with hunger, she felt weak with desire. She wanted to open her mouth and inhale every single piece of food on the table. Not wasting time with biting and chewing, she just wanted to eat and have the feeling of being full. She had never seen so much food. Long gone were the days when she could afford a feast such as this. It occurred to her that the food had distracted her from her situation. Should she try and escape? Looking at the back door, she wondered what the chances were that it was unlocked. Jack followed her gaze and shook his head, a sad expression on his face.

'It's locked, Adina. There is no point trying to escape. Just enjoy your meal and then we will talk.' His voice was kind and he was once more the gentle old man she had first met. Gone was the man that took pleasure from torturing her. Jack picked up a plate from the side and filled it with food, gently drizzling gravy over the top. He placed the plate in front of Adina and then filled his own plate. He looked out of the window once more, before shaking his head and sitting down.

'Dig in,' he said.

Adina looked down at the food. She wanted to eat. The need was visceral. But she needed answers. She needed to understand what the hell was happening here. Jack appeared to read her mind as he answered her unspoken question.

'I promise, we will talk once you've eaten. Please, just eat.'

Adina picked up her knife and fork. A brief thought of using it as a weapon rose in her mind. Maybe she could hide it after she had eaten. She was about to cut into the slice of beef when Jack interrupted her.

'But first, let us pray.'

He bowed his head and she hastily copied, putting down her cutlery.

'Lord, bless this food to our use, and us to thy service. Fill our hearts with grateful praise. Amen.'

Jack looked at Adina expectantly.

'Amen,' she muttered. It felt fraudulent. She had understood people with faith. After the life she had had, there was no room for anything but survival. But she was sure non-cooperation was not an option.

When the beef entered her mouth her senses exploded in pleasure. With a ferocity she couldn't control, Adina stuffed forkful after forkful into her mouth. It was pure ecstasy. Jack chuckled quietly and placed a warning hand on her arm.

'Careful, Adina. You haven't eaten in a long time. You don't want to be sick.'

He was right, already her stomach was rolling uncomfortably. Unused to digesting anything apart from her own body for the last few days. It was panicking at the sudden appearance of a whole roast dinner. Adina picked up her glass of water and sipped at it. Waiting for her stomach to settle. Jack ate quietly, looking out the window every few minutes. Apparently hoping his father would change his mind and come to dinner.

Adina picked at her food, fighting the urge to pick up the plate, open her mouth wide and let the food slide in. It was the best meal she could remember having in years. Although, her opinion might be skewed given she hadn't eaten in days. It was quite likely he could have given her cold pea soup and she would have thought it a culinary masterpiece. Jack emptied his plate and rubbed his stomach. He smiled over at Adina and touched her hand. It was almost fatherly the way he was looking at her.

'Have you had enough?' he asked.

A sudden feeling of fear rippled through her. Reminding her she wasn't at a friend's house for dinner. She was eating with the person that had held her captive for the past few days and hurt her whenever he felt like it. Who had revelled in her suffering and probably killed Dan. Her mind had been clouded by the lure of the food. Now she was full, the real danger of her situation hit her once more.

Jack took her arm and led her to the sofa in the lounge. The fire was crackling and the smell of woodsmoke filled the air. After a hearty meal, it would have been easy to have fallen asleep to the mesmeric sound of the fire. But sitting next to a murderer was an antidote to her fatigue. Adina's mind was racing. Could she pick up that poker fast enough to hit Jack with it? He was in a genial mood now, but if she tried to hurt him, he would almost certainly kill her. Was her best hope to try and reason with him?

Jack sat on the sofa opposite hers. The old-fashioned print hanging on the wall and the flat cushions made the room feel like she had stepped back in time. There was no television and only an old-fashioned radio on a shelf by the fire. Modernity was not welcome here. He leant his arms on his knees and looked at her.

'Adina. Can I just apologise for how I have treated you these last few days?'

The words were hard to absorb. Of all the things she was expecting her captor to say, this was not one of them. Jack continued; his eyes filled with sincerity. She could sense no trick or deception.

'I feel that I owe you an apology and an explanation.' He looked out of the window; the sky was darkening, a beautiful pink hue on the clouds. *Red sky at night, shepherd's delight.* The words came to her automatically. Would she be alive to see the next day?

'This is really hard for me to talk about. But you deserve to know.' He clenched the arm of the sofa, as if fighting back tears. His eyes were watery in the light of the fire. It was too hot. The heat of the flames was cooking the right-hand side of her body. It was an uncomfortable feeling but she didn't want to break the spell. She needed to hear what Jack was going to say. To understand why he was doing this to her. And most importantly of all, what he was going to do next.

'My wife…' Jack's voice broke and he coughed, took a deep breath and began again. 'My wife, Elsie.' The way he said her name told her that theirs was a great love. The depth of his feelings for his wife imbued in just one word. 'We were married for thirty-seven glorious years. Until she died on Black Friday.' Anger pulsed in his voice as he spoke of her demise. 'She was killed. Right in front of me. By the most disgusting, depraved people in this world.' Jack was almost spitting with revulsion as he spoke. 'I-I watched her die. Right before my eyes.' The tears were back. Adina's own emotions seemed to see-sawing; one minute she felt desperately sorry for him and the next she was cowering at the ferocity lighting up his eyes.

'After her death, I was bereft. I wanted to kill myself, to end the grief that was slowly killing me. But then my father helped me realise that everything happens for a reason. The Lord never gives us more than we can handle. He helped me to see that Elsie's death whilst cruel and devastating, happened for a reason.'

Adina looked at him in confusion. Not sure she was liking where this was heading.

'Elsie was taken from me by the greedy, gluttonous scum of humanity. And she was taken from me in this way to give me the strength I needed to carry out the Lord's mission.' He looked at Adina with passion in his eyes, he was begging her to understand. 'The Lord has charged me with eradicating gluttony from the world. With punishing the sinful, that put their own needs and desires above others. Those who live their lives committing sin without repenting. I have to remove their stain from humanity before it causes an epidemic. Before there are more greedy, evil people in the world than there are kind and good.'

The way he was looking at her, it was like he was expecting her to agree with him. To say she completely understood and was happy to join in and help. But Adina had no idea what she could say. She actually felt sorry for him. It was obvious that his grief had sent him crazy. He had had some kind of psychotic breakdown. What exactly do you say to someone like that? Do you agree with their delusion? Would that help her escape? Maybe this was good for her. If he was deluded enough to think the Lord was talking to him, then maybe he would believe her when she said she wouldn't tell anyone if he let her go. But his father must be even more crazy, given this was his idea. She looked out the window, terrified he might come inside. He sounded more deluded than Jack. At least Jack kind of had an excuse, he had lost his wife and it had made him lose his mind. But what were his father's reasons for doing this?

'The Lord has been showing me the way. He has been giving me signs of who I should be targeting. But I am afraid I made a mistake when it came to you.' Jack reached for her and took her hand. She stared at her hand in his, then looked back up at him.

'I overheard that conversation you had and jumped to the wrong conclusions. Granted you should not have lied. This would never have happened if you had not lied. But I can understand how you might be driven to tell a white lie. And I believe that you are sorry and have been punished enough. I think you are a good person, Adina. I am sorry for the pain that I have caused you. Just know, I was doing the Lord's work. It was not my intention to hurt an innocent. I am not that person. Can you forgive me?'

Adina couldn't speak. She felt like she was on a tightrope a thousand feet in the air with certain death one wrong move away. She nodded at Jack and his eyes lit up and he beamed at her.

'I knew you would understand. Father didn't think you would. He said you would think I was crazy but I just knew if I sat you down and explained it all you would understand.'

'Are you going to let me go?' As soon as she said the words, she knew it was a mistake. Disappointment flashed across his face and he let go of her hand.

'I thought you understood.' He glared at her accusingly. She had to fix this. She wracked her brains for the magic words that would put a smile back on his face. That would un-sign her death warrant.

'I do understand. I know that your mission is really important. That God has given you a really important task. But you just said that I am innocent. That I don't deserve to be punished. So surely that means you have to let me go?'

Jack sighed and stood up. He looked down at her, his expression regretful.

'No, Adina. I have to kill you.'

'Kill me.' Just saying the words sounded ludicrous. Words she never thought she would say in her entire life. An uncontrollable bubble of laughter burst from her. This was ridiculous. She must be in some sort of dream.

'I have to, Adina. I can't let you go. My mission is too important to risk that you might tell someone. I cannot take a chance that you might be lying to me. That as soon as I let you go, you will call the police and tell them all about me. Which means I have no choice, Adina.' He knelt down in front of her, like a parent trying to make a child understand something important. 'It will be a good death, Adina. I won't let you suffer. You've had a nice meal and now you're going to drift off to sleep. A permanent sleep.'

'But I have a child. She needs me,' Adina cried. Tears cascaded down her face.

'I know you have a child. But children are resilient.

Sacrificing your life will ensure that she grows up in a world unblemished by depravity and sin. Isn't that worth it? To know your daughter will be untouched by sin. You'll be rewarded, Adina. You will be welcomed into the Lord's arms. You will have eternal life. And when it is time, you will see your daughter again. Have no fear.'

Adina suddenly pushed Jack's shoulder with all her weight. He fell flat on his back, unbalanced by her unexpected attack. In a split second she reached for the poker and raised it above her head. Before she could bring it down on his head, Jack roared and tackled her around the waist. She tried to swing the poker down on his back but it glanced off him. Adina bucked and kicked and screamed at him. She would not die. She would escape and get back to Poppy. Jack pinned her to the sofa. He grabbed each of her wrists and used his legs to trap her legs. Once he had secured her in place, he pushed himself up so his face was inches from hers.

'I guess Father was right. I was a fool.'

His hands grasped her neck and squeezed. Instinctively, she tried to prise his hands away from her throat. She looked up into his eyes, trying to beg him to stop. She was stunned to see he was crying. Almost as quickly as he had started, Jack stopped squeezing. He looked at his hands like they had been burned. Was he going to let her go after all?

'Susan,' he mumbled.

Adina had no time to react before she was picked up and flung over his shoulder. She was marched back down into the pit of hell: the cellar.

CHAPTER FIFTY-TWO

Jack was fed up with his father being right all the time. He had been so sure he could convince Adina that her sacrifice was a vital part of his mission. That she would willingly accept it in order to ensure a better world for her daughter. But he had been a fool. She had no faith, there was no way she was going to understand the bigger picture. If you had no understanding of eternal life then how could you willingly embrace death? Having faith meant you knew that this life was just a waypoint, not the main event. Even so, he was not going to strangle her. He couldn't do that again. Jack would continue with his original plan. Adina would just be an unwilling participant instead. He could adapt for that.

As he laid Adina back down on the cellar floor, he reached for the ropes he had left behind when he'd untied her. She kicked and screamed as he tried to tie her arms, like a feral cat. It took all his strength to subdue her. He winced inwardly as he slammed her head against the concrete floor. She went very quiet and still, dazed. Tying her hands behind her back, he left her legs free this time. Confident she would be unable to escape.

He turned and left the cellar to find his father. It was time to move on. He found his father in the church.

'You were right, Father. It is time to end this. Tonight.'

As they walked back into the kitchen, Jack's mobile was ringing. He looked at the screen and saw the reverend's name. His finger hovered over the send-to-voicemail button but he answered. Better to get it over with. He was sure the reverend was just checking in. If he didn't answer the reverend might decide to track him down. He couldn't have that.

'Hello, Reverend.'

'Hello, Jack. How are you?'

'I'm bearing up in the circumstances.'

'I just wanted to check how you are. I thought I might see you at Sunday service. But no one has seen anything of you. We are all worried about you, Jack.'

'I'm sorry, Reverend. I'm staying with my father. It's too painful being in the village. Too many memories.'

'I can understand. But don't stay away too long. Memories are painful but they are what we have left when someone we love leaves us. They will soon become your most treasured possessions. Plus, it would be good for you to be around people that love and care about you. It will help you move on.'

'Thank you, Reverend. You are very kind. I'm just not ready yet. I will be. Just not yet.'

'Okay. Well I am always here to talk to.'

'Thank you.'

'Oh, before I go. You've not heard from Susan recently, have you? No one has seen anything of her and we are all starting to get concerned. She was supposed to be at the church today and never showed. Very unlike her.'

It was like the floor had disappeared and he was falling through the air. He couldn't breathe. Susan's face, her eyes almost bursting from their sockets as he strangled her. The phone slipped in his hands.

'Jack? Jack? Can you still hear me?'

'Yes, Reverend. Sorry, the signal is a bit patchy here. No, I've not heard anything from her. I'll let you know if I do. She might be visiting one of her sons?'

'Hmm. Maybe. I might give them a call tomorrow and see if they know where she is. Failing that I've got a spare key so I'll go over if I still can't get hold of her.'

CHAPTER FIFTY-THREE

J ack spent the rest of the day preparing. Once he was ready, he headed to the cellar. Each step down the stairs strengthened his resolve. He had to end this now and move on. Jack had no idea where he was going to go but he knew that both he and his father had to leave. They couldn't stay here, not now the reverend was asking questions. He had been so lost in his grief and shame over what he did to Susan that he had not stopped to realise that she was bound to be missed. She was considered a founding member of Winterford. No one could really remember what life in the village was like without her. Yes, she was extremely annoying, interfering and loud, but deep down, Jack knew she was also a kind, generous Christian woman. People would notice when she wasn't around to spread gossip, like a farmer spreading seeds in their fields. The village needed her in order to grow.

Reverend Sam wouldn't be the only one looking in Jack's direction soon. His mission was not restricted to Worcestershire, he could travel anywhere and find people that he needed to take care of. The virus of gluttony had spread nationwide, he would not be short of targets. The only difficulty Jack could foresee was convincing his father to leave.

His father was born in this house. He had ruled his family and nurtured his relationship with God from here. The body of his mother was buried in the land that they owned. A Danvers son or daughter not living here would be unfathomable for his father. But his father was the one that had been telling him over and over again that this mission was too important to let anything get in the way. Surely he would understand that it was necessary. An awful thought struck him; what if his father decided to stay? If he told him to leave and carry on without him? Jack wouldn't be strong enough to do that.

At the bottom of the stairs, the women looked up at him, both were crying and staring at him with eyes full of dread. He sensed that they knew this was the end. He could almost smell their fear. Jack avoided looking at Adina, he knew she did not deserve this. But he also knew he had no choice. Despite her failure to understand, he would make sure that she did not suffer. It would be quick and painless.

Jack had brought an extra rope with him and he unwound it from around his waist. Reaching down, he grabbed Adina and forced her to stand up. Keeping an eye on her, in case she bolted for the door, he grabbed Isabella and dragged her to a standing position.

'Get off me, you psycho!' she screeched at him. She looked feral as she bared her teeth at him, her hair messy, her face dirty, covered in blood and dust. Isabella lurched forward at him, spitting with rage. He was going to hit her but the bindings around her legs caused her to lose her balance and she fell on her face. Her bound hands offered no protection and her nose crunched into the floor; the sound echoed around the empty cellar.

Adina cried out and tried to reach for Isabella, but Jack was faster. Disgusted, he heaved the woman to a standing position. Jack was pleased to see that her nose was bleeding profusely. The red blood dripped from her face, staining her clothes. Isabella's face was scrunched up in pain.

'Serves you right,' gloated Jack. Isabella spat at him. Bloody phlegm landed on his shirt. Jack breathed heavily, he wanted to lash out, but in the back of his mind, he knew he had to get on with his plans so that he could work out what his next steps were.

'You disgusting bitch,' he said. Taking the rope from around his waist, Jack tied one end around Adina's waist and one end around Isabella. He pulled the rope as tight as he could around Isabella's waist, satisfied when he heard a hiss of pain as the rope bit into her skin.

Taking the rope dangling from Adina, he took out his penknife. He pressed his face straight in front of Isabella's and hissed at her.

'I'm going to untie your legs, any funny business and the next thing I cut will be your throat.' He put the blade to her throat. He pressed until a bead of blood appeared, coating the tip of the blade.

'Do you understand?'

Isabella nodded her head, the attitude from her had fled when faced with the glinting blade. Jack sawed at the rope until it fell to the floor, freeing Isabella. He watched for a moment, warily. Worrying that she might mess up his plan. He was going to kill her anyway but he didn't want it to be an easy death. She did not deserve that.

Holding the rope dangling from Adina's waist, he pulled them towards the staircase. He kept his knife out in case of trouble. His father was already waiting for them outside. Jack quickened his step, wanting to get this over with. They had to stop a couple of times as Isabella kept falling.

'Get up!'

'If you had wanted me to be able to walk across the countryside maybe you shouldn't have broken my nose and you should have fed me,' she yelled at him, her voice nasal and muffled due to her swollen face. He ignored her and tugged the rope. 'It would be easier for us to walk if our hands weren't tied behind our backs,' she shouted. But Jack just ignored her. He wouldn't rise to it, he just needed to get this over with.

When they reached the clearing, Jack was pleased to see his father was already there, a satisfied smile on his face. Since Jack had announced his plan to get rid of the women tonight, his father had become a lot happier.

Jack led the women to a magnificent elm tree, the gatekeeper of the forest. He pushed Adina up against it and then untied the rope from around Isabella's waist and used it to tie Adina to the tree. In a flash, Isabella turned and ran.

He sighed inwardly and wheeled around.

'There is no point, Isabella,' he called, spreading his arms wide, 'I've lived here my whole life, I know this land like the back of my hand. There is nowhere you can go where I won't find you. You'll never get away. The nearest neighbour is over two miles away. You'll never make it.'

Ignoring him, Isabella continued to run. Her arms still bound behind her back made it look like she was waddling.

'Father, get her.'

But his father didn't move.

'I'll watch her.' His father gestured to Adina.

Jack picked up the shovel that he had left by the side of the grave he had dug for Isabella. He charged after her, but he needn't have wasted so much energy. A few metres away, he found her lying on the floor. She was wriggling like a worm, unable to use her arms to get up. Her knees were failing to get purchase in the wet mud from yesterday's rain, slipping and sliding. He could hear her gasping for breath as she fought to stand.

Just as she managed to get to her feet, Jack brought the shovel down through the air. He aimed at her legs, using the shovel to sweep them out from under her. Isabella slammed to the floor with a satisfying thump.

'You see, Isabella, I have the Lord on my side.' Jack strolled over to Isabella, shouldering the shovel. She groaned as he kicked her onto her back. 'You were identified by the Lord as being sinful, greedy and despicable. I have to kill you, before your depravity hurts more people. Stealing from others. Who knows how much you have taken from your neighbours? You live in a fancy house. Isn't that enough for you? That you have to steal and take what isn't yours? We were put on this earth to love thy neighbour not steal from them. How can you even live with yourself?' Jack spat in her face. His saliva hit her cheek.

Isabella whimpered.

'I'm sorry. I know I did a bad thing. I'll never do it again.'

Jack knelt down.

'No, Isabella, you won't. I am here to make sure of that.'

Jack dragged Isabella back to the clearing by her feet. Enjoying the screams of pain and fear. It was helping him to forget the screams he imagined Elsie would have made. It felt good to be punishing the guilty once more. To know that someone who deserved it was going to pay for their sins. They would be unable to harm anyone else.

Reaching the clearing, he bent down and rolled Isabella into the waiting grave he had carved out of the earth. Her body fell and hit the bottom of the grave with a satisfying thud. Isabella's screams pierced the night. He saw the barbed wire tearing holes in her clothes, drawing blood as it clawed at her skin whilst she struggled to escape.

'Don't do this, Jack,' Adina wailed. 'God wouldn't want you to do this. He is all about forgiveness, isn't he?'

Jack turned his head to look at her, sad that still she wasn't understanding. But then, God had not talked to her, he had not put His faith in her.

'He forgives those that repent.' He pointed down at Isabella who had stopped moving, realising that the more she struggled the more entangled in the barbed wire she became. 'She did not repent. When I took her, she had just stolen something else. She would not have stopped. It would probably have worsened until more and more suffered from her greed. She just had to have more. She had to have what other people had.'

'She doesn't deserve to die for stealing a few parcels,' cried Adina. Jack wheeled around and marched towards her.

'My Elsie did not deserve to die because someone wanted a cheap TV,' he bellowed. 'My Elsie was good and pure. Not like this loathsome, disgusting sinner.' Jack's throat was full of unshed tears and he turned and strode back to retrieve his shovel. When he returned, his father placed a hand on his shoulder, the gesture warming his heart. His look said, *I'm with you, son.* His father stood next to Adina, keeping watch over her. She threw Jack an angry look and continued to struggle pointlessly at the rope pinning her to the tree.

Under the glow of the lamp, Jack dug his shovel into the mound of earth waiting to entomb Isabella. The only sounds in the clearing were the rush of the wind through the trees, Isabella's soft whimpering, and Adina's grunts of frustration as she fought with the rope – and the sound of Jack's shovel crunching into the earth.

Jack had half-filled the grave. Only Isabella's head and torso remained exposed. The soil compacted over her legs, pinning her in place. The callouses on his hands screamed with pain each time he thrust the shovel into the soil. He watched as wriggling, pink worms and black beetles fell off his shovel and into the grave, burrowing back into their home.

Panting, Jack stopped and rested, holding his weight up by leaning on the shovel that he had pushed into the ground. He looked over at his father.

'Father, can you take over for a bit? I'm exhausted.'

Adina was watching him, tears pouring down her face. She looked more terrified than he had ever seen her.

His father shook his head.

'You know that this is your burden to bear. You were the one that was chosen.'

Was that resentment in his eyes? Was he not happy that Jack had been chosen instead of him? Jack dismissed the thought. His father had been the one that realised the message the Lord had sent them. The one who had encouraged Jack to fulfil his destiny. Jack stood upright and ignored the pain detonating throughout his body. The sooner this was done the better. His hands burned with pain. It became hard to grip the shovel as blood was trickling from the blisters on his hands. But he carried on, forcing his brain to focus only on lifting the shovel. Soon all that was left was Isabella's face. Jack stood up and bowed his head. His father did the same.

'Isabella, you are sinful. You are a thief. Your gluttony is a poison that must be lanced from this world. But he that doeth wrong shall receive for the wrong which he hath done.'

Tears poured down her face. She no longer screamed, her breathing was fast and shallow as the soil pressed down on her lungs.

'Please,' she implored him, 'don't do this.'

'For the wages of sin is death. You have sinned. You must die.'

Jack lifted the shovel and tossed the dirt over her face. She coughed and spluttered as the dirt splattered over her, shaking her head in an attempt to dislodge it. Jack threw another shovelful, then pitched two more clumps of soil onto her head, ignoring the sounds of her choking. Isabella disappeared from sight.

Adina let out a scream that shattered the silence of the night. Jack twisted around to look at her.

'It is God's will, Adina. I've told you. Please try and understand.'

CHAPTER FIFTY-FOUR

J ack untied Adina from the tree. She flinched from him,
visibly trembling. He didn't have the energy to care. Ready
for this to be over, he could sleep for a thousand years.

Slowly, Jack and his father led Adina to the clearing where
he had buried Susan. He didn't want Adina's resting place to be
anywhere near Isabella and Beckett's. She deserved better than
that. Just the thought of digging another grave was exhausting. It
wasn't getting any less tiring no matter how much he did it.

Adina was violently shaking as they entered the clearing
and she saw another grave. Hers was not lined with barbed wire.
He had covered it with leaves and plants, a small token of his
respect for her. But judging by the look on her face, it was not
appreciated. Jack turned to Adina. He took the penknife out of
his pocket and cut the bindings on her wrists.

'I promised you a peaceful death and despite your
unwillingness to understand the importance of my task, I will
honour that promise.'

From inside his pocket, he withdrew a bottle of sleeping
tablets and some packets of paracetamol.

'Lie down.'

She didn't move. Frozen in fear. Her eyes darted past him, as if imploring his father to help. Jack sat down and forced Adina to the floor. Pulling her head into his lap for a moment, he was reminded of all the times he had done this with Elsie; when they would sit in the living room, she would rest her head on his lap and watch the television and he would watch her. As he stroked Adina's hair, he let himself pretend she was Elsie. But Adina's sobs ruined the moment and pulled him back into reality.

Jack unscrewed the cap on the sleeping pills and began to pop them into Adina's mouth. She resisted at first but he forced her lips apart and deposited five pills in there. Adina spat them out. Jack sighed. Some people really did not understand what was best for them. He pushed her off his lap and she lay on the floor, staring up at him, her eyes wide with panic. He picked up the pills on the floor and with one hand he prised her mouth open and with the other placed the pills inside. Fixing his hand across her mouth he stroked her throat, hoping to encourage her to swallow. Adina bucked and thrashed against him but he held fast. He watched the horror fill her eyes as she accidentally swallowed. Jack could feel her coughing against his hand but he would not let go; he wasn't going to let her spit out the pills again. His whole body was aching, he craved his bed.

'I don't know why you are insisting on this charade,' said his father. 'She could be dead right now if you had the strength of a real man to do what has to be done.'

Jack felt irritated.

'What does it matter how I do it, as long as I do it,' yelled Jack, his fatigue making him quick to anger. 'Anyway, you don't really get an opinion given that all you have done this whole time is lecture me whilst standing and watching whilst I do all the hard work!'

His father bristled, the veins in his temple bulging.

'How many times have I had to tell you? It is not my place to do any of this. You are the chosen one. I'm just trying to support you. Guide you. It's not my fault you are making everything harder for yourself and not listening to me.'

Jack ignored him. He let go of Adina's mouth to get more pills from the bottle. As he was twisting the lid off, Adina rolled over and was up before he could fully register what had happened. He dropped the bottle to the floor and dived after her. When he was close enough, Jack threw himself forward and tackled her to the ground. He landed hard on top of her. The aches and pains in his body screamed to be acknowledged. Jack took a deep breath and heaved Adina to her feet. His exhaustion was overwhelming him now. He wanted nothing more than to lie down on the ground and sleep. He had had enough.

Jack dragged Adina back into the clearing and she resisted with every step. His father was stood over Adina's grave with a smug grin on his face. Jack shoved Adina down into the grave. He had not wanted to do this again but she was giving him no choice. She kicked at him as he lowered himself on top of her. Straddling her, he placed his hands around her throat. Susan's face flickered in his mind. Revulsion swept through him, but he was just so tired, he needed to go home. He needed this to be over.

Adina clutched at his hands as he squeezed her throat; her eyes were bulging grotesquely and he looked away. He felt her go still. A twig snapped. The hairs on the back of his neck stood up. Jack let go of Adina's neck and stumbled to his feet. Someone was walking towards him.

CHAPTER FIFTY-FIVE

The figure grew closer. A woman. Slim with blonde hair, greying at the roots. Her face like a white wrinkled napkin, she was easily in her seventies. The strangest thing was, she was smiling at him.

'Who are you?' he shouted, feeling territorial and furious that this woman had the audacity to be on his land. The woman didn't respond. She was staring at him intently as if drinking him in. It had started to rain and droplets were splattering through the trees, jumping onto her green coat.

Her face was instantly recognisable to him. But he didn't know why. Where had he seen her before? It was like trying to remember a dream; his recollection of her was slippery and evaded his attempts to capture it. Jack stared at the woman, familiar but unfamiliar with her.

'You are trespassing. You have no right to be here. Leave now.'

The woman just stood and smiled at him. The droplets of rain fleeing from the tree branches were landing on her blonde hair, flattening it to her scalp. Her blue eyes stared straight at him, unflinching.

'Actually, Jack, I think you'll find I have every right to be here.'

The sound of her voice brought him to his knees. He didn't even notice the pain as his knees slammed into the cold, wet earth. Fireworks erupted in his mind as the memories were unlocked. Memories he didn't know he had, as though they had been locked away and her voice was the key.

'Mother,' he gasped.

CHAPTER FIFTY-SIX

I t felt like all the oxygen was being sucked out of the air. He was on his knees, staring at her. She reached for him, falling to her knees and taking his face in her hands. The delicate scent of her hit him and he burst into tears. He didn't care if this was all in his imagination.

'Son, you need to get away from her,' said his father. Jack looked up at him, confused. His father looked wary; he looked at the woman anxiously.

His mother gently pulled his head back so that he was facing her.

'Jack, you need to listen to me. I need you to hear what I am saying. Can you do that?'

Jack nodded.

'This is going to be hard to hear, but I promise you. I am not lying. What I am about to tell you is the truth.' Her voice was like warm honey on a sore throat. He wanted her to keep talking and never stop. He gazed at her, drinking her in.

'Your father is dead.'

He had not really been listening to her, just staring at her and trying to commit every detail to memory. This was obviously his mind playing tricks on him but he didn't care. But then her words penetrated his mind and he reeled backwards. He pulled his face from her hands and stood up, backing away.

'What are you talking about? You're the one that's dead. My father is right there.'

He pointed at his father whose lip was curled back in disgust. He looked minutes away from attacking her.

His mother looked at him sadly.

'There's no one there. The only people in these woods are you, me and this woman.'

His mother glanced down at Adina, a flash of concern on her face. But then her gaze returned to Jack.

'Liar!' roared his father.

'You're lying! Father killed you. This is a test. You're trying to trick me. You're the Devil. You've come to sabotage me,' he said and stepped behind his father, seeking his protection.

'Tell her, Father!' he begged. But his father just stood there, glaring at his wife with such ferocity it was a wonder she did not melt under the force of his gaze.

'Jack, I am not dead. Your father did not kill me.' His mother stepped forward and his father moved out of the way as she stopped in front of Jack and took his hand. She placed it on her chest and he could feel the thump of her heart under the tips of his fingers.

'I escaped, Jack. I ran away from your father. Unable to cope with one more day in that prison.' Tears were streaking her face, working their way down her wrinkles and falling to the ground. 'I am so sorry I left you. But I had no choice. I knew that if I didn't leave I would end up dead. Either by my own hand or by your father's.' She looked down at her feet and when she met his gaze again he could see the shame and agony in her eyes. 'I wanted to take you. I really did, but I spotted an opportunity to escape and I took it. I didn't know if I would ever get the opportunity again. Your father had gone to see a friend. That morning, he'd beaten me black and blue and I think he thought I'd be too weak to do anything. He was confident that he'd find me lying on the kitchen floor when he returned. But I woke up, bleeding and bruised and, realising he was gone, I ran. I escaped him once and for all. But I broke my heart doing it. Because saving my own life meant losing my child.'

The sincerity in her voice and the pain in her eyes captivated Jack. As she spoke, memories of his mother were rising in his mind. His mother putting him to bed with a split lip. Visions of him hiding under the covers whilst his mother's screams reverberated around the house downstairs.

Jack looked over at his father who was staring at them both, obviously enraged but strangely quiet. *Why wasn't he saying anything?*

'I wanted to come back the minute I left. But I knew if I did that your father would kill me. I prayed. I prayed that you would be okay. I made a plan. I was going to wait until you were eighteen and then I would come and find you.'

She stroked his face once more, he felt her need to touch him. He felt it too. He wanted to be wrapped in her arms.

'I came back on your eighteenth birthday. But there was no one here. The house was dusty and the door unlocked. It was exactly like I'd left it. Nothing had changed except it was obvious no one had lived there for a while.'

Jack looked at her in confusion. But his father had lived there. What did she mean, no one was there? He opened his mouth to speak but she raised her hand and continued.

'I went to the village and asked around, trying to see if anyone knew where you were. That's when I found out that you had married Elsie. I was so delighted to find out that you had broken free of your father and found love.' She let go of him and began to pace up and down the clearing. 'I went to your house, I sat on the other side of the street and watched and waited. I saw how happy you were. My heart nearly burst when I watched you together. I agonised over whether to come and see you. But I didn't know where your father was. I was so scared of seeing him again, of what he might do. I didn't want to risk your happiness. I didn't want to do anything to hurt you again. So I stayed away, I went back to my house and tried to live my life, to be content with the knowledge that you were safe and you were happy.

'But fate intervened. I met Elsie at a farmer's market. I saw her and I couldn't resist. I told her who I was and we went for a walk. Sitting on a bench in front of a lake. She told me everything.'

'Elsie?' Jack felt so confused, *Elsie had met his mother?* His head throbbed painfully, this was so much to take in and a part of him wasn't sure what was true anymore. He sank to the floor. His mind boggling at her words. He longed for Elsie.

'I told Elsie why I left and that I was desperate to reunite with you but did not want to cause you any upset. But Elsie told me to stay away.'

'W-why would she do that?' Elsie knew how much he had struggled with his mother's death. How could she have thought he would not want to see her?

'She had a very good reason, Jack. Nothing else would have kept me away. You see' – his mother took a deep breath; she looked apprehensively at Jack – 'Elsie told me that when she met you, you were well and truly under the hold of your father. He had indoctrinated you. Immersed you in his warped view of religion. You worshipped your father almost as much as the Lord himself.

'Elsie realised that your father was a megalomaniac and that she needed to get you away from him if you were ever going to have a life together. But before she could hatch a plan, your

321

father came home early one day and caught you being intimate on the sofa.'

Jack nodded his head. 'I remember, he went mental and he cast me out. I had to go and live with Elsie's family until their family helped us to get our own house after we were married.'

His mother stared at him. Her gaze felt penetrative, like she was trying to see inside his mind.

'Elsie told me that that is what you remember.' His mother bent down in front of him and took his hands. The look she gave him, full of love and affection, it was just like he remembered. 'But, sweetie, that is not what happened. Elsie told me that you were unable to cope with the guilt of what really happened that night. In fact it broke your mind. It fabricated a memory and convinced you that your father was alive.' Jack looked over at his father; he stood there, unmoving, shaking with anger, but still he was not speaking or moving. Why wasn't he moving? Why wasn't he shouting and protesting that what his mother was saying was lies?

'Jack, the night your father caught you and Elsie together, he tried to kill her. He would have succeeded if you hadn't stopped him.' She bit her lip, tears brimming in her eyes again. His mother seemed to be finding the right words.

'Jack, that night, you killed your father.'

'No!' whispered Jack. He stood up, pushing her away. 'Father. Tell her, she's a liar.'

'Your father isn't here, Jack. It's all in your head.'

'Get her, Father. She's a liar. Make her stop!' Jack begged. But his father didn't move. Just stood as though he had been petrified, unable to move.

'Tell her, Father,' Jack begged.

'He can't tell me anything, Jack, because he is dead. He has been dead for thirty-seven years,' his mother said from behind him.

Slumping to his knees in front of his father, Jack pressed the ball of his hands into his eyelids; memories were stirring that he had never seen before. Memories he could not bear to be true.

'Jack. Please. Just think about that night. Let yourself remember what really happened. You know I am telling the truth.'

Jack opened his eyes and looked up at his father.

'Is it true, did I kill you?'

CHAPTER FIFTY-SEVEN

A memory so vivid erupted in Jack's mind and he lay back on the forest floor.

Jack watches in horror as his father grabs Elsie by the hair and throws her to the ground.

'You are a tramp. A whore. Throwing yourself at my son. You are not worthy.'

His father kicks Elsie in the stomach, she doubles over in pain, crying out for Jack's help. He kicks her again. And again. Her cries reverberate through the house. For a minute, Jack is stupefied. He cannot disobey his father. But as his father's hands clasp around Elsie's neck and he sees her terror, it releases him from his paralysis. A fury unfurls in him as he sees blood vessels in Elsie's eyes burst; she looks at him with bloody eyes, begging him to save her.

Jack bellows at his father and runs, the strength of his tackle sends them both rolling onto the living-room floor. Before his father can move, Jack grabs his father by the neck and drags him over to the fireplace. Jack isn't making conscious decisions, acting purely on instinct. The only thought governing him is that he has to make sure his father never hurts Elsie again. His father's head is inches from the eager flames bouncing happily in the hearth. His father's eyes are filled with anger.

'I'm your father. You will obey me!'

But Jack doesn't listen. All he can see is his father trying to kill Elsie. Without any second thought, Jack uses all his strength to plunge his father's head into the flames. His father's screams are piercing and Jack watches emotionless as the yellow flames leap across his father's skin, feeding hungrily. The smell of burning flesh permeates the room but Jack just holds his struggling father's body in place. He is unsure how long it takes. Jack watches as the flesh is melted from his father's head until he can see the bones in his face and what looks like brain matter.

When he is sure he is dead, Jack lets go of his father's body. He turns around to see Elsie clutching her stomach. Angry red marks in the shape of giant fingerprints are a grotesque necklace. She is crying and gasping for air.

Jack picks her up and carries her to his bedroom.

'Stay here,' he instructs.

Returning to the living room, the smell almost causes him to vomit. Holding his breath, Jack pulls his father's body out of the fire. He wrenches his father into a fireman's lift and carries him outside. Jack puts him down in front of the outbuilding and picks up a shovel. He then picks his father back up and takes him to a clearing in the woods.

At the clearing, Jack digs a grave. He is numb. He has no thoughts. It feels like he is being remotely controlled by some unseen entity. His limbs are acting of their own volition. He digs. He has become so lost in the process of digging it could probably fit two bodies, the hole is so deep.

Jack rolls his father's body into the hole and begins to toss the soil back in after him. The repetitive action of filling in the hole stops him from hearing Elsie coming up behind him. When he tosses the last shovelful of soil over his father's grave, Jack sinks to his knees.

'Jack. Are you okay?' asks Elsie. She moves over to him and he feels her hands on his shoulders.

Her touch restores his brain functions and the reality of what just happened floors him. His body convulses as he sobs. He throws himself on top of the grave.

'Father. Father, I'm sorry. What have I done?' he screams. Tears choke him, he can barely breathe. Elsie clings to him, her tears matching his. They lay there until the sun goes down and they are both shivering with cold. Elsie sits up.

'Jack. We have to leave.'

'How can I leave, Elsie? I murdered my father. I have committed a crime. I deserve to die.'

'You saved my life. You have not committed a crime. You saved me.'

Elsie wraps her arms around him and repeats this over and over again, whispering in his ear. Eventually, she gets up and tells him to wait there. After a few minutes, she comes back. Jack stares at her, unsure how they can possibly move on from this.

Elsie proffers her hand.

'Come on. I've cleaned up the mess inside the house. Come home with me. I'll tell my parents you have had a fight with your dad and you are staying with us. They won't suspect anything. No one will as your dad keeps himself to himself.'

Jack stares at Elsie's hand, not able to bring himself to take it. His mind cannot reconcile itself with what he has done. He cannot live with himself after this.

Elsie falls to her knees in front of him, wincing in pain and clutching her stomach.

'Please, Jack. Let's leave this place and go and live our lives together. Do you love me?'

Jack nods his head. Incapable of words. Elsie stands up and once again offers her hand. 'Then get up and come and be with me. Forget this ever happened. Let's leave and be happy.'

The memory faded and Jack was back in the clearing.

His father was gone.

CHAPTER FIFTY-EIGHT

H is mother knelt in front of him, waiting for him to open his eyes. When he did, she smiled sadly.

'I-I remember,' he croaked.

'Elsie told me that the day after it happened, you woke up and she realised you had blocked it from your memory. That you were convinced your father was still alive. Every year, you made her go to Oakdale Farm to have Christmas dinner with your father. She would watch you have heated arguments with him. Elsie was terrified. It was obvious that you were sick. That you were hallucinating about your father. But how could she do anything about it without implicating you in his death? If she took you to a hospital, the truth would come out. So, she kept quiet. You believing he was alive stopped anyone from being suspicious of the truth. So she went along with your delusion. She loved you so much, son. The strength she showed. Putting up with you thinking the man that had tried to kill her was still alive. I only met her a few times but I can see why you loved her. She was an incredible woman. It made me so happy to know that you had found someone who protected you and took care of you when I couldn't.'

His mother's eyes shone with tears. Jack's mind filled with memories. He saw himself, sitting at the table arguing with his father. Only now, revisiting the memory, he realised that he was arguing with no one. With fresh eyes, he saw the tears in Elsie's eyes and the way she kept her head bowed. The plates empty. As his father had not been alive to cook the meal. His mind felt like it was fracturing; one minute he could picture his father there. But then the picture changed and he was shouting at thin air.

'She loved you so much. That night, when your father kicked her, it caused damage to her uterus. She lost her ability to have children that night. But still, she stood by you. It was the type of love I wished I could have had with your father.'

Jack's heart broke. The revelation of how much Elsie had loved him, the depths she had gone to protect him was breaking him. He wanted to talk to her. To thank her. His heart was fracturing as he felt like he had lost her all over again. Jack threw himself into his mother's arms and cried. He felt her tears falling onto his neck. Elsie had always wanted to be a mother. But his father had taken that from her. Anger stopped his tears. He wanted his father to come back so he could kill him again. Once wasn't enough.

Sensing his anger, his mother drew back to look at him, gripping his hands in hers.

'I've been following you, Jack. Ever since I learned of Elsie's death. I knew that it would have been devastating for you. I only had Elsie's insight into your marriage but I knew that your love was strong. To have that taken away when you were already unstable was only going to destabilise you further. I watched you, I followed you. Waiting for the right moment to talk to you. But when I realised what you were doing. When I–' His mother put her hand to her mouth, swallowing back her tears.

'When I heard you talking to your father I was scared. I

should have done something. I should have told someone. But I didn't. I was weak. Just like I was when I ran away from you and left you in the hands of your father. I watched and agonised over what to do. I didn't know how to help you without making things worse. I don't want you to go to prison. To suffer more than you already have. I don't want you locked up, all alone. But then I saw Adina's sister appealing for her safe return on the TV. When I realised you had her, I knew I had to act. I should have acted sooner.'

Jack's mind was reeling. Then it hit him. The woman at the post office. He remembered he had been struck by a feeling of recognition.

'The post office?'

His mother nodded, her face sorrowful. She ran a hand down his face. 'I was about to tell you who I was then. I saw the recognition in your eyes. But I ran away. I was scared. I didn't know how you would react. I couldn't find the right words. I panicked and ran. If only I hadn't. None of this would have happened. I knew I had to help you. But I didn't know how. You'd already suffered the loss of Elsie. Would it have been fair to have you committed?'

Everything he thought he knew was wrong. His brain felt like it was on a rollercoaster, he didn't know what twist or turn was coming next. He couldn't think straight. Memories were throwing themselves at him: his father was standing over him, lowering the door onto him to trap him in the hole. But then his father was gone and it was himself that was lowering the door; his father locking him in the church. But then he saw his own hand turning the keys in the lock; his father had been standing on the roof of the hospital, telling him not to jump. But then no, he was standing alone. Talking to himself. His memories were scrubbing all traces of his father. He was never there. But he had been. How could he not be? No. Jack hit himself on the head.

Over and over. Trying to knock some sense into himself, to work out what was real. He couldn't trust his own mind. His mother reached for his hand and held it tight.

'Jack, you have to stop. You need to hand yourself in. You need help.'

'N-No, I was chosen. Elsie died so that I would be strong–'

'No, Jack,' she interrupted. 'That is just a lie your mind has made to help you deal with Elsie's death. To give you a way to cope. Elsie died. It was a tragic accident, not a sign from God.'

'No! You are wrong!' he roared. This could not be true. If that was true, then he was a murderer. He was not a murderer; he was God's disciple. Ridding the world of evil. Jack turned, looking for his father, needing his reassurance and support. But he was gone. Then he remembered what his father had done to Elsie and anger at his father flooded his system. Jack's brain was pulsating. He was being assaulted by memories and varying emotions. He wanted to scream. But he needed his father. No, he hated his father. No that wasn't right. His father helped him grieve for Elsie. He was a good man.

'You got rid of him. How could you do that? You've taken him away from me. Father! Father! Come back!' Jack blundered around the clearing, searching desperately for him. His mother was lying. His mind was lying. She was poisoning his mind.

'He's not coming back, Jack. Not now you know the truth. You killed him, like you killed all the others. You need help, Jack. This has got to stop.'

Jack lumbered back towards her.

'No! Stop saying that! It's not true!' His hands were around her neck before he knew it. He squeezed hard, needing her to shut up. Her eyes were swelling in their sockets. She looked up at him with such pity.

'I'm s-s-sorry, J-Jack,' she choked.

The gunshot spooked all the birds from the trees. He

looked up and watched them fleeing the sound. It was only when he looked down, that he saw the blood spreading across his white shirt. His hands dropped from around his mother's neck and he clutched his stomach instinctively.

His mother was staring at him, fresh tears tracking down her face. He looked down and saw the gun in her hand. His father's gun. She'd stolen his father's gun.

'You shot me,' he said. Staring at her in disbelief. He just had time to wonder why he felt no pain, when his legs lost all feeling and he felt himself falling. The world began to swim in and out of view.

He saw Elsie standing over him. She was smiling at him. He watched as she knelt down and stroked his face. There were tears in her eyes. Her beautiful brown hair shone and she was wearing a pure white cotton dress.

'Elsie. I'm sorry. I love you.' He tasted blood in his mouth and felt it trickling down his face.

'Shh, Jack. Don't talk. Be at peace,' whispered Elsie. She reached out and closed his eyelids. Jack inhaled her smell and basked in the feel of her skin against his. Before the world went black...

CHAPTER FIFTY-NINE

When Jack's hands had been around her throat, she had been sure she was going to die. The world around her dissolved and her last thought had been of Poppy. When she had regained consciousness, a woman was talking to Jack. Adina listened as hard as she could. The more she heard the more everything made sense. She thought back to all those times he had 'spoken' with his father. Adina had presumed he was communing with the Lord. But now she thought about it, she recalled him looking right at someone.

Jack's mother was trying to talk him down, to save Adina's life. She slowly adjusted her position so that Adina was able to see what was happening. Jack was lost in his conversation with his mother, screaming for his father. When he lurched at his mother and grabbed her around the neck, Adina was about to go and help her when the sound of a gunshot blasted through the clearing.

Jack's mother had cried out as Jack collapsed to the ground. She cradled him to her. Adina clambered out of the grave. Slowly, she crept towards them. The woman looked up at her,

her eyes full of pain. Blood had bubbled out of Jack's mouth. He was unmistakably dead.

'It's all my fault. I shouldn't have left,' Jack's mother murmured. She cradled Jack's head, stroking his hair. Tears flooding from her eyes.

'I'm so sorry,' Adina said.

The woman started. She twisted around to look at Adina.

'You need to leave.'

'Come with me.' Adina held out her hand.

'No. I'm not leaving him. I'm exactly where I need to be.' A bad feeling rose in Adina's chest.

'Go!' yelled the woman.

Adina's insides went cold. She needed to find Isabella. But if she left, she was pretty sure this woman was going to kill herself. She still had the gun in her hand.

'You don't have to do this. It isn't your fault. I heard everything.'

'I can't live with this, Adina. The knowledge that I brought this man into the world and he killed all these innocent people. I just can't. You heard me. I could have intervened earlier. I wish I had. But I did nothing. Their deaths are on my hands. I've made so many poor decisions. It's about time I made a good one. Now listen, I called the police when I went to the farmhouse to get the gun. I told them everything. They should be here any minute.' She looked at Adina, eyes begging. 'I'm an old woman, I may have left Jack's father but in my mind I never escaped. I have no family, no friends. Nothing. Please just go. Let me end a lifetime of misery.' The pain in the woman's voice visceral. Adina made a split-second decision. She had to help Isabella. She turned and ran. The sound of the gunshot blasted through the trees, chasing yet more birds from the forest.

Adina tore through the field, tripping over branches and rocks, slipping through the mud until she reached Isabella.

Throwing herself onto the grave, she ripped at the soil covering Isabella's face. She had no sense of time and didn't know if there was any hope the girl could still be alive. Her arms burned and her hands windmilled as she ripped huge handfuls of soil away. Adina's fingers scratched at skin and she knew she was close. Adina heard sirens just as she revealed Isabella's face. Her skin was deathly white.

Voices rang out and Adina screamed for help, the sound bouncing off the trees. She got up and ran to the edge of the clearing, relief seeping through her as she saw the fluorescent jackets of the emergency services. A young woman came up to her.

'Are you okay?'

Adina pointed to Isabella. 'Forget me, you have to save her.'

The woman ran over to the grave and started digging frantically. More people joined her and Isabella was lost from Adina's sight. A young man in a green-and-yellow uniform led Adina away from the clearing. The adrenaline was fading. Adina realised that Jack's mother must have rescued her for she couldn't recall climbing out from her barbed-wire grave. She only hoped that Isabella could be saved in the same way. She closed her eyes for a few seconds; she felt like she could collapse at any moment.

It was only when she was sitting in the back of the ambulance that Adina started to laugh. It had started with a bubble of giggling until she was laughing hysterically, her sides heaving. She couldn't believe she was still alive. The events of the last few days felt so farcical. Shaking with laughter, she felt like she was cracking up.

Adina apologised fervently to the young paramedic but she held up a hand to stop her.

'Don't worry, it's just your mind trying to cope with the trauma. I can only imagine what you've been through.' She examined her, cleaning her cuts and bruises, helping her out of her soiled knickers. A testament to her professionalism that she didn't recoil at the disgusting mess. She helped her into a hospital gown and proceeded to stick wires and monitors to her.

A voice from outside had her stumbling to her feet. She pulled off the wires and jumped out of the ambulance, ignoring the protests of the paramedic.

Poppy sprang into Adina's arms and they sank to the floor. Adina breathed in the scent of her daughter and fresh tears fell from her eyes. All those times in the cellar, she had dreamed of this moment. Never believing it could ever happen. They stayed that way, both of them crying. Poppy's fingers dug into Adina's skin. Adina was never going to let go. She pulled back, she needed to look at her beautiful daughter's face. Poppy's eyes were filled with tears. She was smiling and crying. Adina wiped away the tears.

'I love you so much, baby bear.'

They held each other again until a voice interrupted them.

'Adina!'

Her sister was staring at her, with a look that Adina had never seen before. Love. Her sister's eyes were red from crying.

Poppy whispered in Adina's ear. 'Aunty Scarlett has been looking for you, Mummy. She put out a reward, she's been out on the streets handing out missing posters. She's even been on the TV and radio.'

Adina stood up and holding Poppy's hand, walked over to her sister. Scarlett threw her arms around Adina, almost knocking her off her feet.

'I'm so glad you are okay,' breathed her sister. 'I was so scared.'

Adina's shock was followed closely by a bubble of happiness. Her sister and her daughter holding her, now she could deal with anything. Her attention was distracted by the sight of a procession coming into the driveway from the fields. Two paramedics and two police officers were carrying a stretcher containing a black body bag.

'Isabella, no!' Adina broke free of her sister and ran over to them. 'You have to save her. She can't be dead.'

A police officer restrained her, stopping her from getting to Isabella. Adina resisted, sure if she could just get to her then she would wake up. The paramedics must somehow have got it wrong.

Scarlett grabbed Adina and dragged her away.

'Adina. Stop.' But Adina couldn't stop, she had to save Isabella. 'You're upsetting Poppy.' It was the magic word. All Adina's fight was sapped from her body in an instant. She turned to see her little girl standing alone, tears seeping from her eyes. Adina swept Poppy up into her arms and held her tightly.

Scarlett's arms came around both of them and they stayed that way until a paramedic insisted that Adina come with them to the hospital. For a moment, Adina was terrified.

'No. You can't take me away from them.' She clung to Scarlett and Poppy.

'Don't worry, Adina. We are never letting you go.'

Adina lay in the hospital bed. Warmth from the blanket and Poppy's sleeping body curled into her, made a welcome change from the dank, cold cellar. Adina stroked Poppy's hair, revelling in a touch she never thought she would make again. The detective inspector left the room, congratulating Adina for being so brave in the face of such a terrifying experience.

Adina's throat burned from talking. It had taken what felt like three hours to give her statement of events. She was so grateful to be rescued that she had forgot to be embarrassed when she told them how she had been tricked by Jack because of her desperation to earn more money. Scarlett had cleared her throat, clearly uncomfortable on hearing the reality of her sister's dire economic situation. But Adina didn't care about that now. The only thing that mattered to her was the little body lying in her arms on the hospital bed. Money or no money, all she needed was this little girl in her arms.

It struck her that that was exactly how Jack must have felt about Elsie. Despite everything he had put her through, Adina could recognise the power of losing someone. The grief at being away from Poppy and the thought of never seeing her again had tormented her in that cellar.

Scarlett stood up and perched on the edge of Adina's bed. She stroked her hair and Adina basked in her touch, glad that something good had come from the nightmare she had been forced to endure.

'You must be so happy that monster is dead. Can you believe there is such evil in the world?'

Adina considered her sister's words. Laced with hatred and disgust.

'I hate what he did. What he did was horrific.' Adina chose her next words carefully. 'But I can't help but understand why it happened. I don't think he was evil. He was just an ordinary man who had the love of his life snatched away from him. And it broke him.'

CHAPTER SIXTY

BLACK FRIDAY

J ack had always loathed shopping centres. Had he known
that it was going to be the place he would watch his wife's
brutal murder, he would never have let himself be coerced
into going there.

Shopping centres were a unique type of punishment for
Jack. It was as though someone had gathered everything that
had ever irritated him in one place. At every corner he was
greeted by screaming children and shoppers in such a rush they
thought nothing of forcibly bashing people out of their way,
happily invading anyone's personal space as they sought out
overpriced junk. Cheerful tinny music played through speakers
assaulting his ears no matter where he went. That's when he
wasn't being accosted by salesmen who would not take no for an
answer. Or shrewd charities' employees scanning the crowds
trying to make eye contact with their next victim who they
would shamelessly guilt-trip into parting with money. There
was only one reason he tolerated being in this cesspit of human
deprivation. And that was because of the beautiful, broad smile
on Elsie's face when they were there. She thrived on the
atmosphere, almost giddy with excitement. People-watching

and loving every minute of it. Her smile split her face as her eyes darted around. A smile powerful enough to melt away the thirty-seven years that they had shared together. Transforming her back into that radiant eighteen-year-old girl she had been when they first met.

Elsie loved people. Jack did not. She would unashamedly watch people as they passed her by, wondering what their lives were like. Elsie thought nothing of listening to conversations around her when they stopped for a coffee.

'Jack, that man just came in with a woman, had a coffee and left and then came back in ten minutes later with another woman!'

But for Elsie, he would shelve his dislike of society. Most would consider him whipped. That it wasn't manly to do whatever a woman wanted. That she had him by the 'proverbials'. But Elsie wasn't just a woman to him, to him she was everything. Loving her and seeing her happy was his oxygen. So, if he had to suffer a couple of hours being used as a shopping-bag holder while Elsie cooed over frivolous rubbish she was planning to buy their friends and family then he'd do it. After all, that was nothing compared to what she had done for him. She had opened the world up to him and saved him from following in the footsteps of his neurotic father.

It was getting close to Christmas. A season the world had been celebrating since October. It was now November and Jack was more than ready for the sweet relief of normality that January promised. Christmas spirit was in abundance as they walked around the centre, more akin to a maze with its uniform and endless corridors. Each corridor was full of Christmas lights that lasered him with their cheerful glare. Snowmen and Santas waved at him from every shop window. He thanked his lucky stars that it was just the tinkle of chart music playing through the tannoy and not the usual barrage of Christmas songs offending his ears. Kids screeched, running around like a pack of monkeys on steroids. He wrinkled his nose in disgust. Their shrieks pierced him the same way someone scraping their knife on their plate did.

Elsie smiled genially at the children, a wistful look on her face that broke his heart. He knew that she was thinking about her empty womb. It was a taboo subject between them. But even so, the sadness in her eyes when she saw a child told him how she really felt. It was the black cloud hovering around them that he fought tooth and nail to distract her from. Hence, his concession today, visiting this melting pot of humanity when he'd rather be anywhere else. He just had to hope that Elsie wouldn't leave him for another man who could give her a child. They had tried for so long. Each month, when her cycle informed her there was no baby, he would watch her grieve. His throat clogged with words, none of them good enough to comfort her. Nothing he could say would take the pain away, so he said nothing. Part of him was scared that if he acknowledged it, if he gave voice to his failings, it would give her the permission she needed to leave him.

Spotting a store window full of ornamental rubbish that looked right up Elsie's street, he diverted her attention from the children over to the shop. Delighted, she dove inside, eyes zipping between the shelves, hunting with the keen eye of an eagle for something to buy. His knees twinged in disappointment as he followed her dutifully, even faking a laugh at the sign that read 'Visitors welcome, family by appointment' that she had pointed out to him, smiling up at him with those twinkling brown eyes that liquefied his heart.

Finally, once she had everything she needed, Jack took the bags back to the car. *It's almost over*, he promised his aching knees. Soon he'd be at home watching TV with Elsie, drinking a cup of tea and holding her hand. His happy place. Jack left Elsie outside Barclays bank, insisting she didn't need to walk all the way to the car park and back. It would appear he was being a gentleman but to get to the car park they would have to pass at least five more shops and he knew he would end up being dragged into one. It was much safer if he went alone. They agreed he would go and get the car and then they would go for some lunch at one of the restaurants in the shopping centre. Jack walked off in the direction of the car park, not realising it was a decision he would regret for the rest of his life.

After playing a game of Tetris with the shopping bags in the boot, he retraced his steps. Jack was wondering whether he could persuade Elsie to drive home so he could have a pint, when he caught sight of Elsie at the opposite end of the corridor. It was starting to get busier. Huge crowds of people dashed to and fro. Elsie was still outside Barclays bank, two Starbuck cups in her hands. She spotted him and gave him a cheeky smile. He returned it despite his frustration that in the five minutes he had been gone she had found a way to spend yet more money.

Before he could set off down the corridor, Jack looked up to the ceiling as a bodiless, female voice blared from the tannoy. It echoed off the walls. Jack saw an elderly man covering his ears, frowning up at the speaker nearest to him.

'Ladies and gentlemen, we trust you are having a good day. As a thank you for shopping with us at the Kingfisher Centre and in the spirit of goodwill this Christmastime, the shopping centre has a one-of-a-kind offer for you on behalf of Electronics4U. For the next thirty minutes only, the Samsung OLED TV will be on offer for only £99 for the first ninety-nine people that come into the Electronics4U store. Usually £999, but for the next thirty minutes it can be yours for £99 if you are one of the first ninety-nine people. Merry Christmas everyone!'

There was a brief silence. Everyone around him seemed to take a collective breath whilst they processed the announcement. Then, like a starter pistol had been fired into the air, chaos erupted. As if a virus had activated in their brains, Jack watched frozen with shock as human decency and civilisation was replaced by a frenzied greed.

People ran in all directions, choosing which way they thought would get them to the store fastest. He watched as parents dragged their children behind them, the children looking up at their parents in confusion, not understanding their sudden urgency. A woman with brown hair used the pram containing her baby as a battering ram, clearing a path through the running crowd. Squeaks of shoes, screams and shouts battered his eardrums as the people thought only of their desire to possess.

Jack looked back up the corridor to check on Elsie. He expected to see her staring at him, his own shock mirrored on her face. But she was hidden by a sea of bodies. The bank was at the end of the corridor, the same corridor that led to the electronics store. Naturally, most shoppers had run in this direction and it had caused a bottleneck as around five hundred people tried to get around the corner to the next corner. More people ran out of shops and joined the throng of shoppers trying to push, pull and kick their way down the corridor.

Jack was launched sideways and only just avoided falling to the floor. He turned to see two men punching each other. Their fight was savage, their faces contorted with a fury that made him back away. No one stopped them. In fact, no one appeared to have noticed. Every single person was focused only on getting out of this corridor and getting to that store. Jack was about to intervene and stepped towards the men when he heard a voice that he knew better than his own.

'Jack!'

Elsie sounded terrified. Jack took a deep breath and, bracing himself, he jogged into the crowd. Unable to see her through the solid wall of bodies that was getting thicker, all Jack could do was use the blue Barclays sign hanging above the doorway as his compass.

'Elsie!' he roared. He wanted her to know he was coming. But the sound of pandemonium drowned him out. Jack cut a path through the crowds. He had no choice but to push people out of his way, ignoring the pain as elbows and feet collided with him. It felt like he was trying to cross the path of a hoard of stampeding animals in the jungle. The closer he got to the bank the more tightly packed the shoppers became. Hot, sweaty bodies pressed at him from all sides. It was getting harder to make any progress.

A sudden gap in the crowd appeared in front of him and he saw her. Jack stopped short; someone rammed into the back of him, not expecting him to stop.

'Idiot,' someone yelled and carried on pushing past Jack.

But Jack was unable to process anything apart from the sight of his wife lying crumpled on the floor, her light-blue jumper stained with coffee. Jack watched as Elsie tried and failed to get off the ground. He could just make out the fear in her eyes as she looked around her for help. A stout woman with black hair tripped over Elsie, her black high heels hitting Elsie in the head. Jack expected the woman to apologise, to help Elsie to her feet and ask if there was anything she could do to make amends. But the woman scrambled to her feet and dashed back into the crowd. More people moved towards Elsie as they noticed the gap she was lying in, thinking there might be a way to cut ahead by going in that direction. Fear pulsed through Jack and broke through his paralysis. He shoved hard at the bodies around him, unable to take in any details. They had become obstacles rather than people to him. But Jack could not break free from the net of arms, legs and torsos that were refusing to move. No one even looked in his direction as they yelled at him.

'Hey, get off me!'

'You're hurting me!'

'Hey, dickhead, stop pushing.'

Jack could no longer see Elsie. Frustration lanced through him. He was so close to her, yet so far. Anything could be happening to her.

'My wife! I have to get to my wife!' he screamed at the crowd, but no one listened. His eyes found Elsie again as the crowd shifted slightly. Aghast, he watched as an older, balding man used Elsie's head to push himself to his feet. His hands then pushed down on Elsie's back, pressing her face into the floor. Did he realise she couldn't breathe? The man stood up and without a backward glance, rejoined the foray. His black shoe crunched Elsie's hand as he went.

A powerful combination of fury and fear was fuelling Jack as he clawed at the people around him. A man tried to elbow him out of the way but Jack ducked and dove into the crowd. He used the gaps between people's legs to crawl through. The closer he got, the easier it was to see why Elsie couldn't move. She was pinned down underneath a pair of legs. Elsie was pushing fruitlessly at someone wearing blue jeans and red trainers. Her progress halted when a passing foot struck her in the face. She clutched her jaw, cowering on the floor in fear and pain.

The staccato of his heartbeat eclipsed the echoing shouts and screams that surrounded him. All around him people were crying out in anger and pain. Wave after wave of shoppers were running and tripping over and stamping on his beautiful wife. Not a single one of them was stopping. Blow after blow struck her and Jack was forced to watch in glimpses as Elsie winced and cried out in pain. She was trapped in the path most people were using to try and skip around the side of the crowd with no escape. He had almost reached her but it was slow progress. A network of limbs and hostility kept trying to bar his path.

'Oh no you don't, mate,' said a voice. Jack felt a hand grab his coat and pull him back. Jack shrugged off the coat and sank to the floor. He crawled his way through more legs, not stopping to wipe the blood from his split lip, a gift from a brown leather shoe he had got too close to.

Jack's panic was building. He pushed past a middle-aged man with a Santa hat perched jauntily on his head, not stopping when he fell to the floor, a thud followed by a moan. Jack was breathing heavily, and his joints were screaming in pain as he kneeled on the floor to climb through yet more legs. A foot kicked him in the face and he felt an explosion of pain as his nose broke. But his fear for Elsie dulled the pain and he ignored the dripping blood and carried on crawling towards her.

'I'm coming, Elsie! I'm coming, Elsie!'

He jostled past a man in a suit who was on his phone. The phone flew from the man's hands. He turned to Jack with a fury that was lost on him as Jack was only thinking of Elsie. Her voice rang out and he heard her screaming his name. He barged past the angry suit and was just in time to see a foot connect with the side of her head and her eyes roll back, exposing the whites before they closed. Pure terror flared inside him. His body was flooded with adrenaline and he felt his muscles grow stronger. He ripped through the people like a tornado, violently kicking, grabbing, and thrusting people out of the way. Oblivious to the shouts of pain and anger that followed in his wake.

At last, he was there. Jack fell to his knees and reached for his wife. Elsie's eyes were still closed. He took her head in his hands, caressing her cheek. His tears fell on her, merging with the blood dripping from an angry cut on her head. The blood changed from a vivid red, to a watery pink. He screamed in her face.

'Elsie!'

'Elsie!'

Pulling her close to him, he breathed in her familiar vanilla scent. Blows rained down on him as he shielded her from the charging crowd. Elsie was limp and lifeless in his arms. With one hand, Jack tried to move the legs that were pinning her down. They belonged to a bald man; he could see a belly bulging over a *Star Wars* belt. He was lying on his back, eyes closed. The man must have fallen backwards over Elsie and hit the back of his head on the floor. Blood was pooling underneath him. Jack's attention was drawn to a teenage girl who was lying on top of the man's right arm. She was pinned by a boy with black hair and a nose ring. She was alternating between stroking the boy's face and trying to push him off her. But he was a dead weight and her pale matchstick arms were no match. Jack took his eyes off the human Jenga in front of him and focused on Elsie.

With a jolt, the bottle jam cleared. People cried out as they were suddenly thrown forward. The atmosphere intensified as people realised that they were now closer to getting their hands on a cheap TV. Many became more desperate to get there first and didn't think twice as they trod on people who had fallen over or even tripped people up to get around them. This was no place for the timid who were either lying on the floor or cowering in shop entrances.

Reluctantly, Jack let go of Elsie's head and used both of his arms to move the man off her. Carefully, he lifted her into the air. Thoughts of the last time that he had done so rose unbidden in his mind. It had been his wedding day when he had carried her across the threshold. Ready to start their new life together.

Jack walked awkwardly to the entrance of the bank, the

doors sensed his approach and opened automatically. Before he could take more than a step inside a force knocked into him from behind. Jack fell hard, unable to use his hands to break his fall. His knees took the brunt of the impact and Elsie slipped out of his arms and he heard her head strike the concrete floor and rebound. Lying on the ground, Jack saw a large man standing over him from the corner of his eye. The man was wide as he was tall. In his arms, he was holding a large box with a picture of a TV on the front.

'I've got one. I can't believe I've got one!' he shouted at the top of his lungs. His face beaming. Looking around for someone to congratulate him. His eyes fell on Jack and Elsie on the floor. A ripple of unease spread across his face.

'Oh dear. That wasn't me, was it? Can't see where I'm going with this thing.' He patted the box.

Jack had no words. Ignoring the agony in his knees, he crawled over to Elsie. Her eyes were still closed. Apart from the cut on her head, she looked unharmed. As if sleeping serenely. Jack felt movement at his side and a lady wearing a blue shirt knelt down beside him. A member of staff at the bank.

'What happened?'

Jack couldn't talk, his throat was choked full of fear. His hands were shaking violently. As he cradled Elsie's head, the woman put her head over Elsie's face and turned to listen.

'I can't hear her breathing,' she whispered, looking up anxiously at Jack. The lady, Trish, according to her name badge, placed two fingers on Elsie's neck, moving them around.

'I can't find her pulse,' Trish's voice squeaked. 'But I haven't done first aid in a while. I might be wrong?' Trish looked around at the gallery of colleagues watching them. Waiting reassurance that never came.

'No, she's fine,' Jack insisted. He pushed Trish aside and drew Elsie into his arms and rocked her gently.

'Elsie. Wake up, sweetheart. It's okay now.'

He sobbed into her brown hair. Her hand was lifeless in his. But still he held her. Willing with everything he had for her to wake up. Trish's hand rubbed his back gently. He placed his face next to Elsie's, silently begging her to open her eyes.

'Elsie. Please. Wake up,' Jack whispered in her ear.

Speaking caused fresh waves of pain that made his vision go dark. He gripped Elsie tightly and settled down to wait for her to wake up.

It took several paramedics to forcibly remove Jack. He snarled at them as they prised his fingers off his wife. Jack was taken to a chair further inside the bank, his shoulders gripped by two police officers preventing him from going back to Elsie. A paramedic crouched in front of him, examining his nose. Another paramedic came over. His face was grave, and the look he gave Jack told him. Pain like he had never felt before exploded inside him. Jack's heart shattered into a million pieces whilst Trish from Barclays Bank put her arms around him. His anguish could be heard from outside and some of the shoppers stopped in their tracks. But Jack saw and heard no one. His pain was an inferno that was burning him, blinding him to all else. Jack shook off Trish and staggered past her to see the paramedics lifting Elsie's body up on a gurney. He lowered his face to Elsie's, rubbing his cheek against hers. But there was no tinkling laughter that usually accompanied the gesture.

Elsie was gone.

Jack's scream was loud enough to shatter the glass windows of the bank.

THE END

ACKNOWLEDGEMENTS

This is my third time writing acknowledgements and it is sadly still impossible to find a way to thank every single person that has helped me achieve my dream of being a writer. If I haven't mentioned you specifically then please know I am so thankful for everyone that has read, reviewed or supported me in my writing journey. Book reviewers are the unsung heroes of the book world. They are happy to shout about your book and soothe those pesky doubts that plague many authors. I have had the pleasure of turning some of these reviewers into my friends, Suze, Emma and Daisy. I must give a special shout-out to the lovely, amazing Daisy – I cherish our friendship. Also, thanks to Jen Lucas for being there anytime I need a brainstorming session, you are one of the people that I know will always be in my life and I am beyond thankful for your friendship. Also, thank you to Karen of Hair Past a Freckle for recommending my book on her book review radio segment. It was one of the most emotional moments of my life, listening to that with my mum in the middle of a supermarket car park. It meant the world to me.

The biggest and most important thank you that I want to say is to my best friend Kelly Lacey. I met Kelly when she agreed to help me promote Save Her through her business, Love Books Tours. Little did I know that this would turn into a friendship I will treasure for the rest of my life. Since we became friends, Kelly has become my biggest cheerleader, I've bounced ideas off her with this book and she gave me the motivation to keep writing it and not give up. I can honestly say this book wouldn't be what it is without her positivity and unwavering support. There are many blessings being an author has given me but getting to call Kelly my friend is probably one of the best.

I'd also like to thank my publisher, Bloodhound Books. They have an amazing team and the support they give me is amazing. Also, a thank you to my editor Ian Skewis for your patience, support and feedback.

Lastly, as always, I want to thank my rockstar team of friends and family that are always there for me. I've thanked you all individually in my other books, so I'm hopeful by now you realise you mean the world to me and that I wouldn't be where I am without each and every one of you. I do have to thank my mum and my husband in writing as they deserve it. I've been diagnosed with an autoimmune condition, and I've been having pretty gruelling treatment and without my mum and husband, I would have curled up in a ball and stayed there. They have looked after me and given me the strength to carry on writing. Without them, this book would still be a figment of my imagination. I love you both.

A NOTE FROM THE PUBLISHER

Thank you for reading this book. If you enjoyed it please do consider leaving a review on Amazon to help others find it too.

We hate typos. All of our books have been rigorously edited and proofread, but sometimes mistakes do slip through. If you have spotted a typo, please do let us know and we can get it amended within hours.

info@bloodhoundbooks.com

Lightning Source UK Ltd.
Milton Keynes UK
UKHW012225191122
412485UK00007B/58

9 781504 072724